OVER THE BRIDGE

OVER THE BRIDGE

Leann M. Rettell

LeeAnn,
Thanks for being a awesome fan!
Leann M. Rettell

Over the Bridge Copyright © 2018 Leann M. Rettell

All rights reserved. No part of this book may be reproduced in any form by any electronic or mechanical means including photocopying, recording, or information storage and retrieval without permission in writing from the author.

This is a work of fiction. All the characters and events portrayed in this book are either products of the authors' imagination or are used fictitiously.

Melissa Gilbert, editor
Susan H. Roddey, interior design
James Christopher Hill, cover art

ISBN-13: 978-1987460773
ISBN-10: 1987460774

Acknowledgements

The saying "It takes a village to raise a child" holds true for books as well.

Thank you, a thousand times, and more to Melissa Gilbert at Clicking Keys for wading through the mine field of misplaced commas, passive voice, and dangling modifiers. Oh my! This book could never be what it is without you and your ever-watchful eye.

To James Christopher Hill who helped me bring Ora to life on the amazing covers for the Conjuragic Series. More of his amazing work can be found at www.jameshillstudios.com

To Dallas Hughes for taking care of our beautiful children those many, many hours while Ora's story turned from voices in my head to words on the page.

To my children, Nicholas, Katie, and Nathan for loving me even when I'm away and knowing I love you more than anything else.

To Cheri and Makayla Prince for reading all versions of Ora's journey.

And to all who read this…thank you. It was all for you.

Chapter One
Sabrina

SNAP. A TWIG BROKE IN the distance. Sabrina halted in her tracks. A moment later leaves rustled and a bush shook. A rabbit bounced across her path. She let out a breath and observed the scene for a few more minutes. Distraction was a Hunter's ultimate weapon. She wouldn't fall for a simple diversion like a rabbit.

Shaking off the jitters, Sabrina resumed her walk of the perimeter. The security enchantments held, but with only Naiad magic any Hunter would blast through them like tissue paper. Sure, they would hold against humans, but they would be nothing against a Quad or even a Hunter. Once again, she broke out in a cold sweat thinking about being without the rest of her Quad.

Dawn broke over the horizon as she rounded the last arc of the perimeter. The sky turned a lighter shade of purple, and the dew twinkled on the leaves like diamonds. The temperature here in North Carolina had settled into a comfortable seventy degrees instead of the blazing heat of summer.

The chirps of the birds overhead broke the morning's silence as they, too, awoke. *Progress*, she thought. Perhaps they could make it through one night without Ora Stone's nightmares. As if summoned, an icy blast—foreign and unnatural, tinged with magic that singed the air—ripped through her thin, un-spelled yoga pants. The temperature plummeted. Her jaw chattered in response. She would've felt nothing in her leathers.

The air grew colder—cold enough to bring snow. She didn't know much about weather on the human side of the Veil, but she didn't think the temperature would drop forty degrees in seconds.

Over the Bridge

The change in temperature must have pissed off the clouds because a second later, lightening flashed, and a boom of thunder tore through the sky.

Sabrina rolled her eyes as the rain dumped upon her head. As she huffed, her power sizzled, and the water jumped off her skin. The rain fell around her as if she stood under an invisible umbrella.

Lightning struck again, turning Sabrina's thoughts to Ora. She rolled the blue teardrop birthstone between her fingers, thinking. The jewel held a piece of her magic and marked her House, not that there was any question. She had the classic blue eyes and blond hair of the Naiads. But what would Ora's birthstone look like?

Not that she'd ever have received one. At birth, babies in Conjuragic are given a bead of glass, and their magic slips inside it, bending it into the shape of their magical core. A drop of water for Naiad, a green orb for Sphere, a ruby flame for Ember, and purple tornado for Tempest. Ora's magic disturbed Sabrina. With Perdita being a Geminate, an illegal witch born with two cores instead of only one, what else could Ora be? As a Protector, Sabrina's job had been enforcing the laws of Conjuragic, including eliminating the forbidden Geminates, but she had broken her vows when she helped Ora escape. What choice did she have? Ora had been wrongly convicted of being a Nip, a human who steals magic. If she had been recaptured, the other Protectors would've killed her. Sabrina couldn't let that happen, but now she was stuck in the human world, the Veil sealed, and had found out that perhaps Ora wasn't so innocent after all.

Ora's awake, she thought as the cabin came into view, and the storm calmed. Sabrina entered the cabin just as Perdita closed the door to Ora's room. They shared a heavy look. Bacon sizzled in the kitchen, and Sabrina's stomach rumbled.

Sabrina reopened Ora's bedroom door to the roar of the shower coming from the bathroom and called out, "Breakfast in five. Training in ten."

She heard Ora moan, and she smiled. *Oh, today is going to be fun.*

Chapter 2
Ora

"AGAIN!" SABRINA STOOD WITH HER hands behind her back reminding me of a drill sergeant. I glared at her crystal clear blue eyes, set in steel, framing her perfect face and her long blond hair. She wore it braided, hanging down her back, and I imagined using it as leverage to throw her to the ground. If I could ever get close enough.

Sabrina had become our friend since she betrayed her world helping my mother and I escape from Conjuragic. I respected her even more because she saved my best friend Charlie while I had been unconscious after sealing the Veil. But I couldn't stand her during Naiad training.

I'd often wondered during my imprisonment in Conjuragic how she ever managed to make it through Protector training. She had been so kind, so different from the others. I'd had a hard time imagining her on the job until our training began. As a member of the first Quad, the highest ranking of the Protectors, her job had been taking down dark witches and wizards. *Glorified magical policemen*, the sneaky thought flitted across my mind. She hates when I call her that, and I smiled.

"Think my training is funny, do you?" She lifted her hands, and the air cracked as she sucked the water from the sky. My hair stood on end before a newly-formed wave crashed into my left side, knocking me onto my back, three feet from where I'd been standing. I pushed the wet hair out of my face, and she smirked. "I told you to braid that hair. If you can't see in battle, you're dead."

Over the Bridge

"I'm tired," I said, though I knew it wouldn't do me any good. Sabrina, ruthless and unforgiving, pushed me until I couldn't take any more and then some.

"This was your idea." She flung the braid behind her, not looking the least bit sorry. I tried to stand, but my muscles protested. I flopped back onto the ground and laid my head in the mud. "John," she whispered.

John's face rushed into my memories. Images of him smiling at me, eyes full of love, then changing to cold and empty, dead. The boulder crushing him after he threw himself in front of my mom. Rage filled me. The magic inside me rolled in anger. Ready to slash and maim.

I rolled to my feet, concentrating on the air in front of Sabrina as she'd instructed. The power reached out, calling the water from the air. Molecule by molecule, the water pulled together, forming a long lasso. My magic and I together, concentrating hard, flung it around Sabrina, who deflected it as easily as if it swatting a gnat.

"Good. But you use too much magic, which takes time and makes your moves slow. Anticipated even. Your rage helps you concentrate, to reach the core of your power, but what you need is small amounts to allow you quickness and surprise." Her hands, which spoke as much as she did, stilled by her sides as her eyes rose to the growing twilight of the forest sky. Shades of purple cascaded down amongst the trees and steady cadence of crickets grew louder as our battling subsided.

"That's enough for today. Tomorrow you will do nothing but this—" She made a jerking motion with her hand, and a small line of water appeared by a nearby tree and flew across the bark, slicing it. "Small amounts of magic can do tremendous damage if you can control it, which is way harder than sending a tidal wave."

She turned, braid flying around her, and left me alone in the woods where I collapsed against a tree. Sweat trickled down my neck or perhaps drops from the waves of water Sabrina kept knocking me over with. A massive headache gripped my skull, and every muscle in my body ached. The surge of anger and adrenaline disappeared. I'd been training with Sabrina for weeks now, trying to master the Naiad magic within me and still failing.

After my display of magic, essentially destroying Conjuragic, the great magical city, and sealing the Veil between their world and the human one, I thought this would be easy. But the more I worked at it, the less I improved. I wanted to blame it on my powers being locked away for so long by my mother's amulet or because I'm learning to use them as an adult, but I really feared I sucked at magic. I felt for my power, resting deep, rising and falling, in constant motion, as if a sleeping giant. If only my power didn't react to my emotions and instead obeyed logic. I swear it behaved more like a nonchalant cat than an obedient dog. The process felt as if I'd grown new legs and had to teach my brain the neurological pathways to walk.

Arameus, my Defender, or lawyer, explained to me a few weeks ago that even though all the people in Conjuragic possess magic, the levels of talent varies from person to person the same way everyone can sing, but some sound like angels while others embarrass themselves on *The Voice*. Pretty sure I knew which category I fell in.

Mom, ever the optimist, thought I concentrated too hard, but it didn't help that my magic didn't like picking out the parts to make water. Much easier to shove things together than to form a functional weapon.

I wanted to stand up, pull myself together, and do the exercise Sabrina had set out for me, but I knew I wouldn't. Fatigue settled over me in every way possible. My days consisted of waking from nightmares leaving me unrested, followed by hours of training with Sabrina, stopping only for lunch, then collapsing into bed for another restless night. I didn't know if she pushed me so hard to distract me from John or so I could get better at magic. *Perhaps both?*

I'd made a vow to seek revenge for John, but I had no idea how. This thought depressed me almost as much as losing him. I had all this magic inside me but still felt powerless. I also knew deep down, even if I got my revenge, it wouldn't bring him back. Everyone expected me to have the answers. We'd become stuck at an impasse, not knowing where to go or what to do. We couldn't simply go back to our lives. We'd sent my best friend Charlie's grandparents into hiding while we chilled out in limbo. Sabrina never shut up about Hunters, which sounded like bounty hunters to me, and how we should be on the move or they'd find us. How they even knew anything about us stumped me. I'd sealed the Veil in a fit of rage. It'd never been done before. It hadn't been planned, so how would the Hunters have found out about us? Another nagging thought pressed on me. The people stuck in the Veil. I'd sensed them, and some made it through before the Veil sealed. Perhaps one could've been a Hunter or had allies living in the human realm?

The subtle pain behind my eyes grew. A nice stress headache to round out the day. As if we didn't have enough to worry about, a mysterious man who called himself Master who might have his own goonies chasing me as well. Master had a bit of a god-complex, if you asked me.

That wizard had kept my mother imprisoned, hurt her more than I ever really wanted to know. Anger rose, and with it, the cocoon of power. I stood and repeated the small movements Sabrina had shown me.

Over and over, nothing happening, except standing in the middle of the darkening forest looking like an idiot. I puffed out a breath. My annoyance triggered something, and a thin line of water emerged out of the air. Instead of a nice slice like Sabrina made, my pitiful little thing only got the bark wet.

"Seriously!" I screamed at the magic inside me. "If you were going to be this uncooperative, why didn't you stay put? But noooo," the word came in a nice long, mocking drawl, "you had to levitate a pen and get me arrested!" I paced around the tree, throwing my hands in the air, while talking to myself. "If that shit wasn't bad enough *I* almost died after the freaking prejudiced tribunal found me guilty. All because of you!"

I halted, feeling deep to discover my power indifferent as a cat. It could've been laying on a silken pillow grooming itself while I complained. "You don't even care, do you? You don't even care that John died."

My magic reared up, merging with my consciousness. The world grew smaller. Smaller and smaller until only particles remained in the air as I picked out the hydrogen and oxygen. I made, not a small line of water like Sabrina's, but instead, a blade. So sharp I felt it could cut me if I looked at it the wrong way. My magic and I, as one, moved it across the tree, a thirty-foot oak, thick and strong. It sliced the tree in two pieces in seconds. The large trunk tilted to the side as if in slow motion. We focused on the pieces of the tree, noting which parts had been disconnected. We grabbed onto the tree mentally, placed it upright, and sealed the edge by reconnecting the particles as if they had never been apart.

I stepped back. "Holy shit!"

I had used Naiad magic to cut down a tree and Sphere magic to put it back together. I laughed. Could we do it again? I concentrated. It took a while at first, but something clicked into place, and the world descended particles once more as if the world had been painted in the pointillism style. Instead of being stationary, the world remained in a constant state of flux. The painting *A Sunday Afternoon* by George Pierre-Seurat sprang to mind. We could pick out the water from the particles and slice it through the tree. As the tree fell, it pushed the other little specks of color out of the way. We pushed the tree back, put it back in its place, and joined the top and bottom. Viola! A whole tree once again.

My magic and I did this again and again. Each time it got easier. I didn't use fancy arm movements like Sabrina showed me, but only thought, as if I were an artist of a living canvas with an invisible brush.

We turned our focus on the molecules that made up the air, picked a small section, and moved it around, blowing the dirt from the forest floor. Shifting attention once again, we inspected a nearby bush and could make out the flecks within each leaf. Concentrating on one area, the dots moved, slow. We pushed them faster, increasing their speed, faster and faster until, *whoosh*, the little leaf burst into flames. My heart skipped a beat, and I snatched water out of the air and threw it on the leaf.

My mom shouted my name from a distance. I jumped at the sound and the worry echoing in her voice. *Was something wrong?* The faded twilight of earlier had disappeared, and night engulfed the forest. "Coming!"

I turned and rushed back toward our cabin. My mouth watered and stomach grumbled as the smells of cooking meat intensified as I drew closer. No screams or commotion came from the cabin. Mom must have been worried about me being alone in the dark. Though hunger gripped my empty stomach, I wanted something much more important than food. It was time my mother and I had a little talk about what I really am.

Chapter Three
Perdita

ORA BURST INTO THE CABIN after being left alone for nearly an hour. Sabrina left her after practicing Naiad magic and shook her head when Perdita had grabbed her jacket to go and check on her.

"Give her some time," Sabrina said before going into her own room to change.

Ora lingered in the doorway, covered in mud and exhausted, but instead of the usual tear-stained face, this time she stood with her back straight and steel in her eyes. The room quieted, and Perdita paused in the middle of plating the spaghetti on the table for dinner.

"What am I?" Ora asked.

The words hung in the air between them. The words she'd hoped Ora would never ask. As Perdita had always feared, she didn't know exactly how to answer. She cleared her throat. "Why don't we eat first, dear?"

"I don't think so." Ora crossed her arms, not budging from the wide-open doorway.

"It's about time." Sabrina flung her boot-clad feet onto the kitchen table, stretched her long body, and placed her hands on her head.

Perdita stood, moved to the door, and closed it, guiding Ora inside. Perdita looked around, and all eyes stared at her. Charlie with her round face, brown hair, and green eyes saddened by the loss of her brother, an odd expression on her face—a mixture of curiosity, confusion, and overwhelming sadness. Arameus tried not to stare as he pushed his hand through his curly red hair, but as his penetrating green eyes met hers—they too were full of questions.

"Very well." Perdita gestured to the table. "Everyone sit down. Fix yourselves a plate. This is going to take a while."

Perdita abandoned the food and took a seat on one of the bar stools in the kitchen. She took note of the shabby cabin that had become their home since escaping Conjuragic. She listened to their rustling movements, avoiding eye contact, instead letting her focus migrate to the yellowed curtains with faded pink flowers to the wooden walls into the small but modest kitchen. Her eyes settled at the kitchen table where everyone had taken a seat, the food forgotten. Not that she could blame them because she, too, had lost her appetite.

"Some of this you all will already know, but it's best if we all start at the beginning. The truth is, I don't know what you are." Perdita took a sip of sweet tea to fix her dry mouth. "As far as I know, there has never been anything…" She paused seeing the sad look flash on Ora's face. "Sorry, there has never been any*one* like you before." Perdita looked away, staring at a small spider crawling along a web in the corner of the room. She found watching the small insect easier than saying this in front of everyone. "As you know, I was born and raised in captivity. Master…" She shuddered as goosebumps rose on her arms at the thought of him. "I don't know the right word exactly, but rescued is all I can come up with, men and women who were in prison and scheduled for execution. I think he let the world think they were dead and he…made them have…children." The spider turned upside and slid across the web. No sound penetrated the silence of the room except the old grandfather clock in the living room ticking away the seconds. "Sabrina and Arameus will tell you, when people of two houses have babies together, most do not survive. The two cores of magic reject each other. There were a few who survived, and these were called Geminates."

Arameus sucked in a breath.

Perdita continued. "Geminates are illegal. We're harder to control and capture. It's harder to teach us to use magic because, I later learned, the two cores want to conflict. We are often dangerous when we try to wield magic, but Master didn't care. We were his slaves. Only alive because he wished it. After we reached a certain age and there were enough of us, our parents were killed."

Perdita wiped a tear from her cheek. "Master wanted us to create a rock that would allow the person holding it to use all four cores of magic. We worked on it every day, all day. There were many accidents, and we didn't make much progress because we were never taught to use our magic. Mostly, we relied on instinct and what little we could teach each other." Perdita took another sip of tea, the ice clinking in the cup. "You know my cores are Naiad and Tempest. Your father's were Sphere and Ember."

"No!" Sabrina whispered.

Arameus took a sharp intake of breath and exclaimed, "I knew it."

"What? You knew what?" Charlie asked, looking at Arameus for an answer.

Perdita looked at her daughter as her eyes turned back toward her and finally uttered the truth. The truth even she had never uttered aloud. "When two people of different houses have a baby, if it survives, it has both cores of magic. You, my beautiful daughter, were born from two people who had two cores of magic. Which means…"

"I have all four," Ora whispered, looking away in the distance. "I knew it. Sphere, Tempest, Ember, and Naiad. Which makes me a…?"

She gazed at her mother looking for the answer. Perdita shook her head. "I don't know what you're called."

"I do," Sabrina hissed, as she stood up from her chair, and walked toward the door.

Ora turned in the chair. "Well? What am I?"

Sabrina halted at the front door, turned on her heel. "An abomination. The most illegal and feared thing in our world. Worse than even a Nip. You should never have been born!" Sabrina turned, opened the door, and slammed it shut behind her, leaving her words stinging everyone in their wake.

Chapter Four
Perdita

THE MORALE IN THE GROUP plummeted in the week following Sabrina's explosion. Sabrina had been off on her own most of the time, deep in the forest sulking, and refused to train Ora anymore.

In the meantime, Arameus and Ora worked on Tempest magic, but as he himself explained, he could do rudimentary spells, but he never learned to master complex magic. Charlie accompanied them into the forest during these training periods while Sabrina remained aloof.

The distance between Sabrina and the rest of them couldn't go on any longer. Perdita made up her mind to say something to her, but Ora shook things up. She walked into the cabin after training alone, the door slamming against the far wall. "Charlie and I are going to the movies."

Sabrina stormed from the kitchen, the half-eaten apple in her hand. "Absolutely not. Have you freaking lost your mind?"

Ora's eyes flashed, a look of pure teenage defiance in her expression. "Oh, so you're talking to me again?"

Ignoring Ora, Sabrina gestured with the apple. "Perdita, you can't possibly let her go."

"You're not my boss, Protector." Ora flung the title like a curse.

The fluid drained out of the apple, shrinking beneath Sabrina's grip. "As the only fully trained battle witch here, I *am* your boss. I've risked my life for you, and I'll be damned if you're going to throw that away on something stupid!"

Ora's eyes vibrated, a slight side to side movement, and the color bled from the amber shade to motes of blues, reds, and yellow. The hair on Perdita's arms stood on end. The thick scent of ozone rose in the air, reminding Perdita of an incoming storm.

"Ora, honey. Calm down," Perdita said.

Arameus stepped between them, palms up, one pointed at each of the women. "Everyone needs to calm down. Let's discuss this."

Charlie cowered on the edge of the worn-out brown leather couch. She pulled her legs underneath her and hugged them to herself. Her eyes held no fear, but instead a vacant expression. She didn't need this drama to worsen her depression.

Perdita's hands slipped on the cookbook she'd been holding, wrestling with a need to run or hide. Her whole life she'd done nothing but run, and it had to stop. Surprising even herself, she took Arameus's place between Sabrina and Ora. "You two may go."

The room fell into silence, broken only by Sabrina's shout. "What?"

"Ora's right. If all we do is hide and not go out and live our lives, then what was the point of escaping? If we sit here, fighting and hating one another, then John died for nothing. We rescued Ora for nothing. You two left everyone and everything you know for nothing!" Perdita slammed the cookbook on an end table. "Today, this ends. We're here, and we're together. Sabrina, if you feel Ora and I are abominations—" Sabrina flinched at her own words thrown back in her face, "—and you feel you've made a mistake, then rectify it. Arrest us all now, take us to whatever authority still resides in the human world. Let them kill us, put Arameus in jail, and erase Charlie's memories of all of this. Or get over yourself. If you can't do that, then *leave*. We'll manage on our own." Perdita stopped pacing.

Sabrina's shoulders slumped. "I'm not going anywhere." Sabrina spoke so softly that Perdita almost hadn't heard her words. She flopped onto the couch, all fight leeched away.

A weight lifted off Perdita's shoulders. "Then things have to change. We're a family now, and I, for one, am tired of hiding. Ora's right. Even though I escaped from my prison, I hid the two of us our entire lives. Though we had happy moments, I could never let my guard down."

"You two are in even worse danger than ever before. You can't let your guard down now!" Sabrina jumped to her feet. "She," Sabrina jabbed a finger at Ora, "still doesn't know what she's going to do. She's making little headway with magic, and she's keeping us all in limbo. We don't have a plan, and she's just a child. Untrained, dangerous, and relying too much on her emotions

"I know," Ora whispered.

Sabrina's mouth snapped shut, facing Ora with her hands across her chest, waiting for her to continue.

"I didn't ask for this, you know. I never wanted to be special or different. I never even wished for magic, and besides Charlie and," Ora gulped, "and John, no one else accepted me. My existence is illegal in the magical world. I have no home, no place where I belong, and now, at eighteen years old, I'm faced with having to figure all this out, when I didn't even know any of this existed until a few weeks ago, and you expect me to...know what to do?"

"Ladies..." Arameus rubbed Ora's shoulder. "This is a horrible and unfair situation for all of us. But Sabrina, as much as you want, you cannot forget you chose to be here. You believed Ora innocent and hated yourself when she was found guilty at the trial. I saw you hiding your tears as she was placed into the Kassen for execution, and when you found us trying to escape, instead of stopping us, you helped us escape and came across the Veil with us." He paused for dramatic effect, a tactic no doubt learned as a Defender.

Sabrina rolled her eyes. "I know that."

"The question you have to answer is this: if you knew then what Ora was, would you still have done the same thing?" Arameus made a rolling motion with his hand.

"Yes." Sabrina glared, recognizing his Defender tactics.

"Why?" he asked like questioning a witness.

"Because no matter what she is, she didn't do anything wrong. Just like Geminate babies are killed. It isn't their fault. I've seen a...

Geminate. A perfect, beautiful, healthy little boy, and a group of Protectors came, took him away, and…" She left the rest unspoken.

"Conjuragic is so barbaric." Charlie shuddered, not meeting anyone's gaze. "You honestly think you're better than us?"

Sabrina said nothing, but shrugged as if to say, "You've got a point."

Ora stood, walked to the window, and gazed out into the forest beyond. She turned and called to the group, "That's part of the answer then, isn't it? About what we're going to do."

No one spoke, sharing the same confused expression.

Ora rolled her eyes. "We have to find this Master," she motioned with air quotes, "and expose him. We have to free his Geminate slaves. But what we really have to do is change the very foundation of Conjuragic. To teach them how to live with not only each other, but to allow Nips and Geminates, and eventually more of…whatever I am. The prejudice and genocide have to stop."

Ora strutted back to the couch and sat. "I know that's what we have to do, but I don't know how, and it's overwhelming. That's why I want to go out. I need to go out, to see a movie, to live. To see what it is I'm fighting for. But mainly, I need a break from trying to figure this out."

Sabrina opened her mouth, but Ora held up her hand to stop her. "I know it's dangerous. But it's what I need."

"Absolutely not," Sabrina uttered again. "I can't protect you so exposed."

Perdita cleared her throat, ignoring the twinge in her chest at Sabrina's words. "You can't protect her, but if she doesn't get this break, she'll won't be able to move on. We're going to let them go to the movies, but not tonight since it's late. Tomorrow."

"What gives you the right to make this decision?" Sabrina leaned forward placing her elbows on her knees.

Perdita smiled. "Because I'm her mother."

Chapter Five
Ora

I'D WON THE ARGUMENT. CHARLIE and I walked into the theater. The smell of buttery popcorn wafted around the ticket counter. My mouth watered in response. The ringing and whistling of the video games made me smile. This was what I wanted. Normal. Just two teenage girls going out to the movies on a Saturday night.

Charlie agreed sitting around the cabin all day sucked. At least during the day, I practiced magic, but Charlie had nothing to keep her thoughts from her brother. She jumped at the smallest noises, chewed her nails down to the quick, and had a chronic stomach ache.

At night, screaming voices plagued my dreams, not to mention reliving John's death over and over again. The constant depression would eventually drive us all crazy.

Sabrina said, "The paranoia is good for you. It'll keep you alive."

I didn't agree, but now that we're here, the crowd felt too close, as if enemies lurked everywhere. My heart jumped like a skittish rabbit, and my chest felt tight. My skin tingled as my magic stirred from somewhere deep inside me. I wanted to run right out of the theater. I stole a sideways glance at Charlie and saw the same feelings mirrored on her face. This stopped the panic. We definitely needed to get out. I couldn't imagine how much worse we'd be if we stayed cooped up another couple of weeks. She flinched when our fingers touched and met my gaze, her shoulder-length brown hair laying over her green eyes and smiled. The smile looked so much like her brother's. Pain squeezed my heart, and more than ever, I understood how someone could die from a broken heart. I forced another smile and asked, "So are we getting popcorn with extra butter, nachos with extra cheese, or…both?"

"Both and a blue Icee," she giggled.

We took our seats, munching on our popcorn and nachos as the previews played. The theater lights dimmed, and I felt relaxed for the first time in a while. As expected, guilt slithered in like a snake. How could I even think about having fun and watching a movie when John was dead? I'd said I'd avenge him, and here I was having a good time. Trying to ignore the rising guilt, I took care grabbing one piece of popcorn at a time, chewing slowly, savoring each bite. I tried to tell myself John wouldn't have wanted Charlie and me to stop living. He'd want us to move on.

The stinging of tears burned my eyes, but I fought them away. Anxiety, just in a different form. That's what this was. *Okay, Ora. You're going to sit in this theater with your best friend and eat popcorn, dip your chips in the nacho cheese, and watch this comedy. Now, chill out.*

The anxiety prickled off and on during the movie, but I ignored it. Charlie and I even managed to laugh at the funny parts, and for a few hours, life was normal again.

Chapter Six
Perdita

PERDITA SAT BACK DOWN ON retaining wall outside the movie theater while pretending to stand guard. Sabrina would be none too happy when she returned after her next patrol around the perimeter of the theater. Sabrina would tell her off for allowing Ora out of their sight and storm off to the other side of the theater to check on Arameus. Perdita knew this was dangerous, but she couldn't stand the haunted look on her daughter's face, a look that had only gotten deeper since their talk from last week.

Minutes later, Sabrina strolled around the building again, drawing way more attention to herself than she realized. A gaggle of teenage boys stared at her. They catcalled as they admired her model-worthy behind.

Sabrina shot them a look of pure venom, and their smiles faded. There were four of them, each wearing jeans and faded t-shirts in various states of dishevelment. Three of the four turned away, but one stared on. His jovial expression faded into something deeper, meaner, before his attention switched to another pretty girl.

Sabrina marched toward Perdita. The scowl she'd been wearing all day deepened. Perdita half expected Sabrina to run sideways, peek around the corner, and roll between the parked cars in a jaunt worthy of James Bond. This brought a smile to her lips. Oh, how Sabrina would hate that comparison. The women made eye contact, and Sabrina was about to turn around the back of the building when Perdita motioned for her to come over.

Her head darted back and forth, searching for danger, every muscle on high alert. When she found no immediate threat, she joined Perdita.

"We shouldn't have let them go!"

"You know you really should try to relax as well. The movie is almost over, and nothing bad has happened. The stress isn't helping you either."

Sabrina scowled deeper, which Perdita didn't think possible. She patted the Protector's shoulder. "Didn't anyone tell you if you keep that up, your face is going to get stuck like that?"

Sabrina glared before sitting on the two-foot-high concrete retaining wall to the side of the parking lot. "I'm a Protector. That's what I do."

"Perhaps, my dear, you should try to be Sabrina. Just Sabrina."

"Maybe you're right," Sabrina agreed. She let out a heavy sigh, gazing into the sky. "I miss home."

Perdita nodded and waited for her to continue. Sabrina wasn't someone to push for answers.

"I know Conjuragic has its faults, but it's my home. I miss my sister, my nieces, my best friend. I miss the Haven. Watching the dolphins swim by my room. The way the Haven sparkles and shimmers underneath the sea. How my magic regenerates there. We're not all bad. There is love and kindness, and I don't know if she can see that."

"She's more insightful than you realize. She's met you and Arameus and seen the kindness that's possible there." Perdita resisted the urge to keep touching Sabrina's shoulder.

"Maybe." Sabrina shrugged. "I'm also scared it's gone. You saw it, didn't you? The thing she threw out?"

The memory flashed before her eyes, Ora's body forming a ball of searing light that flew away from her. Her eyes sparkling, and her face contorted in rage. Perdita had been avoiding thinking about this image of her daughter, completely overtaken by anger and magic. The ball of pure power swept out of sight, only to be followed a few moments later with a loud bang, and the light that flowed through all the buildings and streets of Conjuragic vanished, and the buildings cracked as the ground rumbled. Perdita shook her head. Yes, she'd seen it.

Over the Bridge

Sabrina blurted out what Perdita had been thinking. "What if there isn't anything left? What if she destroyed my whole world? What if my family is gone?" Her voice cracked on the last word.

Sabrina's steadfast resolve broke. Her body bent over shaking with silent sobs, and a heartbreaking squeal escaped her lips as Perdita wrapped her arms around the young woman. She held the poor girl and allowed her to cry. They sat this way for a long time until her crying ceased, and she pulled herself together.

Perdita stroked her hair and asked her, "What do you feel in your heart, dear? Do you feel they're gone?"

Sabrina unfolded her body, took a deep breath, and shook her head. "No, but I want to *know* they're okay."

The sounds of distant conversation broke the moment. The theater doors opened as people filed out. They both stood and made their way to the front to meet the girls. "You must hold onto that feeling. The feeling they're still alive and work with Ora to learn Naiad magic, and you should teach me as well so I can help more. We'll do all we can to find out the truth of what happened to Conjuragic. But I can't promise we can ever get you home."

Sabrina shook her head. "I can never go back home. I'm a traitor. I'd be executed And I've accepted that. I want to find out about my family. My friends."

"We're your family, too. We'll always be here for you." Perdita gave Sabrina a short hug. As the two women separated, Charlie and Ora walked out of the theater, looking more relaxed than either had since before this whole mess began. Getting out in the real world had done them all some good. When Ora saw Perdita and Sabrina hugging, a questioning look flittered across her face, but it vanished in a second.

"Hey girls, how was the movie?" Perdita asked.

"Not bad." Charlie's gaze swept from left to right. "Where's Arameus?"

"Around back. Let's go get him, shall we?" Perdita took Charlie by the arm, leading her around the theater. Perdita took a small glance behind her, locked eyes with Sabrina letting her thoughts show, and disappeared around the corner of the brick building.

Chapter Seven
Sabrina

Sabrina stood with Ora in an awkward silence. The two women avoided eye contact, neither wanting to admit their feelings.

"So, you think we'll hitch a ride back to the cabin?" Ora asked, staring down the alleyway between a retaining wall and the theater. "Or get a cab?"

"We shouldn't let anyone know where we are. We've been lucky we haven't been found in the cabin yet."

"That old man had been nice to give us a ride here, and I really don't want to walk all the way back in the dark." Ora's head tilted upward. The clear night had disappeared during the movie, and thicker clouds had rolled in, bringing with them the damp smell of approaching rain.

Sabrina reigned in her retort. Ora never consider all the obstacles and outcomes of her actions. Even bumming a ride had been a horrible idea. They shouldn't have brought attention to themselves. Especially in some small town in North Carolina. The place only had a rundown theater, one grocery store, one gas station, and five churches.

At the end of September, what few tourists this town got from camping and canoeing would be wrapping up any day. They'd have to move on and soon, but the question remained on where they would go. Sabrina would have to convince them all to move and stop relying on a teenager for direction.

"Let's catch up with the others." Sabrina strolled onward, not liking sitting still.

They rounded the corner of the run-down theater, passing the stinking garbage can full of stale popcorn. Arameus, Perdita, and

Over the Bridge

Charlie waited for them around the back corner. Sabrina's pace slowed. "I'm sorry I've been so hard on you."

"Thank—" Ora started, but stopped short seeing the anxious looks on everyone's faces.

They huddled together, Perdita's arm around Charlie. Arameus's eyes darted over his shoulder then to the side. Sabrina got the message. Someone was behind him. How had she been so stupid? Distracted by emotions. Talking to Perdita and crying like a pathetic child instead of forcing them to stay out of sight.

Sabrina pulled her magic close to the surface. Her fingertips zinged with power, and she let it fill her, rising with a swarm of rolling sea. The attackers stayed hidden behind Arameus and the girls. Using the smallest tendril of power, she scanned the water in the air, wrapping around them, tasting. Definitely a wizard. She sent another tendril to the side. Pain seized around her throat. Her body hurtled forward, pulled by a giant invisible hand. The toes of her boots dragged along the pavement. Three other attackers came into view. She recognized the young man, no, another Naiad, who held her own magic against her. He had been one of the men who had cat-called her earlier.

The young Naiad had short blond, brown-tinged hair. He couldn't be full-blooded Naiad. A Hunter. A halfsie. The thoughts raced through her head in mere seconds. Two others flanked him—an auburn-haired man with the hint of a growing mustache and a dark-skinned boy of no more than sixteen. He had no business being a Hunter.

"Well, well, well… What do we have here?" The Naiad raised his outstretched hand, lifting Sabrina off the ground. The grip around her throat tightened as she struggled for breath. Her face turned a violent shade of purple.

"Let her go!" Charlie shouted, surprising everyone.

The Naiad's magical grip slacked a fraction, letting Sabrina draw in delicious oxygen. He focused on Charlie. "What will you do about it, little human?"

Charlie stuck up her chin, not backing down. "I've seen your magic, and you don't scare me." She might have been convincing if it weren't for the quiver in her voice.

The four Hunters laughed without mirth.

Arameus held up a hand. "Now, if we can talk about this. We think you've made some sort of mistake."

"Mistake?" the teenage boy spat. "You must be the traitorous Defender." They knew more than Sabrina expected.

"I'm no traitor." Arameus lifted his chin higher. "I honor the truth."

"You chose a Nip over your own kind." At the end of his words, the Ember's hands caught on fire, and his brown eyes glowed red.

"Steady," the Tempest beside him warmed.

"Let me burn them all." The Ember raised his palms to the sky, flames growing hotter.

The Naiad held up his free hand and squelched the Ember's fire with water from the air. "You'll get your chance. We don't need the spares. You can have your fun with them." His gaze scanned past each of them, but his eyes settled on no one.

Ah, they don't know what Ora looks like, Sabrina thought. They couldn't attack until they knew for certain which one was Ora. They had a chance.

Sabrina's power reached out, testing, and felt the weakness in the magic around her throat. The halfsie's pathetic power could never match hers. He'd only gotten her because she'd been taken unaware.

What she wouldn't give for her Quad.

Sabrina met eyes with Perdita. They knew what had to be done. She nodded, and then all hell broke loose.

Sabrina's power shot outward in all directions, deflecting the others' power like a blade through silk. At the same moment, Perdita shoved Charlie to the ground out of the way. Perdita whirled around faster than Sabrina thought possible. Her hands pushed toward the others. Perdita's Tempest magic pulled on the incoming storm. A rolling thundercloud zoomed outward, gathering the water in the air, churning with lightening. Three lightning bolts shot out in quick succession. Two hit the young Ember in the chest. His limp body flew backward.

Over the Bridge

The third bolt stuck the Tempest, but he deflected most of it. Only a small burn mark showed on his shoulder.

Sabrina, continuing her momentum from her first attack, spun her arms in a great circle. The air, stripped dry of water, crackled with static electricity. The hairs on her arms stood on end. She followed the arc, throwing a pinpoint precision of water, sharper than a blade, straight at the Naiad. He threw his hands up, but her stronger power dominated his pitiful attempt to deflect. The water slowed. Instead of slicing through him clean, the magic blade inched inside his chest. His screams permeated the night air. Blood oozed into the water-sword turning it crimson. His stupidity made his death slower and more painful.

The ground shook. Sabrina dropped to her side and rolled toward the others. She caught a glimpse of Perdita battling the Tempest.

The Sphere behind Arameus and Ora bent over, his hands on the concrete. The ground continued to shake and break apart. Ora finally came to life and screamed. Like a child, her powers rose and spluttered in uncontrollable fits. Blips of magic sparked, hitting no one. The concrete around them turned to soggy liquid, trapping Arameus and Ora in thick mush.

Arameus pointed his hands downward. Air blasted into the ground. Rather than helping, he managed to harden the concrete once again, trapping them in place. The Sphere jumped to his feet, an evil smile upon his face.

He faced Sabrina, eyes glowing a faint green. Glowing from immeasurable power or from lack of control, Sabrina didn't know. The air vibrated with magic, tinged with the smells of burning rubber and sage. They eyed each other. Calculating the threat. Movement from the Sphere's left caught her attention. Charlie brandished a rusty jagged piece of rebar. She swung like a baseball player. The rebar struck the Sphere in the temple. He fell and no longer moved.

The alleyway descended into a silence save for their panting. Perdita pinched her nose as blood ran down her face. The Tempest lay a few feet away, eyes staring up into the starless sky, water oozing from his mouth.

"Filled his lungs with water?" Sabrina jerked her head toward the Tempest.

Perdita gave a single nod before rushing over to Ora and Arameus. While the others worked on breaking Ora and Arameus free from the concrete, Sabrina checked the bodies. None had a pulse, including the Sphere Charlie had slugged in the head.

Charlie leaned against the brick wall of the theater, hands covering her mouth, face pale. She lowered her hands. "Did I?"

"Yes."

Charlie broke out in sobs, mumbling to herself, "What have I done? What have I done?"

"What you had to do. Do not mourn the loss of someone who would've killed you. We have to leave and now."

"What about them?" Perdita asked, arm around a pale Ora, who wouldn't look at anyone.

"We'll have to leave them. We've already made too much noise. The human police will be coming."

Arameus pulled Charlie into an embrace, her head buried in his shoulder. "How will we get back?"

Sabrina glanced back toward the parking lot. "We're going to have to steal a car. Who knows how to drive?"

Chapter Eight
Ora

A FAST AND FURIOUS THIRTY minutes later, we pulled away from our cabin. An emptiness filled me as the car bounced along the unpaved road. Arameus, a flash light in his mouth, stared at an old map he found in the glove compartment. He gave Mom directions, keeping us on back roads. The last thing we needed was to be pulled over or caught in a stolen car.

The cabin disappeared as we rounded a large turn, our safety for the last few weeks gone. If only I wouldn't have suggested we go to the movies. But those Hunters had been close. Surely they would've found us anyway. Guilt and embarrassment surged through me again and again. I had been useless. Scared out of my mind. Even Charlie had taken one of them down, and I'd done nothing.

"Sabrina?"

"Yes?" She didn't look away from the side window in the backseat.

"I need you to train me like you were, like a Protector," I explained.

"Okay. What did you think I was doing?" Her gaze never stopped moving as if she expected another attack at any moment.

Ignoring this comment, I said, "There's something else."

"What is it?" Mom peered at me from the rearview mirror.

"I know what I have to do."

"What's that?" Charlie shifted in the middle of the back seat.

"I have to find more teachers. I have to learn to use and fight with all of my magic." I pivoted in my seat facing Sabrina. "Do you know of anyone who might help us? Might train me with the other cores?"

She turned to look out the back window, forehead constricted as she thought. "I know of someone. He could teach you Sphere magic, and he may lead us to others."

"Great! Where is he?" I asked.

"Last I heard, he was in Tennessee," she said.

"We're going to have to ditch the car. Make our way to a bus station." No one said anything.

Tomorrow, I thought, *the real mission begins.*

Chapter Nine
Ora

The trees flew by in a green blur as we rode down the interstate on a big Greyhound bus. I took a sip of my sugary, watered-down gas station coffee and opened my overpriced yogurt for breakfast. Charlie slept with her mouth hanging open, her wavy brown hair lying in tangles across her face. Arameus sat in the row beside us, gazing out the window and sipping coffee. Sabrina rested her head on his shoulder. Her hardness dissolved during sleep, and she appeared to be nothing more than a delicate and innocent young woman. She would hate it if she knew my thoughts. I loved getting under her skin. Tormenting her was a great distraction. In the seat in front of me, Mom rummaged through her plastic bag from the gas station we'd pulled out of. She flicked her blond ponytail behind her, turned, and handed me some string cheese and a cereal bar. I had to admire her. Even on the run for our lives with this half-schemed idea of mine to be trained as a warrior, she still found ways to make me eat healthy. Her wrapper crackled as she opened her own bar.

I attempted to stifle a yawn while rubbing at the dark circles under my eyes. I couldn't sleep sitting upright in the best of circumstances, so I wouldn't be indulging in a cat nap on the bus. Plus, I didn't dare doze off. Every time, the image of John dying replayed in my mind. His blank, lifeless eyes stared at me. Sometimes he blinked, which jerked me awake. Other times, the tailless black cat that used to visit me in my prison cell dragged his body away.

If the nightmares weren't over John, then voices screamed for help—scared and haunted. The memory of them lingered long after my eyes opened.

I tucked my coffee and yogurt in between my legs and rubbed my neck. A constant headache went with me everywhere. Losing sleep had always done it. Now coupled with a stiff neck, the pain reached migraine proportions. We had about another six hours before we reached our destination. Sabrina insisted we take several different buses, changing randomly, and not proceeding in a straight line to throw off anyone who might be following us. I thought this had made this trip longer and harder on all of us, not to mention more expensive since my mother's life savings funded our traveling. She said she cashed out all her accounts when she and John traveled to Conjuragic to rescue me. Good thing, too, since using a credit card now would be out of the question. Although I couldn't help worry that she'd run out of funds soon.

This wasn't something Sabrina or Arameus had ever had to worry about. Travel in the human world had essentially been free for them, other than a small fee to use the Veil. What I wouldn't give to be able to travel anywhere you wanted for little to nothing.

Something clicked in my head. *You could go anywhere you wanted.* The guys at the theater. Where had they come from? Who were they? Sabrina had called them Hunters, but what was that? With the Veil closed, they had to have already been here, so how had they known where we would be? I turned. "Arameus." He met my gaze while my mother turned in the seat to look at me as well.

"Yes?" he asked.

I checked to make sure no one was listening. "How does the Veil work?"

Charlie stirred. "Yeah, we human-side natives can't figure out the physics of it."

I shot her a look. We'd been friends long enough that she caught my unspoken message that said, "I thought you were sleeping." She shrugged and focused on Arameus. "Sure, it's probably a stupid idea thinking about the physics, since, well, magic. But inquiring minds wanna know."

Arameus hid his surprise well. He leaned in closer. "Each gate is attached to a different region."

"How do you know which gate to take? How do you know you aren't going to end up inside a mountain or a volcano or in the middle of traffic?"

"Valid questions. I don't know all the details myself. But that's what the gates are for. They are a built-in safety net. Not only do they allow you to go wherever you want to go within their region of coverage, but they make sure you end up there safely and without being seen."

"Doesn't that mean it can track you?" I lowered my voice further.

"Yes, but most of the time no one minds because it isn't a secret where they're going."

Ora tapped a finger on the bus seat. "Someone said you could lose yourself in the Veil."

"Yes." He nodded. "Your body is pulled apart in the Veil. Down to the molecular level. Probably even sub-molecular. If you can't hold onto your mind, you'll dissolve into nothing."

"Your mind as in your brain. Organic. Also stripped down to the sub-molecular level. So, does that mean the Veil is full of floating brains?" Charlie asked.

I shuttered at the comical and disturbing image.

"No, not your brain. Your essence. What makes you, you."

"He means your soul," Mom said, one arm hung over the back of her seat.

Arameus shrugged. "I don't know about that. But going through a gate helps. It allows people who would never be able to travel a means to do so. Don't get me wrong, it's still dangerous, but it helps."

Charlie wrinkled. She looked at me and then at Arameus. "Didn't you tell me when you all came back you didn't use a gate?"

He nodded. "Yes, we were lucky. Anyone of us could have died going through without the gate."

"What happens if you die in the Veil?" Charlie asked. They stared at each other, and all at once, I felt an intruder in my own conversation. I looked away, but I heard him say, "I don't know."

Charlie asked, "Since you didn't come through a gate, how would anyone on either side know which region to look for us?"

His face drew up in concentration. "I don't know. With the Veil closed, I don't know what information either side can gather. But I would assume the gate we were nearest was the region the Hunters began searching."

I considered his words. "How big are the regions?"

"It depends. Some are only a few miles apart, say if you're going somewhere like a big city. Others are larger areas, in more rural places," he finished.

Sabrina's eyes opened as if sensing the intensity of the conversation.

"Do we have any idea what gate we were near?" I asked.

"What does it matter?" Mom asked.

I looked at her in surprise, but Sabrina answered for me. "If they know what region we should be in, they will be sending most of their forces to search the area. They would descend upon us."

That's what I'd feared. "So, it's good we left, right?"

Sabrina looked at me, her face grave, and uttered my worst fear. "No. The Hunters communicate with each other. When the group who attacked us is discovered, the others are going to come looking for us. It's best to assume nowhere is safe." She stretched her long legs, grabbed a coffee out of the tray, and a cereal bar from my mother. She ripped open the wrapper.

Charlie sighed. "There's food?"

"Not much, my dear." Mom handed her a bottle of water.

"I'm starving." She opened the lid and gulped down half of it while reaching for her yogurt in Mom's outstretched hand.

Watching my friend, I wondered yet again if I should send her into hiding with her grandparents. I'd miss her every day, but every minute she stayed with me she put herself in danger. I finished my breakfast, laid my head against the glass, and closed my eyes, hoping for a dreamless nap and perhaps the answers would come.

Several hours later, we stood in the lobby of a semi-nice hotel in Knoxville, Tennessee, with shining tile floors, several oversized floral-patterned chairs surrounded a large fireplace in a common area, and a. buffet-style bar with several tables and chairs for the continental breakfast in the mornings. A twenty-something-year-old man whose nametag read Mark manned the front desk.

Mark had short brown hair, several acne scars, and typed on the keyboard while speaking to Mom. I walked the short distance away to a self-serve popcorn machine and made myself a large bag. It wasn't bad either, warm and buttery.

"We just need a credit card and your driver's license," Mark said.

I rolled my eyes, walking back to the polished front desk. *Of course, we need a credit card.*

"But, sir, it's only for one night, and I have cash." Mom removed a roll of hundreds from her purse.

"I'm sorry, ma'am. It's company policy," Mark said, not sounding the least bit sorry. I walked up and pulled on Mom's arm, but a crazy idea struck me. I moved Mom out of the way and pulled my magic under the surface. I looked Mark straight in the eye and waved my hand in front of his face, releasing a tendril of power. "We can have a room for the night." The magic stretched out from me, caressing, seductive even.

Mark's eyes glazed over, and he looked sleepy. "Of course you can, darling."

I smiled and looked over at Mom, who looked shocked.

"As soon as you show me a credit card," Mark shook his head, focusing again on the computer screen in front of him.

My shoulders slumped in disappointment, but Charlie burst out laughing. Mom motioned for us to leave from the entrance. Charlie stifled her giggles. Outside, she asked, "What were you trying some Jedi mind trick?"

I smiled lopsided at her and shrugged. "What? It didn't hurt to try."

We erupted into a fit of laughter. I hoisted my backpack farther up my shoulders and strolled away from the hotel wishing we hadn't sent the cab away. Arameus asked, to no one in particular, "What's a Jedi mind trick?"

We lost it again, holding onto each other, doubled over in laughter. My belly hurt from laughing, and tears blurred my vision. It felt good to laugh.

Several blocks later, my magic rolled and sat up, attentive and wagging like a dog's tail. I tried to shake it off, but it fought me. It seeped into my muscles making every movement hard, like walking through water. "Guys, I need to go in there."

The magic guided me. A bell rang above my head as I entered the dim, dusty shop. A voice called from the back, "Hello, can I help you with anything?"

Mom called out, "No, we're just looking, thanks."

"Okay, let me know if you need anything," the owner of the voice said.

The sound of footsteps grew louder as the woman walked to the front of the store. She had big hair, large eyes, and wore a sundress with bright flowers. She smiled, but I turned away, heading down the aisles, as my magic searched.

I passed rows of old couches, dining room tables, and other miscellaneous furniture. Other aisles held old clothing and shoes. The very back row shimmered with the unknown power calling to my magic like a twin. A cabinet full of old jewelry stood in the middle of the aisle. One piece in particular caught my eye—an oval necklace. A thin yellow strip of paper below it labeled the necklace, "The Lamè Amulet," written in calligraphy.

An asteroid, a cross between a diamond and a square, hovered in the center of the oval. Inside the asteroid, a jewel sparkled like a rainbow. Swirls of silver fanned out from the asteroid and five silver strands hung from the oval with tiny rainbow gemstones rippling down the strands.

The beautiful amulet pulsed with power in time with the purring of my magic.

Mom put her hand on my shoulder and sighed. "Excuse me," she yelled. "We would like to buy this necklace."

Over the Bridge

After completing the purchase, we eventually found a hotel room. Or rather an older, run down, roach-motel. We couldn't expect much from a place that didn't require a credit card. I'd bet it was one of those rent-by-the-hour places. It looked clean on the surface, except for the huge roach that scampered up the brick wall outside. The scratched and dull end tables had seen better days. The faded comforters smelled clean. I grabbed a pair of cheap flip flops at the convenience store beside the hotel so I could take a shower without worrying about foot fungus. I had enough problems. Sabrina couldn't quite understand what I found comforting about a shower. "You have magic! You can clean yourself better than any human shower," she said. But she didn't understand getting under the hot water, letting it run over your head and shoulders, and taking away some of the stress with it. Of course, magic, for her, came naturally; whereas I still had to concentrate to control it. It would be like me to suck the water out of the air, run it over my body, and flood the place.

I got out of the shower, flipped my long red hair into a towel, and wrapped another around my body. I cracked open the door to let out the steam. Arameus had left to find us some dinner. I leaned against the door frame, cooling off, and surveyed my group. Charlie lay on her stomach, her hands holding her head while her feet were in the air, curled together. Mom sat on the other bed, hands in her lap. They watched some old TV show. Sabrina sharpened a hunting knife at a cigar table by one of the windows. If ever there was a more ragtag group of people out to change the world, I'd never seen it. It occurred to me this may very well be the last night we were safe. Tomorrow we'd meet the man who hopefully would teach me how to use my Sphere magic. "Sabrina, how do you know about this guy?"

Without looking up, she murmured, "He's Leigh Stewart's uncle."

Mom, Charlie, and I stared at her. "So, he could fight us. Or turn us in to the Hunters?"

"Or what if he refuses and sends us away. Then where would we go?" Charlie asked my next thoughts.

"He's a good man, and," she looked out the window, considering her words, "he doesn't exactly see eye-to-eye with The Man. He got into a spot of trouble not too long ago. Leigh and I helped him out."

"He lives here? Like all the time?" Mom asked.

Sabrina nodded. "That's why he's likely to help?" I couldn't wrap my head around Commander Stewart, the head of the Protectors, with an uncle living in the human world as a rogue, or her breaking the rules to help him out. I had only a vague understanding of the Protectors. But, basically, they were like the FBI and traveled in groups of four called Quads, one from each magical house. "How did you and Commander Stewart get to be on Quad One? You're both so young."

Sabrina raised one eyebrow. "You know we age differently in Conjuragic, right?"

Charlie and I both shook our heads.

She put the knife on the table. "Every year in Conjuragic equates to around five human years."

"So since you look twenty-five," I waved my hand, doing to math in my head, "then that would make you a hundred years old?"

She laughed and corrected, "Not exactly. For some reason, and no one knows why, our children age rapidly in the beginning, year for year, until about age fifteen or so. Then the aging process slows."

"So for someone to look twenty-five, then they would age the first fifteen years."

Sabrina nodded.

"After that it's five human year to everyone in Conjuragic. So ten times five is fifty, plus the original fifteen. That would make them around sixty-five?" I figured in my head.

"Give or take," she said.

"So Arameus is like seventy?" Charlie asked, face pale.

Sabrina nodded, turning her attention back to the knife.

"Too weird." I shook my head and disappeared into the bathroom to get ready. The zing of Sabrina's blade struck a chord inside me. Something both familiar and not. A plan brewed in my head. Charlie, always on cue to my mood, stood from the bed and followed me to the bathroom. I motioned to close the door, and she complied.

"What?" she asked.

"We're going out." I pulled makeup out of my mother's bag.

"Where?" she asked, but picked up the hairbrush and ran it through her hair.

"Anywhere." I put on lipstick. "This is our last night before everything really begins. We need some fun."

"Sounds good to me." She tugged out the tangles in her hair, and I couldn't help but love her. This was my best friend, going with the flow, and getting ready for a night out. Now to convince everyone else.

Chapter Ten
Ora

CHARLIE AND I STRUTTED OUT of the bathroom. I'd French braided my hair and found a cute pair of jeans and a blouse, tied at my waist. Charlie discovered a snug pair of hip huggers and a sparkly t-shirt. Mom, Sabrina, and Arameus paused from eating burgers from a fast food chain.

"We want to go out," I said.

"No!" Mom and Sabrina said together.

"Why?" Even the whining sounded pathetic to my own ears.

Sabrina tossed her half-eaten burger on the paper. "Do you not remember what happened the last time you got the brilliant idea to go out?"

"She's right. We could've been killed," Mom said.

I flopped on the bed, bouncing one leg with the tips of my toes. "But we weren't. Don't you think we all need a break?"

"No." Sabrina gripped the hilt of the hunting knife.

"Arameus?" I turned my full attention to my former Defender, who'd always been a bit more lenient than Mom or Sabrina.

He moved as if to shake his head, but Charlie cleared her throat. "We passed a night club on the way here. Wouldn't dancing be fun?" She flushed a deep shade of purple, and to my astonishment, so did Arameus.

The new amulet around my neck hummed and warmed against the skin on my chest.

"Perhaps going out wouldn't be such a bad idea."

"Have you lost your mind?" Sabrina gaped at him.

Over the Bridge

Ignoring her, he popped the last chicken nugget into his mouth. He chewed and swallowed. "I'm going to the lost and found to see if I can find something for everyone to wear."

"Arameus! You can't be serious." Sabrina stood from the chair.

The necklace pulsed once, then twice, and Mom stood. "I'll help you distract the manager."

"As if he'll care." Arameus held the door open for Mom.

Sabrina shook her head as if clearing away bad thoughts. "What did you do to them?"

"Nothing," I said, but wondered at the power in the amulet.

"I guess I'm out numbered, but this is..." A muscle in her jaw clenched.

"Foolish," I finished for her. "Yes, I know."

Twenty minutes later, we stepped out of the hotel room, heading for the night club. Mom wore a simple skirt hanging down to her ankles with a brown sleeveless top. Dark blue jeans and blue dress shirt looked as if they'd been made for Arameus. He'd even let me cut his curly, unruly red hair with Sabrina's hunting knife. Conjuragic used hair length to acknowledge rank, so for Arameus, shorter hair meant more than just a haircut.

Sabrina, as always, didn't have to do anything to look beautiful, but the tight black dress that only went to her mid-thigh took her to another level of astonishing. Her long blond hair cascaded down her back in perfect wavy curls.

I eyed my own outfit, feeling underdressed and outclassed, except for my new necklace dangling on my chest, my magic content. I didn't realize how much I missed the weight of a necklace. Until very recently, I'd worn a necklace every day. Losing it had released my power and gotten me into this mess.

A short walk later, we arrived at the club as twilight fell. The tension in my shoulders eased as we stood in the already long line that a cute guy in front of us said was typical of a Saturday night. Little did I know, we were walking right into the dragon's mouth.

Chapter Eleven
Ora

Sárkány's nightclub glistened like a diamond in a night sky. The rest of the street's businesses had closed for the evening, their store fronts dark and empty. Two muscular bouncers flanked the blood-red doors, a velvet black rope blocking the entrance. The two men could've been contenders for the WWE. My pulse sped up as I overheard them ask several people in front to show ID. I seriously doubted anyone would be looking for us here. But still, perhaps we should invest in some fake IDs. I made a mental note to ask Sabrina if the Hunters had any connection with local or federal law enforcement or if the Conjuragic community that resided in the human world used some technology to track credit cards. How strange to be on the run but from an unknown foe. Shaking it off and trying not to think like some TV criminal drama, I decided to focus on having fun.

The line inched closer to the door. Despite my efforts to shake off the nerves, my fingertips felt like ice. Although with one look at the sultry Sabrina in her skintight dress and flowing hair, the bouncers waved us right in. Without giving the rest of us a second glance, the bouncer closest to me stamped my hand while the other unclicked the velvet rope and opened the door. A gust of cold hair mingled with a subtle aroma of overripe fruit and latent sweat swept across my face.

Loud music flowed through the night club's doors, which only moments before had been devoid of even the remotest touch of bass. Those doors must be super soundproofed or blocked by magic. There went my wild imagination again. It wasn't as if magic was everywhere. Paranoia, just what I needed.

Over the Bridge

The rich dark wood floors shined with the overhead lights. The walls alternated between metallic black and blood red. The club had not one but two bars—one on my left, the other on the right. Hundreds of bottles of liquor lined the walls behind each of the bars each stacked on long shiny black shelves. A scratched mirror behind the shelves peeked between the bottles. Three women swathed in skin-tight black leather with hair so black it couldn't be real, pale creamy skin, and ruby red lips manned each of the bars. One smiled, showing off white fangs. Dracula's brides came to mind. *Overkill on the goth look.*

Dozens of people leaned against the long wooden bars. Many held wads of cash and screamed drink orders, but the pounding techno music drowned out their words. The bartenders whipped around, flipping bottles, and shaking drinks as if in an intricate dance. The whole charade looked easy, but if I'd tried to replicate it, shards of broken glass and spilt liquor would cover the floors.

In the very center of the club, the huge dance floor crawled with sweaty bodies swaying and grinding to the pounding electronic music. A rainbow of lights swirled around the place, bouncing off a faint mist that hung in the air. Between the movements of the dancers, rows of tables and booths became visible in the back. Using hand gestures, I pointed them out. Weaving between the periphery of dancers and those making their way to and from the bar, we made it to the seating area. An intricately detailed mural covered the back wall. A massive scaling dragon with black shimmering scales and piercing green eyes perched on top of a mountain. The beast looked down as if observing the crowd with silent judgment.

I shivered and slid into a booth. The rest followed suit then stared at me, waiting. Now what to do? The noise, amount of people, and atmosphere of the place crowded my senses. I retreated into myself as the typical awkwardness that defined my life returned, and the standard feeling of not belonging snapped into place like a well-worn glove. Just like in my hometown of Raleigh, West Virginia, I was a regular fish out of water. At least here I could be conspicuous, unlike at home with the population under a thousand

and everyone knowing each other, whether you wanted them to or not. The melancholy inside me grew as the realization hit me. There wasn't anywhere in the world—worlds—where I would fit in. What did I expect when I was a one of a kind...thing? There isn't a name for what I am. An entirely new species—just what every teenage girl dreams of. Go me.

Arameus, always comfortable and cool in any situation, clapped his hands. "Who's ready for drinks?" Without waiting for a reply, he slid out of his seat, heading for one of the bars. Charlie and I looked at each other and laughed. We needed a guy like this to pull us out of our shyness.

Within a matter of a few moments, Arameus made friends with two attractive twenty-something women, a group of men, and a young couple. These people almost tripped over themselves to let him skip them in line. Unlike everyone else who shouted to be heard, Arameus leaned in, and the others quieted to let him speak. The barmaids abandoned everyone else to serve him. Soon, he managed to balance five drinks, making it look easy, and returned to our booth. He radiated coolness. If he hadn't also been selfless and kind, I might have succumbed to jealousy.

He handed each of us a drink, and immediately my mother reached over and snatched the drinks away from Charlie and me. "Hey!" we both yelled at the same time.

Mom put up her finger and shook it at us. "Nuh nuh nuh nuh no."

"But, Mom."

"You two are not twenty-one." She shook her head, arms crossed.

"You have to be twenty-one to drink alcohol?" Sabrina raised an eyebrow. "It is allowed back home at age sixteen."

"We aren't at your home." Mom looked away and muttered under her breath, "Insane. Giving hormonal teenagers with magical powers alcohol."

"Perdita, my dear." Arameus pulled out the charm.

"Oh no you don't, Arameus. Don't you try and sweet talk me. These girls are underage." "I understand your feelings, Perdita, but you must admit these girls may only be eighteen, but they are far more mature than their biological age. Ora herself was almost executed only a few short weeks ago. Charlie has been attacked, and they have both lost someone near and dear to their hearts. If anyone deserves a drink, it's these girls. Besides, we're here. It's not as if they are unsupervised."

I saw rather than heard Mom *humph* to herself. Almost against her will, Mom gestured toward the drinks, and Charlie and I reached for them before she could change her mind.

Mine was a mixed drink, red, looking more like a slushy than a drink, covered in whipped cream. A frozen strawberry daiquiri. As I lifted the cool glass, Mom put her hands up halting us.

We sighed, thinking we had lost out again. But instead, she raised her glass, and we followed suit. She said, "To John."

Tears filled my eyes, and something squeezed around my heart as I replied, "To John."

This must be part of grief. Moments would go by and happiness would sneak in, but before I had a chance to enjoy it, something would remind me. A scent. A memory. Some other tiny random thing and the pain would wash over me once again. My magic slipped upward, comforting, like a warm blanket. The pain eased as my lips surrounded the straw and pulled. The drink caressed my tongue with a sweetness followed by a bitter aftertaste, which could only be the alcohol. Holding the magic close to me like a shield, I let my thoughts wander. What would things be like if he were here? Would he be sitting beside me, holding my hand, or have his arm wrapped around my shoulder? Would he ask me to dance or kiss me? Would I feel safer? Happier?

A young attractive man, tall with brown hair and green eyes, strolled up to the table and asked Sabrina to dance. It took all my self-control not to die laughing at the look on her face. She gathered her composure and said, "Sure."

Her answer and condescending look she shot my way drove the amusement from the moment. I never would've imagined she would accept. Her hand slipped into his outstretched hand, and the two disappeared onto the dance floor. The two of them went in and out of view, and as she glided with perfect moves, the earlier jealousy wiggled again. Not only was she gorgeous and a badass witch, she could dance, too. Some people get all the luck. They disappeared into the crowd again, and I lost sight of them.

An uncomfortable silence followed as the four of us sat there staring at the table drinking our drinks. One song ended and another one started without the return of Sabrina. As a third song began, this one slow, Arameus broke up the silence and asked Mom to dance. She agreed, and I didn't watch them go.

I watched the dancing couples trying to ignore the intense loneliness threatening to overtake the magical shield. How I wished John was here and we could be dancing. I wrapped my hand around the cool glass tinged with condensation and finished the last of the drink in several quick swallows, hoping perhaps the alcohol could dampen the overwhelming despair lingering out of reach. Charlie stared onto the dance floor, her expression one of deep sadness with tears sparkling in her eyes. I opened my mouth to ask her what was wrong, but a waitress approached. The woman's goth style was a little more watered down than the barmaids, except for the fishnet panty hose disappearing underneath a super short black leather skirt. She placed two fresh frozen daiquiris on the table. "Evening ladies. Courtesy of the gentleman on the dance floor."

The woman motioned behind her shoulder, and I followed her gaze. Arameus held Mom, her back to us, and grinned slyly. With a wink, he whirled Mom away so we could have more than one drink without Mom noticing.

"He's awesome." Charlie took another big gulp, raised her glass to him, the sadness gone from her face. "Sooo," she said grinning with mischief dancing her eyes.

"Yeah."

"*The Fifth Element?*" She wiggled her eyebrows.

I shot her a sideways glare. "I'm not the perfect being."

She nodded. "True. *Avatar?*"

"I don't see a big arrow on my forehead. Do you?"

Over the Bridge

"So, Sphere, Tempest, Ember, and Naiad?" she asked.

"Yup."

"Um S.T.E.N... stepping?" She tapped her temple.

I could smack her right now. "No."

She chuckled. "She who must not be named."

"Oh shut up!" I reached over and pushed her.

"I know! We could name you a muggle. Totally mess with all the Harry Potter fans." She stifled a laugh when I rolled my eyes.

She looked at me, her expression serious. "I know what you are."

"What's that?" I asked.

"You're an Ora," she said, looking very satisfied with herself.

I shook my head in confusion. "But that's my name."

"Exactly, whenever you discover something, you get named after it. So, this can be named after you. An Ora."

"Isn't that what you get before you get a headache or something?" I asked her, still not convinced.

She rolled her eyes at me. "Nooo, that's an aura, A.U.R.A., not an Ora."

"Really? Because that's not at all similar." I shook my head, chuckling at her.

"Whatever. That's what you are," she said with a finality.

Why not? It was a good of a name as any. An Ora.

Mom and Arameus returned to the table after the song had ended. Sabrina had moved on and danced with a different man. Out of the corner of my eye, yet another man approached the table. He stopped, hovering above me, awkward and shy. He had short brown hair and kind brown eyes. "Would you like to dance?"

Shock flooded my system. What should I do? It was a dance, not a proposal. Besides, I was supposed to have fun, right? "Okay."

A remix of a pop song blared from unseen speakers. Thankfully, no slow song played, and the young man led me to the edge of the dance floor. Without meeting his gaze, I moved in tune with music while he did the same a few feet in front of me. He kept his hands to himself, which suited me fine. The guilt of another man touching me would've been too much. I spied Mom chewing on her fingernails, not letting me out of her sight. Arameus interlaced his arm with Charlie's and led her to the dance floor. The smile on her face made me happy. As I moved in time with the stranger, I let my vision blur and pretended he was John.

He and I had only danced one time, and that had been at prom before we became a couple and he had still been just my best friend's older brother. It had been embarrassing then, a time when no one else would dance with me except a lifelong friend, and a chaperone to boot. As the realization hit that that would be our one and only dance, the sadness rose again in a wave.

No, I wasn't going to keep doing this. Not tonight. I used the magic inside me and shoved the sadness away, hard. With a forced smile plastered on my face, I picked up the pace. Letting the self-consciousness go, my hips swayed in time with the music. Who cared what I looked like? I'd never see this guy or anyone else in the bar ever again. Even though I may not dance in public very often, I love music. Whenever I hear it, I let myself go.

A new song came on with a great beat and electric sounds. I'd never heard it before. I liked it at once, as did the magic. With my eyes closed, my body swayed with the music as if I'd practiced the moves for hours. The Lamè Amulet bounced on my chest. My fingers wrapped around the firm stone, and it warmed beneath my fingertips. It vibrated along with the music. The music sped up as the beat intensified, and my dancing followed it step for step.

A gasp to my left made my eyes pop open. A little crowd around me stared. *Oh no! I must be a terrible dancer.* Everyone stared. My cheeks flushed red as I spun to run back to the table, but Sabrina met me on the dance floor. She grabbed my arm, nails biting into my flesh, and turned us toward the door. She practically dragged me out of the crowd toward Mom, Arameus, and Charlie, who had grabbed our things and waited near the door.

My dancing couldn't have been that bad. Tears filled my eyes as I leaned toward Charlie and asked, "How bad was it?"

Over the Bridge

She looked at me, her expression grave. "Ora you were...hazy."

"What?" I asked, confused. What the hell was she talking about?

"You were in a magical meditation." Sabrina held my arm and yanked me toward the door. I glanced behind me, and the crowd had resumed dancing as if forgetting what happened. This terrified me, and I couldn't explain why.

"A what?"

"I'll tell you later. We have to get out of here now!" Sabrina answered. Inches from the door, two bouncers appeared out of the shadows.

"Stop right here," one of them said.

The air zinged with magic as Sabrina gathered the water out of the air and flung it like a whip to strike the bouncers. Only instead of hitting them, the lasso stopped midway. The water dissipated, crashing to the floor. Sabrina grabbed her chest, her eyes wide with pain, and I watched in utter shock as she fell to the floor in convulsions. A seizure!

Arameus flipped his wrist, and a blast of air flew from his fingertips. His spell never reached the target. The bouncer on the left threw up a hand, and Arameus fell to the floor, writhing, mirroring Sabrina. Mom tried, too, but the other bouncer tossed his head, and Mom fell as well. The entire thing had taken less than five seconds. No one paid any attention to the three people seizing in front of the door.

Charlie and I screamed. Two more bouncers circled us from behind. A cold hand clamped over my mouth. A fifth bouncer appeared. I squirmed against my attacker. Charlie's screams muffled beside me.

The bouncers dragged Sabrina, Arameus, and Mom into a back office. They turned me, and I caught a glimpse of the club. No one looked our way. My heart hammered even harder in my chest.

The bouncers escorted us to an office in the back. The door snapped shut, taking the sounds of the club with it. The blood-red décor of the walls jumped out at me. A man with dark skin, dreadlocked hair, and black merciless eyes dominated the room.

His arms rested on a black leather circular couch in the middle of the office. Handcuffs dangled from either end of the couch. Two women lounged on either side of him—one blond, the other brunette, each covering his neck with loud kisses and rubbing their hands on his chest.

"Well, well what have we here?" His voice matched the rest of him, dark and dangerous. The bouncers let go of Sabrina, Arameus, and Mom. Their pale faces shown with sweat making their blue lips stand out. The convulsions had stopped, but I had a feeling that wasn't a good thing.

The bouncers who had dragged in Mom, Sabrina, and Arameus said not a word and left. Now only the two who stopped us at the door and the two holding Charlie and me remained.

"This one," the bouncer on the left gestured toward me, "was ruminating."

He towered over me at almost six feet tall, with dusty blond hair, gray eyes, and huge football player arms laced with scars.

I attempted to control my breathing, but it wasn't working. My vision darkened at the edges, and I knew I should do something, but everyone else used magic and failed. Foam trickled out of Sabrina's mouth, and it finally occurred to me what happened. Their magic had been stolen. Nips! Real live Nips. The bouncers had taken their magic. I understood Conjuragic's fear of them.

Even if it had occurred to me to use my magic, which I'm ashamed to say it didn't, it wouldn't have worked anyway.

"Rumination. Really?" the dark man added with an air of curiosity about him. "I've never seen that on a dance floor before." He chuckled without mirth. He nodded toward the bouncer who spoke. "You didn't take her magic then?"

"No, sir. I have them." He pointed to Sabrina and Arameus.

The man looked to the other bouncer, this one dark skinned, bald, with gold teeth. "What about you?"

"She didn't try to use her magic. But sir, there is something different about her. I can sense magic, but it keeps moving. It's like its slippery, and I can't grab it, but I do have the older one."

Over the Bridge

He looked afraid to admit he didn't have my magic and added he had Mom's to save face. Out of the corner of my eye, he glanced at Mom and licked his lips. Sweat beaded on his brow, and a pained expression flitted across his face. Unlike Sabrina and Arameus, her twitch had all but disappeared, and her color had returned to normal. Her magic must be different as well, not so much he couldn't take it, but as if it took concentration to hold onto it. *He can't hold her!* Her magic was returning to her, and he couldn't stop it. His eyes moved from her to the man on the couch. He didn't want him to know.

The leader stood from the couch, pushing the two women to the side, and waved his hands, dismissing them like telling a dog to shoo. He took his time coming toward me, reminding me of a snake slithering to a mouse. He towered over me, grabbed my chin, forcing me to meet his gaze, searching for an answer that I hoped I could hide. After a very long time, his eyes left mine and moved from my hair, down my body, and back again to stare at my chest. Dark thoughts swirled in his eyes, and my terror arose anew.

"Sárkány, don't they match the description Master gave?" the Nip who held Sabrina and Arameus asked.

Master?

"Indeed," answered Sárkány, eyes still on my chest.

"Shouldn't you call the Hunters then?" the bouncer said.

"Not until we're sure." Sárkány's pupils widened. "After I've had my fun."

"But Master will be upset if we delay."

Master? As in Mom's Master? It couldn't possibly the same man. Could it?

Sárkány broke his gaze from my chest and glared at the bouncer. I took that moment to look at the other, who trembled as Mom stirred. We wouldn't have much time.

"Master is cut off from us with the Veil sealed. I have no allegiance to the Hunters. I will call them when I'm sure and when I know we'll be rewarded for finding them."

"But sir—"

Sárkány released my chin, flicked his wrist, and a line of sparks shot from his hand. Immediately, an uneven line of blisters formed on the bouncer's arm. The bouncer hissed once before reigning in his pain.

"Do not question me again, Devil," Sárkány threatened.

"Yes, sir," Devil's face an expressionless mask.

Sárkány returned his attention to me. "I wonder," he said more to himself, eyeing my body, expression hungry. "They say you're a Nip, but Nips can't ruminate. So, what are you?"

I stood in silence as he watched me. I flinched as he reached outward. His lips twisted in a delighted smile. He leaned in, slowly, as if enjoying tormenting me. Instead of where I expected, his fingers grazed my necklace. A spark jumped out of it and zapped him. He jumped back a few steps, releasing a string of colorful curses, and put his fingers in his mouth.

"I knew it! There is something about *that* necklace. It's blocking you from taking her magic." He turned to the second bouncer and noticed him swaying. "Rouzier, what's wrong with you?"

The bouncers holding Charlie and me slackened their grip, turning toward Rouzier. Instinct screamed that this was the only moment I had to escape. My focus shifted, and I called my magic. The world descended into tiny sparkles of moving light. For once my magic and I acted in tandem. Our intentions matched.

The magic ripped out of me in different directions. Quick bursts of power hit three out of those four targets. The three bouncers few backward hitting the floor with a thud.

Sárkány ducked at the last second. He rolled to the side and emerged standing. With quick jabs of his hands, balls of flame flew toward me. Charlie screamed as one whizzed past her head. One flew past my cheek. It crashed into the wall behind me with a roar. The smell of singed hair wafted around my head. I dodged more fireballs.

We had to get out of here. Out of the corner of my eye, something shimmered. A rainbow oval screamed into existence, carrying the thick smell of ozone. The magic quivered, insistent. I understood.

Over the Bridge

I broke into a run as a fireball missed me by inches. A forest lay beyond the rainbow.

I burst into a run. At the same moment, the magic shot tendrils out like a lasso. It wrapped around bodies, securing them to me. I stumbled under the new weight, tripping into the abyss. My feet left the red shag carpet behind, and wet grass squished beneath my feet. I swerved at the last second to avoid a tree and skidded to a halt.

I spun toward the rainbow. Sárkány ran toward it, a look of rage plastered on his face. His mouth opened in an unheard scream as the rainbow snapped closed like a rubber band.

The magic let go of the lassos that had pulled my family with me. Charlie sat on the wet grass, covered in mud. Mom scampered to her feet on shaking legs. Sabrina and Arameus lay unconscious on the ground. I spun, looking for my last target.

Mom screamed, "Look out!"

Devil ran straight for me, prepared to tackle me. The magic shot out like a baseball bat. The force of it sent his body flying up feet first, and he crashed upon the ground with a thump. He didn't move. I sprinted to his side. Knocked out, but breathing. Mom stood next me and asked, "Oh Ora, what have you done?"

Chapter Twelve
Perdita

DEEP WITHIN THE FOREST, ORA emerged holding several strands of dogbane. She dropped them on the ground, propped one up, then used her foot to snap them in half. Once she'd done several, she sat on the ground, Indian-style, and peeled the bark exposing the soft fibers underneath.

"What are you doing?" Perdita asked.

"Making rope." Ora didn't look up.

"Why?"

"To tie him up, of course." She gestured toward the bouncer from the club.

"That's not it. I mean why did you bring him with us?" she asked.

A twig snapped. Charlie, calmed down, strolled toward the two women and the unconscious bouncer. She picked up a branch, stepped on it, and sat beside Ora with her legs crossed. She removed the bark and asked, "What I want to know is *how* you brought any of us here?"

Ora lips twisted in a half smiled. "What did you want me to do, Mom? Leave the Nip who has their magic behind so we can watch them die?"

Perdita turned and eyed Sabrina and Arameus. "A Nip?" Her eyes fell on the huge unconscious man. "I suppose not."

"I don't know how I brought us here. There was a, um, rainbow-ish portal thing and, well, I took a run for it, and here we are."

"A rainbow-ish portal thing?" Charlie furrowed her brow. She glanced at Perdita as if she could give a better explanation.

Over the Bridge

"You mean you ran into something and you didn't know what it was? Do you know how dangerous that was?"

Charlie tapped Ora's arm. "Uh oh, there goes her one raised eyebrow. You're in trouble now."

Ora resumed stripping the tree branches into sections. "Look. I know it wasn't the best decision, but we were trapped. All three of you were unconscious, and we were surrounded. That guy, Sárkány. He was beyond dangerous and an Ember. Plus, they were talking about a Master," she cocked her head so the name would sink in, "and Hunters, and he has Nips under his control. My magic saw an opportunity, and I trusted it."

"Your magic saw an opportunity?"

"Yes." Her expression warred on dangerous and daring to be questioned.

"She's right you know," Charlie said. She stood and broke the rest of the branches. An uncomfortable silence settled, interrupted by the continuous ripping sound of the branches being torn to pieces.

"Once you tie him up, then what? He's not going to let them go. They're his leverage." Perdita patted down the unconscious man. She removed a pistol, a switchblade, and a pack of chewing gum. Opening the chamber, the mystery of the man grew. "This isn't even loaded."

"I don't know what we're going to do, but right now I'm going to make a rope and tie him up. Then once he wakes up, we can talk to him and see what happens." Ora, as usual, was being stubborn.

"He has their magic, and he's a Nip." Perdita stuffed the gun down the back of her pants, slipped the knife into her pocket, and shoved the gum into the pocket as well.

"I know." Ora snapped a branch more forcefully than needed, gathered the pieces, and braided them.

"That means he can use their magic against us. He can use their magic to escape from your rope, and then he'll be gone. He'll lead the others right to us, and in the meantime, we'll have to watch Sabrina and Arameus die or leave them behind."

Ora's hands fell into her lap, shoulders drooping. "Your point is?"

Perdita sighed. "This is our only chance. We have to... We have to." She stopped, hesitating, eying Sabrina and Arameus, hating herself for where her thoughts were taking her.

"You want to kill him," Charlie said.

Ora's head flew up in surprise. "Charlie!"

Charlie swallowed. "Your mom's right. These won't hold him, and he isn't going to let them go. If we do it now, Sabrina and Arameus will get their magic back, and we'll be safe."

Ora's mouth dropped open, eyes traveling back and forth between Perdita and Charlie, disbelief etched in her expression. So much had changed. She shook her head, focusing on braiding the strands. "So you want us to...kill an unarmed, unconscious, helpless man in cold blood?" She didn't meet their eyes or even look up.

Perdita crossed her arms, avoiding looking at the man, who couldn't have been more than twenty.

Ora whispered, "So, who's going to do it then?"

No one would answer, and Ora's lips squeezed together in a thin line. She snatched the branches away from Charlie, who didn't even resist. Ora's eyes glowed rainbow hues as her magic rose to the surface. Perdita took a step back, alarmed, and for the first time, afraid of her daughter.

The bark peeled from the remaining branches, the fibers split into tiny strands, and the water inside flowed out. The strands weaved themselves around each other, making several long ropes, braided together. The hairs on Perdita's arms stood on end as Ora's magic extended, flowing through each rope, giving off a soft golden glow. *Where had all this control come from? Anger? The necklace?*

Ora rolled to her feet, pulled the rope behind her, and strolled toward a large oak tree. Perdita jumped back in alarm as the unconscious man moved. She thought he'd woken up, but no. His body remained limp as Ora dragged him with magic. At the base of the tree, she forced him into a seated position with his back against the bark. His head dipped forward, touching his chest, and she grabbed his arms, pulling them behind his back, and fastened the rope around his hands. After grabbing a second rope, she walked around him several times securing him to the tree, and finally securing his feet together. She pulled on the robes, then stepped back, satisfied, and lifted her hands. The rope glowed red this time. *Blocking him from using magic?*

Ora faced Perdita, a tear running down her cheek, and said in a dead, hollow voice, "They wanted to kill me for being a Nip! Now you want me to do that to him?"

"No." Perdita's voice had no fight. "It's not for being a Nip, but for doing that to them." She pointed to their friends. Arameus and Sabrina lay as still as statues upon the ground, eyes rolled up in their heads, breathing ragged.

Ora sucked in air as if she couldn't breathe. Her hands shook as the war raged inside of her. She fell to her knees, hands covering her face. Perdita understood. This was something different. Ora wasn't fighting or defending her life. This…this would be murder, and she'd never be the same. She sobbed in her hands, words muffled.

Perdita inched closer, sagging to her knees beside her daughter.

Over and over Ora whispered, "His name is Devil. His name is Devil."

Perdita's heart broke. This young Nip had a name. An odd one, but a name. She couldn't let Ora be the one to do it. If anyone's soul had to be destroyed, it would be hers. Ora's breathing slowed, and she wiped the tears and snot from her face. With shaking breaths, she placed her hands on her knees.

Charlie crossed her arms, hovering out of the way. "You know you really are an ugly crier."

Ora laughed, a short quick sound. "Like you're any better."

Night had fallen. The air became colder with growing moisture. The gentle clicking of crickets tumbled out of the trees, and the deep hooting of an owl echoed in the distance. Not for the first time, Perdita's hands grew sweaty. She didn't like not knowing where they were. She went through a mental checklist of everything they didn't have. No food, water, shelter, no other clothes. Everything they had was back at the hotel. They'd landed in the middle of a forest clearing with no sounds of civilization. No echoes of talking, purrs of car engines, or the hum of air conditioners.

She closed her eyes and listened hard. A rush of water rumbled not far off. *A stream or river?* Perdita struggled to her feet, knees and back aching, and fatigue growing. Having her magic ripped from her hadn't been easy. She shuddered as the memory rose—like a thousand needles stabbing into every part of her while getting the air knocked out of her. Being yanked through some magical portal and landing on the hard forest ground hadn't helped either. Before now, she'd been running on adrenaline and fear.

She had to keep going. Ora hadn't used all the rope. She gathered another strand, rolled into a lasso-shape, and headed out toward the sound of water.

"Where are you going?" Charlie asked.

"To try and find us some food. There's a stream or river up ahead."

Ora shook her head. "No, you look beat. I'll go." She took the rope and the knife Perdita offered. At the edge of the clearing, she called over her shoulder, "Mom, watch him. I guess kill him if you have to. Charlie, you can come with me."

Chapter Thirteen
Charlie

Charlie caught up as Ora picked up a long stick and tied the knife to the end of it. They walked together in silence, each lost in her own thoughts. Finally, Charlie spoke, "I'm sorry, O. I wish you didn't have to go through this."

"Thanks."

They made it to a river bank. The water rushed by, lapping against the rocky bank as it passed. Fishing by night wasn't ideal, especially with a knife tied to a stick, but what choice did they have? Ora stripped off her socks and shoes, rolled up her pant legs to above her knees, and waded into the water. Charlie bit her lip, thinking perhaps warning Ora about snakes wasn't a good idea at the moment. Ora waded a few feet into the water, shallow enough so the water didn't get her pants wet, before lifting the makeshift spear above her head. Charlie had no idea how she'd even see any fish.

Charlie and Ora said nothing for a long time, not wanting to scare away any potential fish. Charlie jumped when Ora flung the stick, breaking her still stance. It flew into the air and landed in the water. It stuck and wobbled. She pulled back and checked the end. Nothing. She repeated the process, and on the fourth try, a slimy fish wiggled on the end of the knife.

Ora pulled it off and tossed it to Charlie, who screamed and almost dropped it. By the end, Ora'd caught four fish. After cleaning them, Charlie slipped the rope through their mouths so they wouldn't have to hold each one.

Ora used her Naiad magic to pull the water away from her feet, along with the mud and grass. While they walked back, Charlie asked, "How did you learn to do that?"

Ora paused as if considering the question before answering. "Sabrina."

"Not the magic. Fishing."

"Ohhh. John taught me."

She paused, taking it in. "I still don't understand how I had no idea."

"You were busy with the summer tutoring program, your job, and volunteering at the church."

"I just..." She huffed. "I wish I could've seen the two of you together. I bet you were really happy."

"We were." Ora sniffed.

"I really miss him," Charlie said. "It doesn't feel real. You know? That he's gone."

Ora nodded, the movement too fast, and Charlie knew to drop it. Ora had watched him die.

They made it back to the others, and Ora ran off to gather firewood. Perdita gathered nearby soft grass and made beds for each of them. Together they lifted Sabrina and Arameus and laid them on the beds.

Perdita placed the beds in a circle, and Ora returned with several pieces of wood. She tried but couldn't start a fire. She huffed as her aggravation showed on her face.

"Problems?" Charlie asked.

Ora shrugged. "Ember magic scares me, so my magic, acting like an aloof cat, isn't letting me use it."

Charlie giggled, imaging Ora's magic like something separate from her. "At least you have magic." Charlie found two rocks and hit them together, creating a spark, forcing away memories of camping with her grandparents and brother. Once the fire was roaring, the three of them managed to make a spit and set the fish upon it. While they prepared the fish, Perdita gathered some wild mushrooms, onions, and a few roots. Since Ora had gotten better with Naiad magic, she pulled water from the air into floating balls for them to drink. The look and feel reminded Charlie of drinking like an astronaut.

Perdita moved the food to hover between two rocks after it'd cooked to let it cool down. Rustling of leaves and the soft hooting of owls broke the near silence—save for soft snores from the unconscious prisoner. Large mosquitos flitted around the fire, and she swatted at them every few seconds. "I hate bugs."

Perdita smiled, and a gentle breeze swirled around the group, driving the bugs away. Charlie's gaze returned to Arameus again and again. Each time he didn't sit up her stomach clenched. She understood Ora not wanting to kill the tied up man, but her anger simmered beneath the surface. Arameus's condition got worse every minute. Gentle, kind, and ever selfless Arameus was in pain and dying, and they could stop it by eliminating this man. Not that Charlie thought she could do it either.

Perdita laid the fish with vegetables over large leaves. They ate with their fingers. The fish wasn't bad but had a leftover dirt taste and dried on her tongue. It wasn't a terrible meal but could use some salt and pepper.

"Man, I'd pay some good money for some tartar sauce," Ora blurted out.

Perdita and Charlie nodded, but said nothing. The events of the day were catching up with all of them. The fire crackled and gave off a pleasantly warm heat. Despite the worry, a yawn escaped Charlie's lips, and Perdita's own answered not long after.

The camp-out feeling would have been pleasant if not under these circumstances. Charlie's heart clinched when her thoughts drifted again to Arameus and what wonderful anecdotal stories he would've told.

The comfortable, peaceful mood vanished. Devil yelled a colorful tirade of profanities. The women jumped to their feet waiting for a fight to begin.

"What have you done to me?" He glared at them after the profanities had ceased.

Little sparks flew out of his body as he wrestled with the ropes. He must be trying to use Sabrina and Arameus's magic, but he couldn't. Charlie had no idea what Ora had done to the rope, but it worked.

An inappropriate laugh slipped out of Charlie's mouth. Ora and Perdita shot her a strange look. He swore again, which made Charlie laugh even harder.

"That will be about enough of that." Perdita glared at the man.

"Untie me!" he screamed.

Ora squatted in front of him. "I will untie you when you give them their magic back."

He barked a laugh, bitter and condescending. "Never."

He scowled at her, defiance etched in every feature. Not even his chapped lips and small cut on his forehead could diminish the hatefulness of his expression. The cut had stopped bleeding, but a small amount of dried blood stuck to him. His stomach growled as the women watched him. Ora's expression shifted into one of compassion. Anger flared hot in Charlie. How could she feel compassion for *him*, but forget so easily about Arameus?

The air in front of Ora shimmered, and another small water ball hovered above her hand. She touched it to his forehead, and he flinched and jerked his head away.

She paused, squatting next to him, and said, "I'm not going to hurt you."

He didn't say anything but didn't move when she advanced her hand again and rubbed the water over his wound, washing the blood away. He winced in pain as she wiped his wound with the hem of her blouse. "Sorry," Ora said.

Rage at her best friend rose at an alarming rate. She hadn't done any of this for Arameus or Sabrina. She hadn't even glanced their way more than a few seconds.

Gathering more water from the air, she asked, "Thirsty?"

His eyes narrowed in suspicion, so Ora took a sip. Charlie wished it'd been poisoned. He drank all the water in two big gulps the next time Ora offered. Ora's audacity continued as she grabbed some leftover fish from the campfire and returned to him. His lips remain closed when she held the fish to his mouth. Rolling her eyes, she ate some herself and held the cold meat to him again. This time he took a small bite. He chewed, eyeballing each of them the whole time.

Charlie stomped over to Ora's side. "Can you put some water on this, please?" She had to force out the last word, her tone dripping venom. Ora didn't bother hiding the confused hurt in her expression, but complied.

Charlie left them to check on Arameus. For a long while, Ora fed the evil man fish and some of the roots while helping him wash it down with water. Charlie cared for Arameus and Sabrina and ignored Ora's disgraceful behavior. Perdita came to help. She reached out to pat Charlie's hand, but she jerked away, taking extra care to wipe away all the dirt and grime from Arameus's face. But no matter how many times she wiped, his forehead always prickled with sweat. Every so often he moaned, and his stomach clinched as if in pain. All the while, images of stabbing the Nip kept intruding in her thoughts. Despite what Ora wanted.

When the prisoner would eat no more, Ora returned to the fire pit. "Everyone had enough?"

Perdita said, "I'm good. Thanks."

Charlie could only nod, not trusting herself to speak.

Ora formed another ball of water, put the rest of the food inside it, and moved it closer to the fire. The concoction dissolved into an unappetizing mush of floating soup.

Ora bobbed the fishy soup mixture toward Sabrina. "Sit her up."

Perdita and Charlie maneuvered to either side of Sabrina and raised her to a sitting position. Ora sat down in front of her and bought the broth toward her. She siphoned off a tablespoon full and placed it into her mouth. Sabrina swallowed. Ora repeated this over and over until Sabrina had swallowed half of the soup.

Charlie wanted to cry as she moved on to Arameus, and Ora did the same, giving him nutrients and fluids.

Afterward, Ora used her magic to dampen their skin and pull dirt off them. Ora's forehead furrowed as she concentrated, the strain of using magic getting to her. Controlling her magic to this degree had never been easy, and this evening she'd done more than any of them had ever seen. Charlie couldn't help but notice the faint glow of Ora's new necklace under her blouse. Perhaps this helped her gain control of her powers. Thankfully, the stranger remained quiet through this, watching, and when he thought they weren't looking, testing the ropes.

"How long can they last like this?" Charlie asked, wiping Arameus's face again, worry gnawing at her stomach.

"A few days to a week at most," Perdita answered.

Ora looked as desperate as Charlie felt. Darkness surrounded them, and even the crickets' sweet melody hushed. Exhaustion creeped through every muscle and joint, but Ora looked worse than any of them.

Charlie agreed to take the first watch, not leaving Arameus's side, staring with hatred at Devil. Ora checked on the vile Nip and his ropes one last time before she tried to get some sleep. He yelled at Ora. "Why?"

Charlie didn't exactly understand the question, but without a pause, Ora said, "Because I'm not a monster like you."

As if to prove her right, Sabrina and Arameus let out a scream of pain.

Chapter Fourteen
Perdita

CHARLIE SHOOK PERDITA AWAKE A few hours later. She rubbed her eyes, yawned, and got to her feet. Perdita stretched and rubbed her lower back. She sat down on a nearby rock as Charlie lay down. Perdita asked, "Everything quiet?"

Charlie nodded her head and yawned. "Yes. He's been dozing, and they're pretty much the same. The mosquitos are having quite a feast." She scratched at several new welts on her bare arms.

Perdita nodded as she looked over at their fallen comrades. Their skin paler than earlier with sunken eyes as if they needed to drink more. Their prisoner slept, his head cocked to one side, snoring. Perdita could walk over right now and end Sabrina and Arameus's suffering, but Ora would never forgive her. She hoped it wouldn't be too late before Ora decided to act.

She looked up at the clear sky with bright stars shining and a full moon lighting the clearing. She turned to Charlie. "No storms yet?"

"Not yet." Charlie looked at the sky herself. "She's been tossing and turning, but no nightmares yet."

Perdita nodded. "Hopefully she'll be too exhausted."

Charlie turned over and rested her head on one hand, nodding her head toward Ora. "Do you think she knows she can make it rain?"

"No," she said. "I don't think any of us know what all she can do."

"She'll be something when she learns it all. I'm so amazed every time she does anything." Charlie's expression turned thoughtful. "Something scary powerful. Glad she's on my side."

"Me too." Perdita rubbed the goosebumps on her arms, unsure if from the cold or nerves.

"But you know what? It's not weird. It's like I've always been waiting for her to do it. Does that make sense?" Charlie asked, brow furrowed.

"It does." Her daughter looked so young sleeping on a bed of grass. Her long red hair spread around her, face relaxed and peaceful.

Perdita's heart constricted, knowing she failed to protect her from all of this. She couldn't help but blame herself, thinking if maybe she would have had the courage to tell her daughter about their past, then maybe none of this would have happened. She would be safe in her dorm, lost in her studies, and maybe going to football games. Perdita's worst fears would be her meeting the wrong boy instead of running for their lives.

Charlie interrupted her thoughts. "What are we going to do about him?"

Perdita's eyes traveled to Devil, and she shrugged. "I don't know. We'll have to wait for Ora to decide. But when the time comes, I'll be the one to do it." Her heart grew heavy at the thought. Ora would never see her in the same light again.

"Arameus would know what to do." The wistful expression she always wore when talking about him showed even in the dark. Perdita wondered how long it would take her to figure out she had a crush on him.

"He would." If Sabrina had been awake, she would've killed him the moment they'd escaped. No questions asked. No objections allowed. Always the quickest to act with no hesitation in her decisions, except perhaps helping Ora.

"Okay, kiddo. You better get some sleep."

Charlie yawned. "Yes, Grandma Perdita."

Perdita smiled, remembering hundreds of sleepovers over the years. How many times she'd heard that same reply? Each time she'd stick in her head in Ora's room when they got too loud, and they'd call out, "Yes, Grandma Perdita," and burst into a fit of giggles when she closed the door. She loved Charlie as much as her own daughter.

It had definitely taken some getting used to being called Mom rather than Grandma. For the last ten years of Ora's life, she'd pretended to be her grandmother. Now that the spell was broken, she looked thirty years or so younger. Better than any facelift. She would trade back her old face in a minute to be back in Raleigh sleeping in her own warm bed with their cat Brooke sleeping at her feet. She longed for the afternoons spent sitting on her old front porch in her rocking chair shucking corn or snapping peas from the garden.

Pushing away the melancholy, she stood, wiped Sabrina's and Arameus's foreheads, kissed Ora on the cheek, and whispered, "I love you," before returning to her seat. Her gaze rose to the stars as she listened to the gentle song of the crickets as the wind caressed the leaves. She sat this way a long time, not thinking, staring into space until her back and right hip ached. Needing to move, she stretched, then checked on Devil. She knelt in front of him, reached out to check the ropes, and yelped as he spoke.

"Here to kill me then?"

She jumped backward, scanned his body, but he hadn't gotten free. Her breathing and heart rate slowed. Her cry of alarm hadn't woken Charlie or Ora.

"No!" She gritted her teeth, trying to put as much venom in the word without getting loud.

"Why not?" he asked. "No one will come looking for me. No one will pay any ransom for me, and I can't let them go, so the only hope of saving them is to kill me." No emotion flickered across his face as he delivered the final words as if he already expected to be killed.

"Don't try to make me pity you."

"I'm not. It's the truth. I matter to no one except for Master, and he is cut off from us, and he has plenty more of my kind." Again, with the same flat tone.

Perdita felt the slightest pang of pity for him. "I'm not going to kill you because she doesn't want me to."

He looked over at Ora and after a long time said, "She pities. Her heart is a weakness. It's going to get her killed. She's an enigma to me."

Perdita wished he would stop staring at her daughter. Only when he looked at her did his face show a thread of emotion. If she hadn't been looking, she would've missed the odd longing in his eyes.

"She doesn't look Naiad."

"She isn't." Perdita crossed her arms.

"But she calls the water, and she's no Nip."

Perdita didn't answer. The less he knew about her daughter, the better.

"Her light is brighter than anyone's I've ever seen," he said more to himself than to her.

"Her light?" she asked.

He scoffed, looking between the two of them, as if deciding to answer. "I'm different than the others. Most Nips can't sense wizards until they use magic, and then it feels like static electricity. The hairs on their arms stand up. I'm able to see the light of magic inside. I can spot them instantly whether they're using magic or not."

Perdita shivered at his words. He stared at Ora again. She wanted to smack him to make him stop, but instead, she followed his gaze to her daughter imagining what he saw when he looked at her.

"It's beautiful. Her light. The Hunters are after her. Both of them." He finally turned to look at Perdita.

Perdita's head whipped around to stare at him. "What do you mean both of them?"

"Both the Counsel's and Master's."

"Why are you telling me this?" she asked.

"Because Master is looking for her, and I can see you want to protect her, but that is what he'll do. He'll save her." The gratitude in his voice made her stomach roll.

"I know your Master," she said. "He's no savior."

"Then you don't truly know him. When I was a boy, I came across a woman, and I could see her magic glowing inside her. It called to me, and I reached for it." He scoffed. "Next thing I knew she lay before me screaming while the glow within her belong to me. Then the Quad came. I let it go. I couldn't have held her anyway, but they took me. Made my mother and father forget they ever had me. They put me in their prison and on trial. They sent me to be killed, and all I did was cry for my mom. They put me in the Kassen, and when the murky water poured into that wooden box, someone showed up and took me away. They brought me to Master, and he told me that as long as he could, he would hide me. He would protect me, but I must learn to use my powers to help his cause, but never use them on him. That's what he's done."

She hadn't wanted to pity him, but she'd failed. Imagining a small boy, a child Nip, innocent, much like Ora using her own magic, and having him sentenced to execution.

"Did you ever try to find your mother?" Her heart ached for the lost boy he'd once been.

"No. She wouldn't even remember me." His emotionless tone had returned.

"How do you know they erased her memories?"

"Master told me."

Perdita wondered if a Quad really could erase someone's existence or if somewhere his parents still looked for their little boy, never knowing what happened to him.

"Don't you see what he's done? He saved your life to turn you into a slave," she said.

"No." He shook his head, brainwashed.

"What better story to tell a child slave than his mother wouldn't remember him? Why would he ever go and look for her? How painful would it be to not be recognized by your own mother?"

"You're wrong." His eyes set in a glacial stare.

"I'm not. He uses you, all of you, to do his bidding." She wouldn't stop hoping she could make him see reason.

"Shut up!"

Leann M. Rettell

The wind burst into life, blowing fast and furious. Storms clouds swarmed in the sky. The sky groaned under the weight of the thick, dark clouds lit up by a flash of lightning. Less than a second later, thunder crashed. The sound left Perdita's ears ringing and the ground shaking with the ferocity.

Charlie snapped awake and scrambled off the ground looking for the source of the sound. Beside her Ora screamed, "Nooooo! Nooooo!"

Perdita ran over to her daughter's side as the rain poured from the sky. She shook her and shouted, "Ora, wake up! Ora, wake up!"

Chapter Fifteen
Ora

My body weighed a million pounds. My limbs moved as if shifting through thick tar. Dark fog surrounded me, drowning me in an impenetrable darkness that I couldn't see through. I drudged on blind, no knowing up from down or left from right. Soft whispering of a thousand voices surrounded me as my heart beat in an erratic rhythm mimicking a haunting symphony. Step after step, the mystery fell away and recognition replaced the darkness. A dream. The same dream that came every night, and like every night, the ending drew closer like a hunter stalking its prey. I couldn't stop. If I did, the ground would swallow me like quicksand. My body succumbing to the depths of nothingness. Breathing became impossible, even though I shouldn't need to in this place of fantasy. My limbs failed to work and hung useless at my side. A slow death pulled, edging me toward an eternal abyss. Turning back the way I came wasn't an option. The thickness under my bare feet gripped the soles of my feet like iron fists. The only way was forward. Toward the voices. Toward those who hated me. Toward those who sought to destroy me.

The whispers escalated, replacing the wisps of sound dancing out of reach.

Clear, concise, fearful voices rolled inward and receded like an ever-changing tide.

Where am I?

Help me!

Fear and confusion laced through each word. These hurt my soul, but there would be more voices, each more terrible than the last. Voices would mutate into screams. Perhaps if I moved faster, I could finally get through them. Each painstaking step burned deep in my thighs. An invisible hand clenched around my ribs making every breath harder and harder to draw. Abandoning deep breathing, I resort to panting. A distant and sleeping part of me realized this wasn't real.

"They're here," rang out in my head like a song, pulled, no doubt, from the cobwebbed recesses of my memory. The voices. Too many to count, screamed over and over, in pain, in desperation, in anger.

I want my mommy!
Help! Someone help me please! Please!! Pleeaseee!
I hate you!!
Leave me alone!
Get off me!
Let me out!
I'm sorry!
Help!
Help!
Help!

The cacophony of disembodied voices blended into a mantra repeated over and over. *Help.* The deeper I ventured, the louder it got. Hot tears ran down my face. They needed me, but I couldn't pull myself out of this lost place, let alone anyone else. From amongst the fading darkness, silhouettes of faceless bodies emerged one by one. A palpable thread of red anger tinged with the murky scent of gun powder filled my senses.

They pulled closer, their movements clumsy, slow, and jerky, reminiscent of classic zombies. I couldn't get away. If I stopped, I'd sink.

The only way was forward.

Into their clawing fingers.

The sharp, scratching claws of their fingers grazed the skin over my shoulders, belly, and back. If I went any farther, they would rip me apart, pull me in deeper, and I'd join them lost forever in this land of limbo.

Over the Bridge

Tears burned down my cheeks in rivulets. The scratches sank deeper. Blood joined the hot rush, but in this place, it rolled upward.

Something changed.

A subtle shift in the reality of this place. The gun powder scent wavered under the new smell. The odors raffled through various brain cells like an old school rolodex. Peppermint. No. Something spicy and warm. Cinnamon and browned butter. Yes, that's it.

The voices retreated.

This new entity spoke. *Hello, Ora.*

"Hello?"

It isn't safe for you here.

The word "duh" sprang to mind, but my galloping heart didn't allow the flippancy to escape. "I can't stop or go back. I'm lost."

But you can go sideways.

As if a damn broke open, the epiphany flooded into each movement. In mid-step, I paused, shifting left, before replacing my foot on the sticky, sodden floor. I crossed my right leg over the left, then left over right. No sinking. Not frozen in place.

Step after careful step, I shimmied sideways.

You're going the wrong way, the voice corrected. *But for now, keep going. There is something I want to show you.*

It never occurred to me not to trust the guide. The pitch and tone of the soundless voice flowed smooth and masculine, directly into my mind. The darkness faded. Traces of light floated ahead like beacons to a ship lost at sea. Hundreds of lights loomed in the distance, and indecision cost me. Which one should I choose? The ground sunk a fraction of an inch.

Almost there, the guide urged, insistent and worried.

Grunting and struggling, a warmth surrounded my ankle, and between the two of us, my leg flew from the muck with a thick slurp like the release of suction. *The guide can touch me?*

I inched along, the lights blossomed into gas giants. I squinted against the rising sting in my eyes from the ever-increasing light. The ground beneath me hardened, shifting from the previous unnoticed freezing cold into something warm.

Stop. Tell me what you see.

At his words, an opening into an enchanted forest loomed before me. A rainbow hue shimmered around the edges like before when we'd escaped the club. *Were these portals?*

A beautiful and hauntingly familiar forest lay just beyond the opening. Small rabbits hopped through the bushes, beautiful exotic birds never seen in the human realm sang in the trees, and beyond, a waterfall cascaded down off a rocky cliff leading into a small pond.

The water shimmered like crystal and glistened like diamonds. "It's beautiful."

Interrupting the calmness of the pristine water, a man's head erupted out of the water. He shook the water out of his hair and climbed out of the water. Something familiar about him grabbed my attention. I took a step closer.

It couldn't be.

John!

Alive and healthy with only a scar above his right eye, exactly where the boulder hit him. I yelled out his name and ran. My guide touched my arm. Before its touch had been warm, now it burned the tender flesh of my arm, a warning. *Wait.*

At that exact moment, John looked to the top of the waterfall and yelled, "Come on, chicken."

A woman appeared at the edge.

She yelled back, "I'm scared."

"Come on." He waved. With a scream that followed her the whole way down, the woman jumped. She landed into the water with a splash and emerged a few feet away. She swam toward John, and he offered her his hand. She took it, accepting his help.

Anger and betrayal ripped through me.

His sideways grin mocked me. "See? I told you you could do it."

She laughed and smacked his arm. She shifted her body closer, molding herself to him, and looked into his eyes. Passion and lust screamed in her gaze.

Over the Bridge

The world fell away.

Not her!

The cat woman who tried to kill us. The woman who killed John.

As if in slow motion, she wrapped her arms around John's neck. *My John!*

He leaned forward, and his lips touched on hers. A bucket of ice hit my heart as rage consumed me. My magic hidden in this place boiled like lava. A demon of fire and vengeance. Lighting and thunder erupted behind me. The murky darkness vanished underneath unearthly flashes of blazing light.

Someone, somewhere screamed, "Nooooo! Nooooo!"

Beside me, the guide urged, *Ora, stop. You have to wake up.*

The voice grabbed my shoulder and shook me, screaming, *Ora, wake up! Ora, wake up!*

My eyes flashed opened. The surreal, empty place had vanished taking John with it.

Mom hovered over me. Her hand rested on my shoulder. It had been her who'd shaken me and not the guide. Real tears poured from my eyes as cool cleansing rain poured down upon us. Each droplet matched the strength of my sobs. Her loving arms enveloped me as she murmured into my ear, "It's okay. It was only a dream."

Images of the boulder slamming into John flashed in my mind's eye. Now his hand shook and his eye lids moved as if to blink.

The longer I sat there, and the dream faded, the truth returned. He hadn't moved. His eyes didn't blink. He died. My subconscious was playing tricks on my sleeping brain. That woman killed him. She stole him from me, so my mind changed it into something else. Like he chose her over me. Like he cheated.

The other emotions I'd been feeling over John's death had fought their way to the forefront of my mind. Namely, anger.

I felt guilty even thinking it, but I was furious at John for dying, for leaving me. He died saving my mother. Lost his life to rescue me and I had the audacity to be angry with him.

Leann M. Rettell

I was angry at John.

Naming it relieved the ache in my heart. My sobbing subsided as the rain died.

Charlie knelt beside me, her hand on my shoulder, also comforting me. Rain dripped from her hair and smoke drifted from the sodden fire. The ground squished underneath Mom's knees.

The magic inside me, still simmering from the dream, came to my call. I stood, stepping away, and turned in a slow circle, my arms outstretched, pulling the water from the ground, our clothes, the wood from the fire, and also Devil, who had been watching with an unsettling intensity.

Charlie collected more fire wood as the sun peered over the horizon. "You didn't wake me for my watch," I said.

"I thought you could use the rest." Mom shrugged.

"Then let me get breakfast. How does fish sound?"

Without waiting for a reply, I headed into the woods in search of breakfast. Mom and Charlie stayed behind as if sensing I needed to be alone. The dark storm clouds had cleared, and a beautiful sunrise comprised of a natural rainbow of colors danced across the morning sky like a painting.

It was a nightmare, I told myself again. John died.

Right?

Chapter Sixteen
Ora

DEVIL CHEWED ON WILD BLUEBERRIES, taking each one slow and deliberate, turning the simple act of feeding him into something awkward. I took solace in the knowledge that he was the guinea pig of the group. Part of me hoped they weren't poisonous, but what do I know about berry picking? Perhaps declining to join Girl Scouts had been a bad idea.

With each berry, I half expected him to bite me. He knew this, of course. *Cocky bastard.* On the last bite, he moved in fast for the berry, startling me, and I dropped the dang thing on his stomach, where it rolled down to his, um, lap.

His chuckle, tinged with mockery, stuck a nerve deep in my core. The smile wiped off his face when I glared at him. I caught the glowing light in my eyes reflected in his. Instead of fear, his eyes burned with some dark hunger, twisting the side of his mouth, before shifting his eyes to the berry and returning to mine. "Are you going to get it?" Challenge laced every line of his face. Even tied to a tree, he commanded my attention.

My eyebrows rose as I studied the far from innocent blueberry. "Nah, that little thing isn't worth it." I flicked the berry off into the woods, leaving Devil stewing in his own juices, and Charlie coughing to hide her smirk.

"Nice," she said as I returned to the little campsite.

With a flash of a grin only she could see, I struck the rocks lighting the fire, preparing for the night. The late afternoon sun faded, leaving long shadows as the twilight neared ever closer. Wild onions growing nearby let off a strong odor mingling with the muggy evening. Cool breezes rushed over my skin, making me wish for the not-so-long-ago days hanging with John by the lake. How many evenings had the two of us spent with the air smelling like this? If I closed my eyes, I could almost smell his mixed scent of Ivory soap, his grandfather's aftershave, and a lingering aroma of mint.

Devil called from the tree, breaking my daydreaming. "You know I do have to relieve myself sometime."

"We're going to have to figure out a plan. We can't stay here forever, and they aren't getting any better." Charlie wiped Arameus's brow as I liquefied the berries into a juice.

Sabrina and Arameus's sweating had diminished, not a good sign. Despite giving them water and broth, their lips chapped, a sallow sheen tinged their cheeks, which if anything, looked worse with the accompanied dark-rimmed circles around their eyes. Sabrina, normally fair and exquisite, now looked as diminished as an old woman. The golden locks hung in drab waves around her face looking more like dirty old hay. The sight took me back to the cell in the Nook.

Charlie brushed a lock of hair off Arameus's brow. "You know how easily they could be back to us." Her tone held a dark and sharp edge I'd never heard before.

"I know." I snuck a look over my shoulder at the prisoner.

His expression flashed in a brief show of concern before vanishing to the expressionless mask that he typically wore. Other than the earlier jibe at me, he had no emotions, other than cruelty or intimidation. I supposed being a minion didn't allow for such things. But he certainly couldn't want to die.

"What if we make a deal? You release them and then we release you? We'll go our separate ways?" I stood, placing my hands on my hips.

"No." He couldn't even give me the curtesy of looking at me.

"Why?" I hated the slight whiny quality it came out.

"Because if I let them go, you'll kill me." He closed his eyes, wiggling against the ropes.

Over the Bridge

Blood drained from my face.

"I'll have no leverage, and I'm outnumbered."

"You're the biggest idiot I've ever met. You're outnumbered now. We could've killed you already. You were unconscious, bound to a tree, and helpless. You're helpless now, and for every second I waste trying to reason with you, my friends suffer."

"Then why don't you?" he asked.

"Because I'm hoping you'll come to your senses and release them. No one has to die here." I stomped closer to the tree.

"You're a very strange person. But I won't release them. I'll do what I must. I will not betray Master."

I stared at him with pity.

"He'll help you, too. He's a friend. He protects Nips. He'll save you and you won't need these people anymore."

Finally, some wisp of emotion, an almost god-like worship. He would never release them. We would have to kill him after all. I'd pity him, but it would be like putting someone out of their misery.

I twisted on my heel, heading away from him. "I'm not a Nip. Your evil Master is no friend to me," I called over my shoulder. "My friends have to be cleaned of their own filth because of you. It seems only fitting you do the same. Since you can't see reason, I won't help you anymore."

"Letting me starve to death is still murder," he screamed as I left the clearing, grabbing the long stick, and using the knife to cut it into a sharp edge. We needed more fish, and I needed space.

Chapter Seventeen
Ora

The next twelve hours passed, ticking away like an eternity. At night, we took turns keeping watch. Mom and Charlie had followed my instructions to let me sleep long enough to get some rest, but short enough to avoid dreaming of the Shadow Land. Tacky name, but that's what popped in my head. I didn't dare speak of it lest Mom or Charlie thinking I'd lost my marbles.

We gathered nuts, berries, roots, and edible grasses while swatting at the millions of bugs that lived in the forest. We fished, and I figured out how to hollow out two tree trunks. One we filled with drinking water and the other with live fish so when it was time to eat, we didn't have to walk far. We fed Sabrina and Arameus regularly, but they faded fast. Their cheeks grew gaunt, their moans and screams faint, and they urinated less and less. We cleaned them and did what we could, but it wasn't enough. Remembering my own stent with starvation and dehydration, I knew they couldn't last much longer. At least they were unconscious.

Devil, as promised, had been left tied to the tree. We avoided him as much as possible. If his curses and hateful comments weren't enough, he reeked of his own filth. We didn't feed him, give him water, or even acknowledge his existence other than to keep watch. The magical ropes held him, but soon, there wouldn't be a need for them.

I, too, could barely eat. It was one thing to say what you would do to someone. It was quite another to watch. Why couldn't those first berries be poisonous? Accidental poisoning would be better than murder or neglect.

He couldn't hold his own head up and slept most of the time. Still, he wouldn't budge. Despite cracked lips and sunken eyes, each and every time I asked him to give Sabrina and Arameus their magic back, his reply was always, "Never."

Even Mom, Charlie, and I couldn't get comfortable. At night the temperature dropped, fighting our little fire, making our teeth chatter, followed by the scorching days mingled with thick humidity. Speckled tiny red welts from numerous bug bites covered Sabrina's legs. She still wore the skimpy dress, and we had nothing to cover her with.

Something had to change. We couldn't stay like this. Over and over like a broken carousel, the discussion came up about what had to be done. One of us should leave and discover our location and get some provisions. But who would go? It couldn't be me, they insisted, because my magic secured Devil's ropes. It couldn't be Charlie. She didn't have magic or weapons. She'd get lost for sure and Mom's sense of direction left a lot to be desired. Around the final curve the discussion would steer. If only I'd let them outright kill Devil. But I still couldn't do it.

As if reading my mind, Mom waved her hand toward the large tree. "Ora. Look at him. How's this any better?"

It wasn't, and I knew it. We couldn't stay here much longer. If Sabrina and Arameus weren't released soon, they would die. Killing Devil was the only answer.

Charlie settled beside me on a rock. She didn't say anything for a while before nudging me. "O?"

"I know." I wouldn't meet her eyes. "It's time."

My shoulders sagged as if a thousand pounds settled over them.

Charlie reached into her jean pocket and removed a small object that she concealed inside her curled fist. She eased her hand toward me, peeled her fingers backward, revealing a knife balanced on her palm, very small and innocent.

The decision loomed over me. Never in a million years would I want to take the knife from her palm, but I did. I couldn't let the weight of this rest on anyone else. I wouldn't let it taint anyone else's soul. The tiny light blade felt like it weighed a thousand pounds. It shook in my hand in time to the rapturous beating of my heart.

"I could do it. If you want," Charlie said.

"No. This is on me." Her relief rolled off her in waves as I let her off the hook.

Decision made, I stood on shaky legs. Each step felt like my legs weighed a ton. A hundred times worse than walking in the Shadow Land. I would take that nightmare over this.

The world vibrated under the pressure of my nerves and adrenaline coursing through my veins. Devil dozed but sensed me coming closer. His eyes popped open, and he stared at me. He must have seen something in my eyes because he froze looking like a deer in headlights. I debated how to do this. Should I knock him out? At least it would be quiet, but when I saw the fear in his eyes, I straddled him, putting the knife to his throat. Desperation clung to me like a second skin. His eyes grew wider, and his breathing sped. Our expressions matched, eyes battling in a silent debate. With mine, I begged him to save me. Save me from having to do this.

"Ora!" Mom screamed, fear in her voice.

I didn't turn away or acknowledge her at all. I stared at Devil, unsure whose face held more fear, and moved the knife to his chest, in between the ribs, right above his heart. I took a deep breath to steady myself and set my resolve. It was now or never. "Release them."

"No." For the first time, I heard fear in his voice.

"Release them." The *please* in my words wrapped around every syllable.

He shook his head.

"Do you want to die?" I couldn't understand him.

"Ora, don't. Ora, I thought this was the right thing to do, but Sabrina and Arameus wouldn't want you to become someone you're not. Don't do this!" I didn't turn toward Mom, fighting back the burning in building in my eyes.

"I'll let you go. No one will hurt you. Just release them. Please!"

He stared at me, searching for something, hope dancing in his eyes before emptiness descended in them again. "No."

"Release them!" I gritted my teeth.

He shook his head once.

"Why?" I pushed down on the knife, through his shirt, and a small dot of blood blossomed on his shirt. He winced.

His eyes cast downward, already dead. "I won't release them. Just do it."

"Ora don't!" The pain leeched from Mom's voice.

"She has to, or they'll die." Charlie said, voice flat and empty.

I tightened my grip around the blade, set my face, and steadied myself to push. The world ground to a halt. Mom and Charlie argued with each other, but their words were lost to me, voices in the distance, meaningless. Devil's head hung low as he waited to die with no fight in him at all.

I couldn't do it.

My hand fell limp to my side. Devil's head jerked up, staring at me in surprise. I rolled off his legs and used the knife to sever the rope at his feet.

"What are you doing?" Mom and Charlie shouted in unison.

"Letting him go," I said.

"My, my, my. Look what we've found," a man's voice spoke from behind.

I spun around. Three figures floated three feet in the air at the edge of the clearing. The owner of the voice, a redheaded man in black leather pants and a green shirt, held his arms to his sides, palms up. Twin boys, no more than sixteen, floated beside him with pale faces and messy brown hair. Their wide eyes swept the ground as if they expected to fall at any second. The man in the middle held them in the air. A Tempest.

"You're the Hunter," Devil said. "This is who Master is looking for."

A look of annoyance passed across the Tempest's face. "I know that, boy." He flipped his palms toward the ground, and the three men inched downward until their feet touched the hard earth. He put two fingers in his mouth and whistled.

Mom and Charlie stood frozen while I positioned myself behind Devil and placed the knife at his throat. The Hunter barked a mirthless laugh and eyed Sabrina and Arameus. The look of malicious amusement never left his face. A few moments later, crunching of grasses and fallen leaves grew louder, as the trio waited. The Hunter wore a calm and somewhat bored expression. A total façade I wouldn't fall for. The twins' shoulders shook, faces pale, and they wouldn't meet anyone's eyes except each other's. What were they waiting for?

As if in answer, a rhythmic crunching sound appeared and escalated in volume with each step. Across from the newcomers, a stunning woman appeared at the edge of the clearing with long dark curly hair and eyes black as onyx.

"Aaah, Charity, look what we've found." The Hunter swept his arm in a grand gesture as if showing off prized possessions.

Her hawk-like gaze jumped from one to the other, sizing up everyone and everything in her path. Without slowing her pace, she continued into the clearing. As she neared Arameus, Charlie burst into a sprint and threw herself over his body. Charity paused for only a fraction of a second, long enough to grip a large sword swinging on her hip, before meeting up with her companions, taking her place beside the Hunter on his right side. The position was no coincidence.

"Hunter, release me, and I'll help you." Devil's voice crackled like a toad.

"You think I care what happens to you?"

"I work," Devil swallowed, trying to get more saliva, "for Master."

The Hunter eyed him with distain and tilted his head. "Charity."

Charity moved like lightning. In a flash, her body twisted. Her sword sang as she yanked it from its sheath, swishing through the air, and stopped. She bent, scooped some few fallen leaves, and wiped off the blade. The leaves came away red.

Over the Bridge

Just as one of the twin's head fell to the ground.

His twin screamed, ran to his dead brother's side, and sank to his knees in tears. Surprise flooded my system. Charlie screamed only once—one single cry. The brother's panicked wails filled the deafening silence.

Charity's expression bordered on indifference. Without giving either twin a look, she resumed her position beside the Hunter, who wore his smugness like a crown. "Charity, how many Nip boys has Master given to me?"

She shrugged.

"Guess."

"Fifty-ish." Her eyes never stopped moving.

"How many have you killed?" he asked.

"Dozens." She slid her blade back in its sheath.

"What has Master said about it?"

"Nothing." Her eyes bore into Devil as if imaging taking his head as well.

The Hunter's eyes grew even colder. "You see, boy. You're a dime a dozen to Master. He doesn't care about you. You're a pawn to be used at his will. He passes you all out to his Hunters to do with as we please. You're better off dead. Being captured at the hands of women. At least I'd give you the gift of a quick death. Master wouldn't be so forgiving."

The Hunter turned his eyes on me, an evil, inhuman smile, changing his would-be handsome face into that of a monster. "Do it."

I jerked the blade away, pulled my magic upward as the amulet at my neck warmed under the contact, and entered the clearing showing no sign of fear. Sabrina laid very still, her breathing shallow, a ragged pulling of air permeating the silence that descended upon the forest. The squawks of birds and the rustling of small animals muted. Hell, even the air had stilled into nothingness. Charlie sprawled overtop of Arameus, protecting him, and a single tear ran down her cheek. Mom stood to my left, her face expressionless, staring at the Hunter. I made my face like hers.

"I'm no killer," I answered. The magic reverberated inside my chest, raging against my words, ready to fight, ready to prove me wrong.

The Hunter threw his head back in laughter. "Really? Weren't you about to stab the pathetic boy in the heart, but you're all noble now that you have an audience?"

Charity blew a stray hair out her face. "Taylin, get on with it."

His laughter died. The twin, wrapped around his brother, squealed like a wounded animal as his body shook in a pain I recognized. Taylin threw him a look of annoyance. The Hunter paced. "Now what to do with you? What do you think?" he asked Charity. "Want to have some fun?"

She blew a large pink bubble. When it popped and she returned it to her mouth, she gestured with her non-sword hand. "Kill them all but those two," she pointed to Mom and me, "and leave the unconscious ones."

"But what about these two?" Taylin motioned toward Arameus and Sabrina.

"No fun. You know I like it when they squeal. Besides, it'll hurt them more knowing they'll continue to die slowly."

Charlie stifled her muffled cry into Arameus's shoulder as if proving Charity's point.

Taylin nodded, raised his hand, and the wind pulled in from nowhere, answering his call. My magic stretched and rose, preparing for a fight, permeating every cell in my body. Before anything could happen, the twin boy rose and let loose an unearthly scream that could raise the dead. His face twisted in rage and agony with venom bleeding in his eyes.

Taylin flicked his wrist as if swatting a fly.

The twin's face contorted into an evil, satisfied smile that made the hairs on the back of my arms stand on edge, the magic flickering, unsure. The twin cried out again. This time affecting everyone. It halted the world. But none reacted the way Taylin did. As the scream tore through the clearing, Taylin fell and crumpled in a heap, limps contorting in a violent seizure, as an animalistic cry escaped his lips, followed by sickening cracks accompanied an impossible twist of an arm, followed by a leg.

The twin's scream intensified with each step he made toward the Hunter's side. More snaps and pops as Taylin's bones shattered. The boy swung his foot, not satisfied, over and over, landing blow after bloody blow over Taylin's face. The scream ended descending the clearing into silence. "You killed my brother! Die you son of a—" He paused mid-sentence. A zing resounded from behind him as Charity's sword left her sheath.

"Try it, you bitch. I have his magic, and you can't take it from me."

Still she looked bored.

"Jeremiah, I do as I'm told. As you should have. But now you'll have to die." She twirled the sword around in an impressive controlled arc. "You may have his magic, but are you faster than my sword?"

"Let's find out." He raised his arms.

Two sets of wind crashed toward her. She rolled out of the way. The air hit nothing but each other, the resounding boom louder than any natural thunder. On her feet, she sprinted straight for him. Her sword held at the ready.

To my surprise, Mom raised her hands and released a wave. It rushed upon the ground toward Charity. She saw it the same time as I did. She smiled as Mom's body stiffened and fell upon the ground. *She's a Nip, too!*

Using Mom's magic, she extended her arm. A giant hand of water gripped the sword and swung toward Jeremiah. He saw it, too. The wind he commanded dissipated. He paused, waiting for the end, the sad look of finality and relief mingled on his face.

That did it. Magic erupted. It shot straight out, through my amulet, toward Charity. She shifted her stance.

"Catch this!" I yelled as it slammed against her chest sending her flying backward.

Twinges of pain ripped through me. Like someone had dragged a corkboard of nails over and into me. Weakness followed while my arms and legs shook attempting to move. I reached for my magic. It wasn't gone, but paler. I leaned forward, placing a hand on the ground, unaware of having fallen to one knee. Refusing to give up, I fought to stand. Jeremiah stared in shock as Charity got to her feet. A streak of blood ran along her hairline.

She shook her head and said, "Thanks for the Ember."

A blue flame ignited out of her hand. It snaked its way through the grass. The flame wrapped itself around her sword. She must have dropped it during the confusion. The sword rose, covered in flames, and flew toward Jeremiah. She raced it as if making sure either she or the sword would end him.

Pain and weakness still coursed through me. Every thought, movement, and breath a battle. The magic slipped through my fingers. *Come on.*

Charity and the blade inched closer. Time slowed. Charity bent her knees and launched herself in the air, her sword high, ready to deliver the final blow. Out of nowhere, a tree branch creaked and swung.

It smacked into her like a baseball bat. Her body crumpled with a loud crack of ribs snapping. Her limp body flew into the distance.

She disappeared from sight. Within moments, a pulling sensation washed through me. At first low, then faster and faster. With each second, the pain vanished, my strength returned, my magic whole once again. Mom sat up. Her magic back as well.

Jeremiah stared behind Devil. Following his gaze, a new man observed us from beside the tree. A Native American with long dark hair, olive skin with a pointy face, and a woven necklace hanging around his neck. Hiding in plain sight, a green Sphere jewel had been woven into the necklace nestled into the middle. Now I knew who had swung that branch.

"Why you come to dis place?" he asked in a thick accent.

Jeremiah turned and ran as fast as he could away from the clearing. He looked back only once toward his brother's body.

"We were hiding," I said.

"You bring Nips?" He motioned with his chin toward the crumpled remains of Taylin.

Over the Bridge

"No. They found us," I said.

"Who are you?"

"My name is Ora. This is my mother, Perdita."

"Your full name." He interrupted me, waving a hand as if shooing a fly.

"Ora Stone."

"Perdita Stone," Mom said.

Charlie scrambled off Arameus body. "I'm Charlie McCurry."

"Who are they?" He hobbled farther into the clearing using an old stick as a cane.

"Sabrina Sun and Arameus Townsend. They're with us."

"Sun?" He furrowed his brow. "That one knows my niece, Leigh Stewart."

I couldn't believe it. Here was the man we'd been searching for, and he'd found us. "Yes, they worked together. We've come here looking for you."

"Ehhh." He shrugged his shoulders as if he couldn't care less. "There you are."

He hobbled without another word past the oak tree, disappearing into thickening forest. Were we supposed to follow him? After a few moments, his voice called out from the forest, "You coming or what?"

The ground below Sabrina and Arameus rose and formed a gurney. The legs walked, carrying them into the forest, controlled by Leigh's uncle.

Charlie, pale but chin set, followed the walking tables, not letting Arameus out of her sight.

The ground beneath Taylin and the dead twin rumbled. Great heaps flung themselves upward, forming a deep hole, before jolting the two dead bodies. They rolled into the ground and the earth rippled over them, almost tender, like a mother covering a child. The sight of the young boy's grave tugged at my heart. The nameless twin had been so young and loved by his brother. How could we leave him here in an unmarked grave?

"Ummm..." I gestured toward the grave.

Leigh's uncle paused barely visible through the trees. He shrugged. "Ohhh, all right."

Small piles of rocks sprang to life from all directions. They surrounded the twin's burial spot melting and rising higher, before solidifying into a headstone. As soon as I imagined flowers, white lilies grew upon his grave. It hadn't been much, but I hoped one day his brother would return and find him.

Mom and I shared a look. We had to follow. She caught up with Charlie and held her hand. I bent down to Devil, still tied to a tree, pale faced and for once, looking stunned. The knife still somehow in my hand slid through the rope, freeing him. There had been too much death today. I offered him my hand.

Almost as if in a daze, he took my hand and rose on shaky legs. His expression never wavered, like a boy who lost his puppy. A flash of another red-headed young boy in a snowy clearing much like this one popped into my head. *Dodger*? I shook my head, clearing the random, and strange, image.

"Release them," I pleaded.

His eyes met mine, and with one slow release of air, he deflated. A second later, what little he had drained from his face. "It's done."

A huge weight of relief came off my shoulders. "Thank you."

Leaving him behind, I stepped into the forest, unsure of my fate, but I paused, turning to the Nip I'd freed. He hadn't moved but stared at me looking so utterly lost and unsure.

"You can come with us if you want. Devil." The name felt odd on my lips.

His eyes locked onto mine, and a moment passed between us. His head twisted toward the twin's headstone, and then returned his gaze to me, a slow smile spreading there. "I think I will." He caught up with me as we walked farther into the forest. "By the way…"

"Yeah?" I asked.

The soulless man from the nightclub had gone as if he too died back in that clearing. The new man's gray eyes pierced into mine and shown like a light had been turned on. "I'm Damien."

Chapter Eighteen
Charlie

THE GROUP WALKED FOR WHAT seemed like hours. Sabrina and Arameus, still unconscious, regained some color and each breath became less ragged than the one before. Charlie hoped they would improve, but they had been down for a long time. Her legs burned, and a numbness had settled over her heart. She wished Leigh's uncle would make a walking gurney for all of them as well, but she would never ask such a thing.

Besides, Charlie hadn't taken her eyes off the stranger who'd saved them. He walked with a knobbed wooden stick, favoring his right leg with each step, although he hid it well. He had long black hair with thin streaks of gray, large bushy eyebrows, and a pointed face. Every so often, he stopped and chanted, lifting his arms above his head, and shook the stick. Whatever his reasons for this, he didn't share with them. They could only pause when he did this and wait. Sometimes it lasted only seconds and others took several minutes. The current chant lasted longer than the others. Charlie perched on a rock, resting, until his little foreign ceremonies completed. She did her best not to look over her shoulder.

Betrayal.

That thought kept ringing through her head. How could Ora have brought along that bastard?

Leigh's uncle hadn't said a word during their journey, and neither had anyone else. Perdita's sunken eyes surrounded a pale, ashen face, showing the subtle white lines around her eyes. Losing her magic twice now had taken its toll on her. Ora hadn't faired any better. Something had shifted in her—died a little. If Charlie hadn't felt the same, she'd have attributed it all to the Nip stealing their power.

No, it could only be the atrocities they'd witnessed. Until recently, Charlie had never seen such brutality. Bizard had been one thing, but Charity was pure evil. Absolutely no conscience. She'd killed that guy without hesitation or remorse.

Ora's voice rang out behind her. "Will I always feel like this? As if my magic is all twisted up inside me?"

"It's normal," Devil said. "The magic has to rearrange itself again. It'll take time."

Charlie bristled at their conversation. As if this wasn't his fault! How could Ora think of letting him go? He'd almost killed Arameus and Sabrina. Charlie wondered how many times he'd used his powers. How many he'd killed.

The chant ended, and without a glance, he resumed walking. Charlie rose and yelped for about the hundredth time. She'd almost fallen because her feet kept getting snagged on roots.

Ora's hurried footsteps resounded beside her before the red of her hair flashed in Charlie's peripheral vision. "Are you okay?" Ora asked.

Her face scrunched up as she fought to keep herself from crying and shook her head from side to side. Tears swam beneath her lashes, trying to break free, and at last, she lost her internal battle. Two hot angry tears ran down her cheeks. She wiped them away with a rough hand. "It's just…" She paused as her voice broke.

She took deep breaths to steady herself. "I feel so useless." More tears rolled down her cheeks, and she didn't bother to stop them this time. They left small clean lines down her dirt-stained face. "I mean, I just sat there, and I couldn't do anything." Her voice cracked as she fought to hold it together. "In the club, I stood there. Back there, I sat there. I can't…I can't." She fought back sobs. "I can't help anyone. I can't help him. I can't do anything. I don't have magic. I'm not a Nip. I can't use a sword. I can't even fight. I'm useless. I'm nothing. Just a pathetic human who gets in the way." She wiped tears away with the back of her hand. "I'm so stupid!

Over the Bridge

What am I even doing here?" She put her hands over her face. The group stopped, even Leigh's uncle, but he hadn't turned around.

Ora didn't know what to say. The moment to say something brilliant and exceptional wasted. She didn't think Charlie was pathetic. If anything, she'd been cursing herself, able to destroy an entire city with all this magic, but she couldn't even fight off a couple people. "We all watched that boy die and didn't do anything. Charlie, I..." She paused as Leigh's uncle appeared at their side. Neither of them had even heard him approach.

He stared into Charlie's eyes. "You're not nothing. You're a Vessel. Come. We are not far now." He hobbled away again.

The girls looked at each other and stifled back a nervous laugh at the eccentric old man. But what had he called her?

A Vessel? What on earth could he mean by that?

After a few more minutes of walking, the trees thinned, and they emerged into another clearing. A small lake off to one side caught Charlie's attention. A large oak tree sat to another part, forming a makeshift barn. The tree bent over as if in a bow. The top branches formed a large hand with leafy fingers touching the ground. The whole structure shaded the herds of animals—sheep and goats—and a quaint fence of infantile crepe myrtles kept everything confined to one area.

Beside this a large garden held an assortment of vegetables, herbs, and flowers. Charlie recognized corn, tomatoes, and zucchini from her days helping her Grandmom garden. In the center of the clearing, a large rounded building, if you would call it that, made from wood and dried mud sat as if overlooking everything. A large rectangular opening had been carved in front of the structure making a doorway. On the side of the doorway, a long tree trunk, hollowed out to make a bench, gave the entire oddity a welcoming appeal. Wildflowers grew underneath the bench and surrounded the structure while several free-roaming chickens clucked and pecked along the ground. They weaved in around various rusted old pots and a single black boot. Commander Stewart's uncle lived in the coolest place!

Charlie, Perdita, Ora, and Devil halted in their tracks as high above them, a loud crack sounded followed by several more in quick succession. Expecting an attack, they raised their arms, planting their feet, but couldn't stop the chorus of cries as two more hollowed out benches fell out of the nearby trees. They landed with a rumbling thud. Instead of attacking, they cantered along, skipping like happy dogs using wooden legs, and chased the chickens. Stewart's uncle whistled, and the benches trotted toward him and came to rest beside the bench by the front door. Arameus and Sabrina's gurneys joined the three benches.

The benches formed a small circle by the door. Stewart's uncle sat down on the original bench, leaned his cane beside him, motioned for everyone to sit down, and then lit a brown pipe. "You," he pointed toward Devil, "stink. Go clean up." He nodded a head toward the lake behind the mud house. "I'll send you some clothes."

Devil staggered toward the lake while Charlie took a second to appreciate the weirdness of her life before following the others to the benches. Another wooden bench trotted from inside the structure with a pair of blue jeans and what looked like a shirt sitting on top. Devil returned several minutes later, sliding beside Ora, looking as if he might collapse.

Leigh's uncle had an air about him of stillness and peace. He spoke little as if he was used to being alone and had no problems keeping his own company. The sheep and goats bleated as they wandered around their pen, munching on the grass, while the chickens reemerged from being chased by inanimate objects. Or what should have been inanimate objects. Their strange host puffed on the pipe, turned his head, and blew a smoke ring. The place definitely had a Hobbit/Beauty and the Beast vibe about it.

"You going to sit there all day or tell me why you search for me?" His old and raspy voice confirmed he didn't use it much.

Ora's back straightened as her brow furrowed, a look I'd seen some many times as her mind whirled inside searching for the correct response. Ora's gaze flicked between Sabrina and Stewart's uncle. They had all expected Sabrina to explain everything once they arrived, but she couldn't since she still didn't have her magic.

"Maybe if Devil would release their power, she could explain!" Charlie glared at the Nip, shocking even herself at the outburst.

Devil flushed red. "I've already given their powers back, and my name is Damien, okay?"

"Changing your name doesn't make you any less of an ass…" Charlie's words died away at Ora's venomous stare.

She cleared her throat and turned her attention back to Stewart's uncle. "Sir, um, I don't know your name…"

He stared at the pond for a long time as if forgetting they were there. "Fox."

"Fox? Really?" Ora asked.

He only stared.

"Is that a nickname?"

"No." He puffed on the pipe, letting smoke slide out of the side of his mouth. The sweet, almost tangy smell of the tobacco wafting around his head spread toward them on the breeze.

"Right. Well, um, Fox…" Ora paused, collecting her thoughts.

"Just spit it out, girl," Fox said.

Ora flushed under the harsh words. "Your niece, Commander Stewart, arrested me with her Quad a few months ago. I was accused of being a Nip, but I'm not."

"That one is." He gestured with the pipe toward Devil.

"Yes, well…" Ora eyed the Nip, trying to find words to describe him. "He's…new."

"Mmm, hmm," Fox nodded, flicking the ashes into the grass, then added more tobacco, and lit the pipe again.

"I was put on trial and found guilty." Ora rubbed her hands together, a nervous habit Charlie hadn't seen in a long time.

"Thought you aren't a Nip?" he asked, looking out at the trees.

"I'm not." Ora leaned forward on the bench, attempting to win back his attention.

"Your niece and her partner, Lieutenant Sabrina Sun, believed me. They tried to find evidence to prove my innocence. But it wasn't enough. My Defender, Arameus Townsend," Ora gestured toward him, "did his best, but we lost."

Fox kept his focus on the surrounding trees, smoking his pipe, and his eyes skimmed the tops of the trees. Charlie thought he'd stopped paying attention until he asked, "Why aren't you dead? Nip punishment is the Kassen, is it not?"

Perdita's hand squeezed again, knuckles pale, as Ora placed her hand over top. "My mom came to rescue me, and she met an oxygenian who helped me escape. We were trying to find a way to cross over the Veil when the Kassen was discovered empty. Arameus warned us. We made a run for it, but the Quads still hunted us. During our escape, we ran into Sabrina, and she helped us."

Fox's eyes left the treetops, flicking to Sabrina, then to Arameus. "Ruined their lives," he said.

Ora's shoulders fell, and her head hung low. "I know."

He rolled his eyes. "*You* didn't do a thing. Their choice, their lives. Damn hard choice, too. Brave to stand up for what's right." Propping the pipe in his teeth, he asked, "What you want from me?"

The moment of truth had arrived. Ora's head tilted. "Before I ask, you need to hear it all."

He nodded his head once.

Ora and Perdita met eyes, finding encouragement, Ora focused once again on Fox. "During our escape I...well...sort of destroyed Conjuragic and sealed the Veil." Her words ran together as she said them so fast.

"Aye, t'was you then." He scratched his chin. "I wondered what happened."

"Yes, sir." Ora folded her hands, placing them in her lap, waiting for his judgment.

"Girl, you still haven't told me what you want?"

"I have magic from Sphere, Naiad, Tempest, and Ember."

Damien's head whipped to Ora She ignored his wide-eyed stare. "I was hoping you would train me to use Sphere magic."

Over the Bridge

To his credit, Fox took the news in stride. He puffed the pipe several more times. "To what purpose?"

Ora recoiled. "Excuse me?"

"Why you want to know?" He waved his pipe.

"Because..." Ora floundered again. "Because it's a part of me. Because I need to be able to defend my family, my friends. Because I need to fix things."

"Learning magic tricks will help you do this?" His attention once again shifted to the woods. A chill crept up Charlie's neck, and she, too, let her eyes roam the treetops as if something was coming.

Ora nodded. "Yes, sir, it will. But it isn't the magic I need to learn. It's wisdom and fighting and any knowledge that you'll share with me. Because I'm up against the entire world of Conjuragic, and I need all the help I can get."

"What's the Vessel for?" He gestured toward Charlie.

"That's Charlie McCurry. She's my best friend. The Quad attacked her when I was arrested, and after I sealed the Veil, the Hunters went after her. I have to protect her, which is another reason why I need to learn magic."

Fox laughed.

"What's so funny?" Ora demanded, red-headed temper rising to the surface. Charlie's hair stood on end. Ora's magic had risen to the surface. It charged the air, leaving a bittersweet tang like baked bread and vinegar.

"The irony, child, is that you, one with all cores, is friends with a Vessel." He continued laughing.

"I'm sorry sir, but what's a Vessel?" Charlie asked, and he stopped laughing, pointed to Devil, and said, "Ask him."

Before Devil, an appropriate nickname for Damien, had a chance to answer, Fox rang out in a chant—the language foreign, his words insistent. Whether due to the chant or his magic, the trees Fox had been watching bent and twisted. The ringing crack of a large tree trunk snapping into pieces ricocheted not far from where they all sat. A horrified scream interrupted the quiet melody of the forest's singing birds. Everyone jumped to their feet, except for Fox. Loud booming footsteps shook the forest, and Charlie expected a giant to emerge or the T-Rex from *Jurassic Park*. The sound grew louder, as did the high-pitched screams. *Boom. Boom. Boom.*

Charlie's heart thundered, siphoning blood to her extremities, readying her to fight or run for her life. With each rumbling step, cascades of leaves flooded the ground, and as she pivoted to run, a tree, whose trunk had split down the middle, emerged from the forest. Its branches twisted into a fist holding the squirming Jeremiah, whose screams hadn't slowed in the least. *Nope, not a T-Rex. It's an Ent from* Lord of the Rings.

"Why you follow me, Nip boy?" Fox puffed on his pipe, still seated upon his bench.

Jeremiah's screams faded into cowering whimpers. His head darted back and forth as his body dangled in the Ent-like thing's grip, thirty feet above the ground.

"I asked you a question." Fox's tone held an edge of annoyance.

Jeremiah groped at the branches, attempting to hold on, and screamed down at them, "I didn't have anywhere to go, sir."

Dirt and tree sap covered his face and clothes. A long scratch glistened red down his left cheek. He focused on Ora. "I want to help you. I want revenge for Gabe."

Gabe? Charlie could only guess that had been his twin brother's name. Not that any of them asked. Ora only glanced at Fox with pleading etched in her every gesture. Only Fox could grant him mercy.

Fox gave away nothing, eying his animals and home, before looking back at the pitiful young man. "I have no fear of you, Nip."

Jeremiah's words barely reached them. "I noticed."

Fox pointed at Ora. "First lesson. Nips cannot take your magic unless you send spells at them. But if your magic's in the environment, in the cores, then you can do anything you wish, and they cannot touch you."

"Oh," Ora said, not yet catching on that Fox meant to teach her. Devil shifted beside her.

"Except if you have one like him." Fox nodded toward Devil. "He is true Nip. He can snatch it right out of you. Isn't that right, boy?"

Devil turned red, not backing down from Fox, and his expression changed as his mind went into overdrive, calculating if he should answer.

"Yes, sir," Devil answered.

Fox pulled the no-longer-smoking pipe from his mouth. He frowned, stood, stretching, and looked up, almost as an afterthought. "Right then."

The tree lowered Jeremiah to the ground, dropping him the last few feet. He sprawled outward as he landed before jumping to his feet, his body poised and ready for an attack.

"This is your one and only warning, Nips." Fox's gaze flicked from Jeremiah to Devil. "Try anything, and I will kill you."

They both nodded, pale-faced.

"What kind of…dwelling is this." Perdita gestured toward the hobbit like hole behind Fox.

Fox raised one eyebrow. "You can speak. Was wondering. This is a Hogan." He clapped his hands together. "First things first. We eat. Then *Hatał* for your fallen friends." As if his words made perfect sense, he turned on his heel and disappeared through the doorway to the Hogan.

"A what for our friends?" Charlie asked.

Fox poked his head out of the doorway, a smile spread across his leathery face. "A *Hatał*—a healing chant."

Chapter Nineteen
Charlie

They walked inside Fox's Hogan. Delicious smells of cooking meat with spices and yeasty bread baking carried on the wind from the carved-out windows much like the entryway. Charlie's mouth watered. Their meals of late had been anything but satisfying. Charlie noted a woven wool blanket on a bed in the left of the large room. She doubted anything of such fine quality could be found in a store. A large table with a solitary chair sat to the right. When Fox passed by the table, a loud boom sounded outside the window. Charlie edged her way forward to spy what the ruckus would be this time. Out of one of the windows, a tree had fallen to the ground and carved itself into chairs. Charlie couldn't help but smile at his extraordinary magic.

At the far end of the Hogan was a kind of kitchen; it had a large stone hearth and a large clay pot inside the opening. Fox reached the hearth, and the pot lifted and floated out to him. The lid floated off as steam rose into the air. Fox peered inside, took a deep sniff, picked up a wooden spoon, and took a small taste. "Tonight," he said to himself as he placed the spoon down, turned his back, and limped to the other side of the kitchen to a long counter coming out of the wall. Behind him, the lid sank back on the pot before returning to the hearth.

Fox faced the counter, and the walls melted away in thick muddy rivulets forming another window. He leaned out as strips of stalk and leaves grew impossibly fast from right outside the window. He gathered strawberries, oranges, bananas, and nuts, as well as some herbs and other leaves. As his hand pulled away, the plants shrank backward and out of sight.

Over the Bridge

The fruit split itself in half, and the nuts jumped out of the shells. An invisible knife chopped some of the leaves. A few other leaves laid on the counter, and Fox turned to Ora. "You have Naiad magic?"

"Yes." Ora stepped closer to the counter.

"Take water out da leaves." He hobbled back toward the far end of the Hogan beside his bed. The wall melted away, and he whistled. A few moments later, a goat trotted up and stood sideways by the door. A small circle of earth rose of the ground, and he sat on it like a stool. He grabbed a small bucket from somewhere underneath the bed and milked the goat.

He waved a hand over his head reminding her to move. "Leaves."

Ora jumped. "Leaves, water, on it."

Ora placed her hand over top of the leaves. She closed her eyes while she concentrated. She formed her hand into a claw-shape and lifted upward. Nothing happened until Fox appeared by her side and smacked her on the hand. Ora jumped, jerking her head toward him. "What?"

Charlie noted a faint sheen of water on top of the leaves.

Fox held the bucket of goat's milk, wagged one finger at Ora, and said, "Don't use hands."

"But I," Ora said.

"Next lesson, no waving hands. Even Protectors have hard time using magic without waving hands." He inspected the still limp but no longer fresh leaves. She hadn't quite gotten them dehydrated, but he quirked his mouth as if thinking they'd do before sitting the bucket down and extracting a tea kettle from underneath the counter, a small blanket hiding the contents underneath. He sat the kettle down beside the leaves. "Put water in pot."

Ora's throat bobbed as she swallowed then moved as if to raise a hand. She halted. "Are you going to hit me?"

"Probably."

Her mouth twisted into a thin line. Charlie would've recognized her annoyed look from a million miles away. Ora stared into the pot, brow furrowed, and nothing happened. In another situation this would've been comical. Ora's hand raised, and fast as a snake, Fox slapped it again.

"Oww!" Ora rubbed the back of her hand. "Why do you keep doing that?"

He crossed her arms. "Why raise hand? Hands do nothing. It's your mind. Raising hand gives you away. In battle you need surprise. Pow. Pow. Pow. Pow." With each Pow, roots shot up from the ground and ensnared Charlie, Perdita, Damien, and Jeremiah.

After the roots grabbed them, each let out a scream. Ora's face paled as her eyes moved to each of her friends and back at Fox. His gaze never left hers.

"What would hands have done?" he asked.

Ora's eyes darted back and forth as she worked out the answer. "It would've slowed you down, and they would've figured out your next move. You'd have ensnared one or two but might've missed the others."

Fox nodded, then poked the kettle. "Again."

Charlie rooted to the spot, literally as they wrapped around her, holding her firm, but not uncomfortable. Ora concentrated on the kettle. As soon as Charlie wished she could sit down, the roots moved, and adjusted her into a sitting position. He could've released them. Charlie didn't like being an example, and by the looks on their faces, neither did the others.

"You can do it," Perdita said.

Ora's face relaxed. Water materialized from the air and moved into the kettle. Ora had gotten good at this little bit of magic, but nerves and not using her hands made it harder. Ora got too much, and it overfilled, splashing on the ground below it. But she did it! She jumped up and down.

Charlie yelled, "Great! Now can you let us go? I've got a vine poking me in the butt."

Ora burst into a fit of giggles as the vines peeled off them. Ora's laughter continued. She bent over, holding her belly, with tears in her eyes. She tried to rein it in, but when she looked at Charlie, she'd burst out into another round. The laughter spread, contagious, and after a while, they all laughed.

The two girls laughed the longest. When they finally could control themselves, they noticed Fox's new chairs creeping toward the table. He sat at the table, chewing, before motioning Charlie and Ora to join the rest of them. Charlie wondered if the trees he kept stealing wood from were outside somewhere, licking the areas of missing wood, as if cleaning its wounds.

Charlie's stomach growled. Fresh ripe fruits, soft white cheese, a steaming kettle of tea, and fresh warm bread with the steam still rising above it laden the table. The table had a plate, bowl, and cup for each. Charlie filled her plate with the cheese, bread, and fruit. Ora fixed herself a spoonful of nuts and made a salad out of the various leaves and herbs. She sniffed at two bottles on the table before pouring what looked like Italian dressing on her salad. Charlie poured them both a cup of tea. Charlie took a bite of strawberry, and it burst full of sweet juice. She moaned, enjoying the best strawberry she'd ever tasted. She chewed while slathering her steaming piece of bread with butter. Not waiting for it to cool down, she took a big bite. Warm, buttery, and so divine it could've been laced with a sleeping potion. With each bite, Charlie's muscles and nerves relaxed.

No one spoke as everyone, Fox included, devoured the food. Charlie had to force herself to take small bites and chew well. She didn't want to waste the food by making herself sick by over eating. Her plate empty, she debated on getting seconds.

Charlie waited for the others to finish. With her full belly, warmer temperature, and plummeting anxiety, her eyes grew heavy. She yawned, mouth wide, and stretched. Everyone's plate emptied, except for Fox. He ate with purpose, taking only small bites and chewing for a very long time. Before long Ora yawned, too. Devil and Jeremiah followed.

Charlie tried to remember the last time she'd gotten a good night's sleep. Or when any of them had. Her constant ache from fatigue had lessoned. The persistent headache, starting at her neck and traveling down her shoulders and upward until her entire head throbbed, had lessened. Interweaved through her, a coldness seeped down into her bones. Even this had diminished. Every muscle demanded rest.

Charlie didn't know what came over her, but she stumbled to her feet, shuffled to Fox's bed, slipped off her shoes, and in one uncoordinated movement, she pulled the blanket back and fell into the bed. The soft pillow caressed her head, and the warm blanket wriggled over her shoulders. Within seconds, Ora joined her on the other side and both of them fell into a deep, dreamless sleep.

Chapter Twenty
Perdita

Perdita leaned over the lake washing the dishes from their meal. Ora was finally getting some much-needed rest. Not that the others didn't need it too. Fox had declared after cleaning up they should all join Ora and Charlie in a nap while he prepared for the *Hatał*. Perdita had to agree. The last few weeks had been more than taxing. Every moment felt like a roller coaster, going faster and faster, turning and twisting, and when you think the ride is over, the bottom drops out from under you.

"You have Sphere magic?" Fox had snuck up behind her.

She screamed and dropped the plate into the lake. "Oh, you scared me!" Her wet hand left an imprint on her already soiled blouse.

He waited for her answer, leaning against his walking stick, never in a hurry.

She answered him. "No. Naiad and Tempest."

He nodded. "You help. Come." The plate rose from the bottom of the lake and rested upon the stack of clean dishes beside Perdita.

"Show off." She muttered and could've swore she heard Fox chuckle beneath his breath. She carried the dishes back inside the Hogan and put them away. Fox had made more beds, and Ora and Charlie remained sleeping.

Fox made the Hogan bigger and divided it into different rooms, separating Devil and Jeremiah from the rest of the group. She peeked inside finding the two in the newly made beds with their eyes wide open. Perdita didn't know how she felt about those two being here, especially while the two girls slept and Sabrina and

Arameus still unconscious. Especially since she and Fox would be outside preparing for the healing chant. She pivoted to tell Fox she couldn't leave the girls alone, but as she turned, he appeared by her side. She jumped and wondered how he moved so silently.

"They cannot leave room unless I permit it." He used his walking stick to point out two plants on either side of the door. The leaves moved as if in a breeze, despite the stillness of the air. Upon closer inspection, she recognized the same plants that had bound them earlier. The leaves slithered like snakes ready to strike. A chill ran down her spine, and she shook it off.

"They're like..." Perdita cut her sentence off since Fox had slipped away again. She caught a small glimpse of a shoe going around the corner from the open doorway. With one last glance at her sleeping daughter, Perdita stepped out of the Hogan in search of Fox.

She found him a few feet deeper into the clearing, or perhaps the trees had moved themselves. It was hard to tell with Fox. She marveled at Fox being so at one with his environment, his magical core, that nature bent to his will. He only had to think something, and it happened. Like growing which foods he wanted to eat, shelter, weapons, anything. No wonder he lived out here. What else did he need? Although for her, it would be lonely not having anyone to talk to, except the sheep and goats.

When she reached his side, he pointed. "We need special Hogan. Bigger, eight sides and round."

She had a hard time picturing this, but instead of trying to figure it out, she asked, "Why do you need my help? Obviously, you can make this without me."

"Two cores magic stronger than one. Will make spell more powerful," he said in his odd broken English.

"Oh. Can I use my hands?" she asked.

He actually smiled. "This time only. You train, too."

He gestured with his stick for her to go on the other side of the field. She turned to face him, and he waved for her to take a step back, and she did so until she reached about thirty feet away from him.

Over the Bridge

They stared at each other for a long time. Finally, she asked, "What am I supposed to do?" He muttered something.

"Can't hear you!"

Then he yelled, talking with his hands. "Use wind to pick dirt up from center; then make dome."

She imagined a large circle and concentrated on the center. She hadn't used her magic very much, but this she remembered. All day long in the prison, she pushed different kinds of earth together with air and mixed it with water, along with Philo, her husband, trying to heat it up to make the all-powerful rock for master. The dirt moving under her will brought back bad memories, but she shoved them away. This felt better, using her magic for good, not for the whims of a madman.

Sweat broke on her brow, but the dirt trembled. The gentle shaking intensified, and dirt from the outsides rolled inward until it picked up speed. The dirt formed a large mound and rose in the air. Using her magic in this way had never felt so difficult. It took all her concentration, and still, she felt as if she carried a heavy load. The strain built higher and stronger until, in one breath, the load lightened.

Fox's magic had joined hers, sharing the load. Shifting her attention, she sensed his magic, weaving in and around hers. She pushed the air, making it rise and roll outward. It fell back toward the earth, forming his dome. His magic controlled the descent and locked the earth back together making one solitary mass.

This had to be why Conjuragic was a powerful city. It had been made by constructing the buildings using all four cores of magic. She compared this Hogan to his main home. Now that her Tempest magic had been reawakened, she could see his magic interwoven into the Hogan, but the magic in this one wound tighter and stronger.

The structure solidified. She smiled to herself, dropping her arms, and strolled around the Healing Hogan as an opening formed on each of the eight sides. She joined Fox on the other side, and he motioned with his hand. "Walk with me."

They proceed to walked around the newly-formed Hogan, and every so often, he pulled out a seed from a little pouch he had in his pocket. He sifted through them, pulled out one, and bent to the ground. When his hand reached the earth, it parted for him, and he dropped the seed. As he stood, the earth closed, and he sang a little chant. A little plant peeked a small stalk and tiny green leaf out of the dirt. It looked like a time-lapse video, only it happened in seconds, instead of the hours or days it really should. He created life.

On the eighth side, he handed Perdita the last seed. She took it and stared at him. What did he expect her to do? The tiny, vulnerable seed waited to be born. Fox gestured toward the ground, expecting what she couldn't guess. So many thoughts flew through her head, all of doubt and insecurity. She fought them, all while he stared at her, waiting to see her reaction. Calmness settled over her. She bent, her magic reached forward, and the air pushed the dirt aside. It formed a small hole, an opening, waiting for life to begin. She took the seed in her fingertips and placed it into the ground, like a mother laying down her sleeping baby, and instead of using magic, she covered this tiny seed with her hands and patted the ground at the end. A tear rolled down her cheek. She lifted her hand and using her index finger, scooped her tear, and placed it on the dirt. With the most natural feeling in the world, the Naiad magic inside her pulled her tear into the ground, her love stimulating the tiny seed.

With her magic, she watched the water move, trickling through the ground, and reaching her seed. The shell cracked open, the small tendrils of roots reaching out into the dirt, like baby arms reaching for their mother. The roots, shining with both hers and Fox's magic, grew longer and sank into the earth, spreading out, and took hold. The stalk elongated and rose from the seed, searching for the sun, and broke through the earth. The little plant twisted and turned, growing branches and leaves and a small bulb. The bulb opened, and a beautiful white flower emerged, pointing straight at the sun. Perdita stood and let the tears fall.

"You're a natural." Fox tapped his walking stick on the ground.

She smiled, pleased. "Are we done?"

"Your part, yes. Ora's is next."

"She doesn't have a lot of control."

"The magical artifact around her neck will aid her."

"The necklace?"

Fox nodded, stepping back toward the main Hogan. "It called to her, no doubt. Pieces like those offer a kind of training wheel when first learning."

Perdita didn't want to know what it did after Ora learned to control her magic. They walked together back inside the main Hogan, and everyone slept. Ora's face had relaxed in sleep, and she didn't toss and turn like she had for months. Even the two Nips snored from the next room.

"More tea?" Fox offered as he handed her a steaming cup. She sipped the sweet herbal tea that held a slight bitterness at the end. They sat together at the table in an easy silence. The tension eased away from Perdita's neck and she yawned.

"Thank you for helping us," Perdita said. "Helping Ora."

He nodded and sipped his tea. The warmth spread through her body, and her eyes grew heavy. On cue, another bed of earth grew beside Ora's. She shot a questioning look at Fox and then at her cup. "Did you?"

But he interrupted. "Give you all sleeping herbs. Yes. Need sleep badly. Especially that one." He pointed at Ora.

Perdita's body tried to fight the tea, alarm thudding along in her brain, but the fogginess won out. Her head drooped, and her protest never left her lips when he took her elbow, guiding her to her feet and into the bed. She tried to fight it, but her shoulders dropped back to the bed when he placed a finger to his lips. "Shhhh."

"How could you?" she mumbled.

His brow furrowed. "You don't trust me?"

She realized she did. He didn't give them the herbs to harm them, but to allow their stressed minds to relax, a thoughtful gift. She tried to spit out a thank you before succumbing to sleep.

Chapter Twenty-One
Ora

THICK NOTHING SURROUNDED ME IN the Shadow Land. This time I recognized the place. The darkness fell upon me but felt different this time—welcoming instead of teetering with danger.

The familiar browned butter and cinnamon smell washed over me moments before the voice spoke. "Welcome back."

"Thanks." I wished for light before remembering John's embrace from last time. The darkness would do.

"What am I doing here?"

"When you're ready, you will know," it said.

"Who are you? My conscience?"

The voice laughed. "If that's what you wish."

"Fine. I'll call you Jiminy then."

The voice made cricket noises. I giggled. At least my conscience had a sense of humor.

I hadn't moved, yet I didn't sink inside the tar-like substance. Taking tentative steps, I found the movements still sluggish, but much easier than before, and I could move in any direction I wished. The angry, scared voices echoed far, far way. A chill ran down my spine.

Jiminy said, "They're far away. Don't worry about them right now."

Warmth touched the small of my back. Following its lead, I pushed through the muck, step after step. I could've walked for days or only seconds. Time didn't have meaning in this place. I wondered where my conscious planned on taking me when a light appeared up ahead.

Over the Bridge

"Not much farther now," Jiminy said.

The closer the light became the fog around me lifted. A fuzzy house appeared through the fog. With each passing step, the beautiful two-story colonial-style home with brown siding and a double door in front became clearer. A cobblestone path led to the front door with small bushes with little white flowers wrapped around the house, and on either side of the porch, large white rose bushes framed the steps. A sign hung from a lamp post that read, "Aryiana's Intuitions." The center of the sign had a large hand with an eye in the palm. To the left of the hand, the text read, "tarot, crystal ball, psychic, palm reading," and on the right, the text read, "oils, brews, charms, incense, and candles." The welcoming sense of the home disappeared as the front door swung open with a bang, and a dark-skinned middle-aged beauty with long straight black hair stuck her head out. She wore a long wool maroon shawl around her shoulders, a pale blue blouse, and soft jeans. Her head swiveled back and forth, alarm etched on her face, before yelling in a thick French accent, "Who's there? What do you want?"

I took a timid step closer, skimming the house and what I could see of the street, trying to find the source of what had disturbed her.

Jiminy said, "Careful."

I halted. As soon as I'd moved, the woman's head whipped around, and she stared straight at me.

"You?" She glared and stomped out of her door, leaving it wide open. Tapping her bare foot upon the wood. "What are you doing here now?" She stalked toward me as if going to stroll right into the Shadow Land.

Jiminy whispered, "You're not ready yet. It's time to wake up."

I didn't want to leave, but something in the woman's body language made me take a step back. All of a sudden, I flew backward as if struck by an invisible hand. My eyes jerked opened. I bolted upright. Fading sunlight filtered through the makeshift windows in Fox's Hogan. Soft snores filtered around the room from my companions sleeping. Mom laid in a bed beside me while

Charlie flanked on the other side. Damien and Jeremiah had been given a new bedroom that hadn't been there when I'd fallen asleep. A trail of smoke from the doorway wafted in the door. Fox's hand appeared from nowhere, motioning me to join him, presumably on his bench.

"Good. You're awake. You must help prepare for *Hatał*," Fox called to me from outside. I slid out of bed still disoriented, stretched, slipped on my shoes, and stepped outside. Dusk settled over the clearing turning the sky a thousand different shades of pink, purple, and blue.

"Beautiful night." Fox stood, wiping his hand down his faded blue jeans, slipped the brown pipe into the pocket of a blue dress shirt, and hobbled away toward a new building. His eccentricity made perfect sense since he lived alone. He wasn't used to talking to people or announcing his movements. He limped, favoring the right leg, while his long black hair swung across his back, secured at the nape of his neck. The cowboy boots scuffed the ground on the well-worn path to the forest's edge.

The new Hogan towered over the old one, and flowers and other plants surrounded it. It had eight openings into the inside. I took a peek inside. Sabrina and Arameus had been placed in the center, side by side, still on the gurneys. My friends had been cleaned, hair brushed, and clothes changed. I decided against asking who had done all that.

Fox handed me a large clay pot. I took it and followed the strange old man into the woods. Somewhere along the way, my life had derailed from normalcy into this maddening chaos. With no way to stop the monstrous train, I had no other choice but to keep moving forward to see where the ride would take me. Fox halted and pointed to some various leaves, grass, roots, or rocks before moving on. He never said a word, leaving me to assume he wanted those objects picked up and placed in the pot. We left the woods and traipsed to his lake. Fox tapped an old, bent, metal ladle, before holding up three fingers. I pulled out three ladles full of water without magic, which seemed appropriate somehow. Fox whistled and snipped a bit of wool from a sheep before entering the goat's pin. He tossed the wool into the pot. "We need blood and bone."

"Say what?"

He pulled a small knife out of one of his pockets. It had a wooden base and sharpened rock instead of steel. It looked like something a caveman might've used. Clicking his tongue, Fox reached for one of the goats, who ran over at his call. The little thing ran over, so trusting, and nestled its head against his hand. "May I," Fox asked, and the goat nodded as if giving him permission. Fox put the knife to its leg.

Averting my eyes, I braced for the squeal of pain. None came. Fox's knife appeared from my side, dropping the tiniest bit of blood into the bowl. The goat licked its leg without so much as a scratch. Relief flooded over me.

Fox left the pin, not waiting for me, moving faster than I thought possible. He held up a hand signaling for me to wait while he disappeared into his Hogan. He returned with a small white piece of bone and placed it into the pot. With deft hands, he took the pot from me and hobbled into the Healing Hogan.

"Where did the bone come from?"

"One of my goats." His shoulders sagged.

"You killed one of the goats today?"

"No. Goat old. Time to move on. Must have known you coming. Waste nothing." He shrugged, but the sorrow surrounded him like an aura.

"What do you mean?"

"Goat died this morning. Offered me its meat."

I wasn't sure how a goat offered its meat, but I thought it'd be best not to ask. We entered the Healing Hogan, which had changed since I'd first peeked inside. A circle of seats made out of dirt surrounded the gurneys, and an altar had risen in between Arameus and Sabrina. He placed the pot upon the altar.

"If they have their magic back, why won't they wake up?" I asked.

"When stolen and gone for long time not enter body right. Like Saran wrap. *Hatał* help put it back together." He motioned for me to come closer. "Send magic into pot."

Send magic into pot? That's it? That's the best directions you've got? I had to try. Closing my eyes, I felt within myself, deep into the madness where my magic lived. In some ways, I felt I'd only scratched the surface. Images of a large cave appeared in my mind's eye. The magic rolled and bubbled looking somewhat like molten lava, churning black and red. I had expected it to look or feel different. Like there should be four distinct parts, but it was whole and singular.

"I see it. There isn't four parts."

Fox chuckled. "You expected different parts. One for Naiad, Tempest, Ember, and Sphere?"

"Yeah."

He shook his head. "'Tis all bound into one. You want to learn each core, but none of what I teach you, what she teach you," he gestured toward Sabrina, "will be perfect. Your magic unique."

I supposed I'd always known that. But I still had to learn what I could from people who did know each core. There had to be a starting point.

I fell into the cavern, called to my magic, and it rose like a living thing, the power vibrating. The enormity of it baffling and horrific, but it could do good. Fox's magic proved how magic was meant to be used. In balance.

As some of my fear fell away, the magic rose, higher and higher. I felt and saw a glowing golden light leave my chest, coalescing through the amulet, and settling into the pot. At first nothing happened, but then the pot shook and glowed. The light grew brighter and brighter until it stung my eyes. The brightness faded after a few more seconds. The contents inside the pot had all melted and formed a golden syrup with tendrils of smoke rising from it. Fox dipped his finger in the syrup and smelled it. "Perfect. We are ready." The aroma of freshly mowed grass, watermelon, and a long-forgotten fruit wafted from the pot. He set the pot down upon the altar.

Over the Bridge

He grabbed my elbow, leading me out of the Hogan toward the main house. "It's time."

He entered the Hogan, calling for the others to wake up, but I paused at the doorway. Something whispered inside my head. I closed my eyes, and once again, I could see the Colonial house with white roses, Aryiana's house, but closer this time, as if I stood on the cobblestone walkway. The incense burned a sweet aroma of lavender. Through the window, Aryiana stood in her small kitchen, cooking. Her head lifted, and her eyes met mind. Her lips never moved, but the voice with the French accent whispered again, "I see you child, and I'll be ready when you come."

My eyes jerked open. I stool mere feet from the Healing one. Mom, Charlie, Damien, and Jeremiah sat inside the Healing Hogan in the seats surrounding Sabrina and Arameus. *What was that?*

Eight people sat in the Hogan, enough for eight openings. Coincidence? I think not. Fox motioned for me to enter and shuffled back toward his Hogan. I found a seat surrounding my sick friends and waited to begin. Damien opened his mouth, but a breeze blew through the Hogan drowning his words as Aryiana's voice whispered in my head, "Remember, I'll be waiting."

Chapter Twenty-Two
Ora

INCENSE BURNED, FILLING THE HEALING Hogan with a sweet woodsy aroma while Fox gathered more herbs and flowers. Sabrina and Arameus lay on the gurneys, groomed, wearing white ceremonial robes that left their necks, forearms, and lower legs exposed. Fox returned, changed from his jeans and blue button-down shirt into black pants and short-sleeved t-shirt, and placed various herbs and flowers around Sabrina and Arameus forming a circle. He picked up the potion of syrup we'd made together and motioned for me to come to him.

Everyone else remained seated surrounding our two patients in the center as I moved forward. Fox took my hand, guiding me beside Sabrina. While chanting in a foreign language he grabbed my index finger and dipped it into the syrup.

Fox used my finger, covered in the potion, to draw different symbols on her forehead, arms, legs and finally on her chest over her heart. Next, we moved to Arameus and repeated the process. We drew different symbols from those on Sabrina and Arameus on Fox's chest, arms, legs, and forehead. His chanting never ceased, and with his free hand, he patted a rhythmic beat on his leg.

Dipping my finger into the potion again, he traced a symbol upon my chest, and motioned for me to move my amulet to rest over top of it. He wouldn't touch it.

He gestured to my seat, and I nodded, not wanting to talk, it felt wrong to break the chanting. Without meeting anyone's gaze, I returned to my seat. Everyone stared, and my cheeks burned. Fox moved directly opposite me with Sabrina on my right, Arameus on my left. I prayed silently for this to work. Fox handed Damien an old drum and instructed him on the beat.

"Why me?" Damien asked, breaking the silence.

"You took their magic. You have to guide it back home," Mom whispered, and Fox nodded.

Damien ducked his head, but took the drum stick, copying Fox's beat. The white scars shone on his arms, the muscles rippling with every strike. It wasn't the time to notice such things, but I couldn't help but wonder where all those scars had come from. Whoever had done it made sure to spare his face.

Fox handed me a small scrap of paper with a note written in tiny, chicken-scratch letters.

Hatal begin soon. You chant too. Always think about making friends whole. Pass to others.

Fox picked up the incense burning on the altar. Instead of the tiny sticks I'd bought in novelty shops, his looked like fat sausages. A large group of herbs bound together with twine. The flame burned bright at one end while Fox gripped the other side. He chanted and moved in a strange dance, bouncing from one leg to the other, turning in circles while waving the smoking stick around in weird circles. If everything in my life hadn't been so crazy, this might've been funny. Charlie and I shared a "what the hell" look, but Mom leaned forward and mouthed, "Sage." Fox completed the circle and stood at the altar. All eyes trained on him.

He motioned with a rolling gesture of his hands. I wasn't sure if he wanted me to join him or something else. By the clueless looks on everyone else's faces, they didn't know either.

Charlie handed the little note back, and I read through it again. "You chant, too." Then I heard it, the repeating pattern of Fox's words, *"Lumen de Lumine Eck Ong Kar Sat Nam."*

I repeated his words, stumbling over the new sounds, *"Lumen de Lumine Eck Ong Kar Sat Nam."*

The others joined in. At first our words were mumbled and distorted, but as we got the hang of it, our chant became stronger and faster. I closed my eyes, losing myself in the chanting, imagining Arameus awake and smiling and Sabrina sulking and beautiful.

Over and over, we chanted the words, and as time wore on, the individual words faded. We were no longer individuals but a new entity chanting together to one goal. A cool, vibrant gust of air flowed around the Hogan, the ground trembled at my feet, sweat rolled down my neck, and a warm sensation spread across through my chest. At the periphery of my consciousness, the magic inside me rolled out and away from me, swaying in time with the chant, as if dancing, slithering into every nook and cranny of the Hogan.

The chant grew faster and faster. Fox's words shifted, building off ours, which remained the same, almost singing the new chant over the old one. The air in the Hogan rang with static electricity. The very pressure from the energy pulsated through the room. My eyes opened. I had to see it. Sabrina and Arameus glowed. The brightest spots shined over the markings on their bodies. Fox's markings glowed, too. As did mine. A blue tinge of light shimmered underneath Sabrina's skin while Arameus had something similar, but less bright and purple. Their magic.

Fox had been right. Their magic was crumpled like an old shirt thrown in the laundry, twisting in and around itself.

Fox stomped in an intricate dance, weaved around the altar, and shook the sage stick over top of Sabrina and Arameus. He tossed the remaining stump of the stick on the ground. It landed and exploded into a thousand pieces, which flowed upward and swarmed like dancing fireflies. Fox clapped, chanted, and danced back to the altar. He lifted the pot and spun. The fireflies of sage swarmed down, landing on Sabrina's chin, and her mouth opened. Fox stood above her head and poured half the golden syrup in her mouth. Without pausing, Fox moved to Arameus and emptied the remaining thick syrup. A small part of me panicked thinking they would choke, but my magic warmed as if soothing me.

All the while the words, *"Lumen de Lumine Eck Ong Kar Sat Nam,"* poured through and out of me. With each word, my own power settled, growing outward, like a root gaining access to the deepest parts of the soil. Here, in this place, no fear could reach me. No doubt. My magic welcomed it. Celebrated and merged with me. Reaching out from the darkest, stillest depths within me, stretching, and celebrating. It wanted this, needed it like oxygen.

Fox returned to the altar, settling the pot on top, and raised his hands to the sky. Using the Sight—a word which stirred more visions of the past—the world of whole shapes disappeared. Underneath everything, small individual atoms moved together in the perfect harmony of life. Atoms, that's what I could see, I understood now. I'd seen this before, as a child, before the spell that locked away my power, only I hadn't known the word for it.

I let the Sight expand. The golden liquid inside my friend's mouths shined like a beacon. It slid down their throats, bypassing the trachea, and entered their stomachs. The syrup broke apart into the tiniest of atoms, passing through the stomach into the blood stream, which carried it to every cell in their bodies. With it, the magic followed.

My magic touched everything and everyone, light tiny tendrils spun outward like spider silk. Around Damien, my power quivered, recognizing the foreign power. I'd have thought it would've retreated, escaping from the potential of danger, but it didn't. His power held its only vibration of energy that mirrored mine, like two halves of the same coin. In response the power cooed, wrapping around the Nip power inside him. Damien shuttered as his shoulders dropped, relaxing the ever-clenched jaw, but never missed a beat of the drum.

If my magic gave off a golden light, his absorbed it in an inky blackness. I couldn't look any longer as my pitiful human eyes were incapable of seeing the true reality. In this moment, magic broke all barriers, taking me into higher plane of existence and understanding.

At the release of restraint, my power reached toward Damien, in offering and question. His black power grasped mine and rose out of Damien, mingling with mine. This blackness could never be terrifying. Unlike the monstrous darkness where nightmares lived, this blackness personified an endless starry night sky filled with fireflies and the sweet scent of dew and promise.

Our magics danced, swirling and dipping until holding onto each other, we dove into Sabrina and Arameus. Their magic rough and jagged, but as the two of us swam through them, carrying with us the love, and harmony, and connection of every person in the Hogan, the wrinkles and clumps straightened. With each adjustment of their magic, their mortal bodies twitched and shook like a seizure, but with every jerk, their magic righted itself. A whistling sailed through the Hogan, as the magic moved within them, growing louder and louder until every sound ceased as Damien and I sailed out of them, releasing each other, and settling back into ourselves. The chanting, the drum, the whistling all gone. The Hogan descended into a silence so complete I might've gone deaf.

At the same moment, Arameus and Sabrina both bolted upright and screamed.

Chapter Twenty-Three
Sabrina

Sabrina stared at Ora's shocked face. Confusion like she'd never known rolled over her in waves. Ora sprinted to Sabrina's side, as Perdita and Charlie went to Arameus. Sabrina recoiled while her eyes darted back and forth. The nightclub had disappeared and dissolved into pain. Pain unlike anything she'd ever experienced. A pain so complete it blocked out the world, but now that too had gone. Ora scooted backward, giving Sabrina some space, as an unsteady weariness took the place of blind panic. Ora eyed her like a wild animal. This more than anything gripped at Sabrina, bringing back the logical side, not ever wanting to not be out of control.

Sabrina took in the strange structure she found herself in. At least fifteen-foot-high ceilings with walls made of clay and dirt and openings all around like some weird gazebo. A circle of benches surrounded the two beds in the center. A timid young boy she didn't recognize stared at her, but his eyes darted to the floor when her gaze passed over him. A familiar tall, blond man dropped a drum and stick on the ground. He stood, not watching any of them, and hurried out of the place. The back of her neck prickled at the sight of him.

Arameus panted, eyes wide as saucers, also taking in the new surroundings. Sabrina swiveled to look behind her. Fox, Leigh's uncle, bowed his head. She met the man only once but trusted him.

Some, but never all, of her suspicions sank away. As she didn't seem to be in any immediate danger, other sensations slid their way into the forefront of her mind. Her stomach churned and craved food. She grabbed Ora's hand, as if desperate for something to cling to, and asked, "What happened?"

Ora and Perdita shared a look.

Perdita leaned forward. "You and Arameus were attacked by a Nip." She placed a hand on Arameus's knee. His face paled.

Sabrina swallowed, noting the odd symbols painted on Ora and Fox. "The Nip is dead then?"

Perdita stammered, "Um. The thing is…"

The blond-haired scarred man from earlier stepped out of the shadows. "Not exactly."

Sabrina's eyes narrowed, but exhaustion crept along her muscles. She wiped her brow, taking the last of the markings with it. Sabrina swung her legs around, dangling them to the floor, and moaned as the room spun from even that little effort.

The mousy young man appeared at her side and placed a hand on her wrist checking for a pulse. "You need food." The boyish, mousy look of him faded as he stared at her with something akin to worship in his eyes.

She glared at him, and asked, "Who are you?"

"Oh, that's Jeremiah. He's a new friend. It's a long story," Perdita said.

"One that needs told by the warmth of a fire and with a full belly." Fox waved from outside the Hogan, leaning on an old, twisted walking stick.

Behind her, Charlie and Perdita whispered. At last, Sabrina heard Arameus's voice. Although he sounded hoarse and weak, his voice reassured her that he too would be okay. Perdita took Ora's place, steading her with an arm on her elbow, as Ora gently pulled Arameus into an embrace.

"Thanks," he said, voice hoarse like a frog's.

"I think I owed you one…or a hundred," Ora said.

He moaned. "If this is what I have to go through for repayment, consider us even."

Ora, Charlie, and Perdita laughed.

Ora said, "You all want to try to stand?"

Ora and Charlie each took one of his arms, guided him to the edge, but even that wasn't enough to help him stand. Damien and Jeremiah took over. Charlie, Ora, and Perdita helped Sabrina. Sabrina's legs screamed in pain and quivered with the slightest effort. Rage aided her, but even that sucked what little energy she had.

Inside another mud-filled structure Sabrina recognized as Fox's home, she slumped in the chair. She caught her breath and rolled the back of her hand across her forehead, annoyed at the sweat there, pointing out her weakness. Her eyes roamed Fox's place. The place had done a complete one-eighty since the last time she'd been there. It had doubled in size with a big table already set with bowls and cups for everyone, and more chairs, a large sitting area, new openings for bedrooms, and a privy.

Fox sat with his hands folded on the table in front of him. He nodded at Sabrina. "Tell me your name."

Ora held out a hand. "We told you, this is Sabrina Sun."

Fox stared at Sabrina ignoring the others. Sabrina understood his intention even if the others didn't. Arameus nodded in her periphery also acknowledging the necessary custom. Sabrina rested her palms on the table, pushing, trying to stand. Ora took her elbow, but Sabrina gave a quick jerk of the head. Ora's arm retreated as Sabrina braced herself and pushed. The room tilted, but she fought down the vertigo, closed her eyes, and breathed through her nose. When the nausea rolling through her stomach settled, she said, "I am Lieutenant Sabrina Sun. House of Naiad. First born of Rebekah and Robert Sun. Former Protector. Quad One."

Fox nodded his head as she bowed and sank into the chair. What little color she had recovered faded with the effort.

Fox's gaze shifted to Arameus even as he pushed himself to standing. Sweat glistened on his brow as he said, "I am Defender Arameus Townsend, Esquire. House of Tempest. Third born of Destine and Geoffrey Townsend. Defender Conjuragic Law." He, too, bowed before collapsing in the chair.

Fox stood, nodded to either Sabrina and Arameus. "I am Fox Stewart. House Sphere." He gave a small bow. The formal introductions complete, he said, "I welcome you to my home. May you be safe and content in your time here. What's mine is yours."

Sabrina and Arameus said together, "We thank you for the hospitality. May your house be ever strong and true. We accept your grace and offer our own."

The rest stared at the foreign custom but said nothing. Fox picked up a ladle and scooped something into the nearest bowl, passing it to Perdita who sat to his right, and she passed it to Charlie. The mousy boy passed his own bowl to Fox, who accepted, ladled in what smelled like stew, before passing this to Perdita. This repetition continued, each picking up an empty bowl, passing to the left, and when everyone had a bowl full of stew, Fox took his seat, grabbed a spoonful, and ate.

Sabrina chuckled at the looks on Charlie and Ora's faces, but this comforted her. This small reminder of home. The hunger inside her won over the amusement, and she took her first bite. She moaned of pleasure. The warm, savory spiced broth swam around her tongue making it the perfect base for the soft potatoes, sweet carrots, and tender meat.

Ora peeled apart a hot, yeasty roll still steaming from the hearth and slathered it with delicious homemade butter. Fox poured them all a glass of red wine. Sabrina sipped the wine, which mingled with her meal and accentuated the spice in the broth. Ora's nose cringed with each taste, but she said nothing.

Sabrina took her time. With each bite, strength and clarity returned to her. Her arms no longer wavered when she brought the spoon to her mouth. No one spoke during the meal. Odd. Sabrina could sniff out secrets like a hound dog.

Her mind whirled through what she could remember, which wasn't much. Her eyes flicked to the scarred blond then away, sizing him up, recalling his loaded words from before. Could he be the Nip? If so, he'd let them go. But why would they let him stick around? What about the boy? Where and when had he come from? Did they think she couldn't handle the truth?

The clinking of spoons on porcelain bowls transitioned from a feverous ruckus to a quiet melody, Fox took the pot of stew to the kitchen area and returned with a large pie with a lattice top still steaming with the aroma of fresh baked apples and cinnamon.

Perdita cut slices and served them while Fox returned with a pot of coffee and ice-cold milk. Sabrina picked at the pie, which on another day she would've devoured, and instead stewed in her growing annoyance. She wouldn't accept secrets when Hunters could be anywhere and now Nips too. She flung her fork on the plate with a clang. "Is anyone going to tell me why he's here?"

If looks could kill, Damien would be dead where he sat. As his eyes met hers, she remembered where she'd seen him before. He'd been a bouncer at the club. He stopped them from leaving.

"Sabrina." Perdita ran a hand through her hair. Sabrina cut her off, not standing the easy and tenuous tone.

"You're the Nip, aren't you?"

"Yes." Damien sat his fork down, keeping eye contact, not backing down. The tension in the room spiked.

"You're a spy, aren't you?" Sabrina's words came out in a snarl.

"No."

"I brought him here," Ora said.

Sabrina didn't waver. Of course one of them had brought him. He had to have swindled them. She'd have to find out.

"Why?" she asked.

Ora squirmed. Her eyes closed, and she shook her head, as if she wanted to be anywhere else in the world. She sighed, leaning back in the seat, and told the story of how Damien took their magic. How she'd fought and escaped Sárkány. Her words sped when describing the standoff with Damien. When she finally got to the battle with Taylin and Charity, she paused, avoiding the boy called Jeremiah's gaze. But she needn't have bothered.

Jeremiah stared at the grain of the table before he said, "He ordered her," the word came out a curse, "to kill my brother,

Gabe." He pulled in deep breaths through his nostrils. "To prove to Damien that Nips mean nothing to them." He glared across the table. "I'll never understand how you didn't already know we're nothing to them."

Damien looked away, redness blossoming on his cheeks. "I do now." The sincerity in his words almost changed Sabrina's mind—almost.

Fox grabbed the plates, piling them one of top of the other. "Much magic nearby drew me to them. This one," he nodded toward Damien, "sensed me and asked me to save you all. He said you can kill me, just save them."

By the shocked expressions on everyone's face, no one else had known that either.

Fox licked pie off his finger. "I saved the big day." He smiled, showing off yellow-stained teeth, and waved his hands in the air. "Brought them to my home. We performed the *Hatał*."

Fox shuffled to put the dishes on the counter and lit his pipe, blowing smoke rings while Sabrina processed the information. The *Hatał*—an ancient and complex bit of magic. Even the healers no longer performed it. It wasn't only a healing of one's magic, but a physical and spiritual one that helps not only those hurt, but those performing as well. Fox would never have done something like that and included Nips if he didn't trust them. He had bound them all in this ancient ritual. Somewhere she remembered something about the binding linking fates, but she couldn't quite get the quote right.

Sharing her fate with a couple of Nips didn't sit well. "We should kill them both and be done with it."

Jeremiah paled. "Wait, can I say something?"

Sabrina raised an eyebrow.

"I may be a Nip, but I never wanted to work for them. They stole us from our parents. They tried to tell us our parents gave us away. Said that our mother didn't want freaks living in her house. But we knew it wasn't true." Grief lined his face as hate brimmed in his eyes. "They showed up at our house one day when we were home alone. They burst in the front door." He swallowed. "Gabe and I were playing video games. They grabbed us, jerked us outside, but we fought back. A few of them used magic." His eyes locked on hers. "It was the first time we even found out what we were."

Goosebumps ran along Sabrina's arms.

"Their magic came at us. Our power grabbed it like instinct. It hurt having all that power shoved inside us." He shuddered. "It hurts every time."

Damien's head moved a fraction of an inch. If Sabrina hadn't been trained in interrogation, she would've missed it.

Jeremiah traced his finger along the table. "We had no clue before that moment what we were. What we could do. But it wasn't enough. There were too many of them. They shoved us into a van and drove away. They didn't think to blindfold us." At this, his face twisted in a hateful grimace. "Our mom's car passed us. I saw the look on her face when she noticed the front door wide open. She knew. Gabe watched her jump out the car, run inside screaming. For us."

His fist slammed on the table, making everyone jump. "Our mom loved us. She never would've given us away. Even if she knew the truth about us. They stole us."

"How old were you?" Charlie whispered, tears filling her eyes.

Jeremiah's pain rolled off him in waves. Without looking up, he said, "Fourteen. That was two years ago."

"You couldn't escape?" Charlie asked the question everyone wanted to know.

"We tried. We refused to fight like so many other Nips. Finally, Master came to us, and he told us if we didn't want his gift of protection, and to be with our own kind, we could leave." His voice faded, lost in his own misery. "We saw it as our chance to escape. It had to be easier if we were on this side of the Veil. But Master told us it would be a shame when the MDA found us, because not only would we be arrested and executed, but our younger brother and two sisters would, too. Maybe even our parents. I didn't believe him, but Gabe did. He was too afraid to try an escape then, and I wouldn't leave without him."

"Then what happened?" Ora asked.

Jeremiah wiped his nose. "We were handed from one of his henchmen to the other. Gabe and I were never one of Master's Nips who worshiped him. They all knew it. Finally, they handed us over to Taylin. None of his Nips last long. But I never thought he would…"

Damien said, "We have to kill Master."

The Nip stared at no one. His words were more to himself. Sabrina didn't know anyone who was that good of an actor.

Arameus shuddered. "I think that's enough for tonight."

"But what about—?" Jeremiah sat back in alarm.

"No one is getting killed tonight," Sabrina said.

Arameus pushed to his feet, stronger than before, requiring only an arm around Charlie to shuffle away toward a room off to the side. At the doorway he murmured, "I think I'm okay. Thank you, Charlie."

Chairs scratched the floor as they got to their feet, taking the rest of the plates, and Perdita finished the last of her red wine. Sabrina prepared to stand when Arameus leaned against the doorway. "This Master, does anyone know his name?"

Jeremiah and Damien shook their heads.

His shoulders drooped. "Uhh! This is so frustrating. Where would we even look?"

Perdita raised the empty wine glass. "I know where his base used to be, but it's in Conjuragic. We can't get there with the Veil sealed."

"Fox, what kind of coffee is this?" Ora asked. Everyone's eyes moved to her at the abrupt change of topic.

She sipped the coffee. "Don't look at me that way. We all know what were up against, but tonight we should be celebrating. You two are healed, and we're with Fox. He's going to help me train. We have new friends and allies. So yes, there's so much to do, but we're one step closer. We should be grateful, at least for now."

"Cambodian," Fox said.

Ora furrowed her brow.

"The coffee," he waved toward the cups, "it's Cambodian."

"Oh…" Ora giggled. "So, can you make any plant you want?"

He rolled his eyes. "I can grow if I have seed. Cannot make something out of nothing."

"Where do you get the seeds then?" Perdita asked.

"EBay." He relit his pipe.

Ora's mouth opened in surprise.

He chuckled. "What? You think I never leave forest?"

Charlie flipped her palms up. "Umm…well…yeah, we kind of did."

He blew more smoke rings. "I go to city sell my," he lifted his hands and did imitation quotation marks, "Authentic Native American woven throws and clothes." He chuckled to himself again. "I also sell potions."

Charlie leaned forward, put her elbows on the table, and asked, "What kind of potions?"

He blew a large smoke ring then another smaller one inside. "Ehh, different ones. Some back pain, some for help sleep, some relaxation, some depression, some weight loss."

"Weight loss?" Sabrina asked. "Thought you were going to stop selling those?" Her last visit to discuss with him the use of real magic potions flashed in her mind.

Fox laughed so hard he started coughing. "Yes, weight loss. That be a popular one. Can't get rid of my best seller. But I toned them down. Yeah." He didn't even bother looking guilty.

"Wait. They work?" Ora glanced between Fox and Sabrina.

"Aye, but they not true spell. They weak." He chuckled.

"But why wouldn't you sell people true spells?" Charlie asked.

He waved his pipe at Sabrina. "Because silly girl, if I sell real spell, I have Conjuragic Quad on me. If not, I bombarded with humans. Dah no good." He swatted a hand as if shooing a bug. "Even dah weak ones got their attention." He gestured toward Sabrina.

Ora stretched and yawned. "But you can make true spells?"

"Aye."

"Healing spells?"

"Aye."

"Poisons?"

His mouth curled on the pipe. "That and a cure for them, too."

"Can you teach me?" Ora asked.

"Aye."

She smiled. "Guys, that could really help us in battle!"

"Battle? Who said anything about a battle?" Sabrina blurted, but as soon as the words were out of her mouth, she knew that was the path they were headed. Regardless if Ora could ever reopen the Veil, the Hunters wouldn't stop coming, and would, at some point, join forces.

If she could get them back to Conjuragic, the Council wouldn't let her walk free. Wouldn't let any of them go. They'd have to fight or stay away.

"This is much bigger than revenge. I know that now. Losing John sparked something that has been going on for a long time. We have to stop Master. We have to stop what happens to Nips. That'll mean war."

Chapter Twenty-Four
Sabrina

SABRINA'S LEGS AND CHEST BURNED as she sprinted along the top of the water. The river about a ten-minute walk from Fox's house extended for miles. She found the exercise perfect to work out both her body and magic. Her anger flared whenever she thought about how weak she'd become. All because of that Nip! A Nip that Ora had allowed to live.

The recollection of him wanting his old Master dead cooled her temper some, but not nearly enough. Her body had once been strong. She could run for hours before she got tired, but now she couldn't run more than a mile or two. Even the smallest things tired her out. Just calling the water from the river and washing herself was enough to have her breathing heavy.

She hated feeling so vulnerable and vowed to get her strength back as soon as possible. Charlie catered to Arameus's every beck and call, stalling his recovery. *Could that girl be any more obvious? Not that Arameus had any clue.*

Sabrina picked up the pace, sank her power into the river, and the water rose into the air at a steep incline. Her thighs felt the strain, but she pushed past it. Instead of focusing on the pain, her thoughts turned to the other Nip—Jeremiah. Perhaps because he hadn't taken her power or because he'd lost his brother, but that one she liked. He reminded her of her sister, and the urge to protect him overwhelmed her. As long as he didn't try to take her magic, they'd be fine.

She stumbled, and the water dipped downward. This fear of the other Nips and Hunters didn't help. If they wanted her magic, she couldn't do much to stop them. Save not actively using her magic on them.

She huffed, remembering Arameus's reminder that humans could feel the same way about her. Did he have to be right all the time?

The water plateaued and spilt over in a waterfall. Sabrina took it at a run, jumped, and landed on the sides of her feet. She skied down the mountain-like waterfall, and at the end, she rotated the water upward in a half pipe shape. She pushed off, twisting her body in a double back flip, and landed on the river bed. She rested her palms on her knees, panting hard, and hating the headache forming above her right temple.

Her head popped up at the sound of clapping. Perdita leaned up against a tree and tossed her an apple. Sabrina caught it with one hand and took a large bite. The apple snapped under her teeth, and sweet juice flooded her mouth.

"You're getting better."

Sabrina scoffed and sank her teeth into the apple again.

"Hey, at least you didn't land on your face like yesterday." Perdita ignored Sabrina's glare. "You think you're ready to train or do you need to rest?"

The fatigue rolled over Sabrina's body like a boulder. She didn't want to be someone who needed to rest, but she didn't want to overdo it either.

Seeing her expression, Perdita nodded, always knowing her true emotions, and said, "You've done a lot today. You're really improving, but it'll take time. I think you should get some lunch, and I'll work on my own. You can join me later."

The relief was palpable. Sabrina could only wonder how Perdita always knew. Could it be part of her magic as a Germinate or some motherly instinct? She finished her apple but wanted more.

Her leg wobbled as she stepped forward. The trees around her swirled as vertigo hit her hard. She'd overdone it. She needed more food.

"Thanks. I'll see you later."

Chapter Twenty-Five
Perdita

PERDITA CONCENTRATED ON THE WATER, glad she'd told Charlie to make some vegetable soup and fresh bread. Sabrina would need the calories when she got back. The river shifted from side to side, sliding onto itself, a peaceful sway instead of the fierce rolling mini-tsunami Perdita intended. The use of her magic returned after a few tries, much like riding a bike, but at least this time, she used her magic for her own will and for good instead of her Master's evil will. No. Not her Master. Not anymore.

From far in the distance, she heard chattering of voices and feet pounding on the ground, but with each passing step, the sound grew louder. Perdita focused and picked out Charlie's voice; the other had to be Arameus. He'd finally gotten off his butt and out of the Hogan. He spent too much time sitting around letting Charlie fetch his meals. As they neared, Perdita yelled, "Hello?"

Arameus and Charlie broke through the tree line. Since losing his power, Arameus had lost some of his luster. It showed in his pale, almost greenish face, and his fire-red hair hung limp and dull. His arm draped over Charlie, not in any affectionate way, but as a makeshift crutch. By the ecstatic expression on her face, Charlie didn't mind. Instead of replying, Arameus grimaced instead. Arameus held none of Sabrina's fire. Charlie helped ease him onto the ground. He huffed and puffed like an old man while Charlie put a bottle of water to his lips. Perdita couldn't allow this to go on any longer. "Charlie, go back to the Hogan. See if you can help with lunch."

Charlie didn't look up from Arameus but shook her head. "I've already finished lunch."

Irritation flashed through Perdita, not that anyone noticed. "Charlie. Go. Now."

At this, Charlie met her eyes, her brow crinkled together, not understanding her abrupt dismissal.

"You're not to wait on Arameus anymore. I know you want to help, but you're not." Perdita turned her gaze on Arameus. "The same thing that happened to you happened to Sabrina, but she's up every day trying to get her strength back. She's miles ahead of you, and it's because you're not doing anything to help yourself. She's not let herself be babied. It has to stop. Now." Perdita took her hands off her hips and crossed them over her chest.

Arameus didn't say anything during her tirade, but his head dipped in concession before shifting toward Charlie. "She's right. You've been great, but I've got to start taking care of myself. You can go on back. I'll be fine."

The happiness faded from Charlie like a cloud covering a sunny sky. She stood and shot Perdita a nasty look of defiance that reminded her of her younger self when she hadn't allowed Ora and Charlie to do something. It almost made Perdita want to laugh, but it wouldn't be helpful in this situation. Charlie stomped off after telling Arameus bye.

Arameus at least had the decency to hang his head in shame. Or perhaps he didn't have the strength to hold it up. Perdita wouldn't be preaching to him again, at least for now. Let him stew in his own thoughts while she turned her attention back to the water.

The sky above had been sunny, but dark clouds had rolled in, and a light rain broke through the clouds. She raised her magic like a shield, protecting herself from the rain, and clenched her fists at her side. Not moving her hands proved more difficult than she would've expected.

Sabrina barely moved her hands. A few droplets of rain fell through the shield as Perdita recalled Sabrina's whispered confession. "I don't actually have to use my hands. It looks cooler." Perdita found joy in seeing Sabrina warm to them and how she'd picked up some of Ora's slang.

Over the Bridge

With much grunting and panting, Arameus got to his feet. Perdita didn't acknowledge this. She usually didn't interfere in people's lives and instead she preferred to watch and wait for them to come to her. So, when she did say something, it was important. She'd held her tongue, but Arameus needed some tough love.

Arameus shuffled to her side, hiding under the magical umbrella, and said, "I'm sorry."

Perdita shook her head. "You should be apologizing to yourself. You've only been getting in your own way, and if you don't have mutual feelings, you may have been hurting Charlie as well."

"Charlie?" he asked, confused.

Perdita resisted the urge to slap her own forehead. Men! "You really haven't noticed?"

He stared ahead with a dumbfounded look upon his face, seeing nothing. The rain dripped off the side of her umbrella, but he paid no attention to the oncoming water. A drip from the tip of his hair onto his nose brought him out of his thoughts. He tilted his head upward as if just now noticing the rain. He pushed the wet hair away from his face. "You know, as Tempests, you and I could push this storm away."

A crack of lightening followed by distant thunder as if challenging them to a dual. Perdita looked from left to right at the blackened clouds. She should, of course, be able to control the weather, but other than using small bits of wind to levitate objects, she'd never really tried. With Arameus's strength gone and his magic still weakened, he must have decided he really had to jump back into the saddle.

She inclined her head to one side and said, "I don't know how."

"To be honest, I was never very good at it. Like I told O, I can do rudimentary spells, but I struggled. Perhaps that's one reason I went into law. That and I like to argue with people." He laughed, the sound deep and rich, welcome even.

Perdita hadn't heard it in a long time and wondered how he'd always appeared so nonchalant about abandoning Conjuragic. "How are you doing with all this?"

The smile vanished, and he shrugged.

She regretted the loss of that smile, but again, sometimes things needed asked. "I don't mean about losing your powers to a Nip. I mean all of it. You left everything behind for Ora. A girl you'd only just met. Nothing more than a client. I realize once you were across the Veil you didn't really have a choice. But if you knew then what you know now, would you still have done it?"

A heavy sigh left his lips as his shoulders sank as if the weight of the world rested on his shoulders. Arameus, hardly ever a man of few words, remained speechless. She wouldn't have blamed him if he said he wouldn't have helped.

"Ora was innocent of her crimes. She didn't deserve the Kassen. If I were a better Defender, she wouldn't have been found guilty. If I'd done a better job, she wouldn't have had to escape. John wouldn't have died, and my home wouldn't have been destroyed. I should've done better."

Perdita shook her head, a hand over her heart. "It wasn't your fault. I know you did everything you could. So does Ora. We don't blame you."

Arameus smiled, avoiding directly answering, and said, "So are we going to get rid of this storm? I'm tired of getting wet."

Perdita didn't press the issue. "Okay. What am I supposed to do?"

"Send your magic into the storm."

It took all her effort not to raise her hands. She pushed the magic away from her and fought her own fear the farther it went. It felt wrong letting it drift so far. She steadied herself and let go. Her power soared higher and higher, singing in pleasure with the electricity in the air. The two mingled in harmony. At times, her power wavered like a kite caught on a wind current. A touch of something similar but foreign danced around the edges of her magic. She recognized the sensation of another's magic near to her own. How many times had she done spells with Philo? But this time it wasn't her beloved. The magic belonged to Arameus.

Sorrow loomed in her and the magic recoiled. The suddenness of it shocked her, but as she'd practice over the years, she shoved the sorrow away and focused.

Over the Bridge

"Good. Now do you feel that? The density of the clouds?" Arameus asked. He stood right next to her, but he could've been a million miles away.

"Yes."

"You push the clouds to the right, and I'll push it to the left."

"Okay."

"On the count of three. One. Two. Three."

She closed her eyes, using her magic to see. She shoved at the fullness. For several moments, the place wouldn't budge. It stood strong against her will like a steel door. She concentrated harder, feeling the drain of her energy, and the place shifted. Inch by inch, the spot thinned and separated. The firmness melted away. She opened her eyes and gasped as the storm clouds flew apart. "We did it." The magic sank back inside her, tired but satisfied.

Arameus's skin paled further, but he'd pushed past it. He needed to get his butt in gear, but perhaps this had been pushing the limits. "Let's head back. It's almost lunch time." She offered her arm, but he refused.

They walked in easy silence during their journey back. Arameus panted, stopped often for small breaks, and stumbled only once, but he'd taken her arm so he wouldn't fall. After he righted himself, he released her. Perdita held her head a bit higher. Perhaps he'd needed a little push.

Quiet followed Perdita and Arameus through lunch time. Only the clinking and slurping of forks on plates made any noise. Charlie sulked at being sent away and pouted whenever Arameus grabbed his own bowl of stew. Fox took his time with each bite, savoring every mouthful, unlike Sabrina who shoveled food down her throat. It had to be her third bowl. Jeremiah wouldn't look at anyone, using the spoon to push around the same uneaten potato, as if he didn't quite belong. Perdita vowed to do something about that.

Ora also only picked at her food. Damien ate fast, tearing into the bread with his teeth, and stole glances at Ora whenever he could. Perdita didn't approve of his infatuation at all.

Sabrina pushed back from her empty bowl. "Ora when you're done, meet me outside. We need to train more."

Arameus stood with Sabrina, and Charlie jumped up as if to follow. "I'm going to go for another walk." He held up a hand to Charlie. "I'll see you later. Okay?"

Charlie blushed, eyes cast downward. "Yeah. Okay. No problem."

Perdita retrieved their dishes, intent on washing them in the new sink Fox had assembled for them, along with the new indoor privy. Fox touched her elbow. "We need to talk."

"Sure. What's going on?"

"I need tell you 'bout my plan. It's a doozy!" He cracked a mischievous grin even the Cheshire cat would envy.

Chapter Twenty-Six
Ora

"Stop waving arms!" Fox fussed.

"I'm trying!" I kicked the forest ground. We'd been training for days, but my magic had reached a standstill.

"You have several things to learn. You must pull out magic in small amounts. And don't use hands. Third, grow plants and make potions."

Easier said than done.

"You have to see your power," he said.

"That's like asking someone to make the nerves fire in their brain to make them walk."

"That is how you walk."

"Yeah, but no one has to think about neurons firing in their head."

"Not everyone's a witch." Fox settled on the newest bench and bit down on the pipe.

Not having a bench of my own, because Fox wouldn't make me one, I flopped down to the ground, sitting in the dirt. His stupid words echoed in my head. "You can make bench." If I could make a bench, I would. My power, the deep cavern of power, sloshed, matching my irritation. Fox couldn't understand that using my power felt a lot like igniting a bomb. The power came, all or nothing.

Spending hours and hours outdoors with Fox hadn't been the fun experience I'd expected learning to use magic. He either shouted, or puffed on his little pipe, or quipped annoying sayings at me.

"Child," he put a hand over his eyes, "how to make you understand. You trying too hard. I told you before. You not Sphere, not Naiad, or Tempest, or Ember. You're all cores. Your power strong. So strong can destroy world only if you wish it. You should use that amulet of yours." He cupped his hands together making an upside-down bowl. "You atomic bomb with teenage girl emotions. Bad combination. *Pwoooh!*" His hands moved outward, mocking an explosion.

I yanked blades of grass from the ground. "Gee, thanks."

"It's true."

"You know I wouldn't destroy the world if I got mad!"

He raised one eyebrow.

"Except…that one time…when I did."

He rolled his eyes, pulled himself up with his walking stick, and hobbled away mumbling something about stubborn girls, leaving smoke trailing behind him.

"It's not like I meant to," I called after him, and he threw a hand up, dismissing me.

Mom's training had been going way better than mine. Perhaps because she'd been raised in Conjuragic. Of course, she'd been in prison at the time, but still she'd some use of her magic.

I huffed, lips quivering, sounding like a horse. I have all this power and it's stuck there. Sometimes it comes out easy-peasy and other times like unraveling twisted cellophane.

The easier times where when I had been pissed. I wondered if I turned green.

I shook my head. That wouldn't do. No Hulk references. With Sabrina, I'd cut down the tree and put it back together. That had been small, precisely controlled power, that I'd wanted to happen. Had I waved my arms?

The difference dawned on me. I'd used the Sight to see the tree in its pieces. The magic rippled inside as if in answer. I didn't have to look for it. Like I'd told Fox, when I wanted to walk, I moved my legs, not concentrating on the neurons in my head. So maybe I didn't have to focus on the magic inside, but on the Sight.

There was no time like the present to test my theory. Pushing to my feet, I ran to a tree with a large trunk. I willed the Sight to open.

Over the Bridge

I searched for the tiny particles, the molecules, the atoms to become a living microscope. The tree warbled as my vision blurred, but laughter jolted me out of the moment.

Damien leaned against a nearby tree with his scarred arms folded across his massive, muscular chest.

"What's so funny?" I demanded.

He smirked. "You look like your head's about to burst."

Irritation flared. Using the emotion, I focused on the tree again. The Sight opened, and in less than a second, the tree burst apart at the molecular level. To the naked eye, it would look like I made the tree disappear. Using my magic like any other appendage, I held the molecules like a hand gripping a glass. Damien screamed and rolled out of the way. The tree reappeared, planted in a new location, inches from where he'd been leaning. I'd have to move it back or else both trees would die, but I'd enjoyed wiping the smug look off his face.

"That wasn't funny!"

"You sure about that?"

He backed away, brushing the dirt and leaves off his clothes. "Fox was right."

"About?"

"You're trying too hard."

I considered his words.

"Penny for your thoughts?" he asked.

I smiled at the antiquated use of words. "Fox said I don't have four cores. I have one all merged."

"You do."

"How are you so sure?"

His expression wavered from curious to intent, inching toward me, and part of me fought the urge to run, but another planted my feet and blew off the fear. He towered over me, face intense, and reached forward. With a tenderness I didn't expect, he pulled a leaf out of my hair. My heart beat a little faster at his closeness.

"I see magic inside of people. Most Nips can't. Like Fox told you, I can take their magic without them sending a spell toward me." His gaze dipped lower. I could've been offended, but I understood it wasn't the outside he saw. "Your magic's unlike anything I've ever seen. It's beautiful." He whispered the end, and I shuddered.

Everything about him overwhelmed and thrilled me. Backing away from him felt like stepping back from a ledge. If I jumped, would I fly, or fall?

The Sight opened, and I moved the tree back to its rightful place, except I cleaved a new bench with rough lines and uneven legs, but Damien and I could sit on it. The heat of his body radiated outward. Every breath and slight shift of his body made me realize how *aware* I was of him.

The silence stretched between us. I coughed and swallowed past the hard lump in my throat. "You know most of the time, I wanted to quit. I want all this to be a bad dream. I mean it's what... sometime in October? I should be in a sorority or going to the homecoming game or studying for midterms instead of...what... camping out in the forest with this strange old man learning magic."

I shifted to face Damien, and he matched the movement, our knees touching.

He leaned forward, putting his elbows on his knees. "What's a midterm?"

"Oh, shut up!" I nudged his shoulder with mine.

"No, seriously. I...I don't know what that is." He blushed.

A deep sadness rose in me. Of course he wouldn't know about those things. He'd been kidnapped at four! What kind of a life had he had before now? "See it's when you say things like that I know I can't quit. What happened to you..." His back straightened as suspicion gathered in his expression. Of course, he didn't know that I knew his history, "Mom told me what happened to you, and Jeremiah and Gabe, and God knows how many other Nips." I shuddered at the thought. "What about the Geminates who are born? Genocide! That's what it is. They kill all those innocent babies. Babies! Because of what they *might* become. But this asshole, evil dude, who parades around calling himself Master like he's some Darth Vader wannabe, roams around free. You know. You've seen him. What house is he in?"

Damien's jaw set. "He isn't my Master. Not anymore."

"You know what I mean."

"He's Naiad."

"Naiad...really? I never would've pictured that." Sabrina's house. Surely, she had no idea who he was. "He has God knows how many Nips at his service as slaves, Geminates, and countless followers in both Conjuragic and here. I doubt the Council even knows about him."

I waggled my finger. "He must be planning something big. It's like he's playing chess and setting up his pieces to strike. Think about it—if he has a thousand Nips and they can take two cores at a time, they themselves could take out two thousand wizards."

"That's not all." Damien interrupted my ranting.

"What do you mean?"

The blood drained from his face. He avoided my eyes as if he'd let something slip.

"Damien, what do you mean?" The Sight opened, ready to strike if he threatened me.

He held up a hand, pupils dilated. "Chill out. It's...I'm not used to talking about this stuff. I wasn't allowed."

My suspicion dampened along with the Sight. "Speaking of things you aren't talking about...you're really going to have to tell me what a Vessel is because Charlie's going crazy."

He hung his head and said, "I was hoping you wouldn't ask." He sighed. "You know I can take a wizard's magic at will." He placed his elbow on his knee and propped his chin with a fist. "I'm called a true Nip. From what I know, true Nips are very rare. Not only can we take magic by will..." He paused, sucking a deep breath, and said, "We can also take magic and put it into a human."

"What would that do?"

"I can take a wizard's magic and put it in a human. The wizard dies like that." He snapped his fingers. "The human usually dies as well, but slow and painfully. Like the magic is poison. But there are some humans who merge with the magic. They become wizards themselves. They're called Vessels."

I sat there in stunned silence for a long time. The sun shined bright, steaming through the trees, as the wind blew through the branches, shaking the leaves, and a small bird landed nearby yanking a worm from the ground. But reality faded into an insane surreal-ness.

"Say something."

"When you said, 'That's not all,' what did you mean?" I waited for the answer I knew was coming.

"If Master had a few true Nips with thousands of humans, he could kill nameless wizards, throw their magic into a human, and move on to the next."

My mind's eye envisioned Damien, this blond-haired, blue-eyed handsome man, leading an army of Nips and Geminates with a band of human slaves to be used as ammunition. The horde raging toward Conjuragic. Those who fought back collapsing, dead instantly, with no chance at all. A chill ran down my spine. They would be unstoppable.

"How would he get these humans?"

Damien smile held no humor. "How many humans do you know who would risk anything to have magic?"

"Even if it means dying or killing someone else to get their magic?" Even as I asked the question, I knew the answer. Was there no goodness anywhere? Maybe I should leave the Veil sealed and hunt the wizards in this world. Perhaps the worlds should be separated. Arameus and Sabrina's faces swam before my eyes, and I knew I could never do that. If there was a chance for them to go home, I had to give it to them. There was goodness in both worlds. I needed to fight against the evil.

A wonderful thought occurred to me. "Hey, Damien?"

He grinned, a shy, lopsided one. "Yeah?"

"You could help me, too. You've used all four cores, right? You could help me since you're the only person I know who knows what's like to have each core."

His smile vanished. "All I know is how to destroy things using magic. I wish I knew how to heal."

Over the Bridge

His sad face made something in my brain snap into place. "I have an, um, interesting idea."

"Oh yeah?"

"Have you ever touched someone's magic and not taken it?"

A look of horror flashed across his face. "Absolutely not. Don't even think about it." He jumped from the bench, marching away.

I followed him at a jog. "What's the big deal? If you take it by accident, let it go. You can do that, right? It'll only hurt for a second. Easy peasy."

"No way!"

"Come on."

"No."

"Just do it. You big chicken."

"No."

"Touch my magic!" I put my hands on my hips. We both laughed. "Seriously, just try."

"Why?" he asked.

"I don't know. I keep thinking about you as a little boy. You saw something pretty and you wanted to touch it. Touch it but not steal it, and you didn't get to." It sounded stupid when I said it aloud.

"I don't want to hurt you."

I took his hands in mine. "That's why I want you to try. To show you I believe you can use your power and not hurt someone."

"If you're wrong?" His pulse quickened the longer our hands touched.

"I'm not."

His breathing heavy, his gaze shifted, looking at my magic. Without hesitation, I closed my eyes, pulling the power forward, an offering. After a moment, I felt him. The intimacy of this took me by surprise. My cheeks burned as if I stood naked in front of him. I peeked. Damien's eyes squeezed shut. The embarrassment vanished. His power held at the edges of mine, close, with barely a caress. The sensation soothed me.

"Ora?"

"Yeah?"

"Can I try a spell I've always wanted to do?" he asked.

"Okay."

He let go of my hand, strolling a short way into the forest, returning moments later with something in his hand.

"Ready?" he asked.

I nodded.

"You have to stop me if I hurt you."

I took his empty hand in mine again. His power reached for mine, but this time his entered mine, guiding, like hugging me. I willed myself to relax and let him lead, like a dance. He opened the palm of his hand revealing a tiny seed. Our intertwined magic breathed into the seed. The pod opened as the tiniest tendril of root snaked outward. He guided the power, and the new plant continued to grow. A small stalk elongated and bloomed into a white and purple flower. Our magic retreated inside as his let go. I felt empty and chilled, as if warm covers had been pulled from me.

Damien squatted, using his bare hands to dig a small hole, and placed the new flower inside. He covered it and patted the earth.

"It's the one spell I know that's creation instead of destruction."

"This is the first time you've got to use it without destroying someone else," I thought out loud.

"Exactly." He rose from the ground, wrapping me in large, muscular arms, lifting me upward and spinning. "Thank you."

I laughed.

He put me down. Something inside him eased. A tiny part of him healed. "You're welcome."

His eyes returned to the flower, grinning like a fool. It made me chuckle.

"What are you laughing at?" He jumped after me.

Screaming, I spun and ran.

Guilt wiggled in my gut but vanished as visions of John with the cat woman popped in my head.

I skidded to a halt, and Damien swerved to avoid crashing into me.

"What?"

Over the Bridge

"When you were with Master, did you ever meet a woman who could turn into a cat with no tail?"

The playfulness vanished. "Strega."

Chapter Twenty-Seven
Ora

THE SHADOW LAND SURROUNDED ME. I must have fallen asleep. No fear accompanied the realization. The angry or scared voices echoed from far off. Moving forward, I whispered, "Jiminy?"

His scent appeared in seconds. "Yes?"

"What is this place?"

"You're not ready to know yet."

This reply should've bothered me, but it didn't. Jiminy's warmth touched my elbow, guiding me forward, around the voices.

"Hey, my feet aren't sticking to the ground anymore."

"You're gaining more control."

Control of what? The voices echoed. I wished they weren't here. They made me feel guilty, and I'd done of that enough while awake.

The un-penetrating darkness of the Shadow Land had gone, replaced by lighter shadows, and a vague grayness, a slight improvement. Jiminy guided me to the left, and I turned in that direction. I wondered if we would go see the fortune teller, but she hadn't called to me.

Damien said, "Strega."

I spun, searching for the sound of Damien's voice, but I couldn't see him. Jiminy gripped my shoulders, halting my circling. "He isn't here. It's a memory. This is a place where you can reflect on things, and apparently, he is on your mind."

I concentrated on the sound.

Strega is Master's favorite pet. She's a Nip, but she has been with him her whole life. The rumor is after her Nip parents had been killed, he kept her, but experimented on her. He did that a lot in the beginning, trying to make us more. As far as I know, she was his only success. She can turn herself into a cat. She is his spy. If you know who she is, then you're in even more grave danger than I first thought.

I shivered, remembering our conversation. "Jiminy, do you know what I am worried about?"

"I believe so." He'd moved farther ahead.

Following the sound of his voice, I followed him. "Do you think he sent her to me because he knows what I am?"

"It doesn't matter what I think, only what you think."

I sighed while I contemplated this. Wouldn't Master have taken me out of my cell instead of letting me stand trial if he knew the truth? Perhaps in the past he let the trials proceed to confirm he could add another Nip to his ranks and to make everyone believe they'd died. Plus he'd gain their trust by rescuing them. Strega could be used as leverage. Couldn't he say he'd always been there with them, via his servant? Had he sent someone to retrieve me from the Kassen and I'd already gone? And since he couldn't have me, he'd found a way to report me missing? Why else had none of the other Nips gone undiscovered? So he must not know about Mom or me.

A huge weight lifted off my shoulders. "I wish we could go back to that hotel and get our stuff back. Would be nice to have more than one pair of underwear." A wave of movement from the right caught my attention—my arm. No longer invisible, I brushed a hand over my shirt.

Jiminy chuckled and changed direction. Instead of being solid like me, he appeared like a shimmering shadow of a man. This made following him a lot easier. A building covered in fog appeared about fifty yards ahead of him. The closer we got, the more the familiar building sharpened in focus. It took me a while to recognize the hotel we'd stayed in before we went to the club. The Shadow Land shifted, moving us from the front of the building to inside our room, which had been emptied and cleaned as if we'd never been there. I wondered what they did with our stuff.

Lost and found, perhaps?

In the blink of an eye, the room vanished, replaced by a shabby office with wood paneling and an old desk covered in numerous coffee-stained papers. A dusty lamp gave off dim light. A man snored, leaning back on an old blue recliner in front of a tiny TV, playing *SpongeBob*.

Old filing cabinets lined the walls, and a large box sat in the corner with the words "Lost and Found" written on the side with a black permanent marker in untidy handwriting. Mom's backpack bulged from the top of the box. I stepped forward, and the ground felt solid beneath my feet, the darkness around me vanishing. I tiptoed to the box, grabbed our things, and examined my book bag, finding all my things just as I'd left them. The same with all the other bags except for Mom's money. *Bastard!*

The office held two doors. One led to a bathroom reeking of old urine. The other led to a front desk area. A cash register rested below the counter. Sitting the extra bags on the ground, I pushed a button, and the register popped open with a jangling sound. My heart pounded as I checked to see if the manager had woken up. He snored and stirred but settled back down. The drawer held only a little cash, but I lifted the sectioned case and found the big bills. I grabbed the bills, counting out the amount Mom had left, stuffed that into my pocket, and put the rest back. I pushed the little drawer closed, which locked with a click. *What a strange dream.*

I slid my book bag over my shoulders and grabbed Charlie's, Mom's, Sabrina's, and Arameus's things. The bulky bags weighed me down, making balancing each step hard.

Just like in the club, the rainbow appeared floating in mid-air not two steps from where I stood. On the first step, Arameus's bag slipped off my shoulder and landed with a thump.

The manager jolted awake. "What the…?" His eyes darted from my face to all the bags. Understanding and anger replaced the look of confusion.

"Thief!" He jumped from the chair.

I grabbed Arameus's bag and jumped into the rainbow, falling to my knees, bags flopping everywhere. I shoved onto my knees and glanced backward, finding the manager staring dumbfounded at the hole. He couldn't see me. I chuckled and picked up our stuff again, which no longer felt as heavy or bulky. The hole behind me closed, and to my left, a light appeared. I shuffled toward the light, giddy with excitement.

I stumbled, landing with a loud thud, Fox's woven blanket tangled in my legs. Sleep walking? I chuckled, the sound nervous, shook my head at my crazy dreams. Sleep gritted in my eyes, and the inside of my mouth felt pasty and gross. I slid out of the covers, stood and stretched, and went in search of a drink. I halted two steps in the living area. Our bags lay on the floor by where I'd fallen! I must still be dreaming. I rubbed my eyes and looked again. They hadn't disappeared. My fingers shook as I reached for the bags, still not convinced they were real. When my fingers grazed the solid fabric, I drew back as if I'd been burned.

"Interesting night," Fox said from behind me and whirled around with a yelp. The look on the office manager's face flashed in my mind's eye.

"It was real?" I whispered to Fox.

He lit his pipe and shrugged. "Your magic unlike any others. There is no telling what you can do."

"But how?"

The fortune teller's voice blew through the room. *I'll see you soon.*

My gaze swept the room in search of the owner of the voice. "Did you hear that?"

He arched his back and moaned. "Hear what?"

"Nothing." If I could travel in my dreams, I definitely didn't want to be hearing voices too. But if I really went to the hotel, then I must have actually traveled to Aryiana's. But who was she?

"Come on then," Fox muttered. The door that sealed every night peeled outward, and Fox stepped out of the entranceway, a trail of smoke following him into the night.

"Where are we going?" I waved the lingering smoke away.

"To train, of course."

"In the middle of the night?"

"Seems that way." He didn't bother turning around.

"Are you crazy?"

I slipped my tennis shoes on and jogged into the forest. With each jolting movement, I wished I'd have put on my bra. The chill in the air, seeping through my clothes, raised goosebumps on my arms. The light of the full moon shined bright, illuminating the world below in a bluish hue. The muggy nights of summer had faded away over the last weeks, and tonight, the ground glistened as if laced with diamonds instead of the night's frost. As I exhaled, steam-like breath billowed around my face, reminding me of childhood and pretending to smoke. With each shiver, the thought of Fox's woven blanket became more and more welcome.

The ground crunched beneath my feet as I lost myself in the rhythm of walking. The sounds of the forest distracted me from the cold. Little nocturnal creatures scurried through the underbrush, fleeing from our approach, an owl hooted above my head as the sweet smell of clean cold air cleared my head. Fox's paced slowed what felt like hours since we'd left the Hogan as the sky transitioned to the dark purplish hue of approaching dawn.

He broke through into the smallest clearing I'd seen. "This is where I come to meditate."

"Won't the others worry if we're gone when they wake up?"

"Your mom knows you're here."

Fox leaned back as if to sit. My hand jerked forward to prevent him from falling, but the ground rose, forming a chair, as he released all his weight. His brown eyes flicked to my hand on the tawny skin of his elbow. I let go as he once again lit the pipe.

"You know those cause cancer."

He only smiled and gestured for me to sit. I knew he wanted me to make my own seat like he'd done.

I stared at the ground, but my magic reacted like a child, rolling over, and pulling the covers above its head. I half expected it to grumble, "But I don't wanna go to school."

"Look inside you."

Over the Bridge

"I can see it. I can feel it. But it's late." I flung my hand at the sunrise. "Or early, and I'm tired, cold, and hungry."

"You don't want training? Ready to face your enemies without my help?" His lips thinned into a small line.

"No. You know that's not what I mean." The tantrum died away. "It's harder calling the magic out or whatever. It's much easier to control if I use The Sight."

His head cocked to the side. "The Sight?"

"It's what I named it as a kid." That little fact snuck out. Where had that memory come from? "Anyway, it's like I have," I rolled my eyes, knowing how stupid it would sound out loud, "microscopic vision."

"You're Super Girl?"

"She has X-ray vision. Thank you very much." I wagged a finger at him. "No. Mine zooms in. I can see the molecules of things. Like the world is made up of trillions of tiny little dots, and I can rearrange them. It isn't pulling the magic out and then directing it. The Sight pulls it toward to where I need it to go."

"Then do that." He shrugged, nonplussed at my crazy description.

It works better when I'm angry, but I didn't want to bring that up again. Definitely didn't want him reminding me how I destroyed Conjuragic. Maybe I could use the anger.

I had so many choices—my arrest, Charlie's attack, almost dying in prison, the hateful looks of the Tribunal, John and Strega.

The Sight flashed open as the necklace warmed against my skin. The dirt and grass vanished into the particles beneath. Shifting under my command, the earth rolled in on itself, rising in the shape of a lopsided, bumpy chair, but a chair regardless. I blinked the Sight away and shot a Fox a glance, searching for approval. I found his expression impassive.

"What? I made a chair."

He pointed at my outstretched hands. I dropped them, and the chair slumped into a shapeless mound.

"Again."

Hours inched by as I assembled, destroyed, and remade the pitiful chairs. By the end of the morning, I'd even managed to do it without using my hands. They had to be the ugliest chairs I'd ever seen, and sitting on them came with substantial risk.

Fox let me take a break, but by break he meant growing trees in order to feast on their fruits. He slid several seeds for apples, pears, grape, and almond trees into my palm. He grew his own apple tree and feasted on his fruit while my stomach grumbled louder than the oncoming thunder. It took another several hours before even one grew large enough to flower and bear fruit. Fox, as with everything Sphere related, made growing a tree in a single afternoon seem easy. The pounding in my head, sheer exhaustion, and stiff muscles told me it damn well wasn't a piece of cake. Stupid, stubborn tree! Every step took insane amounts of encouragement, like trying to reason with a toddler. It didn't want to come out of its seed, extend its roots, and make a trunk. As for speeding the process of growth and photosynthesis—near impossible! Trees liked to do their own thing. Even if it did take years.

"You know this isn't a convenient way to bring your own food when you're on the run. I mean, someone is bound to notice fast-growing trees," I grumbled.

"Who says you are learning this to make food?" Fox asked while eating one of the apples I'd coaxed out of the latest tree. His nose wrinkled. "This is too sweet and mealy." A satisfying image of one of those apples hurtling toward his head and smashing into applesauce filled my head. "Then what am I learning it for?" I asked.

"You'll see," he mumbled while chewing. Rolling my eyes, I returned to the tedious task of growing the other trees. Several hours later, I sank to the ground, rolling to stare upward, exhausted—so much for lunch. The newly-created little forest surrounded me, leaves swaying in the breeze, almost content, and I had to smile. I mean, really, how cool was making full-grown trees producing fruit and nuts from mere seeds in a single afternoon. The sun hung low in the sky, and it had to be after dinner time. Even though I

Over the Bridge

had no desire to eat, Fox insisted I taste the fruit. The headache from earlier had careened over into a full-blown migraine. Using the Sight all day drained me. Fox shuffled over and handed me a small branch. I glared at him. He had another think coming if he thought I'd make another damn tree tonight!

"One more, girl."

I jerked the cutting out of his hand, huffing the whole time, sounding every bit like the eighteen-year-old girl that I am. The irritation building did nothing to stop the pounding in my head. The dirt sprung out of the ground, forming a small but perfectly round hole. The branch soared out of my hand and landed in the hole. I might've been impressed if my head didn't feel like it'd split in two.

The ground rolled over the branch, and the Sight opened with a flash of bright light that mimicked the pounding in my head. The small roots erupted from the branch and extended into the ground. The tree blossomed before my eyes, much more quickly than any of the other trees. The trunk grew tall and wide. The branches reached for the sky. Small beautiful buds of leaves burst open. In mere moments, a full-grown tree stood before me. The grass around the tree withered and died.

I took a step back and admired my work. I glanced to Fox for approval, but he stared off in the distance, legs crossed on his perfect chair, puffing on that infuriating pipe. I huffed, rolled my eyes, and sighed. As if he would notice.

"Remove some bark, girl."

I pushed down the urge to scream, sent my power flying, and a large hunk of bark flew off as if there'd been an explosion.

"Too much!" Fox yelled.

"It's not like you told me how much!"

His hands separated approximately six inches. After retrieving the large chunk, I slimmed it to the right size, wanting to throw the excess at him. I waved the finished piece in the air.

"Crush it to dust. Then mix in water."

I shook my head, and my power lifted some dirt from the ground and pulled water from the air. I mixed the two forming a hollow bowl shape before sucking the water back out of it. I slid the piece of bark inside it and concentrated. The bark settled into the bottom as a brownish white powder. I pulled the water from the air once more and swirled it in the cup, forming a solution that included a bit of mud from my makeshift bowl.

Fox's eyebrows rose. The first and only sign I'd impressed him. "Nice. Now drink it."

It was my turn to raise my eyebrows. As if I'd ever want to drink this stuff. He waved one hand, and I huffed before chugging it all in one gulp, sputtering at the disgusting, acrid taste. Mid-swallow, my body recoiled, turning the swallow into a cough that sent the burning liquid up my nose. "Gaaack!" I wiped my mouth. *He must be trying to kill me.* "That was disgusting!"

"How do you feel now?"

"Besides wanting a real drink to get this nasty taste of my mouth?"

I scowled and looked at myself. I still wore the grubby tennis shoes, jeans, and my button-up blouse from the night we went to Sárkány's, which had been semi-cleaned, but nothing could compare to a nice tumble in the washer and dryer.

The usual tightness in my neck had dissipated. I turned my head from side to side, finding full range of movement, and my back didn't protest when I bent forward. The more I examined myself, the more I realized my blazing headache had gone, too.

"Willow. The bark make great pain killer. Important in battle. Drink it and small improvement all over but can make into paste to put on wounds. Very valuable to have." He made a clean slice through a branch. He handed a sampling to me and ran his finger along the edge. "It must not turn brown here. Keep moist. Keep safe."

He walked around to all the trees I had grown and either took a cutting, as with the willow, or seeds. He handed me small pouches, which I put them into.

"Most important, keep them with you. They are important weapons, give you food, medicine. So much of what you need." He patted my hand. "Are you ready?"

Over the Bridge

I nodded.

"Come, we make paper for books."

For the next three days, we worked almost nonstop. I learned to grow too many plants to count. I filled three books, which I made myself, with copies of spells and potions from Fox's private collections. We went over which plants go in which potions, at what point they needed to grow before they could be harvested, and in what order to add them. We went over simple healing spells for gashes in the skin, to mending broken bones, to extremely complex enchantments like fighting infections, or healing spells for ailments with magic itself.

I learned how to make bowls, cups, beds, Hogans, and even managed a very unstable gurney. I found the more I used the spells, the easier they were to perform. I still had problems not using my hands.

We worked from dawn to dusk, stopping only to eat, and of course, I always had to grow and cook my own food. Which I must say, the first time I made my own porcelain skillet and cooked my own mixed vegetables of onions, broccoli, cauliflower, asparagus, potatoes, carrots, and eggplant with rosemary, thyme, and parsley with olive oil was amazing. I even managed freshly cooked apples with cinnamon. I struck with Fox's flint and steel to start the fires. I still didn't trust myself to not cause a forest fire.

I fell asleep as soon as I laid down and didn't dream. I hadn't even dreamed about the Shadow Land. On the fourth morning, I woke to the sounds of Fox rustling about the campsite. I wrapped myself in the blanket Fox weaved for me while I'd been busy growing things.

The crisp and cool morning smelled delicious as the nighttime frost faded with the morning sun. I yawned and rolled out of my bed, draping the blanket over my shoulders and crossing the short distance to the now almost bare willow tree to make the homemade pain killer.

Daily headaches plagued me either from the uncomfortable bed or using magic so often. I couldn't say which. I mixed the solution with water, from a pitcher I'd made, and added berries to mask the taste. I gulped it down in three large swallows.

Stepping out of our small Hogan, I found most of the plants I'd grown withering away. I made a small noise of protest, and Fox said without looking at me, "They'll die anyway with the cold." Still, it seemed such an awful waste. "Gather your things."

I did without asking questions. Fox wouldn't have answered them anyway, and I'd end up doing whatever he wanted in the end. I placed my things outside the Hogan and stepped away, heading into the woods.

With a massive whoosh, the Hogan collapsed behind me. I jumped and let out a loud yell. "Watch it!"

"It's time to go back." Fox picked up his walking stick, his own bag, and hobbled into the forest, leaving me behind. I rushed to catch up but found he'd waited for me.

We began the long trek back to the others. Could I have finished training already? Surely I didn't know everything, but without even asking, I already knew he'd tell me, "Of course you don't know everything, but you know enough." It still didn't feel that way. We shared an easy silence, having grown accustomed to each other over the last few days. An unnatural quiet settled over the forest. No rustling of small animals or chirping of birds. Something felt different, dare I say, like something magical in the air. Even my steps made no sound along the forest floor. My thoughts wandered in our slow but steady pace. I hadn't dreamed of the Shadow Land since coming here.

I had seen our stuff from the hotel in Fox's living room, which could only mean I actually went back to the hotel. Did that mean John really had been with Strega, the evil cat woman? This bothered me more than I could say. It left a raw feeling in my stomach, a pressure in my chest, and a sour taste in my mouth.

What could it mean if he'd been with her? Could I be so easily replaced, discarded, and forgotten in a matter of a few weeks? Then to be replaced by her! The woman who had tricked me and tried to kill us. Hell, the woman who threw the boulder at Mom.

Over the Bridge

The boulder he jumped in front of...the one that killed him! Or, I guess, almost did. The thing that really bothered me...he looked happy. In love even.

I wiped a tear away in frustration and tried to think of something else. My thoughts turned to the fortune teller. Who was she and what did she want? I heard her laughter echoing through the woods. I whipped my head around looking for her, but the sound came from everywhere and nowhere at the same time. Fox hadn't reacted. *It must all be in my head*, I thought.

We arrived back at the base camp much more quickly than it took to get to Fox's meditation place.

"Ora!" Charlie yelled as we emerged from the woods into the main clearing. She ran, and I followed suit, meeting her in the middle.

"Happy birthday!" I told her and pulled a small pouch out of my new pack.

"How do you know it's my birthday? I don't even know what day it is!" A wide smile spread on her face as she opened the pouch. She gasped as the contents poured in her hand.

"I don't either, but it's sometime in the fall. I didn't want to miss it, and besides, I bet you didn't know I can make coal, and therefore..." I grinned, waiting for her to finish my sentence.

"Diamonds!" She threw her arms around me. "Thank you!"

"Yeah, well, sorry I missed your actual birthday. Busy training and all."

She pulled away, grasping my elbow, and led me into the Hogan. "Look. Our clothes are back from the hotel." I picked up my book bag, placing the pouches of plant seeds and clippings, along with the handmade spell books inside. I slid the straps over my shoulders, vowing never to take it off, and thought longingly of changing clothes.

"We've missed you. Arameus and Sabrina have gotten so much better. Your mom's training is going great, and Jeremiah has been teaching me to play guitar!"

Before I could reply, Mom burst through a new opening in the back of the Hogan, drying her hands on an apron, before pulling me into a tight embrace. "Missed you," she whispered into my ear.

"Me too."

"How did your training go?" Mom tucked an escaped lock of hair behind my ear.

We held onto each other, and the three of us stepped out of the Hogan.

"Good. Intense." Squeezing her hand, I stepped away envious of her clean clothes and shampoo-scented hair. "I think I'll head to the lake to wash up."

"Fox made us a shower, but you might want to wait a minute. Sabrina and Jeremiah went to the river." Charlie leaned sideways. "Never mind."

Following the direction of her gaze, I waved at Sabrina and Jeremiah carrying a wooden stick between them, laden with fish, each smiling.

"Hey!" they said together.

"When did you get back?" Arameus shouted from inside the animal pen. He sat on a little stool milking a goat. He stood, wiped off his hands, and flung one knee over the bushes surrounding the pen. He no longer limped, and his cheeks had filled back out.

Damien jogged from the garden, vegetables piled in his arms, a bright smile spread on his face. He dropped the vegetables at my feet. My cheeks warmed at the sight of him. He placed a small pink flower behind my ear. "Ora."

"Damien."

Fox cleared his throat, and everyone turned to stare at him, faces pale. He tossed aside his still smoking brown pipe. Sabrina and Jeremiah hung up the fish. Mom removed her apron.

"Really?" Damien asked.

Fox glared at him. "Her final test is now. Everyone, attack!"

Everyone, except Charlie, moved their bodies into combat positions. The Nips waited while the rest pulled their magic to the surface ready to strike. Charlie, like me, looked completely surprised.

Mom's gaze flicked to Charlie's. "Run."

Over the Bridge

Charlie spun on her heel, bolting for the safety of the Hogan.

My gaze went to Damien, and he shrugged. "Sorry, beautiful."

All hell broke loose.

The ground gave way under my feet, and I lost my balance. Almost as if on cue, the Sight opened, spying Fox's magic underneath my feet.

My power rushed over his. The ground stabilized. Before I could regain my footing, a wave surrounded my head like a football helmet. I couldn't breathe. My heart raced. I couldn't think.

A voice spoke inside my head. *Calm down. Concentrate.*

The power inside me shot outward. The wave burst apart. I ducked and rolled away. Wet hair flung across my face. A gust of icy wind hit my back. Time slowed. Thoughts died away. Dirt rose behind me, shielding me from the wind. Arameus stumbled backward as the dirt ripped out from underneath his feet. It rolled over him. Burying him alive.

A fury of wind, water, and air clashed against one another. All aimed at me.

Dodge. Roll. Duck.

A rock caught me on the forehead. An explosion of pain followed by a warm wetness dripped down my face. Mom hesitated. The tree beside her encircled her. Two down.

Fox yelled, "Nips!"

Sabrina knocked me aside with a wave. I tumbled under the force of it. My back slammed into something hard. The wave stilled. I wiped the mud from my face hoping to see what I'd hit. Damien towered over me.

"You think Nips won't attack her, too? She has to be ready!" Fox called, and the doubt in Damien's face fled.

His power reached inside me and squeezed. It hurt so badly I couldn't breathe. A cry of pain escaped my lips, but he didn't let up. Spells from the others kept coming. Blackness tugged at the corners of my vision.

The voice spoke again. *You are stronger than this. Look closer.*

The Sight pushed open wider. Pain lanced through my head, but Damien's power could barely hold mine. I yanked my power back and slammed it into the ground. Three cylinders of earth burst around him, pinning him in place.

Three down.

Jeremiah took a step toward me. A wave slammed him into the tree. The branches wrapped around him, followed by roots.

Two left. I spun, searching for them, and noticed something different.

My vision burned white hot with power, and their magic dimmed into comparison to mine. No fear could reach me. Only annoyance at this little game remained. Two streams of magic exploded. One toward Fox and the other at Sabrina. The streams hit the targets at the same time. Their bodies flung into the air. Seeds fell from the nearby trees from the force of the hit. Without thought, my power grabbed the seeds in mid-air, slammed them into the dirt, and seconds later full-grown trees ripped from the ground. The new branches caught Sabrina and Fox.

The last two down.

Their faces all wore the same expression—fear. I raised my head in triumph. My vision cleared.

The voice called to me. *It's time. Come.*

Chapter Twenty-Eight
Perdita

ORA VANISHED. THE FOREST AROUND Fox's Hogan fell silent, save for the bleating of the sheep and goats. Fear crept in Perdita's heart when she realized Ora disappeared. The kind of fear only a parent can feel. Panic chilled her blood. *Where is my daughter? Is she safe? Does she need help?* No answers came. The branches around Perdita crunched and leaned forward, lowering her and Fox to the ground. The other trees released Damien and Jeremiah as if opening a great fist. The dirt rolled away from Arameus. He sucked in large gulps of air. Ora had left his mouth and nose uncovered.

Charlie sprinted from the Hogan. "What the hell were you guys doing? Why would you attack Ora?" Her accusing expression wavered when she saw the looks on their faces. Her head jerked left then right and spun around in a circle. "Where's Ora? What did you do to her?"

Whatever rationality Charlie had left receded. If Perdita didn't say something soon, Charlie would lose it. "We weren't really trying to hurt her. It was her final test with Fox. To see if she could use what she had learned under pressure. We don't know where she went."

Perdita had broken their shocked silence. As if she'd given them permission, everyone shouted at once. Their words mingled, but the theme repeated itself. *Did you see her disappear? Where did she go? Her eyes glowed. They changed colors. How did she do that?*

Only Fox held his tongue. As the ranting died away, Fox whistled. His pipe sailed through the air. He caught it, wiping the dirt on his robes, and lit it. "We know she's powerful. That girl has unimaginable potential. She did good. Where she went? Guess good as mine."

His walking stick flew from behind the animal pen. He landed in his palm with a *thunk*. He puffed on the pipe, smoke trailing, and shuffled along the periphery of the newly-formed trees Ora created in their battle. Dead grass surrounded each tree stretching out several feet. Fox held the pipe in his teeth and stretched his weathered hand to caress the bark. "Grown too fast. These trees are weak. Pushed beyond their limits. She didn't encourage them grow, but forced it. They're afraid." He tapped the dead grass with his stick. "They're ashamed. Had to steal the nutrients and life from around them to obey her." He patted a tree. The bark cracked and flaked away. The trees collapsed in on themselves. Perdita could've sworn she heard a collective sigh of relief as the trees crumbled into dust.

Perdita reflected at his words. Unimaginable potential. She couldn't imagine what Ora could accomplish. Both good and bad. Now that she had some training, her powers would grow even stronger. Her display shocked them all, but her eyes. Her eyes had changed also when she'd sent out that mass of power into Conjuragic.

Perdita assumed that display had been rage coupled with lack of control. But Ora hadn't been angry with them. Or had she? Did she hate them now and that's why she'd left? She couldn't believe it. Wouldn't believe it.

Each time Ora captured one of them, she looked more relieved than angry. When she left, it didn't seem like she had abandoned them. Perdita recognized the look of determination on her face. Yes. It had been Ora's decision to leave. Her eyes weren't glowing when she left. But where would she go? More importantly, how had she left?

Perdita prayed silently for Ora's safety, because she couldn't do anything else. Damien stalked off into the forest without speaking to anyone.

Charlie blinked back tears. "But she just got back."

Over the Bridge

Arameus went to her side and put an arm around her. "Ora's strong. She'll be okay."

Sabrina shook her head and said, more to herself, "She scares me. No one should have that much power."

Perdita bristled at that Conjuragic way of thinking. *Who is to say how much power someone should have?* "It isn't how much power that someone has; it's how they use it."

Sabrina met her eyes and shrugged, conceding the point. "Speaking of using power, what happened to you?" Sabrina placed her hands on her hips and stared at Jeremiah.

The boy's cheeks flushed red. "I tried, but her magic is different. It's like trying to hold onto sand. It slips through my fingers."

Perdita remember Damien describing the same thing. Perhaps it shouldn't, but knowing a Nip couldn't steal Ora's power, at least not for long, relieved her. Still she wasn't invulnerable. Sometimes a few seconds was all someone needed. Fox re-lit his pipe. Nothing bothered that man for very long. He limped over to his goats and sheep. They bleated with wagging tails, happy to see him. He bent and nuzzled their snouts whispering something that sounded very much like *Did you miss daddy?*

Without looking at anyone, he yelled, "What's for lunch? I'm starving."

Chapter Twenty-Nine
Sabrina

CHARLIE AND ARAMEUS LEFT THAT morning to go for their customary jog. The extra pounds that Charlie had carried on her face and hips melted away with each day of training as well as a healthy vegetarian diet. Her girlishness faded every day as she changed into a beautiful young woman. A vast difference from when Sabrina first met her. The memory of Corporal Jabez Bizard torturing Charlie to get answers haunted her. She should've done something then. At least something more than yelling at him.

After their run, Sabrina hoped Charlie would join her gardening with Fox, human style, and cooking lunch.

Perdita appeared from the Hogan, hands damp from finishing the dishes. Sabrina pulled the water from her hands. Perdita shook her head. "You know you don't always have to use magic. A towel would do just fine."

Sabrina smiled. "Any practice is a good thing."

"Please. You're back to your old self. You don't need to keep pushing yourself."

"You're one to talk. Pushing Arameus and yourself every afternoon while Charlie swoons over him."

Perdita shot her a knowing look. The stupid man still hadn't caught on that Charlie had a huge crush on him. It reminded her of how she'd felt about Simeon. Her heart ached at the thought of him. Had he survived the explosion of the Unity Statue? He'd been in MDA headquarters in the heart of the blast zone. A dark look crossed Sabrina's face as she wondered yet again about the fate of her home. Of Simeon, and Leigh, and her sister and nieces.

Over the Bridge

She'd give up her life, her freedom, as long as they were okay. They would've liked Perdita and Ora, even Jeremiah. She still hadn't decided about moody, sulking Damien though.

"Arameus is getting really good," Perdita said, drawing Sabrina out of her brooding.

"Confidence is key." She scanned the animal pins and gardens. "Where are the Nip boys?"

Perdita's lips thinned at Sabrina's racial slur. "Damien is teaching Jeremiah some techniques, and Fox volunteered to be a lab rat."

"Brave man." She shuttered at the remembered pain. She'd never volunteer to lose her magic. "You ready to run?"

"Do we always have to run on the river?"

"Hell yeah. What's the fun of being a Naiad if you don't run on water."

Perdita huffed and scrunched her forehead. "Because unlike some Protectors I know, I am a lot older and out of shape, so running is hard enough as it is without trying not to fall into the water." The image of Perdita crashing into the river with a splash came to mind, and she suppressed a grin. "Did you practice your spell work?"

Perdita removed the apron, revealing a running outfit. "Yes. Still unpredictable." Not unexpected for a Geminate, but she had way more control than Sabrina assumed she would. Sabrina guessed she'd be better if Ora hadn't disappeared and Perdita wouldn't quit bursting into tears at random times.

The two women set off toward the river in an easy silence. Sabrina found herself looking forward to spending time with Jeremiah later in the afternoon. As if reading her thoughts, Perdita asked, "What do you and Jeremiah get up to in the afternoons?"

"I tried to teach him how to fish, but he wouldn't shut up and scares away all the fish."

"He hardly speaks to anyone else. What does he talk about?"

"Video games, which he's vowed to teach me how to play. One night he showed me soccer, and another night I...never mind."

Perdita halted in her tracks, lifting her brow. "You what?

"Nothing."

"Don't give me that."

Sabrina blushed from her neck to her forehead. "Fine. I showed him the songs and dances I used to do for my nieces, but I only did it after he told he and Gabe tried out for a," she searched her memory for the word he'd used, "reality TV show. It upset him talking about his brother, and I'd wanted to cheer him up. He really liked hearing about the shark games at the Haven." If she could go home again, she'd bring him along. He'd become like a brother she never had.

"You're a mighty fine woman, Sabrina Sun."

The blush deepened. "Let's see if you say that after our run."

"Where have the fish gone?" Jeremiah cast his line yet again. His shoulders slumped. "Oh and by the way, what's up with Ora's necklace?"

"What about it?"

"Does it protect her? I saw her magic shoot through it. Back where Gabe…" He shook his head. "Anyway, it seems like no one can touch it."

Sabrina sighed, choosing her words carefully. "I don't know where the necklace came from, but it called to her. She found it in some random human shop. Magical objects like that have been studied, but every so often, after an object has been tampered with by magic, it takes on a life of its own and chooses a particular witch or wizard. The objects could be anything depending on who it's been meant for—a necklace, a ring, a cup. I've even seen a car. No one knows why. So, with Ora's necklace, it has its own power, but it works with her magic, in a symbiotic way. I doubt anyone could touch it, except for Ora, now that it's chosen her. Does that make sense?"

He laughed. "Not in the slightest."

Over the Bridge

She laughed and splashed him in the face.

"Hey!" he screamed, and they abandoned their poles and jumped into the water for a splash war. No magic involved.

"I say she's on an island somewhere, sprawled out in a hammock, drinking out of a coconut, and ogling some cabana boys." Charlie gestured with her fork, a steaming chunk of onion at the end.

Sabrina laughed at this theory. Each night the guesses on where Ora had disappeared to grew wilder and wilder. Damien scowled, pushing his corn around on his plate. Perdita paled, but Fox patted her hand. "I told you she's fine."

"You have no way of knowing that."

His eyes crinkled as if he knew something the others didn't. "Dese things work out. You see." Fox grabbed another roll out of the basket.

Tonight's dinner of long grain wild rice with black beans, onions, peppers, and sweet corn melted on Sabrina's tongue. Charlie sure could cook. She added silky brown gravy and large yeast rolls with her honey cinnamon butter. Fox nibbled on his fourth piece. Sabrina resisted grabbing a third one herself—otherwise she'd have to run extra tomorrow.

"I think she robbed a bank and is off buying a large yacht. Once everything is ready, she's going to come back, get us all, and we'll live the rest of our days out at sea where no one will find us," Jeremiah said as he shoved a huge spoonful of rice into his mouth. "How else did all your stuff get here overnight?"

Sabrina reached over and tousled his hair. "Whatever you say, toad!"

"Toad?" His hand stopped with the spoon midway to his mouth.

"Bullfrog. Same thing."

"Huh?"

Perdita laughed, getting her joke. "You're a good friend of mine, Jeremiah."

"Uhh, thanks." He shot a questioning look between the two women before shoving the spoon into his mouth.

Fox said in between bites, "We leave…tomorrow."

"What?" everyone shouted at once.

Perdita grabbed the table with white knuckles. "We can't leave. What if Ora comes back? She won't know where we've gone!"

Arameus asked, "Where are we going?"

"Time to sell my potions and blankets. We go to city. Nashville. Ora be there."

"What do you mean Ora's there?" Perdita asked.

"Nashville?" Sabrina said.

Fox swallowed. "Ora isn't there now. She's going to be there. In Nashville. We go sell potions."

"Why Nashville?" Arameus asked while Perdita breathed heavy beside him.

"Voice whisper in ear. It say she meet you there. So we go." At his words, Perdita's shoulders slackened.

Great, a whisper in his ear. He's gone mad.

Chapter Thirty
Ora

I glided through the Shadow Land with ease, avoiding the screaming voices. Jiminy's warm presence accompanied me, though he didn't say a word. I arrived in mere seconds at the fortune teller's house, stepping out onto the cobblestone walkway.

The middle-aged black woman waited for me on the front steps, barefoot, holding a steaming mug and a towel. She greeted me in well-worn jeans, a button-up blouse, and a light shawl draped upon her shoulders. Younger than I remembered, her black skin shined in the sunlight, and she wore an easy smile upon her lips. Her dark hair with fine strips of white strands wound in tight braids, flowing down her back.

"Welcome, child. I am Aryiana Ponder, and you are Ora Stone. For your head." She handed me the towel.

I took it from her and wiped my forehead. I'd forgotten the cut I'd gotten during the battle. I winced as the soft, clean towel grazed the wound. I stared down at the white towel, now stained red and brown with blood and dirt. Aryiana pushed the steaming mug toward me, easing the bloody towel from my fingers. I peered inside at the brown creamy drink from which wafted the aroma of Thanksgiving. I sipped before it even occurred to me to be wary of her. I swallowed the delicious tea. It tasted exactly the way it smelled and left a warm feeling in my belly, but also a tingling sensation in my head.

I met her eyes, not questioning how she knew my name or why I trusted her. "Thank you," I said.

She smiled and wrapped her arm around me, ushering me inside. We stepped through her doorway. I'd expected crystal balls and incense and chanting music, but no, her home could've been plucked out of anywhere in the world. A home. Nothing more. I stood in the small but welcoming foyer. Two rooms careened off the foyer as a wooden staircase lined the left side of a long wooden hallway. A formal dining room on the left and a sitting area with one small round table on right side. Nothing sensational adorned the little table. Aryiana stepped past me heading down the long hallway straight ahead, bare feet smacking down on the thin wood floors that stretched to a small kitchen. Antique photographs in large oval frames lined the hallway. Generations of families mixed of every race and nationality.

"I trust you're hungry." Aryiana waved to a wooden chair at her small, wooden table. Like everything in her home, the table whispered uniqueness with its chipped edges and faded lacquer. History and memory had ingrained itself in the wood. Charmed would never adequately describe Aryiana or her home. She wrestled about by the stove and returned with a plate full of eggs, bacon, biscuits, dirty rice, and a small bowl of cheese grits.

My mouth watered. Eating food I'd grown myself, by magic, for the last several days hadn't been tasty. Plus, I wasn't an outdoorsy camp-out kind of person. Even before we'd met Fox, we didn't have the luxury of going to the grocery store and buying whatever we wanted. I shoved bite after bite in my mouth, chewing enough to swallow, suppressing moans as the flavors burst and mingled on my tongue. I plowed through the first plate but took slower bites on the second. Aryiana, like Fox, didn't speak while eating her own plate of food. Although much slower and gracefully than I had.

I sat the fork down on the plate with a clang.

Aryiana refilled my mug before taking our plates to the sink. Despite how much I'd eaten, I couldn't help but sip more of the drink. "I love chai."

"Yes. That was a delightful find when I moved here to the human realm." She spoke with a slight French accent.

"Where is here?" She had to be a remarkable woman seeing as how she didn't react when I appeared from thin air, but then again, she did speak to me in my mind. So, what did I expect?

Over the Bridge

"New Orleans," she replied. It occurred to me I had left everyone behind. I stood, meaning to leave. "I have to go. They don't know where I am. My mom will be so worried."

Aryiana patted my arm. "They're fine. I've sent a message to Fox. When we're done, you'll know where to meet them."

"How do you know all this?"

She smiled. "I just do."

"What am I doing here?" I asked.

"Why, you're here to learn Ember." She sipped her tea.

The thought chilled me. Fire magic held a wildness to it that frightened me. I finished my tea. She took my mug, placing it in the sink before opening a cabinet, and removed a small glass. She took orange juice from the refrigerator and poured some into the glass. She returned with the glass, pulled something out of her jeans pocket, and placed it on the table. Her hand covered the object from her pocket as she slid both the glass and object toward me. She removed her hand and straightened. Before me sat two round reddish-brown pills. I shot her a look.

"For your headache." Her gaze flicked to the pills and then back to me.

I picked them up, threw them in the back my mouth, and took a big gulp of the sweet yet tangy drink, swallowing.

"Ibuprofen?" I asked.

She nodded.

A satisfied feeling swept over me. I'd choose taking an actual pill of Ibuprofen over making willow bark pain medicine any day.

She yawned as she slid once again out of the chair, depositing her own cup, and stepped to the doorway of the kitchen. "Come now, child. You must be weary from all your travels."

I downed the rest of the orange juice, rubbed my full belly, and placed the glass in her sink. I followed her out of the kitchen. Down the hallway, we took the stairs. At the top, Aryiana gestured for me to go through a door into a bathroom—a glorious bathroom. Fox's magical one had beat squatting in the bushes and using Naiad magic to clean off, but a real bathroom, what a luxury!

She handed me two clean big fluffy towels, a nightgown, and some clean underwear. I picked up the towel and pressed it to my face, inhaling the scent of laundry detergent.

"I'm sure you would like a shower, and when you're done, there is a bedroom across the hall where you can take a nap."

That's it, I love this woman. She gave me breakfast with real food, supplied me with a bathroom, a fresh hot shower, clean clothes, pain medicine, and I'd get a nap! She must be a saint.

She left the bathroom, closing the door behind her. I stepped out of my well-worn clothes, dropping them onto the floor, hoping to never wear them again. The shower burst to life with the turn of the handle. While waiting for the water to heat up, I studied my reflection in the mirror. Dark circles rimmed my sunken amber eyes and sallow face. How much weight had I lost? My once vibrant red hair had turned dull and lanky. The gash in my forehead from the battle at Fox's had healed. Perhaps something in the tea had sped the healing?

As the hot water ran over my body, I moaned out loud, feeling my muscles loosening. I washed my hair twice, massaging my scalp. After the conditioner, I moved on to the rest of my body. I scrubbed everywhere from the tip of my nose to in-between my toes. No matter how much magic I had, I'd never get over the pleasure of a shower. As the water grew cold, I turned off the faucets, wishing I could've stayed longer.

I dried off and slipped on the fresh soft clothes. In one of the cabinet drawers, I discovered a hair brush and dryer. Across the hall, the bedroom called to me. I took in the antique luxury of the room in a quick sweep of my eyes. A pretty pink quilt with small flowers covered the full-sized bed. The antique dresser shined with soft lamp light, and on top sat an antique hair brush, comb, and hand-held mirror on a silver tray. Charlie's grandmother would've loved this room. A soft high-backed chair waited in the corner, covered with a warm blanket.

I pulled back the clean, soft quilt, savoring the moment. I rubbed my fingertips over the soft, silky sheets. They felt cool against my body when I slid in the bed, turned on my side, and pulled the bedding over my shoulders, tucking it around me. I pulled the metal pull switch on the beside lamp, and the light went out with a click. The room descended into darkness, despite the sun shining outside. Magic?

In seconds, uninterrupted sleep took me, and I didn't wake until the following morning.

The next day, I got dressed, slipping on the clean clothes Aryiana told me I'd find in the dresser, and revisited the bathroom before padding downstairs to find Aryiana.

"Good morning," I said.

"Morning." She stood from the little kitchen table. "You slept well." A statement, not a question. "Have a seat. You're starving." Another statement, but moments before my stomach rumbled.

I took the same seat as last night, and she sat a large bowl of oatmeal in front of me. She placed several small bowls with toppings, a plate full of toast, and pitchers with milk and orange juice on the table. I piled on brown sugar and butter on my oatmeal, helped myself to two pieces of buttered toast, and poured a glass of milk. I wished for another cup of chai, and without me asking, she poured us both a cup of tea. While I chewed, I wondered what Ember training involved.

"I know you have many questions, but let me assure you the answers will come when you're ready," she explained in between bites. "You see, Ember magic is different from the others. When using the other cores, you simply need to know how to use the magic. What you can and cannot do with it. Ember is different. It's all about control. As you know, fire can be very destructive and almost have a mind of its own. Knowing how much or how little to use is very important. One can try to light the fireplace and end up burning down the house or even the town. It takes no skill to send fire bombs flying at a city, but to do this," she held up her hand, and one blue flame ignited out of her finger, "takes skill."

"Impressive." She already knew I had all cores. She knew I'd been with Fox. This mind reading should've unnerved me, but it didn't.

I swallowed the last spoonful of warm, sweet oatmeal and popped the last of the buttered toast into my mouth. I took the plates to the sink. She didn't have a dishwasher, so I filled one half of the sink with warm water, adding dish soap, and placed my dishes inside.

Aryiana placed her own dishes into the sink. While I washed the dishes, she put away the rest of the uneaten food and drinks. We worked in an easy silence.

"There is another thing I wish to teach you. Everyone knows fire can be destructive, but if you can see the constructive side, then I'll consider myself a successful teacher. Fire can warm your home, cook your food, heat up potions to heal or to ease suffering. This is what most people do not realize."

The prospect of learning Ember overwhelmed me, but unlike a few days ago, I had faith I could master this. But I'd been afraid to try Ember alone for the reasons she had named. Seeing the worry upon my face, she tilted my chin to meet her kind eyes. "I know you have good in you. I can see it's abundance. I know you don't want to hurt anyone. I also know most of your magic is tied to your temper, so learning to be calm and focus your attention is my main goal as opposed to learning magic tricks. There's one thing I worry about, though." She let go and turned away from me to look out of her kitchen window. "You're in a battle. Whether you know it or not, and you've set yourself upon an epic quest. This will mean hurting people. I hope you have the courage to do what is needed when the time comes and the wisdom to know the difference."

"That makes two of us."

"I have faith in you. Go get showered and dressed in something looser. You'll find the best outfits for this in the third drawer in your room. When you're done, meet me at the end of the upstairs hallway."

I wiped my hands on a towel hanging on the cabinet underneath the sink. I took the steps at a jog, excited to have two showers in two days.

I didn't linger in the shower today and dressed quickly in form-fitting black yoga pants with a loose-fitting gray t-shirt and sports bra. I left my bedroom, going to the room at the end of the hall. I knocked and opened the door, finding yet another wooden staircase, and headed upstairs. The old hardwood creaked with every step.

The stairs led to a bright and airy attic, totally unlike most dusty cluttered attics. Lush carpet lined the floor with two cushions facing a large round window with the rays of the morning sun streaming inside. A treadmill, free weights, and a large flat screen TV hung on the wall with an assortment of DVDs on a shelf below it. I hadn't been expecting a sleek and modern personal gym when the rest of the house gave off an antique richness.

Aryiana sat, lotus position, in the middle of the floor on the cushion to the left. She wore orange leopard-print yoga pants and a matching sports bra. She'd pulled her long hair into a loose ponytail at the base of her neck. Despite her age, her legs and arms were long and lean with a firm stomach as if she worked out daily. Music played in the background—a mixture of birds chirping and a rolling river intertwined with music from a piano, harp, and bells. She held up her hand motioning for me to sit beside her.

I followed her lead and sat, crossing my legs and placing my arms on my thighs, palms up. Without opening her eyes, she said, "The first thing we need to work on is your ability to find your magic without being angry. The best way I have found to calm the mind is through the rumination."

The chill of dread spider-walked down my spine. "I've done it once. At a club called Sárkány's. I got us caught, and Sabrina and Arameus almost died."

"Don't let that bad outcome give you the wrong impression. Rumination is something not everyone can do. Especially without practice and focus of the mind. You were able to do it on your own, which is impressive."

"What am I supposed to do?"

"First you relax your mind, and when you're there, find your magic, bring it up, but not out." She smiled, turning to face me, still not opening her eyes.

My eyebrows raised at her quirkiness. "Sure thing."

"Ready to begin?" She faced forward.

Nervous, I took a deep breath, faced forward, and closed my eyes. The sun warmed my face. Behind my eyes, colors and shapes moved in slow circles from the light shining through the window. No wonder Aryiana had kept her eyes closed the whole time.

"Slow breathing. Empty your mind. Relax your body. Starting at the top of your head, moving down to your forehead, then cheeks and jaw."

I tried to follow along, breathing in and relaxing my muscles one by one. Never did I feel a deep state of relaxation. Nor did my mind empty. I tried. I really did, but annoying thoughts kept jumping into my brain. Things like my hip hurts. This is stupid. I wonder what's for lunch. Each time, I gave myself a mental shake, attempting to clear my thoughts, but the subtle whistling sounds of Aryiana's breathing distracted me. Next, I tried to see if I could detect a seagull's call in the background of the music.

I opened one eye and peeked at Aryiana. She sat, perfectly still and calm, even breathing, her face smooth and relaxed with a slight smile, as if all the secrets of the universe had been revealed to her. For all I knew, they probably were. She even had a faint glow about her skin which shimmered. The glow must be her magic, I decided. Jealousy flared, and I closed my eyes and tried even harder.

Rumination and meditation had to be similar. I mimicked something I'd seen in a movie once. I repeated the thought *ohm, ohm, ohm*. Which made me feel stupid, but I kept at it. *Ohm. Ohm, ohm*. Still nothing.

Obviously, that wasn't working. Instead, I tried to take deep breaths and find my magic. As usual, my magic hid in a corner yelling, *I'm not coming out to play!* and blew raspberries at me.

Well crap. Now what? So I did what I thought most people would do when they meditated with another person and weren't successful.

I faked it.

In my head, I sang "Old MacDonald had a Farm," "Twinkle Twinkle Little Star," and "I'm Henry the 8th I am. I am I am."

Finally, Aryiana took an even deeper breath, let it out, and I could finally open my eyes. She regarded me and smiled, looking irritatingly refreshed, and asked, "How do you feel?"

How do I feel? Stupid, like a failure, a cheater, but instead I replied, "Great."

She laughed out loud, and it had a musical quality to it. "Liar." She flowed to her feet, lithe like a dancer. She unfolded the cushion and rolled it out making a mat. "I know you've ruminated before, but I didn't expect you to be successful on the first attempt."

"Oh."

She patted my shoulder. "It takes practice and discipline. Before you'll be successful, you need to condition your body. Not only for rumination but also for any fights you'll be getting into in the near future."

This made me rather nervous since she could, in fact, see the future and all.

She shrugged with a bright smile. "Theoretically."

I hate the way magical people seem to be able to read my mind.

"All right, get up."

I folded out my cushion like she did, making my own mat.

"Okay, first you need to learn yoga." She dropped that bombshell.

I groaned in protest. *What? I'm opposed to exercise.* Don't get me wrong, I've gotten on the treadmill a time or two, but I've always been one of those lucky girls everybody hates because I could eat anything and not exercise and still remain thin. A big argument between Charlie and me for years.

Again, reading my mind. "This isn't to keep you from getting fat. This is to help you increase your strength. You notice you've lost weight?"

I nodded. Working with Fox over the last few days left me exhausted, and while I've always been thin, I'd never been fit, despite playing soccer.

"Shall we begin?" She stood on her mat, feet together, hands in prayer position in front of her heart.

Over the next hour, I twisted and turned at very odd angles, which wasn't difficult, but irritating with the ever-changing motion. *I hate downward facing dog!*

After our workout, Aryiana and I went downstairs for some lunch. Enjoying a chicken Caesar salad and lemonade, my thoughts traveled as they so often do in moments of quiet.

"Aryiana?"

"Yes, dear."

"There was this guy..." I twirled my fork in the bowl. I didn't know how to start. Aryiana waited. I liked this quiet way about her. It reminded me of Mom. "He...uh. He died. At least I thought he died..." I struggled.

"But you've seen him."

"Yes, in the Shadow Land. It's what I call it."

She nodded. "I know."

"I saw you there, and you're real. Then maybe?" I couldn't make myself say it. Because if I really saw him, then he's with her.

"Maybe he's alive?" she asked for me.

I nodded, meeting her eyes. She stared me with a sad expression. "I'm sorry, child. The boy you knew is dead."

At the same time relief as well as devastation washed over me. I fought the stinging sensation in my eyes. Aryiana allowed me to fight my internal struggle in peace. It took me a few minutes, and my eyes watered as I got my emotions under control. "So, what exactly is the Shadow Land?"

"Surely you already know." When I stared at her dumbfounded, she smiled. "It is the Veil, of course."

"The Veil?" I thought about the Shadow Land. "The screaming I hear?"

"Those are the screams of people trapped inside."

My lunch threatened to rise in the back of my throat. Their screams echoed in my mind along with their fear and confusion. They must've been in the middle of traveling when I sealed it. But if I were truly honest, I wouldn't have cared in that moment. But now that I'd calmed down, I felt the horror of what I had done.

Over the Bridge

"It could have been worse." Aryiana shrugged. "They could've died."

I considered her words and realized if they're still alive, then they could be rescued. She reached across the table and grasped my hand. I hadn't even realized I had been shaking.

"This is the true reason why you are here. You have great power. You've even taken down a whole city, yet despite this, you're not master of your magic. You must learn to control your emotions. Remember, despite your abilities, another will always be mightier than you if they can control their temper." She squeezed my hand again, let go, and resumed eating.

"If I sealed the Veil, how can I travel in it?"

She considered my words as she chewed, then swallowed. "I guess you made a bridge. Sometimes you traveled with your psyche only. Others," she waved a hand over my body, "take you great distances."

A Bridge.

Aryiana's chair screeched as she stood from the table, an excited twinkle in her eye. "Come on. It's time to learn to Ember magic."

Chapter Thirty-One
Ora

I COULDN'T HIDE MY EXCITEMENT. I'd been performing magic for months now, but I hadn't tried setting fire. I had been too afraid it would get away from me, but with Aryiana here, she could help. We cleaned up the kitchen and went outside.

She laid out varying stacks of wood from huge piles to others with only a single log that lined up in a row. I shot her a questioning look. She smiled at me knowingly. "With Ember, big is easier. The smaller piles will be harder. Ready?"

A wide smile stretched across my face. "Absolutely." I fought the urge to jump up and down.

She laughed. "Okay, dear, tell me how you let your magic go."

I explained the Sight. "It's like the world moves in tiny patterns, either moving in a circle, or along spiderweb patterns."

She raised one eyebrow at me, and guilt spread through me. "What?"

The concern etched on her forehead didn't fade. "It's nothing. As a seer, I'm able to see how events will unfold. I see the world in much the same way you described. It is ironic that others call what I have the Sight."

"So I'm a seer?" I speculated.

She looked lost in thought. "I suppose that remains to be seen."

This was new. With everything I could already do, I might be able to see the future? As always, she read my thoughts. "It isn't the future, only the possible ways events can unfold. It is murky and hard to predict. Much better to focus on the abilities we know you have."

"Okay. What am I supposed to do?"

She strolled over to the largest pile. "Look at the wood. See the particles moving?"

My eyes unfocused, amulet vibrating, and zoomed on the bark of the wood and went deeper. The particles moved like she said. Using the Sight had gotten easier. I nodded. "Yes. I see it."

"Make them move faster."

I picked one particle and a thin string of magic connected the pile of wood to me. The particles moved, but as if in slow motion. I plucked the string, sending the vibrations rippling down the line, and the particles oscillated. The wood vibrated, and the friction increased, driving the temperature higher inside the wood. Soon a small whiff of smoke rose from the wood. A tiny flame came to life, and my vision relaxed. Once started, the fire grew without any help from me.

"Very good. Again," Aryiana instructed. I did the same thing with each pile until every piece of wood burned making the back yard alight with fire. The heat poured over me, the scent reminding me of camping with John. Responding to the sadness, my power rippled as if a large stone plummeted into a lake. I soothed my power, and it purred, relaxing.

Proud, I smiled at her. She returned my smile and said, "Now, put it out."

My moment of celebration dowsed with her words. What did she mean put it out? "I don't know how."

"You can do it. Just look at the particles, not the fire, and slow them down. Don't you see, fire is the result energy of the particles moving fast, causing friction, bouncing off each other. It's a domino effect that you can stop. Once you do, the energy dissipates, and the fire goes out."

Past the light and flames, the particles appeared once more. They vibrated and bounced off one another, giving off sparks of energy as one hit another. I focused on one particle, watched it move around in an erratic pattern. I guessed if it bounced off here, it would hit there next. When it hit the first one, I redirected it, preventing contact with the second. Opening the Sight further, the vision expanded, showing more particles, and I blocked multiple paths at once. The fire cooled, but the sound of a car door slamming nearby broke my focus. The Sight faded, and the flame roared to life once again.

"Very good for your first try." She patted my shoulder. "Keep at it. I'll be inside if you need me."

"But, what if?" I spun around watching her back as she walked inside.

She called over her shoulder, "You'll be fine. Trust yourself."

I practiced again and again, but as anytime I used a new part of my magic, the results were inconsistent. Although I didn't give up. It had grown darker, albeit no cooler, when Aryiana called for me to come inside. New Orleans heat didn't dissipate, even in October. Add in fires blazing and cooling off and on, and sweat trickled down my back and neck. She had made a simple dinner of potato soup and warm bread. She slid me two more Ibuprofen.

"Thanks. Did you read my future and see I'd have a headache?"

"Somethings don't require using my ability as a seer. Once you see the pattern of events over and over again, some things become predictable."

"What about Fox? Is he a seer, too?"

"He has an uncanny ability to read people. It's how he recognized the differences in Charlie and you."

"I wonder why he lives alone." I dried the dishes as she handed them to me.

"When you can read people, it's easier to be alone." She rinsed the soup pot.

"I don't understand why he'd choose to live in the human realm when he wouldn't age as fast in Conjuragic." I speculated out loud, and it wasn't until the words had left my mouth did I realized Aryiana had chosen the exact same thing.

"Freedom from persecution is worth a shorter life."

This piqued my interest, but I didn't press. I suppose the same had happened to my mother and me. Our freedom is worth settling for a human lifetime, but now if things turned out the way

Over the Bridge

I'd planned, Mom and I might live a long time together. I shook off the premature thought, throwing down the towel on the sink, and pressed my back against the counter.

Aryiana's sad eyes flicked back and forth taking in every inch of my face. "You look so much like you father."

Nothing could have shocked me more than this. My mom never mentioned my father. Ever!

"You knew my father?"

"Briefly."

"Wait, I thought he was born in prison? How could you have known him? Unless?"

"Yes. I met him while he was a prisoner in Conjuragic."

Shock and suspicion flooded my system. My eyes flitted to the door, and I considered running. I met her eyes, and they gave me pause. The kindness never wavered.

"I'm not going to hurt you. I was a prisoner of the Experimenter too, of sorts. I gave him something he wanted, and in return, he helped me to come here." She leaned against the counter and folded her arms.

My heart pounded, and I still didn't know what to do. "What did you give him?"

"The prophecy."

The blood drained from my face. "You mean the prophecy about the Geminates making an all-powerful rock?"

She nodded. "Something like that."

"But because of the prophecy, he captured people and made them have children. Made them have Geminates and enslaved them?" I paced around the kitchen, trying to come to grips with this revelation. "It's why my parents were slaves!"

"I regret the actions he took from my prophecy, but without the prophecy, you wouldn't exist either."

My pacing stopped. I looked to her with pain in my eyes. "Was there... Was there a reason?"

"Yes. You. The prophecy has two potential endings. One is his complete success, and the other his downfall. You are the deciding factor."

"What do you mean?" I didn't want to hear this. It was too much.

"Your choices will decide his fate." She moved toward me, but I inched away from her. She halted, not pursuing me further.

"What choice?" I asked, barely above a whisper.

"That I cannot tell you. It has to be of your own free will. I cannot sway you."

"But you can sway everything else!" I shouted and ran to the front door. Her shouted words halted my steps at the door. "I'm the one who told your father how to escape!"

My hand trembled on the doorknob, but thankfully, the magic stayed down.

Aryiana walked into the hallway. "I came back to Conjuragic because the Experimenter was frustrated his jewel was taking so long. During our discussion, your father had been brought to him. Your father had found out your mother was pregnant and started a fight with the guards. The Experimenter had planned to execute your father, but I stopped him. I told him your father was the key to the prophecy, and without him, he'd never succeed."

I didn't look at her. I couldn't.

"The Experimenter left the room, and while your father and I were alone, I told him how to escape and to come to me when he reached the human world. He didn't survive their escape, but your mother did. I was there when you were born, and I helped her find a place to live. You survived because of me."

Chapter Thirty-Two
Ora

THE NEXT MORNING, MY EYES felt like raisins from crying. I didn't travel through the Shadow Land or Bridge in my sleep via my psyche or physical body, thank goodness. I got out of bed, tiptoed across the hall, showered, and dressed. I headed downstairs away from the bumps from the attic. Childish, but I couldn't face Aryiana, not yet anyway.

A note sat on the kitchen table.

Breakfast is in the oven.
Help yourself.

My stomach growled, and I peeked inside. Pancakes with bacon sat on a warming plate. I fixed myself a plate and a large glass of milk. I found the butter and real maple syrup. I ate with small, careful bites, not really hungry, but delaying the inevitable. I knew I'd have to face her, but I didn't know what to say. She'd helped my parents escape and for us to get settled once in the human realm, but on the other hand, how many others had suffered due to her actions? As I chewed my breakfast, I realized Aryiana wouldn't stop me, and she'd understand whatever I decided, whether to stay or go.

Sighing, I decided I would stay. My parents trusted her and never lied to me. I had no right to judge her when my actions destroyed a city and left hundreds trapped inside the Veil. Everything she'd done had been with good intentions. *But what to do about the prophecy?*

I chewed the fluffy pancakes, weighing the options, and in the end, decided the prophecy didn't make a difference. I couldn't worry about something I couldn't change. The Experimenter's fate was in my hands, but then again, this hadn't really been a surprise. Stopping him had been my objective all along. I'd already learned from Damien he had an army of Nips and God knew how many Geminates. It was only a matter of time before he acted. If I failed, he would win. But I had a chance to stop him. To help all those nameless people. Wasn't that why I'd trained, to fight him? I scraped the remaining uneaten food in the garbage, quickly washed the dishes, and put the rest of the food away. I'd already dressed in a new yoga outfit of green pants and top with swirls of blues and purple.

I wouldn't change my plans. If that meant yoga and ruminating, so be it. I turned on my heel, left the kitchen, and headed to the attic.

Aryiana leaned against the window frame, staring out, dressed in black and blue yoga clothes, her hair swept into a loose braid. She turned as I approached and opened her arms. I embraced her, letting the mistrust go.

"I'm sorry, child."

"I know," I whispered, leaning back, and gestured to the mats. "Shall we begin?"

She laughed as I pulled my hair back into a ponytail, curled into lotus pose on the cushion, and closed my eyes. Behind me, she turned on the music. Today's a techno beat, a dancing song. Her footsteps shuffled along the carpet, and I picked up the subtle shifting of her clothes as she sat on the cushion to my left. "This type of music helped you ruminate the first time. Perhaps it can again."

I let the music carry me away. Unlike yesterday when my mind wandered, today I heard nothing but the beat of the drums and clang of bells. Instead of holding still, my body swayed in rhythm and breathed.

I grasped the amulet, which bobbed left and right. It warmed in my fingertips. The colors underneath my eye lids shined bright and clear as I emerged from the darkness and danced along with the music. Sinking in myself, I pulled my magic up from the depths, rising to merge with me, a partner in the ancient, tribal dance. One song merged with the next, but I kept dancing.

A deep, peaceful energy rose higher, filling every part of me, as thought and time fell away. Sounds and smells, even the feeling of the mat underneath me faded, as if far away. Slowly, thoughts reformed, disconnected and irrational at first, but with each beat of the drum, they cleared. The steady pounding of drums mixed with my heartbeat. My eyes popped open. The sunlight no longer poured through the window. No music played from the speakers. I crept to my feet, now alone in the room, stretching, and wincing at the stiffness in my knees and hips. Outside the large round window, the purplish red hues of twilight cascaded over the skyline, turning the distant trees bluish. I couldn't have been sitting here all day!

I rushed downstairs calling Aryiana's name. She answered from the living room. I found her, curled up on the couch, her feet tucked beneath her, reading a book.

"Aryiana, did I?"

"Yes."

"Ruminated?"

She nodded, holding her place in the book with one finger. I didn't know why, but I screamed with joy and did a little happy dance. She laughed out loud.

"Are you ready for food or to practice magic?"

I felt alive with energy like I could do anything. "Magic!"

"Then let's go." Uncurling from the couch, she placed a bookmark between the pages, and set her book on the end table. I followed her outside, and large glass containers full of water replaced the wooden logs.

"I thought we were working on Ember magic?"

"We are. You think wood is the only thing that burns?"

"No, but water?"

"Everyone is so caught up in what core you have, but there are some things we all can do, but it's accomplished in different ways. For instance, when cutting down a tree. A Sphere would cut the fibers of the tree itself. A Naiad can form a blade of water, or pull the water from the tree outwards, slicing it from the inside. Right?"

"Yeah. I guess."

"A Tempest will use the air to push it down, and Embers can burn it apart. The end is the same."

"True, but what's the point?" I realized that sounded rude. "Sorry."

"The point is knowing your enemy. Their strengths and weaknesses, and by knowing theirs, you can understand yours as well." She put her arms around my shoulders leading me out into the yard.

"I don't understand."

She let out an exasperated sigh. "Okay. If you saw a tree walking toward you, what would you assume?"

I rolled my eyes, thinking of Fox. "Sphere."

She bobbed her head up and down. "Possibly. Possibly, but why couldn't a Naiad be manipulating the water inside the tree?" Of course that could happen. Why didn't I think of it?

"You've been learning the obvious ways to use your powers. Now we need to get you thinking outside the box. Now turn the water into steam." She waved her arm toward the glass.

I opened the Sight, focusing on the small molecules of hydrogen and oxygen. Not that I could distinguish the two. The water molecules sped, but when the unwelcome thought *making spaghetti will be so much faster came*, I lost my concentration.

"Focus," Aryiana said.

"Sorry." I felt my power reach outward, touching the water, moving it faster until it boiled with steam climbing out of the container. I moved to the next one and soon all the containers boiled, steam rising into the cool night air. I watched the molecules dance in a chaotic frenzy, and I wondered if instead of making them move faster I could slow them down. One by one, the particles slowed to my will, and the water froze to ice.

Surprised, I looked to Aryiana for instruction.

She smiled, holding her head higher. "That's my girl."

Chapter Thirty-Three
Charlie

Fox's infernal roosters crowed at dawn while he banged in the kitchen, making coffee, or what Charlie referred to as caffeinated oil. Half blinded by sleep and grateful she'd packed the night before, Charlie grabbed a banana and Fox's trail mix.

The rest packed and readied themselves with little more than grunts. Even Sabrina moved slower than usual. Fox made it abundantly clear they wouldn't be returning with him from the trip into Nashville. Though he wouldn't tell them why. Charlie guessed they'd overstayed their welcome. A loner and a Hogan full of company wasn't a good mix.

As soon as everyone stepped out of the Hogan, the extra rooms caved in on themselves with a resounding *woomph*. The animals bleated at the loud and unexpected noise. Fox cooed to his favorite goat, scratching at her chin. "Daddy will be back soon. I'll bring you a treat."

Fox's place had returned to his former, one roomed, Hobbit hole. Charlie hoped he'd at least close off the bathroom. Fox hurried as fast as Charlie had ever seen him, moving his various little potion bottles and blankets on his Sphere-made carts.

They followed behind him, carrying their own packs, for about thirty minutes or so. No one spoke much. The farther they went, Charlie picked up the rumbling of the occasional car in the distance. They ended at the edge of a road by a blue beat up pick-up truck that to have been made in the sixties.

"You sure that thing still runs?" Damien carried a new pack Fox had made for him.

"What you know about human vehicles, Nip?"

Damien scratched at the wool shirt from Fox's pile. "Driving and fixing cars became a useful skill as I helped in the human realm. Anything to give me more status."

"And to please him." Jeremiah glared.

"No. To make myself less expendable."

"What's that supposed to mean?" Jeremiah threw his own pack on the ground.

"Nothing." Damien lifted his hands as in surrender.

Jeremiah opened his mouth, but Sabrina stepped between them. "He wasn't thinking. He didn't mean you and Gabe were expendable."

Damien's eyebrows rose. "What? That's what you thought? I would never."

Deflated, Jeremiah picked up his pack. "We're cool. We've all suffered. Now we just have to trust each other. Right?" His gaze swept all of them.

Perdita sighed, as if a weight rested there. "I owe you an apology, Fox. I still don't understand why you're sending us away while Ora is still missing, but I'm going to choose to trust you."

"Good. Aryiana be happy. Come. Time to go or we be late." Fox slipped the rest of the things in the back of the pickup and slid into the driver's side.

Perdita paled at his words.

"Who's Aryiana?" Charlie asked.

Perdita tilted her head to the side as if listening to something but shook her head and slid into the passenger's side without a word.

"Guess we're riding in the back." Sabrina climbed over the bed and found a spot against the back window. This left Charlie, Arameus, Damien, and Jeremiah to fill in the remaining spots in the bed of the truck with Fox's things. He pulled out of the run-down dirt road, following an overgrown path for ten more minutes, before merging onto a backcountry road. As they picked up speed, Charlie settled in the bed of the cab, trying to avoid as much wind as possible. They rode, unable to talk due to the roaring of the wind for what she'd guess to be about an hour. The country roads faded away as more and more developments cropped up along the drive leading into a city, likely Nashville. Finally, Fox pulled to a stop.

Arameus climbed out of the opened bed of the truck, extending his hand to her. "Not my favorite way to travel."

"Definitely," she said, sliding outward.

Fox ignored them, removed a table from the bed, and set it up. Arameus moved to grab a handful of Fox's blankets when Perdita's back stiffened. "We need to go. Now."

"What?" Sabrina asked. "Where?"

Perdita pointed down the street. "There's a diner about four blocks that way."

Sabrina rolled her eyes. "Look, I'm hungry too."

Fox waved. "You must go now. Go. Go."

Arameus wavered, looking between the two women and Fox.

Perdita grabbed her bag, tapped Fox on the shoulder. "Thank you." Without another word, she jogged down the street and pressed the crosswalk button.

Charlie picked up her own bag, confused. She stopped in front of Fox. "Will we ever see you again?"

Fox paused for a fraction of a second, fixing this table, preparing to sell his potions. "Time will tell. But now no time for goodbyes." He pulled her in with an awkward one-armed hug. Then shooed them all away.

Perdita never slowed as she guided them into a little café with faded red brick and a large hand-painted coffee mug on the side. "This is the place." She opened the door as a bell jingled. Without waiting for them, she stepped into the café. Charlie followed, as did the others. Perdita stopped, mid-step, spinning to shove Charlie in a two-person table in the middle of the café. "Stay here and keep your head down."

"What?"

"The rest of you, come with me." Charlie watched in confusion as Perdita directed everyone where to sit. When Perdita caught her watching, she swiped with her palm, indicating Charlie shouldn't look at her. She looked away, tucking her head down as the waitress approached her. "My goodness, is it afternoon already? My name is Lynda. Welcome to Connie's. Can I get you anything to drink?"

"Sweet tea," Charlie said.

"Coming right up."

The bell dinged, and Charlie's gaze flicked to the doorway. The blood drained from her face. Charity strolled into the diner, followed by Sárkány, and a red-headed man Charlie didn't know.

Why would Perdita bring us here?

She swallowed as the trio sat down at the table right behind her. Charlie thought Charity should have died after Fox attacked her, but she'd been wrong, though the evil woman hadn't walked away unscathed. A large bruise of faded black and yellow encircled her left eye. Various cuts and bruises lined her chin and arms. Guess getting smacked by a tree and flying through the air would do that to you. Charlie felt not even the slightest hint of remorse. The bitch deserved it.

Footsteps approached the table. Charlie wouldn't risk a glance, hoping it was only a waitress. The chairs behind her scratched on the floor.

Charlie strained to listen, but noted a shiny napkin holder. She scooted it sideways to get a distorted image of the group behind her. They joined a table where a man sat alone, staring at the trio approaching him.

"All right, Sárkány, why have you called me here?" the man at the table asked.

"Straight to the point, Finch. No time for some lunch?" Sárkány slid into a seat opposite him, while Charity sat on the side of the table, facing Charlie's back, and the unknown redhead with them took a spot beside Sárkány.

"There is no point in pretenses. I don't like you. You don't like me. You've called me here, and I've come. What do you want?" Finch leaned back.

"Very well." Sárkány tapped his fingers on the table. "We're on the hunt for one of your kind, and we would like your assistance."

"Why are you hunting one of my kind?" Finch asked.

"This one was arrested, caught in the act in front of…" Sárkány said, but the rest was lost as Lynda returned to the table.

"Here's your tea. Have you decided yet?" Lynda asked.

"Um no. Not yet." Charlie picked up the menu pretending to look.

"Okay. I'll give you a few minutes. Take your time."

Charlie focused on the conversation behind her.

The man called Finch barked a laugh. "So, you're trying to tell me a Gayden escaped the Kassen and sealed the Veil? You know we can't do that."

"Obviously she didn't do it alone. She had her Tempest Defender and a Naiad Protector to help her." Sárkány leaned in close, speaking so quietly Charlie had to strain to catch his words. "I almost had them in my club, but they escaped."

"An unknown Gayden, a Tempest, and a Naiad Protector all escaped from you and your goonies? How's that possible?" Finch's question held more sarcasm than any actual curiosity.

"She's more powerful than we imagined and has unexpected allies." Charity banged a fist on the table.

The unknown redhead who had yet to speak, grabbed her wrist. "If you can't control your temper, you'll be taken care of." The cruelty laced every nuance of the man's bland tone.

Finch leaned toward her. "You know how I feel about our kind serving the likes of Magicians. You disgrace yourself, Charity. Do not speak to me."

Charity pointed a finger in his face, jabbing like her missing sword. "You and the other Nips live out your life on your tiny little island, huddled together, and pretend to be only human, whereas I live with the Magicians, using my abilities, instead of hiding from them."

"Don't *ever* call me a Nip again!" His hand balled into a fist. "We live on our island so we can be with our own kind. We stay out of Conjuragic to honor our agreement with the Council. It sounds to me as if the Council violated *their* end of the bargain by putting this girl on trial. You know any Gayden found is supposed to be sent to us."

Someone made a shushing sound.

What was this? An island full of Nips? An agreement with the Council? Gayden?

"She used the stolen magic in front of over a hundred humans. The Council didn't have a choice but to bring her in. Surely you can understand that? Too many people found out," Sárkány said.

A chair scooted backward, scraping along the floor as Finch stood. Finch leaned forward, placing his palms on the table. "Then perhaps ours will be forced as well. It isn't *our* problem the Council refuses to make our treaty public. We'll not help you look for her."

"You know as well as I do if the whereabouts of your island became public, wizards and humans would descend upon you in mass. The Council may have agreed to a peace, but the rest have not."

Finch stood straight, placing his hands on his hips. "You know as well as I do the fate of your Magicians if they attack my island, but hey, if you want to test your luck, it's your funeral."

A chair scratched along the floor as Sárkány rose. "Finch, be reasonable. Surely the safety of your people as well as mine is worth more than that of one little girl."

"Perhaps."

"If she comes to you?" Sárkány asked, the hint of a threat hanging on the question.

"If she's a Gayden, she'll be welcome."

"Then we may indeed have to pay your little island a visit. Since we're cut off, you no longer have the protection of the Council."

Finch laughed, the sound all menace. "Surely you realize it was your kind the Council was protecting. Not us. Good day."

Finch's footsteps crossed behind Charlie followed by the ringing of the bell as he stormed out. Out of the corner of her eye, she caught sight of Finch turning to the left.

"That went as expected." Charity flung an arm toward the retreating Finch.

"Yes." Sárkány returned to his seat.

"What next, Logan?" Sárkány asked the other man who'd came in with them.

"I don't know if she'll go to the island. From the reports, the Experimenter sent before the Veil closed, this one was brand new. She knew nothing about our world or magic."

"I'm telling you that girl isn't a Nip," Charity said.

"Enough of this. It doesn't matter, Charity. If she caused this much destruction, the Experimenter will want her. Any word on fixing the Veil?" Logan asked.

"No. From the reports I'm getting from our side, it seems it's locked tighter than a nun's hoochie on Christmas. We can't unseal it," Sárkány said.

"If she is a Nip, then we have a bigger problem. The magic she stole will be slipping by now. If she is the only one who can unseal it, she has to be found soon." All three chairs scooted across the floor.

"Right. That's why she needs to be found as soon as possible. Alive. Put a watch on the island. If she shows, let us know. Come," Logan said.

Charlie breathed a sigh as the bell rang. They disappeared, going in the opposite direction of Finch.

Less than a minute after the threesome left, Perdita rushed past Charlie running straight into Ora who'd just stepped into the diner.

Chapter Thirty-Four
Ora

Two weeks passed at Aryiana's much the same way every day. I ruminated in the morning, but not as long. I learned how to go into my state of peace with all different genres of music and the most difficult of all—in total silence. I had more energy than ever before, and my constant worrying over the future had lessened. During the moments of rumination, the universe revealed her secrets, but once I returned to reality, the clarity escaped my attention, as if running around a corner every time I looked for it. After rumination, I did a few hours of yoga and lifted weights. The softness of my body lessened, becoming leaner and strong. The shine returned to my hair. The fullness returned to my face. Before, it had a slight roundness of childhood, but the face that stared back at me now was a woman's.

Each day, my control of my magic climbed. I finished up the rest of the day practicing magic in Aryiana's back yard or she made me travel through the Bridge. Now, I could start and stop fires both big and small. My favorite "little trick," as Aryiana called it, was making a flaming ball of fire float between my hands like I'd seen in movies. Small burns lined my arms. Living proof that while I may have magic, I'm far from fireproof.

"With Ember, you have to always be aware of protecting yourself, making sure the molecules forming your own skin don't move around, too, catching on fire." Aryiana bounced a ball of flame from one hand to the other. "Did you finish making your sword?"

"Yes, but it broke as soon as I tried to cut the log. The metals were too soft." I shot an icicle into a nearby tree as it embedded in four inches in. I'd have to fix that later.

Over the Bridge

"Did you use the wrong types of metal?"

I shrugged. "No offense, but I'm blindly pulling metals from the earth, it's not like I know what kind of metal it is."

I turned my attention to a small bush, which pulled itself from the ground, stumbling around on its roots like a crippled man missing his cane.

"You'll get better. By the way, did you ever find my shutter?"

A blush creeped from my neck, warming my cheeks. My little dip into Tempest magic had been a bit too vigorous. "No. No, I didn't."

She clinched her fist, extinguishing the fire ball with a hiss, and wiped off her burn-free palms. "No worries. I'll buy a new one. You can take me."

The icicle melted as my power knitted the opening in the tree, leaving a slight discoloration to the bark behind. "I'm guessing you don't mean in the car."

"Nope. Bridge time!"

As I'd learned when I'd first got to Aryiana's, the Shadow Land was the Veil. As my power had closed it off, it became a potential place, connecting realms and places. My psyche could travel there as well as my physical body. Using yet another part of my magic, I practiced opening and closing it. Traveling physically required knowing where you wanted to go. Sometimes I'd let Aryiana lead me while I kept the power flowing around us. While other times I'd lead and follow the sounds of Mom's voice. They were still with Fox but were going to move into the city.

The following morning when I got to the kitchen, Aryiana waited for me, with my packed bags on her table. "You kicking me out?"

"Yes, my dear. It's time for you to go."

I nodded. "Am I ready?"

"You'd better be. Come, let's go to the back yard."

I stepped to the back door, paused, turned to observe her welcoming kitchen. How many others had stayed here? Did my mother eat at the same table?

Questions I'd couldn't bring myself to ask. Perhaps one day, when all this was over. If I'd learned enough, now that life pulled me back to my destiny. Prophecy or not, I needed to get back to my group and wherever the future would lead us.

Aryiana made a small sound behind me. Silent tears ran down her face. I hugged her without saying anything. Part of me wanted to ask her what she saw in my future, but a bigger part didn't want to know.

"Here, you might need these." She handed me a baseball cap and a letter. I thanked her and slipped them into my bag.

We walked into the back yard. We hugged once more. "Thank you for everything."

"My pleasure, child."

I opened the Bridge as I'd practiced. The screams still sent chills down my spine. I pivoted in Aryiana's direction to ask a question. Before I could even open my mouth, she said, "You'll help them when it's time."

I nodded, trying to make myself believe her words, and with a shaky breath, I stepped through the Bridge into the Shadow Land, listening, as I'd practiced. Mom's voice appeared louder than the others, and I moved in her direction. Each step brought me closer to her. Closer to my fate. Darkness closed in around me, and Jiminy's familiar presence lingered not far from me. "Hey, stranger," I said. I hadn't felt him in all the times I'd traveled with Aryiana.

"Hello yourself."

"Where were you?"

"Away."

The darkness faded into shadows, brightening into the front a quaint café. The front façade featured a faded red brick, large glass window with a hand-painted mug on the window, and inside several old diner tables. I pivoted the Bridge opening, checking for on-comers, finding no one, and stepped out, leaving the world in-between, arriving at the front entrance. The Bridge closed behind me. A quick glance around revealed an empty city street I didn't recognize. As I opened the door, a bell rang signaling my entrance.

Over the Bridge

The delicious aroma of fresh burgers and greasy fries hit my nose, making my mouth water.

Mom pushed through the door. A smile spread on her face as she bumped into me. She threw her arms around me. "Oh, Aryiana said you'd be here."

"No time," Sabrina said, pushing past us. "Which way?" Sabrina faced Charlie, who pointed down the street to my right.

Damien followed, pulling on Jeremiah's arm, following Sabrina and Charlie. Jeremiah's expression—a mixture of intense sorrow and rage, frightened me more than anything else had.

Arameus emerged from the diner, patting Jeremiah on the shoulder. "Now is not the time."

"But she's right there," Jeremiah said, spittle flying. "She has to pay!"

"She will. I promise, but not right now." Damien held Jeremiah's elbow, firm, but not hard. Jeremiah's arm relaxed, and he turned toward the right, away from the unknown she.

"Will someone tell me what's going on?" I asked. Mom put her arm around me, leading me toward the others. "This way. We'll explain soon."

Chapter Thirty-Five
Sabrina

SABRINA RAN OUT OF THE café and headed in the direction Charlie pointed. "Tell me what you know. Fast!"

Charlie struggled to keep up. Perdita and Ora brought up the rear. Charlie spoke up so everyone could hear. "That guy's name is Finch. He's a Nip. Charity and Sárkány and some guy named Logan met with him asking about Ora."

"What did he say?" Sabrina asked. They rounded the corner of the street, hoping they didn't lose him in the crowd.

"Said he didn't know anything about her, and there is an island of Nips. The Council knows about it and has a secret treaty with them."

Sabrina skidded to a halt, pausing in her haste to stare at Charlie. "I was on Quad One. I never heard of a secret treaty. Or any island of Nips."

"Yes, because governments so readily tell everything to the minions who enforce their laws."

Sabrina bristled at Charlie's comment. "Let's go."

She marched forward, jumping as someone spoke from down an alley.

"Was wondering if you all were going to follow me." Finch leaned up against the building with one leg propped up. The man had short graying hair, a scar across his forehead, and soulful brown eyes with a mouth pulled up in a mocking smile.

Sabrina's magic rose instinctually, but her experience with Damien had taught her nothing if not to be cautious around Nips.

Finch's cocky smile widened. "You going to speak or what?" Sabrina couldn't quite place his accent. It wasn't exactly French but had a similar slowness to it.

"I, uh…sorry," Ora stammered, running her hands down her tie-dyed t-shirt and over her shining, long red hair.

Finch turned his attention from her, reaching into the pocket of the light blue dress shirt. Sabrina's power tingled at the edge of her control, ready to strike. He noticed, meeting her eyes, and slowly pulled out a cigarette from a crumpled pack, and popped it into his mouth. With his other hand, he struck a match against the brick wall behind him then put it to the cigarette, lighting it, and took a deep puff. He blew the smoke out of the side of his mouth, and his attention returned to Ora. "I haven't got all day, girl."

Her head snapped up, determination blazing in her eyes. "Right. My name is Ora. I'm the girl…"

"The girl they were looking for? Yeah, guessed that much. Question is what do you want with me?" He looked at his watch and took another long draw off his cigarette.

"I want your help to take down the High Council." Sabrina's mouth dropped open at Ora's words.

He choked on the smoke and then laughed. "Damn, girl. You are interesting."

"I'm serious."

He shook his head, still grinning. "I know you are. That's why it's so funny, and why does a little witch like you want to take down the big, bad wolf?"

Sabrina stilled. *He knows she's not a Nip?*

"Yes, hot stuff," Finch winked. "I can tell she's no Gayden. But you have magic inside you. A good bit of it too. Based on that alone, I shouldn't consider helping you, but I must say you've raised my curiosity."

"Ora, how do you even know you can trust him?" Sabrina shifted, pushing Charlie farther behind her, shielding them all.

Ora pushed past her, undeterred, and held up her hand at Sabrina's unspoken protest.

"At first I wanted revenge." Ora pushed farther to the head of the group, shoulders straight, head held high.

Finch cocked an eyebrow. "Revenge? For what?"

Perdita said, "She was arrested and accused of being a Nip. She forgot she was a witch."

He raised one eyebrow. "Gayden."

"Um, what?" Perdita arched her brow.

"Nip is the Magician's term for us. It's insulting. They call us thieves. When, in fact, we are the Gayden. Guardians of humanity from Magicians. Their term is derogatory."

"Oh, like a racial slur," Charlie asked.

"Exactly. Now how does someone forget they're a witch?"

Perdita said, "I blocked her powers with an amulet and spelled her."

"She's still got the amulet." Finch lifted his chin, gesturing toward the necklace.

Ora put her hand over Perdita's forearm. "I lost the amulet. It's a long story. But in the end, I stood trial and was found guilty, and sentenced to the Kassen. I managed to escape, but when we were ambushed while trying to get back through the Veil... During the fight, my fiancé—" Her voice caught. "John was killed."

Finch let his foot drop into the dirty concrete. "Fiancé? How old are you, girl?"

"Eighteen."

"You want to take down the High Council over the loss of your puppy love?" He shook his head, flicking the cherry from the cigarette, and tossed it down the alleyway. "Good day to you."

He sidestepped, trying to push past them, but Sabrina would have none of it. She planted her feet. "You need to hear her out!"

His jovial manner disappeared. He rose to his full height of six feet. The only way past was through them. He'd cornered himself down a blocked alley with only a pungent, overflowing trash bin and the scattering of boxes and filthy blankets. Without the woody sweet twang of his cigarette, the overwhelming aroma of rotting fish mixed with sour urine filled the alleyway.

Over the Bridge

Finch squared his shoulders as if ready to barrel through their group.

Ora put her hands together, as if in prayer. "It wasn't puppy love. He was my best friend's brother. I knew him my entire life, and he was a good man. He didn't deserve to die." She paused, an unsure expression crossing her face. "I didn't deserve to be arrested, tortured, and left to starve in the Nook, or almost executed."

At her words, he deflated. "Fine. Get to the point."

Ora relaxed. "Like I said, it started as a need for revenge. But I found out my parents are Geminates and were born and raised as slaves to a mad man trying to fulfill a prophecy."

"This same man is kidnapping Nips, I mean Gayden, to make them do his bidding," Jeremiah growled from behind. Sabrina half turned, not daring to take her eyes off Finch. Jeremiah stepped from around the corner. Damien followed with Arameus right behind.

"Who are you people?"

"I apologize. We didn't want to overwhelm you, so we stayed back. I'm Arameus Townsend. I'm a Tempest, and in my former life, I was a Defender."

"Jeremiah McAlister." Jeremiah stretched out his hand, surprising Sabrina with the confidence in which he spoke to the strange man. Finch bristled at the young man before squeezing the offered hand once.

"It seems introductions are in order. I'm Ora Stone. This is my mother, Perdita."

Charlie gave a little wave. "Charlie McCurry. Lowly human, at your service."

"You're not lowly. Stop saying that." Ora elbowed her friend in the side.

"It was your brother who died?" Finch asked.

"Yes, sir." Her voice fell, as she rubbed her arm, not meeting the stranger's intent stare.

Ora gestured toward Sabrina. "You're up."

Sabrina flicked her long braid behind her back.

"Sabrina Sun. Naiad. Former Protector. Quad One."

Finch's eye narrowed. "Protector, huh? So what do you know of the treaty?"

"Nothing."

Finch's head cocked at this before turning his attention back to Jeremiah. "You were kidnapped?"

Jeremiah stuck his chest out. "Yes. Master kidnapped hundreds of Gayden. My brother and I were taken two years ago. Ora helped me escape."

Finch gestured to Damien with his chin. "What's your story?"

Damien's face hardened. "Name's Damien Snider. I've been serving Master since I was four. I was arrested for stealing a witch's magic. After being found guilty, Master faked my execution. He took me in and convinced me my family wouldn't want me."

"They prosecuted a four year old?" Finch's hands balled into fists.

Ora hushed him as an elderly couple walked by.

Finch lower his voice, but the harsh tone remained. "How old are you now, boy?"

Damien shrugged, raising his eyebrows. "You know how aging is different in Conjuragic. With traveling across the Veil, not to mention celebrating birthdays for Nips, uh, Gayden wasn't a priority, I'd have to say maybe nineteen."

Finch spun and kicked a rock down the alleyway. "The treaty had been in place long before that. The Council violated it."

"Maybe we should take this somewhere a little more private," Sabrina said through gritted teeth.

Ignoring her, Damien said, "Of course we knew nothing about a treaty or of any Gayden other than those under his command. The ones he rescued, like me, were more than happy to serve him. But he had trackers who located Gayden and took them from their homes."

Finch's eyebrows rose, his gaze flicking between Damien to Jeremiah and back again. "Did the Council know of this?"

Sabrina shrugged her shoulders. "Definitely not."

"How did you find the children?"

Over the Bridge

"I'm not sure. I heard they tracked known Gayden and went after their relatives who they tested. When they found a confirmed Gayden, the trackers handed them over to Master. If those Gayden resisted and didn't serve willingly, well eventually they had—accidents." Damien ran a hand through his hair, eyes troubled as if remembering the horrors he'd seen.

"But they were your kind! How could you stand by while they were being killed?" Finch raised his fist.

Damien rose to his full height. "You don't think I know that? You don't think I regret it? At the time I thought they were stupid. I thought he was the only wizard in the world who would protect us, and if they didn't serve him, the Council would kill them anyway. I was wrong, okay?"

"Gentlemen." Sabrina stepped between them, magic stirring, preparing for the fight brewing. She shoved it back, knowing it wouldn't help her if these two Nips started fighting. "That'll be enough of that."

"What happened to the kids who were taken if they weren't Gayden?" Perdita asked, white faced.

The men glanced at her. Damien's jaw clenched. "I don't know." A chill swept through their group as if collectively they knew those other children hadn't been returned home. The two men stepped back.

Finch broke the uneasy silence. "Okay, fine. What's changed then?"

Damien gestured with his chin toward Ora. "Her."

Her cheeks flushed red. To her credit, Ora kept her eyes fixed on Finch.

"What about her?"

"I held those two." Damien gestured toward Arameus and Sabrina. "Before she captured me."

Finch's eyes opened wide in surprise. "You captured this big guy?"

Ora flushed a deep shade of red. "Guilty."

"You didn't kill him?"

Ora stiffened, shifting her gaze to Perdita.

"No, she didn't." Damien smiled, staring at Ora as if she were a priceless jewel. "She tried to reason with me, but I wouldn't budge. She chose to release me, but a Tempest Hunter ambushed us. Went by Taylin."

"Charity's Taylin?" Finch laughed, big and loud. "So that's what happened to her face."

"Ora didn't do that." Sabrina scowled, unsure why she had to clarify that, but she didn't want this Finch guy to think Ora had done that.

Finch continued to laugh. "Serves her right, whoever did it. Then what?"

Damien flushed. "I'd already started to see how different Ora is from any witch I'd ever met. Then with what happened to Jeremiah's brother, everything changed."

Finch wrinkled his forehead, shooting a questioning look at Jeremiah.

Jeremiah recounted his brother's tale along with their capture. Finch listened motionless with his face contorting in anger every so often.

Sabrina touched Jeremiah's arm. When she realized what she'd done, she jerked her hand away as if she'd been burnt. What would Leigh think if she saw how soft Sabrina had become?

Ora cleared her throat. "So, like I said, revenge, but I realize the problem goes so much deeper than that. This man who calls himself Master has to be stopped. He's forcing witches to have Geminate children. He is raising these children as slaves. He's kidnapping your kind to do his bidding, and no one seems to know what his ultimate plan is. People shouldn't be killed because of what they are. The Council cannot let this continue to happen. Things have to change, and I could use your help."

Finch pinched the bridge of his nose and sighed. He didn't say anything, but pulled out another cigarette, lit the match, and inhaled, taking as much smoke as he could. He let it out while they waited for his answer. Finch's gaze flicked to each of them, he finished his cigarette, and said, "It won't be up to me. You'll have to present your case to the Elders. They will be the ones to decide to help you or not."

Ora smiled. "You'll take us there?"

Finch shook his head, pushed past them, and strolled down the street muttering, "I must be crazy."

When no one moved, he stopped and yelled, "Come on! I hope you have money because I'm not buying your plane tickets."

Ora's smile widened. "Actually, I have a better idea."

"What?" Sabrina asked.

"We're going to go through the Bridge," Ora said.

Perdita crinkled her forehead, not knowing what Ora meant either. "Bridge?"

"Yes. Remember when I took us from the club to the forest?"

Sabrina had been told of this but had no first-hand memory of it. Perdita nodded.

"The Bridge is the Veil. I can open it, but not to everyone, and form the Bridge, letting us travel from one place to another. Hundreds and hundreds of miles. I learned it with Aryiana."

Aryiana. There was that name again. Who was this woman?

"You must have lost your damn mind!" Finch shook his head, backing away.

"Will you all trust me? We're going to hold hands and go for a little walk." Ora reached for Finch's hand. "You just have to lead once we're in there because I don't know where your island is."

"Absolutely not. Walk into a black hole, teleporting. Must think I'm stupid," he muttered to himself, walking away.

"Come on, guys. We'll be there in a few minutes instead of hours. It will be so much easier." Ora stared at all the skeptical faces. "I've done this like fifty times. I know what I'm doing."

"Nope!" Finch pushed his way past Sabrina.

Damien caught up with him. "Hey, man. It's free."

At this, Finch paused. "Free you say?" He crossed his arms, bobbing his head, and pointed it at Ora. "I like free. But if I die, I'm going to haunt you to the end of your days."

Ora frowned, jerking her finger at Damien. "Oh, but you'll listen to him." She huffed, spinning around, red hair flying. "Whatever. Come on." She stomped farther down the dark alley.

"Ora," Arameus muttered, "don't you think it'll be suspicious all of us disappearing down a dark alley?"

"More suspicious than opening a black hole surrounded by a rainbow in the middle of a crowded street?"

"Hmmm. I suppose not," Arameus admitted.

"All right. Stand back everyone, and remember, hold hands and don't let go. Finch, you know what you have to do?"

"No, not really." His hands trembled.

"All you have to do is concentrate on home. Listen for someone you know, then follow the sound. Besides, I have a sort of guide if you get lost."

Without waiting for their reply, Ora focused on the brick wall at the end of the alley, irises swirling in a kaleidoscope of colors. The fabric between realms opened wide. The wind whipped through the narrow spaces between the buildings, sending bits of paper and dirt flying. What Ora called, the Bridge opened. Everyone stepped back. The thick scent of ozone drowned out the stench of trash. Sabrina's pulse raced. The smell reminded her of home, of the Veil, but she'd never seen it like this. Only the edges sparkled like the Veil. The middle of the large circle held no color as if swallowing the light.

Ora reached a hand backward, Finch hesitated, but Arameus shoved him forward. He clasped her hand. Arameus grabbed the other, reaching for Perdita. The group formed a chain, holding one another's hands. Ora said, "Here we go." She stepped forward, disappearing into the abyss.

"Shit! What was I thinking?" Finch paused as if he would let go, but stepped forward, disappearing. Perdita followed holding onto Charlie, then Damien and Jeremiah stepped through. Sabrina brought up the rear, hope rising in her. Maybe she could go home, one day. She crossed the threshold and relaxed as the darkness swallowed her up, but no pain came, and Jeremiah's sweaty palm still held hers.

Over the Bridge

A strange voice in the dark said, "Everyone is in."

"Who is that?" Perdita asked, panic in her voice.

"Quiet!" Ora said. "Finch. We have to change places. Are you concentrating?"

"Yes."

After a minute, Jeremiah's hand pulled her, and Sabrina stepped forward. Each step took effort, like marching through water, and this substance wouldn't move away from her the way she could push water away.

Ora's voice spoke near her, but in this place, she could've been anywhere. "Good, now I want you to concentrate and focus on the sound of something familiar, something from home. Got it?"

Finch didn't say anything, but Sabrina thought they shifted direction. They walked and walked. With each step, Sabrina felt they weren't going anywhere, like being on a treadmill.

Finch spoke, startling her, breaking the silence of the Bridge. She couldn't even hear herself breathe. "This way. Jesus, it's so thick in here," Finch complained.

"I know. Jiminy, help him," Ora said.

"Who the hell is Jiminy?" Finch asked. A scent rose from the darkness, like cinnamon and warm baking bread. Relaxation seeped through her muscles, and they picked up speed.

"Is it just me, or anyone else hear screaming?" Charlie's voice reached them through the darkness.

"Those are the people trapped in here," Ora said.

"Unbelievable." Sabrina's stomach rolled.

Ora said, "I'm going to help them. Once I figure out how."

"Will you two shut up! I'm trying to concentrate so we can get the hell out of here!" Finch said.

"Sorry," Ora said.

"We're close," Finch said. At his words, the darkness lightened. Shadows formed, and the fogginess thinned. Sabrina jogged now, keeping up with the others, all excited to leave this place. She should probably be scared, too. Going to a place full of Nips, but it had to be better than this Bridge inside the Veil.

The edge appeared a few feet ahead. Finch stopped. Ora ran into him.

"There a problem?" Arameus asked. Sabrina could see everyone now. Just beyond them, a bright light shown and didn't hurt her eyes.

Finch asked, "What do I do now?"

Ora pushed Finch through the Veil. Ora jumped out after him. The rest followed. Sabrina's foot sank into a soft, squishy surface, reminding her of home. The sun blinded her, but she kept going, shielding her eyes from the sun. As her eyes adjusted, she gazed backward at the Bridge and spotted someone lingering at the edge of the opening. Whoever it was disappeared along with the Bridge shrinking to nothing.

Sabrina scanned her new surroundings. White sand extended for miles. White, frothy foam waves rolled along the edges leading out to an ocean of sweet, deep blue. Rows and rows of empty bungalows ran along the dunes just beyond the beach. Charlie and Ora gazed wide-eyed. Finch struggled to his feet, brushing sand from his blue jeans. Even Finch's swearing couldn't spoil the moment or the beauty of the beach. He finished beating the sand from his pants, straightened, opened his arms wide, and said, "Welcome to Gayden Island."

Chapter Thirty-Six
Perdita

THE ISLAND STRETCHED LONG AND narrow. In some places, Perdita could see across to the other side. She guessed it to only be about a mile wide. The beach glittered with white sand tinged with light pink accenting the long boardwalks and the series of bungalows behind the dunes.

Not a cloud floated in the sky while the sun beat down warmth upon Perdita's back. The salty sea breeze blew her loose blond hair. Arameus helped Charlie to her feet, and Sabrina gazed out into the sea as if wanting to run out into the water as if her heart wrestled with homesickness. Finch scowled, un-phased by the beauty of the island, and wiped swept off his brow. "Damn heat."

"Finch," Perdita asked, "where exactly are we?"

"What?" His face relaxed. "Oh right. Feròs Zile. An island in the Bahamas."

"The Bahamas!" Ora and Charlie squealed together and ran to each other, screaming in childish delight, jumping up and down. "We're in the Bahamas!"

"Oy vay!" Finch shook his head as Charlie and Ora ran up and down the beach squealing.

"Girls!" Sabrina barked in her lieutenant's voice. "We're not here on vacation. Stop acting like blubbering teenagers."

Arameus crossed his arms, watching them with a faint smile upon his face. "Come on Sabrina, let them have a little fun."

"They *are* blubbering teenagers." Perdita laughed, enjoying the brief flash of Ora's former carefree nature.

The girls' smiles vanished. "Sabrina's right, at least for now. The island will be on high alert with our appearance." Finch motioned for them to follow him.

They crossed the boardwalk, and a small child peeked around the corner, spying on them. The young girl could be no more than four. The sweet, long-haired girl slid back out of sight at their approach. The curtains at different houses fell back into place as they advanced farther into the town. The wooden boardwalks gave way to paved streets with small buildings made with white and gray stones. Large towers broke up the monotony at various locations with an abundance of restaurants, shops, a hardware store, and a mom-and-pop's grocery shop.

The tallest building loomed in the center of the island. With its steep angles and large arched windows and a large steeple on the front, Perdita guessed the place used to be a church. At the very back of the building, a tall, circular tower extended high into the sky, reflecting rays of the sun from either a mirror or large window. Finch led them toward the old church. As they neared, Perdita read the sign above the entrance: Town Hall. The place would've been welcoming if an olive-skinned man wouldn't have emerged from the double wooden doors holding a shotgun over his shoulder. The stranger narrowed his dark eyes as they approached. Being medium height and build did nothing to diminish the sense of foreboding.

The man sneered. "Outlaw, there better be a good reason you're bringing Magicians on our island."

"Relax, Wade. They're here to talk." Finch didn't break stride as he approached. The shotgun gave Perdita pause.

"So they say." Wade swung the gun off his shoulder and pointed it at Ora. "There's something off about this one. That one too." He casually waved the weapon toward Perdita.

"I'm aware. They have requested an audience with the Elders and are here as my guests. There are what, four Magicians, two Gayden, and a human? I think we can take them if push comes to shove." Finch jogged up the three steps to the porch and pushed the gun to the side. Wade risked taking his eyes off Ora to glare at Finch.

"What's this about, Finch?" Sabrina's body tensed, gesturing with her chin at Wade.

Finch shrugged. "He's not going to be a problem."

Wade relaxed the shotgun over his shoulder. "You better hope so, Outlaw."

Charlie asked. "Outlaw?"

Finch glanced back. "It's my last name."

Ora smirked, breaking the tension. "Your name is Finch Outlaw?"

"Right!" Charlie said.

Wade clicked his tongue. "There something wrong with them?"

Finch's lips twitched. "That is yet to be determined."

Finch nodded at Ora. "This one is a Magician commanding the four cores, and an enemy of Conjuragic. She has an interesting tale to tell." He dipped his head toward the man. "This is Wade Deaver, my second in command."

Wade's eyes bulged. "Did you say four cores?"

"That's right." Ora didn't back down from the challenge.

He looked away first, eyes scanning the rest of them, before stopping on Perdita. "What about you?"

"My name is Perdita Stone. I'm her mother and a Geminate. Tempest and Naiad. Nice to meet you."

"Jesus Christ, Outlaw. Are you freaking kidding me?" Wade gripped the barrel of the gun, knuckles white. "What about the Magicians? And the traitor Gayden with them."

Damien crossed his arms, rising to his full six feet. "Damien Snider."

"Jeremiah McAlister."

"For the record, we aren't traitors. They got to brainwash me since age four. Jeremiah was kidnapped. You were what? Thirteen?"

"Fourteen," Jeremiah clarified. "Don't ever call me a traitor again. You got that, mister?"

Wade looked at Finch, and they shared an unspoken communication. Finch mumbled, "Mmm hmm."

"Gotcha." Wade looked at Charlie. "Who might you be?"

Charlie shrugged. "Just the human best friend. Nothing special."

"Charlie." Ora raised her eyebrows.

"This should be interesting. Come on." Wade adjusted the gun over his shoulder and entered the building.

Here goes nothing, Perdita thought.

They took their first steps inside the building and toward the future.

Inside the building, the dimness made a stark contrast to the bright sunlight outside. The aroma of lemon furniture polish mixed with candle wax took Perdita back to the few times she had taken Ora to church as a child. The walls held only a few portraits of the town in different eras and a map of the island.

Farther inside the stone building, Wade led them through two more double doors into the meeting hall. Multiple rows of wooden pews divided by a central aisle led to the front of the room. Three steps lined with maroon carpet led to the higher level, more pews facing the others, and an altar. This building had definitely been a church. Men and women scattered around the edges, all brandishing weapons, with tense faces. Perdita's back stiffened. On an island full of Gayden, their power to take magic was way worse than any gun.

Four men and two women sat behind the altar, not speaking, but regarding them as Finch led them up the aisle. The Elders? They varied in age and body size, but none younger than fifty. All dressed in island clothes.

Finch dipped his head in a slight bow. "I apologize with this abrupt, unannounced visit."

An old man with a raspy voice, dark skin, and long, bushy eyebrows interrupted him. "Yes, Finch. We weren't expecting you back for a least a day. How did you get back so soon?"

"I know. I had the meeting with Sárkány. It seems the Veil is indeed sealed—well, of sorts. He asked for our help. He said there had been a trial on an unknown Gayden."

Over the Bridge

"A trial?" An old woman with white hair, dark skin, and a large crooked nose interrupted Finch.

"Yes. Their cover story is they couldn't bring the accused to us because the stolen magic had been flaunted publicly."

"A clear violation of the treaty." The bushy eyed old man banged his fist upon the chair in outrage.

"Indeed," Finch agreed. "The accused, Miss Ora Stone here," he gestured to Ora, "was found guilty and sentenced to the Kassen."

The Elders' focus shifted to Ora. The hair on Perdita's arms stood on end. Power rose in the room, opposite and defiant.

"But she is no Gayden." The old man's eyes narrowed, and the strange power vibrated around him.

"Easy, Winslow." Finch side-stepped, blocking Ora from his sight.

"No, I'm not." Ora leaned to the right, looking around Finch, who moved out of her way.

"I escaped with the help of an oxygenian by the name of Lailie, another victim of the man who calls himself the Experimenter. She told me she was a descendant of Tituba, the first Ni—, Gayden. I owe her my life." She paused, back straightening. "My mother and my fiancé traveled to Conjuragic in hopes of rescuing me. During an attempted break in at the Nook, my mother, Perdita," she gestured toward Perdita, who nodded in acknowledgement, "befriended Lailie. Her soul was released when she helped me. She's at peace now."

"Why is this our concern?" Winslow asked. The other Elders nodded.

Ora retold her story yet again. When she'd finished, the Elders talked amongst themselves with murmuring from the security around the room.

"What did you destroy?" Finch asked through the chatter.

The room grew quiet, waiting for her reply. "I don't know exactly, but it felt alive somehow."

"You destroyed the Unity Statue." An emptiness settled in Sabrina's eyes. "You sent out a ball of magic in the direction of the Guidance Hall. There was an explosion, and afterward, the lifeforce of the city died. The city of light went dark and started to crumble. The man I love was in that building."

Ora's faced turned ashen.

The old woman asked, "You still stand by her side?"

Sabrina turned to Ora. "You weren't there. Your eyes changed. Glowing like those without control. When we got to the human world, you were lost to us for days. So many times, I wanted to kill you where you slept. But as I got to know you, I see now that you never would've done it on purpose. When you finally woke up, and I saw you crying on the riverbank, I knew your pain for John matched mine for Simeon. I knew he would've wanted me to help you because you reacted the same way I would have."

Sabrina faced the Elders. "I stand by her side because of her goodness, her kindness, and her bravery. I have watched her grow, and I urge you to consider her words."

Silence followed these words.

Ora cleared her throat. "When we got back to the human world, we rescued my best friend, Charlie. There were Hunters waiting for us. Since then, we have been finding people to train me to control my powers."

"What do you want from us?" a second man, younger with graying brown hair asked.

"Steve, let the girl speak," the old woman called.

"Okay, Aggie." Steve rolled his eyes.

Ora patted Damien on the back. "During my travels, I discovered the Experimenter is trying to fill a prophecy he'd heard many years ago, a prophecy that would give him the power to control all four cores. He has used many means to achieve his ends, creating Geminates and holding them prisoner. This is how my parents came to be, but nineteen years ago, they escaped him before I was born. I have the powers of Sphere, Tempest, Ember, and Naiad."

All the Elders straightened in their chairs. Ora continued before they'd stop her and demand they leave. "What's more important to you is he is collecting Gayden." She moved to Jeremiah, linking her arm through his. "Not only those who chose to join him, but he is seeking them out and kidnapping them as children. He has a whole army of them on his side, poised and waiting for his opportunity to strike."

"Nonsense."

"That can't be."

"It's impossible."

Words of denial flood the room. Jeremiah spoke up. "It's true. I'm living proof." Once again, he retold the story of his kidnapping. When he had finished, Damien stepped in front. "Mine is a slightly similar story."

When he described his trial, the Elders each swore, cursing the Council and the Experimenter.

"That is a clear violation of our treaty!" the second female Elder shouted, this one with hair as white as snow and shining blue eyes with pale skin.

"How many times has this happened?" Aggie asked Damien.

"Not too often. We barely have Nip trials." Arameus spoke up.

The Elders glared at Arameus. He flushed red under their scrutiny. "Sorry. I have only recently heard the term Gayden. Please excuse my ignorance."

Damien lifted an arm to get their attention. "Trials, no. But I've heard of the Council searching for them. If they find them, they are put to death without trial."

"What's this?" Winslow's lips thinned to a smooth white line.

"There are some who're found using their powers and instead of arresting them, the Council orders them put to death. Master sent his followers to find them first, but sometimes we didn't arrive in time."

Arameus covered his mouth with a hand. Sabrina asked, "What? I've never heard of this. We've always arrested them. According to our laws, if they are guilty they're to be executed, but not without trial. Arameus, you're a Defender. What do you know of this?"

Arameus held up his hands. "Nothing."

"Oh, there was a special group the Council sent." Damien shook his head.

"What of our treaty?" Steve gripped the sides of his chair with white knuckles.

Sabrina swallowed as sweat trickled down her back. "I knew nothing of a treaty. If the people of Conjuragic knew of this place, there would be a panic."

Arameus agreed. "The treaty is news to me as well."

"This isn't anything new." Aggie dismissed their words with a wave of her hand. "We knew the treaty was between the High Council, their closest advisors, and us. But if this is true, the Council violated the treaty."

Ora stepped forward as if she'd been waiting for this opportunity. "This is why we've come. What the Council and the Experimenter have done to your people, what they did to me must stop. They broke your treaty countless times, and the Experimenter used your people. The Geminates are his prisoners. Prejudice runs rampant in the magical realm against Gayden and Geminates. It has to stop. But as bad as the Council is, the Experimenter is even worse. He must be stopped. You asked Finch how he traveled here. I can open the Veil via a Bridge to go wherever I wish. It's under my control. I'm here to ask you and your people to help me cross over into Conjuragic. Fight with me, side by side, to take down the Council and find the Experimenter. Help me free his Gayden and the Geminates."

Her words hung in the air. The Elders looked to one another. They leaned closer to one another, whispering while Ora waited.

Winslow squared his shoulders, sitting straighter. "You've given us a lot of information. We ask you to give us the day to decide. You're welcome to stay here, enjoy the island, and we will give you our decision in the morning."

Perdita couldn't help but feel a bit of defeat. She thought after Ora's passionate explanation, they would've jump to their feet ready to join them. Naïve, but she'd hoped.

Ora bowed her head. "Thank you for your time and consideration."

They left the building without saying a word. The guards stayed out of the way. Finch led them to a section of bungalows. "You guys can stay here."

Over the Bridge

The two suites connected: one side for the girls and one for the boys. The faint teal walls held pictures of lighthouses and sailboats. White down blankets covered the double full-sized beds with light purple silk sheets underneath. The large bay windows overlooked the sea. Each room held a balcony with a sitting area of wicker chairs and table. A large stand-up shower with new tile and a jetted spa tub tempted Perdita in the bathroom. Seconds later, Charlie strolled in and squealed. "I can finally use a real bathroom!"

The sun dipped lower in the sky, close to dinner time. Perdita's stomach growled.

Finch returned with food and an assortment of bathing suits for them to choose from.

Ora raised her eyebrows as he handed her a suit.

He shrugged. "What? It doesn't look like you have had much fun, and this might be your only chance."

She took the suits, tossing them in the bathroom, and met everyone on the patio. Finch had brought them fresh fried fish sandwiches and homemade chips. Perdita enjoyed every bite of the flaky fish and didn't even mind the grease on her fingers.

After they finished the quiet meal, Ora and Charlie disappeared inside to find suitable bathing suits. Perdita and Sabrina followed the girls inside.

Ora handed Perdita a suit. Perdita waved her hands, stepping back. "Absolutely not."

Ora laughed. When Charlie picked up hers, she muttered, "A bikini, really? Don't these people believe in one pieces?"

"Shut up, Charlie," Ora teased. "You aren't fat, and it'll look great on you, so put on the suit and come swimming with me."

Sabrina emerged from the bathroom wearing her leather Protector's outfit. Perdita furrowed her brow, and Sabrina answered the questioning look. "Naiad, remember? Waterproof. Besides, I haven't got to feel like me in a while, and being on an island full of Gayden..." Sabrina shook her shoulders. "Man, that is going to take some getting used to. Anyway, being around an island of them is nerve wracking."

Ora paled, as if something unpleasant touched her. "Sabrina... I..."

She crossed the short distance between them, putting her arms on Ora's shoulders. "Don't. We're okay. Really."

"If I can help," Ora began, but Sabrina stopped her with a nod of the head.

"I know you will. Now come on, get that suit on and let's go for a swim." She opened a sliding glass door and ran to the beach. Arameus, Damien, and Jeremiah tossed a volleyball in the air on the beach. Sabrina ran past them and dove into the sea.

Ora sighed, stepped into the bathroom, and changed into a pretty pink and blue, rather revealing, bikini. Perdita wanted her to cover up but held her tongue.

Ora sighed. "Not my first choice, but all my goodies are covered." Charlie emerged with black boy shorts and a red top. Ora grabbed a couple towels and stepped through the sliding glass door, off the patio, and onto the beach.

Perdita watched from the patio table. Jeremiah and Damien played sand volleyball. As Ora approached, the volleyball landed with a soft *thunk* on the sand, rolling away forgotten, as Jeremiah and Damien stared. Arameus's gaze settled on Charlie, not covering her exposed abdomen. Last summer, she wouldn't have been able to fit in the suit, but now her legs stretched long and trim with a flat stomach.

The volleyball game restarted as the girls laughed when the water rushed over their legs. Perdita smiled, glad Finch had taken this time to let them unwind, and with that happy thought, she returned to their room for a quick power nap.

Chapter Thirty-Seven
Ora

THE SURF ROLLED OVER MY legs and my waist. The last of the sun's rays warmed my shoulders. I would've liked to lie on the beach and get a little tan. But again, perhaps not. The last time I'd laid out, I'd been with John. Part of me realized there would be certain things I could never do again without thinking of him. The loss of John crept up on me at quiet times like these.

A shadow fell over my right shoulder. Charlie settled beside me, eyes glistening, staring into the endless sea. "John would've loved it here."

I could only nod as the tears fought yet again to break through.

"Tell me about you two. How you got together. When?"

The boys resumed their volleyball match. The sky continued the spectacular cascade of colors as the sun set against the sky. As the sun faded underneath the horizon, I talked and talked about John. I felt the healing tendrils easing into my broken heart as I laid bare our secret relationship. Only one secret remained: the dream in the Shadow Land. I couldn't let the betrayal of seeing him with Strega affect her memory of him too.

We returned to the group. Sabrina finished her swim, emerging from underneath the waves like some mysterious mermaid, and her skin and hair shimmered like the waves. The guys had moved onto Frisbee. Mom joined us after Finch beat on the door and made her come out. She perched on a piece of driftwood talking to Finch, who piled pieces of wood in the center of a makeshift fire pit. He brought a cooler, and when we approached, he stopped and handed Charlie and me a Coke. I thanked him and popped the top of the can and took a large sip. I settled beside Mom in silence watching the waves crash along the shore. The air had grown colder, and I slipped on some soft jeans and a t-shirt Mom had brought out with her. The guys had given up playing games since darkness had fallen. Finch also had brought down an old boombox, which made me laugh.

He put on some music and attempted to light the bonfire, but he swore every two seconds as gusts of salty air kept blowing the pitiful fire out. Arameus grinned and Charlie swatted his arm. I took matters into my own hands, reached for my power, which galloped to me, wiggling, like a happy dog, and sent an arc of fire into the wood. It burst to life, engulfing us with light and warmth, and smiled as everyone stared.

"Haven't you been a busy little bee, off learning Ember magic." Arameus gave me a double thumbs up. The burdens weighing on all of our shoulders diminished tonight.

"Guess what else I can do." I rubbed my hands together.

What?" Arameus leaned in, reminding me of our many conversations in his office over good food.

"This." I jumped to my feet, turned around, and for flare, stomped my foot upon the sand. It rose fifteen feet into the air forming a detailed sand castle with towers, turrets, miniature shingles, and even small little flags. I turned back to my crowd and bowed as they clapped and hooted.

I returned to the driftwood and picked up a shawl, throwing it around my shoulders. "So what have you all been up to while I was away?"

Before anyone could speak, Finch excused himself to get us more drinks.

After he walked away, Mom spoke for the group. "Mainly Arameus and Sabrina gathered their strength back. I worked with them both to work on my control. Charlie learned some potion making from Fox."

I raised my eyebrows, and Charlie smiled. "As long as you have the right ingredients, it isn't hard. You don't even need magic."

"I looked through those potion books, and they looked hard to me."

"Oh, but Arameus helped me with some of the words. He was a big help." Charlie flushed red, and I stole a glanced at Arameus, who avoided my gaze. An awkward silence followed. Had I missed something?

Damien stoked the fire with a long stick. "Jeremiah and I talked a lot with Sabrina. They, um, might have had a little fight."

"A fight? Why would you do that?" It shouldn't really surprise me, he did almost kill her.

"Not me. Them two." He pointed at Jeremiah and Sabrina.

"Yes, but we worked it out." Sabrina shrugged and threw an arm around Jeremiah and rubbed the top of his head with her knuckles.

"Gerrooff!" Jeremiah laughed. I didn't know why, but I felt a little sad, as if in my short absence, I'd grown apart from the group.

"So why were you in a city?" I asked, realizing for the first time I didn't know where we'd been earlier. Could it really be the same day?

"We went with Fox to Nashville so he could sell his potions, and to get out of the woods for a while." Charlie twirled her hair.

"Wasn't he expecting you to come back?"

Damien laughed. "He must be a seer because he told us we weren't coming back, and then your mom agreed with him."

"No. Aryiana told me, and she's been speaking," she shot me a meaningful look, "to Fox as well." I knew exactly what she meant about speaking.

"I've always wanted to meet a seer," Arameus said.

I couldn't help but think of Aryiana. "They're certainly interesting."

"Speaking of seers, how did you manage to find Aryiana?" Mom pulled a light jacket over her shoulders.

Damien stared at me waiting for my answer, and I felt my face grow hot. "During my nightmares, my psyche traveled in the Bridge, and I saw her place during one of those nights. After our, um, training session," at least they had the audacity to look guilty, "she told me it was time to come."

Finch returned with more drinks. This time, he brought bottles of beer and liquor.

He lit a cigarette loading the cooler with the alcohol. "Yeah, you guys are supposed to be having fun, not gossiping. Let's get the party started."

He poured some of the liquor on the flames, and they shot higher into the air as everyone laughed. He cranked up the loud, techno beat music with hints of island drums. My kind of music—dancing music, which I never would've expected from Finch.

"Hold your horses, Frenchy Cowboy. You have to tell me more about this island."

Finch grabbed his chest in mock horror. "Frenchy cowboy? Muah?"

Damien waggled his finger at Finch. "Yes! That describes him. I've been trying to figure it out."

Charlie giggled. "As if a Frenchman grew up in Texas."

Finch batted a hand in the air. "Aghhh hell with all y'all. What do you want to know, missy?"

"Everything. How did you all come to live here?" All eyes turned on Finch.

"Not much to tell really. Tituba settled here after she escaped. The rest migrated here over time."

"But how come I haven't heard of this island?" Mom asked.

"That's an interesting question. The Magicians came over, all secret like, when they made the treaty with the Elders. We agreed to stay away, and they helped make our little island hidden from the world. They helped start the farms at the periphery of the island, Spheres of course, so we're able to grow about anything here. We have some animals around, so we're self-sufficient." He picked up a beer. "But we do get a lot of things shipped over from the main islands."

"That's amazing." Arameus leaned forward.

"I guess. Now come on, y'all. Let's dance." He turned up the volume as high as it would go.

Over the Bridge

We jumped from the driftwood and danced around the flames. I yanked on Mom's arm, but she wouldn't dance. After a song or two, she excused herself to the room. I expected Finch to follow, but instead he stayed, drinking bottle after bottle as his speech grew more slurred with every sip. Charlie and I danced together, laughing at him as he stumbled over his own feet.

As the evening grew later and the bottles emptier, our little group separated. Sabrina left us to sit by the sea as the waves washed over her legs. Finch and Jeremiah sat by the fire singing loudly and badly to a slow song. I leaned over to ask Charlie if she wanted to go to bed, only to find her dancing with Arameus, her head resting on his shoulder as they swayed back and forth. A wave of loneliness swept over me in surprise. I didn't say anything but walked down the beach.

I didn't understand my reaction and had to give myself some distance to figure it out.

"You like him, don't you?" A voice from behind startled me.

I let out a small scream of surprise. "Mannie, you scared me!"

"Mannie?" He gave me an odd look.

I shrugged. "I don't know. It's what I've been calling you in my head."

I looked away, but I caught his slight smile before I did.

He muttered, "I can handle that."

I found myself rather aggravated by him, spoiling my private time, and his prying. As if to further annoy me, he said, "You didn't answer my question."

"No, I didn't," I huffed, wishing he would go away.

"Then why did you walk away?" He gestured back toward the fire. "From them."

"To give them some privacy." The lie rolled off my tongue.

"Mmmm hmmm." He didn't believe me.

"Uhh, look, I don't know why I walked away. Okay?"

Damien grabbed my hand and spun me around to face him. I stared at his chest, not wanting to look up and meet his gray eyes. "Ora." He whispered my name, and my eyes met his without my permission.

"You're lonely." His breath smelled of mint.

I shrugged, unable to tear my eyes from his. The memory of his powers touching mine, so intimate, so forbidden, so—exciting crept into the forefront of my mind. My mouth dried while the beat of my heart pounded. His head bent, and I knew what he was going to do. Fear and anticipation paralyzed me. Only taking moments, but feeling like hours, his lips finally brushed mine.

Perhaps his powers slipped into mine again because that brief touch of his lips spread…everywhere. Running like an electric current, waking long slumbering parts of me, as my skin sizzled underneath his touch. More. I wanted more. I leaned into him, wrapping my arms around him so my fingertips grazed the small tangle of hair at the base of his neck. At last he opened his mouth, his tongue finding mine. I stood on my tiptoes, deepening our kiss as I ran my fingers into his blond hair. He moaned against my mouth, and before I lost myself completely, deep down in my consciousness, I kicked myself. *Hello! What about John?*

I pulled away, panting. "I'm sorry. I can't. I just can't." I spun and ran, ran like a coward and a cheater as fast as I could back to our room. Damien called my name, but I didn't stop as the door slammed shut behind me.

Chapter Thirty-Eight
Ora

THE FOLLOWING MORNING, I SAT on the bed of the bungalow, dumbfounded. The Elders turned us down. They didn't even have the decency to tell us to our face. No, they sent a hung over and red-eyed Finch to tell us at first light.

I couldn't say it surprised me. Asking for their help had been nothing but a long shot. Why I thought I could get a bunch of Gayden to go up against the whole of Conjuragic. They had a treaty and to risk their peace for…what exactly? I understood. I hadn't offered them anything in return.

But I'd hoped.

At least they listened to my argument, and if nothing else, we all needed last night. I'd needed last night—except for the kiss. I'd spent hours remembering it after I escaped into our room and fighting guilt. I'd started all of this because of John, and I'd kissed another man. Kissed him and enjoyed it. Reveled in it and wanted more. I'd called myself every possible bad name, but still my blood boiled whenever I remembered it. I pushed it to the back of my mind to deal with later.

"Where are we going to go now?" Charlie paused, stuffing a folded shirt into her backpack.

"Should we look for a Tempest? Or maybe Aryiana would take us in?" Mom brushed a lock of curling red hair behind my ear.

"No. If we were meant to go to Aryiana's, she'd have told us," I said.

"Maybe we could go to my grandparents'. At least we'd have some stability and could fight off the Hunters." Charlie shoved a pair of jeans into the bag.

"No. They're safe, but I'd understand if you want to go back with them." I tossed an extra pair of sneakers into my bag.

"No." Charlie turned toward the boys waiting outside for us. "I'm not going anywhere."

I bent over my bag, folding the clothes, and placing them inside. Charlie stepped up behind me, wrapped her arms around my neck, and hugged me.

"Maybe we should put this revenge business behind us." Charlie rested her head on my back.

The rustling of clothing halted as they awaited my answer. Tempting. Oh so tempting to give up, but I couldn't. Changing things in Conjuragic felt like my responsibility. After all, as the only one with the ability to control all four cores of magic, shouldn't I use my powers for something good instead of wasting it and hiding?

I straightened, disengaging myself from Charlie, slung the packed bag over my back, not saying a word, and stepping out of our bungalow. I strolled out to the beach, wiping at my eyes, and stared out at the endless water. The waves calmed me, and staring into the water felt like staring into infinity. I liked to think the water as a timeless entity that watched the comings and goings of humanity with an indifferent curiosity. The sounds of footsteps approached me along with the smell of a lit cigarette that floated past me, carried by the salty sea breeze.

I smiled in spite of myself. "Here to see us off?"

Finch turned his face away, trying to hide a scowl. "I can't say I agree with their decision."

Appreciation flooded through me. It took courage for him to stand in front of me and openly disagree with his people. "I know, but they are only doing what they think is right."

He crossed his arms over his chest, glaring toward town. "Easy for you to say. I think they're being cowards."

"They only want to protect their people." I patted his arm, but he stood as still as a statue. "Thank you for all your help."

"It should have been more." He scoffed, staring down at the sand, shaking his head.

Over the Bridge

More footsteps ran down the boardwalk. Jeremiah ran at full speed, his bookbag bouncing on his back. "Wait for me."

He skidded to a halt at my feet, sand flying over my shoes. "What're you doing?" I turned him around, pushing him back toward town. "You should stay here. They said you and Damien are welcome to stay here."

He fought me, managing to get out of my clutches. He backed away and faced me with a scowl. "You're not going without me."

"These are your people. They can teach you. Protect you. You could bring your family here."

"Listen, Ora, I might have the power of the Gayden, but I can't sit by and do nothing about what happened to Gabe. To me. To Damien. You're fighting for us, and I'm going to fight too."

"Jeremiah, I couldn't live with myself if something happened to you." Images of Gabe's death flashed behind my eyes.

"I couldn't live with myself if I stayed here and did nothing."

We stared at each other, his eyes pleading with mine.

Arameus joined us, bags in hand, and shielded his eyes from the brilliant sun. "Come on O, let him come. He's earned the right to decide for himself."

Jeremiah had been through more than I had. A prisoner for two years and countless injustices only to watch his twin murdered in cold blood just to make a point to Damien. "Oh, all right, but you'd better not die."

"I'll try not to." His lopsided grin melted any doubts. That boy was too cute for his own good.

Sabrina, Mom, Charlie, and Damien approached from the bungalows with somber, defeated faces. "All right, everyone. Let's go." I reached inside myself to open the Bridge when thunder crashed above me. I jumped. It couldn't be thunder. Moments before, the sky had been a clear baby blue with only scattered, white, fluffy clouds. In seconds, the sky darkened as large, black, angry clouds rolled toward us sending bolts of lightning rippling across the sky in rapid succession. The cracks of thunder shook the ground beneath my feet.

Magic swirled within the clouds. My own power reared to the surface, scanning, and finding the source of the foreign power deep in the ocean. A gigantic wave rose out of the depths forming a tsunami. Twenty feet above sea level, a woman rode the wave like a queen, spreading her arms wide, directing the unnatural surge of destruction toward the island.

Finch sprang into action, racing toward town. "Sound the bell! The Magicians are coming!" He jetted past the bungalows, rushing toward town.

Seconds later, the rest of us followed. Sabrina cat-called behind me, excited for action. My feet pounded upon the boardwalk. I slid to a halt, jerking open the sliding glass door to the bungalow, and slung my bookbag inside. "Charlie, get to the Town Hall. It'll be the safest place."

"She's staying with me," Arameus shouted.

Catching their stubborn expressions and held hands, I shrugged, pushing past them. "Keep her safe."

He put a protective arm around her. "With my life." The power inside me coiled, ready to strike, and I stroked it down. *Not him.*

"Not the time, Ora. It's time to fight." Sabrina peeked her head around the bungalow, eyes alight with excitement. She looked the same as I remembered her from our first encounter: aquatic blue leather and hair swept back in a braid. Her body tensed, on full alert—Protector mode. I only spared a half second to ponder how the hell she'd changed so fast.

Sabrina and I hauled ass toward the center of town, not looking back to confirm the others followed. At the front of Town Hall, Finch gathered the fighters, at least thirty men and women. Finch yelled orders to his well-oiled troops. "You three, get as many women, children, and elderly as you can in the shelters! You all, confirm the Elders are in the defensive chamber and stand guard! The rest of you with me to your stations! No mercy!"

The troops hollered, "Hurrah!"

"How many?" one of the group asked.

Over the Bridge

"I don't know, but be prepared for anything." Finch checked the magazines of various pistols strapped to his legs. A large automatic weapon I didn't have a name for rested over one shoulder.

"What can we do?" I screamed as I crossed the last few feet to his side.

Wade burst out of the Town Hall. His eyes turned down into slits when he spotted me. "This is all her fault. It's her they want. We should hand her over."

Guilt threatened to swallow me.

Finch pushed him to the side. "To your post, soldier."

Wade stood his ground. "The Elders voted no. We can still salvage the treaty. Just hand her over, Finch."

As unsurprising as his words were, they still stung. Mom and Sabrina stepped beside me, crossing their arms, blocking me from Wade. Sending him a clear message that they'd have to go through them first. The wind picked up behind me, blowing my hair forward. I shouted to be heard above the howling wind. "Don't you understand? The Veil is sealed. This isn't the Council. It's the Hunters, and with them, you have no treaty. I'll fight with you if you let me help."

Wade glared, but Finch held up a fist. "Of course you'll help. You all will. Arameus, to the towers—your magic will be amplified there. Sabrina, to the sea. Jeremiah, go with Wade to the mountainside, and you three, stay with me."

Finch's demands sent Sabrina and Arameus fleeing, Charlie in tow. A brief moment of panic rippled in me as my best friend left my side.

Wade gritted his teeth.

Finch's patience disappeared. He lifted a pistol, pointing at Wade's foot. "You either do as you're told, or I'll remove you from the equation. She can open the Veil. She could've disappeared at the first sign of trouble, but she didn't. You know she's more powerful than any Magician we've ever seen. We could use her on our side. Now go!"

Wade and I met each other's eyes and reached an unspoken understanding. This wasn't over. Wade jogged away, gun held at the ready, and Jeremiah followed him.

Finch pointed toward the largest tower of the Town Hall. "This way! Come on!"

Damien, Mom, and I followed Finch inside the Town Hall. We ran past the meeting hall where we pleaded our case only yesterday. We headed upstairs. At the end of a hallway, Finch pressed something, and the wall slid sideways revealing a secret stairwell. As we climbed, a loud bang and rumble shook the ground. I fell into the wall beside me. Something very big and powerful had hit the island. *The tsunami?*

"Hurry!" Finch screamed as I steadied myself. Behind me, Mom staggered to her feet, using my offered hand to right herself. We continued up the winding staircase. At the top, another loud boom shook the building. The wall behind us exploded into debris. Dust flew through the air, and a buzzing noise lingered in my ear.

Finch screamed at the people at the top, but I couldn't hear him. A quick glance revealed a circular room, one large window surrounding the room, like a lighthouse. Shoulder to shoulder, people stood in front of the window, overlooking the island at every angle. Gayden defending their home.

I squeezed in between two people. What I saw terrified me. Lightning bolts pelted the island. One after another. *Boom. Boom. Boom.*

The sky outside descended into a darkness as black as midnight. The tidal wave hovered above the island, poised to strike. Why wasn't it falling? I grabbed a pair of binoculars and searched the beach. Sabrina stood on one the dunes, hands held high, holding the wave back. The hairs on the back of my neck stood on edge to see the full strength of her power.

I pulled the binoculars up to search for the woman on the wave. I found her and another Naiad bobbing in and out of the water. I followed her with my eyes, but my power had other thoughts. The Sight opened, the full measure of its power overwhelming. I fought off the vertigo and let it take control. It flew away from me, like a snake cast out into the world. Hungry. Powerful. Ready to devour. The Naiad disappeared, and my magic shifted, anticipating where this stranger would appear next. As she appeared, my power seized a piece of seaweed. It wrapped around her body. Tighter and tighter, like a python choking its prey.

She flailed underneath it. The wave shrunk in size. The Naiad shifted her power away from the wave and into the seaweed. Water swelled inside, and it imploded, freeing her.

My magic and I moved in synchronicity. I couldn't tell if I controlled it or if it controlled me. Trying a different tactic, I gathered the air above her and plunged it into the sea. This magic she couldn't defend against. The air moved under my command, pushing her from underneath. She kicked, unable to find an opening, helplessly watching herself be pulled toward the island.

The Naiad still controlled the wave. Sabrina kept it in check. The woman dropped onto the pink sand of the beach. A horde of Gayden awaited her. Her back arched as if in pain as her magic was ripped out of her.

The great wave crashed back into the sea. I searched the sky, looking for the next target, the source of the lightening.

"What's going on with the sky?" Damien yelled from my left.

"Tempest!" Finch called from somewhere to my left.

"They can control the weather?" Damien yelled. No one answered him.

The lightening beat across the island. Thor's greatest weapon unleashed. Neither the Sight nor my power searching could find the Tempest.

Damien grabbed my hand. "Let me help."

His powers blended into mine. At first, my magic reared back, prickling in alarm, and I sensed his sharp intake of breath. I soothed the power, and it yielded, giving him access to the deep chasm inside. Together we directed our combined power into the air. Four Tempests floated in the clouds, miles away from the island. Our power hit them. One by one, they fell unconscious from the sky.

One second, they were hundreds of feet in the air. The next, they splattered against the ocean's surface. The horror of our actions tore through the curtain of this surreal reality.

"We had to," Damien said, reading my thoughts.

They were here for blood, innocent blood, because of me. I had to stop them. With another jet of power, the last of the Tempests fell. The black, dangerous clouds dissipated. The crystalline blue sky shined bright once more. For the briefest of moments, I thought it was over.

Fireballs, like cannonballs, catapulted to the island. They crashed into buildings. Wood and plaster exploded. Smoke and flames roared to life. The smoke threatened to darken the sky once more.

Damien's power retreated as I pulled water from the air. The deluge poured from the sky dampening the fires, the damage of soot and grim still apparent. Each time one fire went out, three more appeared. I had to find the source and take it out. The brief outline of an Ember caught my attention, running toward the towers, straight for Charlie.

"Charlie!" I screamed. As all logic fell away from me, I ran from the window, jumping over the missing stairs, my body rolling and crashing into the bottom wall. Someone screamed my name. I couldn't stop. I had to find her.

I scrambled to my feet, hobbling through a limp, before bursting out of the Town Hall. A brown-eyed Sphere waited for me with a living tree. The branches ensnared my waist. I screamed, enraged this creature tried to stop me, to get in my way when I had to get to Charlie now! My power pushed inside. The tree exploded into tiny fragments. The Sphere dropped to his knees. His mouth dropped open in shock. A streak of blood trickled from the side of his mouth. His head dropped, staring at the tree limb plunged into his chest. He fell to the side and moved no more.

Not giving him a second look, I bolted toward the towers. Toward Charlie. Who I couldn't lose. Another Sphere jumped from behind two buildings, hands raised. Using this as my advantage,

Over the Bridge

I froze a spear of ice. The deadly weapon shot toward her throat. The sickening squishing sound followed me as I passed her.

The *clomp clomp* of running footsteps closed in behind me. My magic reached backward, retreating as it sensed Damien. With his longer strides, he caught up with me, and we ran in time. He slipped his powers in and out of me to take down enemies on his side while I cast spells toward mine.

We rounded the last corner as a fireball struck the towers. The entire building erupted in flames. I stumbled. We were too late.

Damien grabbed my arm. "No, look!"

He pointed about a hundred feet away. Arameus and Charlie raced toward the beach, Sárkány, Charity, and another man right on their heels. Damien grabbed my arm. We raced toward them. A stitch in my side caught me. *Not like this. Please God. Not like this.*

Charity twirled her sword as she jogged. "Come, little girl. We only want to play with your insides."

A movement from beside them caught my eye. Wade and Jeremiah pulled up alongside them. They would reach them before I would. The others saw them at the same moment I did. The pain in my side doubled. I cried out, bending over, clutching my ribs. The pain and sight of my enemies paralyzed me.

Charity stopped, facing Jeremiah, and yelled to the others, "You go on ahead. I need to finish what I started with his brother."

Jeremiah's face contorted in rage. The stolen Ember and Naiad magic inside him flickered. An arc of fire, like a lasso, flew from his hand toward her. She ducked out of the way, laughing, and swinging her sword. This only made him angrier. He shot two more spells at her. She dodged the first, but the second hit her. The smile faded as shock took over. Ice started at her feet and crackled as it moved upward. It covered her face last. She stood, unblinking, dead, a frozen statue. Jeremiah reached her, triumph gleaming in his eyes. He pried her sword from her hand. Two of her fingers snapped off and fell to the ground. He raised it high, staring into her frozen eyes. "For Gabe."

He drove the blade into her chest. The end of the blade stuck out of her back. The ice receded from her body. She collapsed to the ground, blood pooling from her wound.

Sárkány and the other man stopped their pursuit of Charlie. They spun sideways to face us. We stared at each other in a standoff. The stranger smiled, lifted a hand, palm upward, and pointed at Charlie. The spell rolled out from his hand.

"No!"

There was no time to stop it. It would hit her.

Wade bolted from nowhere. He jumped into the air, the spell colliding into him. The stranger's face contorted in pain. He screamed, shaking, and fell to his knees. Wade rolled to his feet.

Sárkány glared. "You can only hold two, and you're full."

Sárkány lifted his hands, flames licking his skin, and flung fire at Wade.

Wade pivoted, and something left his hand as the ball of flame stopped in midair in front of him. The flame wavered before vanishing. Sárkány dropped to the ground. At the same moment, Charlie collapsed.

"No! No!" Arameus screamed as he pulled Charlie into his arms.

The sight of her falling snapped me out of the paralysis. I crossed the distance to her side. Her beautiful face had turned blue. Her eyes shut. My legs could no longer support me. Arameus screamed, clutching her to him.

I couldn't believe it. I'd lost her, too. Lost her to Wade, not an enemy.

Wade had done this. Rage filled me. The Sight erupted, scorching the world in white. On my feet, I faced the man who'd done this. "You son of a bitch."

The magic inside me boiled like lava. It seared through every part of me, rising higher and higher. There would be nothing of him left. Damien grabbed my elbow. "Ora, stop!"

"He killed Charlie!" I said through gritted teeth.

"No, he didn't. She's a Vessel. He put magic in her. She's not dead. Look, she's not dead."

He forced me to turn around. The magic thrashed, burning to be set loose, to destroy the source of my anger. I'd kill him too if I had to.

Arameus's voice doused the seething demon inside. "Come on, baby. Come back. Come back." The white haze of the world disappeared.

I forced myself to look at Charlie. The blue faded as the pinkness of life filled up her lips. Her chest rose, and Arameus cried out, "She's alive. She's alive."

Damien let me go, and I knelt once again by my best friend. She opened her eyes, and I learned the true meaning of relief. I flung my arms around her as Arameus hugged us both.

Damien asked, "We got them all?"

Wade replied, "I think so. I'm going to head back the main island with Jeremiah. Survey the damage."

My body quivered as adrenaline coursed through me. We survived the attack. I looked down at my friend as she opened her eyes.

"What happened?" she asked, her voice hoarse.

"Um¬...you remember when I told you you're a Vessel?" I began, not sure how she would take the news.

Her eyes opened wide. "You mean I have magic now?"

"I believe so." I watched her closely for her reaction.

A wide, but tired, grin spread across her face. "Awesome!"

Chapter Thirty-Nine
Ora

The smell of burning debris filled my nostrils as I put out yet another fire. Tired didn't even begin to cover what I felt. Every muscle ached while something squeezed around my head making the bright light of the fire torture. After the attempted invasion, I'd have thought it would've grown quiet, but if anything, the island bustled in an array of activity. Finch regrouped everyone, and as leader of the island's defense, he had assigned groups.

Some groups cleaned up the debris while other groups treated the wounded and put out the fires. Another group had the unhappy task of gathering the bodies. Relief washed over me when Finch hadn't picked me for that particular assignment. I couldn't face that. However, no matter where I went, the wails of the grieving echoed around me, each cry like a knife to my heart. I kept busy, putting out fires, trying to avoid the stares of the Gayden, and the guilt. Sárkány and his people came because of me. Everything was always because of me.

Finch tried to reassure me that no one blamed me, but regardless, he lied. I could see it in their eyes. If I hadn't come here, the Hunters wouldn't have dared.

Charlie remained in the hospital, slipping in and out of consciousness. After she'd realized she had magic, she'd fallen unconscious. Arameus, face set in a grimace, carried her to the local hospital, no bigger than a little clinic.

"What will happen to her?" I asked.

Wade cringed, wallowing in the knowledge of what he'd done. "She'll be dangerous for a while. Not only to herself but to others. She has to adjust to this. Learn how to control it."

Over the Bridge

White hot anger gripped me. "What if she hadn't been a Vessel? You would've killed her."

"I know." Wade refused to meet my gaze.

"Did you know? Before you threw that magic into her, did you know she was a Vessel?"

"I suspected."

Damien pulled me away, as the world once again hazed white.

"Calm down." His hands raised in mock surrender under the scrutiny of my glare. "I'm not saying what he did was right. But Charlie is okay. She'll be happy now, right? How many times has she felt useless? Now she's a witch."

"Yeah, if she doesn't kill herself or someone else trying to control it." My own power danced beneath the surface, a constant reminder of the struggle of control. If I'd been born with magic and had so much trouble, how would Charlie ever manage?

"Tell her that. She acted like she'd won the lottery."

I said nothing, stomping out of the hospital to kill the fires still raging over the island. Hours had passed, and still I'd heard nothing of her progress. Mom stayed with her at the hospital. I held to the naïve belief that no news was good news.

Mom, yet another reason to feel guilty. I'd left her in the middle of the battle and admitted this to Damien.

"Ora, if you are going to do this, you have to stay focused. I know you don't like it, but you can't be everywhere at once. You can't protect everyone, and someone is bound to get hurt. But everyone is an adult. They're here by their own choice. It isn't up to you to protect everyone."

I jerked around, yelling at him, "What about you? I went after Charlie, but you followed me. Why?"

That shut him up. The look he'd given me still confused me. It wasn't one of defiance, but sad, like a lost puppy.

"Arrgh!" I screamed, wanting to start fires instead of put them out. I paused, strolled out on the beach, and surveyed the island. Buildings caved in, rocks littered the ground, soot and grime everywhere. People worked together in small groups. I had been mercifully left alone to stew in my own feelings.

Guilt rose again. I should be with these people, comforting them, and assuring them everything would be okay, but I sighed, turning away from the buildings like a coward, and gazed out at the sea. The waves, unlike the island, appeared unchanged by what happened here today. No sign of a Naiad slipping in and out of the water, raising a tidal wave to destroy us all. Just the waves rushing in toward the land, gathering sand, and receding back into itself. Back and forth, in and out, like breathing.

I sat upon the sand, crossed my legs, placed my hands upon my thighs, palms upward, and closed my eyes. I quieted my mind, seeking the state of rumination. If ever I needed a mental cleansing, it was right now. I'd been avoiding the worst of my thoughts. I killed people. The images of the Tempest falling from the sky, those I flung spells at as I raced to Charlie, and the Sphere who tried to stop me as I left the Town Hall flashed before my eyes. Aryiana's words echoed in my brain. She'd been afraid I wouldn't be able to do what was necessary. I'd certainly proved her wrong, but how would I go on living knowing what I'd done?

As I closed my eyes, the answer appeared of what truly bothered me. This was only the beginning. If I continued on this path, many more would be put in danger. I would have to hurt or kill again and again, and those I love and care for may die. *Can I continue?* I let myself go and sent my question away from me and entered a state of rumination to find my answer.

Chapter Forty
Perdita

THE HARBOR HOSPITAL, A QUAINT brick building, was tucked away in the center of the long, slender island. Charlie rested in one of the triage rooms. Perdita had to find her. The wounded poured in after the attack. Without a Sphere or Sphere magic, healing would have to be done the human way. One Gayden had managed to get Sphere magic, and he'd treated the worst of them with the stolen magic, the ones the doctors felt could be saved. The losses weren't as bad as she had feared.

The island had succumbed under the attack to almost total ruin. Most of the buildings were burnt or collapsing, debris lined the streets, and to top it off, the city's water and sewage lines had been damaged, and the island had lost power. The Elders directed those with Sphere magic to repair the damage, but the doctors wouldn't hear of it. No way they'd let them leave to fix buildings when people needed healing. Not that Perdita blamed them. At least the hospital had a backup generator. The place could barely be called a clinic, much less a trauma center, with minimal capability and bed space. The parking lot had been converted to a triage area.

Ora hadn't stayed to watch over Charlie. Her guilt wouldn't let her. Perdita wished she could take some of the weight off her daughter's shoulders, but no matter what she said or did, it wouldn't change how Ora felt. So, she left her alone to process her feelings.

Ora went with the Gayden who had captured Ember magic to try and do some damage control.

Arameus hadn't left Charlie's side. Perdita wasn't sure when it happened, but Arameus had finally noticed Charlie. An uneasy feeling rested in the pit of her stomach. She wasn't sure if Ora had any feelings for Arameus. She didn't think so, but one could never know.

By a lucky twist of fate, the clinic sustained only minor damage in the fighting, but it fought a different kind of battle now. Chaos reigned inside. The waiting room burst at the seams with screaming children, people holding bloody bandages around wounds, and still others called in panic at the desk, demanding to know if anyone has seen their daughter or son, husband, mother. Perdita's heart ached for these people. She understood Ora's need to stay away from this. Perdita would've gladly joined her, but someone had to stay with Charlie.

Once Perdita had gotten over the initial shock of the pandemonium, she noted several women behind the check-in desk trying to answer questions. Doors perched on either side of the large desk. Each had a tiny window. Through one, Perdita caught sight of Wade. She tapped her knuckles on the window, and he glanced her way. His eyes wavered, but he pushed back from the nurse's station and strolled toward the door.

The door opened with a click, and she slipped through. She half expected the crowd to follow, but no one paid her any attention. *Thank God.*

The thought spiraled into a flood of feelings. The terror during the battle held back and chose that moment to come steaming at her. She held onto the knowledge that Charlie survived, and no one else in her group had gotten hurt. But Charlie had magic inside her now. A Vessel—otherwise she would've died.

Perdita grabbed Wade's arm, halting him. "Did you know she's a Vessel?" She did nothing to hide the accusation in her voice.

Wade paled but said, "I... She wasn't quite human."

"But you weren't sure?"

Wade hung his head low and shook it once.

"She could have died!" Throughout the commotion of the clinic, people stopped to stare at them.

"I know! Ora's already made me feel guilty about it." He ran his hands through his hair. He wouldn't meet her eyes and instead stared at the wall, his guilt eating at him. "I didn't think. I—I had two cores, and there was one man left. He was about to kill me, and I—slung it away from me. It was instinct. I never meant—I didn't intentionally direct it toward her."

She felt her anger slipping away. She didn't want it to. She wanted to remain angry, to make him pay for what could've happened to Charlie, but he truly felt bad. She couldn't stay mad at him. It wouldn't undo what had been done.

"It's okay." She patted his arm, trying to rectify the situation, hating the sadness weighing on him. They all had enough sadness to last lifetimes.

"No, it isn't."

"You can't take it back. You have to learn from this so it doesn't happen again."

"You're right."

Perdita moved past Wade to find Charlie in one of the rooms to the right. Charlie occupied the one of the two twin beds. She struggled to get up, but Arameus eased her back down.

"Honestly, I'm fine. I don't need to be here. They need to give this bed to someone who needs it." Perdita's hair stood on end as the unnatural wind circulated the room, Charlie's new power slipping away from her.

Arameus shook his head. "You have to be checked out."

"I'm not hurt. Look, no bleeding or anything." She held out her arms so he could see.

"It's not physical injuries they'd be looking for." Arameus touched the side of her face, the move so gentle.

Charlie folded her arms. "We're in a human clinic. You really think they have anything here to check for magical injuries?"

"She's right," Wade said from behind Perdita.

Arameus and Charlie broke off their conversation now they realized they weren't alone. Charlie used Wade's statement to her advantage. "See? Now let me go. I'm getting up."

Arameus didn't stop her this time. She swung her feet over the side of the bed, flinging the covers to the side. She swayed as she stood. Arameus grabbed her arm and gave her a stern look. Charlie waved him off and said, "Chill out. I got up too fast. That's all."

Wade cleared his throat. "Charlie. I..."

Charlie stopped him by holding up a hand. "We're good. You gave me magic. Now when do I get to use it? Oh, I wonder what core I have. Do you know, Wade?" The wind pushed from behind her blowing her brown hair forward.

Arameus grabbed her arms. "Whoa there, sweetheart. You're getting ahead of yourself. We don't know how stable your powers are."

Charlie gave him an angry face, which looked more like a pout.

"He's right. You'll have plenty of time for that later. Right now, we need to talk. All of us."

Perdita jumped at the sound of Finch's voice. He appeared behind her without making a sound.

Perdita settled on the empty bed beside Charlie. "Talk about what?"

"I think we need to go talk to the Elders again. Change their mind."

Before she had a chance to answer, panicked shouts grew louder. Finch said, "What the hell is going on now?"

Finch and Wade went sprinted down the hall and through the doors leading to the waiting room. Perdita followed them with Charlie and Arameus on her heels. She burst through the doors, and the crowd moved opposite the check-in desk to point out one of the large windows. Various voices from the crowd rang out louder than others.

"What's going on?"

"Are the Magicians back?"

"Not again."

Finch and Wade disappeared out the automatic glass doors. Perdita drew out her powers as the doors opened and she stepped out onto the cement landing.

What she saw stopped her in her tracks, her hand falling to her side, as Finch said, "What the hell?"

Chapter Forty-One
Ora

I OPENED MY EYES AFTER only a few moments. I'd tried to reach the state of rumination but hadn't made it. I arched my back, shocked to find a dark night instead of the afternoon I'd left behind. A blanket had been draped around my shoulders. The soft crackle and gentle warmth of a fire warmed my left side. Damien leaned against a nearby rock—snoring.

The sight of this large man with his face relaxed in sleep made me smile. His intensity dampened, and behind it, the lost innocence. His blond hair stood out at different angles. His arms folded across his chest, feet crossed, head dipped to the side. He must've brought me the blanket and built the fire to keep me warm. He'd stayed with me. I sighed. This shouldn't make me happy.

I stood and stretched, pulling the blanket tighter around my body. The sea breeze chilled my damp skin. The tide had moved in while I'd ruminated, and with each wave, a fine mist coated me. My shirt and pants clung to me, heavy with dampness. I didn't want to wake Damien, but my teeth chattered, and I desperately needed a bathroom. I tiptoed over to him, difficult in the sand, squatted, and shook his shoulder. "Damien."

He startled awake and looked around. Once he'd gathered his bearings, he dazzled me with a smile. "What happened to Mannie?"

Warmth crept up my cheeks at his gibe. Thank goodness he couldn't see my blush in the dark. I chose to ignore his comment. "Come on. Let's go inside. It's cold."

"Okay." He pushed himself to his feet, dusting himself off. "By the way, what did you do?"

"What do you mean?" I asked. He knew what rumination looked like from the club.

His brow furrowed and waved behind me to the town. "You fixed everything."

"What're you talking about?"

From what little I could see in the dark, the fires no longer burned, no debris littered the streets, and the collapsed buildings had been rebuilt.

"How?" My hand flew to my lips. Had I imagined the fight? Surely not.

"I was hoping you could tell me."

He must have gone crazy, thinking I did this. "I sat down and ruminated. I didn't do this."

His eyes softened. "Yeah, O, ya did. You sat down and then your magic left your body and swept over the land. Pretty damn amazing, if you ask me. The bricks and stones rose into the air and settled back into place as if nothing had ever happened. The fire damage vanished, and the dust flew into the sea."

I didn't like how he looked at me with worship in his eyes. I didn't do anything. "It wasn't me."

"I know what your magic feels like. I've touched it, remember?"

This also made me uncomfortable, like he described me naked or something. I shifted my weight from one foot to the other.

"But I didn't do anything. I—ruminated. That's all."

"That's not all you did."

"No. I hid from everyone. I'm a coward. I'm supposed to be this powerful witch, but I'm so tired of feeling afraid, and weak, and guilty all the time. People shouldn't die because of me! I'm not worth it!" Tears, hateful, betraying tears, threatened to spill over.

He crossed the short distance separating us and gathered me in his arms. "Listen to me, O. I've seen your magic, and you're powerful. But what makes you worth fighting for and dying for is your heart. You protect the innocent. You protect those weaker than you. You stand for what's right. You're worth it *because* you feel this guilt and because you're afraid, but you keep fighting anyway. That is why so many people—love you."

I didn't know what to say as he held me in his strong arms. I didn't feel like any of those things. I pushed him back and looked up into his eyes. "But I didn't mean to fix the city."

He only smiled. "Your head gets in your way. When you ruminated, your heart knew what to do and did it."

The smile wavered when his gaze fell on my lips. I knew before he leaned down that he was going to kiss me again. This time, I didn't stop him.

"Ora, wake up!" Mom's fingers dug into my shoulder.

"Uhhh. What?" My sleeping brain surged to full alertness as memories of yesterday popped in my head. I jerked upward, glancing around and recognizing the bungalow. Mom rummaged through my bag, yanking out clothes, tossing them on the bed.

My heart skipped a beat. "Is it Charlie?"

She slowed as her body softened. "No. She's okay."

The words eased my tension, which kicked in the exhaustion. I yawned, rubbing my eyes, wishing I could go back to sleep. I'd lain awake long after returning to the bungalow. Thoughts of John and Damien conflicting in my mind.

"Get dressed. The Elders want to see you."

Oh crap. I bet they're going to ask us to leave. I flung the covers away, grabbing the handful of clothes, and disappeared into the bathroom. Ten minutes later, I stepped out of the bathroom, dressed and wrestling to get my wet hair into a braid.

Mom and I left, heading to the Town Hall, Sabrina and Charlie meeting us at the corner. I knew the Elders waited, but I threw my arms around my best friend. "Are you okay?"

"I'm fine." She squeezed me back, hard. Her gentle warmth reassuring, and I couldn't let her go for a full minute.

"We've got to go," Sabrina said.

I pulled back, squeezing Charlie's hand and resumed our trek to the Elders. Damien hadn't been kidding. The island looked as if nothing had happened. Except for the new graves. Even the most powerful magic can't bring back the dead.

Wade guarded the door, shotgun over his shoulder, dark eyes staring. A strange sense of déjà vu washed over me. The underlying guilt was the only difference, and quite possibly respect, in Wade's expression.

Wade's gaze moved to Charlie. His eyes clouded as he battled his own inner demons over what he'd done to her. I wondered if anyone had figured out what kind of magic she had yet. No one stopped as we entered the Town Hall. Lemon, candle wax, and a slight charred smell wafted around. The long hallway that held the hidden stairs told no tale of yesterday. How could I have possibly done all this? Even the pictures remained in place, unscathed. The double oak doors opened into the church-like room.

The Elders faced us, perched on their individual chairs in the front, along with several bodyguards positioned behind them, including Finch. Jeremiah, Damien, and Arameus sat in the front pew, and turned in their seats, watching us as we progressed up the center aisle.

I bowed, not sure if this was customary, but I caught Finch's smirk as I righted myself. "You wanted to see me?"

Steve said, "We want to thank you for helping us defend our home, and for fixing it, too."

"You're welcome." It sounded so lame, especially when I hadn't done it on purpose.

"In light of yesterday's events, and at our Head of Defense's urging," Aggie flicked her eyes in Finch's direction, "we have changed our minds. We will help you."

"We would like you to work and train with Mr. Outlaw and the others in charge of our security to formulate a plan of action. We're reaching out to the other Gayden to see who will join you. This will be a strictly volunteer basis only, but we give our blessing," Winslow said.

So many questions raced in my mind. *Other Gayden? Train?* Mom nudged me with her shoulder.

"Thank you."

"There are a few things we want, of course." Steve leaned forward.

"Such as?"

Winslow pulled out a piece of paper from a file he held in his lap. "In exchange for our help, we require you, Ora Stone, to fight for the lives and freedom of Gayden. We expect, if we win the war, for you to have the Council renew our treaty and make it public. We want a seat on the High Council, and all Gayden currently in Conjuragic will come to us for judgment and punishment. Any future trials will have a Gayden on the tribunal as well."

This seemed reasonable to me. I asked, "This is all depending on the outcome of the war." *War? Crap. Was that what I was starting?*

"Yes. We are aware. You agree?"

"Yeah. Sure."

"You must sign."

Sign? Like a formal contract. As if I'm some politician signing a law.

Winslow handed the paper to Finch, who stepped down the stairs. Panic set in as I stepped forward, hands shaking, lips numb. My hand trembled as Finch held out a pen. I felt like a fish out of water. Mom smiled, full of pride, and nodded once. Charlie's skin glowed with a new radiance. Sabrina shrugged. Arameus's head tilted to the side, as if not unsure about this outcome, but resolved. Jeremiah stared at me with something akin to hero worship, which I didn't feel like I deserved. Damien didn't move at all, but I remembered his words from last night. People were willing to fight with me. I bent over, staring at the innocent appearing paper, and signed.

Finch clapped his hands together. "All right, boys and girls. Let's get training."

Chapter Forty-Two
Sabrina

"ALL RIGHT, EVERYONE. THAT'S ENOUGH for today. Pack up your things and move on to your next station." Sabrina wiped a towel over her sweaty face.

The blazing sun beat down on Sabrina's neck as sweat rolled down her back. The cool breeze blowing in from the sea released the built-up heat in her cheeks. She opened the large red cooler that rested upon the sand, pulled out a bottle of water, and downed it in seconds. The group departed, chatting amongst themselves. No stragglers stayed behind to ask a question or two.

As she stared at the waves, she could only shake her head. Never in a million years would she have dreamed she'd be a traitor to her kind, let alone as big of one as she'd turned out to be. Yet, here she was, teaching Gayden after Gayden how to wield stolen Naiad magic. To top it off, she cheered with each improvement they made.

The next group would be here in fifteen minutes, so she had time to rest. Sabrina kicked off her leather boots, thankful to be rid of them. Boots were not meant to be used while walking on sand. She ran on tiptoes to the surf. The sand burned her feet, but the cool salty water helped. She pulled the water up and around herself, washing away the sweat, and relishing in manipulating the water. Jeremiah asked her the other day why she did it. She said, "It's like stretching your legs. It feels good."

At the thought of him, Sabrina smiled. He'd turned into the brother she never had. She wished he could meet her sister one day. Like all siblings, sometimes they got into arguments. Of course, what had happed at Fox's had been an accident. She could see that—now.

They'd been fishing together for a while, and she'd forgotten, stupid of her, about his power. Playing, she sent her power at him, to splash him with water, but he had reacted on instinct, ripping her magic out of her. Of course, he released it right away and checked he hadn't hurt her, but as she came to, she'd been overcome with rage and attacked him. She'd jumped on top of him, punching his face. She lost count how many times she hit him. She might not have stopped if Arameus and Damien hadn't pulled her off him. His nose had twisted at a weird angle, blood had smeared all over his mouth and nose, and both eyes had already started turning black. Only then did she hear his cries and the realization of what she'd done had hit her. Fox healed him in seconds, but that did nothing for her guilt. Jeremiah forgave her, even apologized for hurting her, before she could say anything. After that, she vowed no one would hurt him ever again, including her. So, they worked together, all of them, sending spells at him, teaching him to control his power, and not use it by accident.

Now he trained to use his powers and how to manipulate the stolen magic, and she helped him. What was one more treason on her record? Helping an escaped prisoner, allowing the existence of Geminates, and helping plan the invasion of her world. Besides, she remembered something Simeon said to her the night before Ora escaped. She'd been trying to recover, thinking she'd let Ora die, knowing she was innocent, and he'd asked if she had to do it over again, what she would do different. She didn't want to ever feel that level of guilt again. While a part of her felt the guilt over betraying her own kind, she couldn't sit back and do nothing while Gayden, like poor Jeremiah, continued to die, or be handed over to Master.

She'd never set out to be a traitor, but now her path lay bare before her, and she wouldn't balk at it. When Damien announced that this "Master" was Naiad, she felt somehow personally responsible. Dirty and betrayed because that someone like that shared her core, tainted it.

Jeremiah jogged down the beach. Sabrina smelled him before she saw him.

"How's training going?" He leaned over, hands on his knees, panting.

"Good. We'll be separating them into teams soon."

"I know you don't approve of how I've learned, but do you think I'm good enough for the aquatics team?"

Sabrina bristled. She avoided thinking about how the Gayden learned to use their powers. On one hand, the witches and wizards Ora rescued from the Veil had volunteered to have their magic ripped out of them all day instead of remaining trapped in the Veil, but what choice did they have? All the ones she'd personally talked to said they'd lose their powers for a time to a Gayden any day over being stuck in the frozen Veil.

"I might be able to make space for you. If you're lucky." She nudged his shoulder.

Jeremiah had developed an affinity for Naiad and showed talent at Ember. Perhaps it was the hours of training or being away from his kidnappers, but Jeremiah's tiny arms had filled out. He'd grown about two inches, and stubble grew on his face.

"We've been training for weeks and weeks. Do you think we'll ever be ready?"

"We'll be ready. What all did you do today?"

"Tempest, Sphere, some Ember, but it was cut short."

"Another fire?"

He wiped sweat from his brow. "Yeah. Think they need to go ahead and choose teams. Some Gayden can't handle certain cores. Sphere is not my forte."

"They'll pick teams when we're closer to figuring out where we have to go over."

"Is there anywhere that's really remote?"

"Not really, and our other problem is we need disguises. Robes so we can blend in if we need to."

"Anywhere in the human realm make robes?" Jeremiah squatted, sinking his fingers into the sand, sculpting it as if trying to make a sand castle.

"No. At least not in enough quantity that we'd need." Sabrina knelt beside him.

Over the Bridge

"Right! Twenty thousand Gayden. The citizens of Conjuragic would shit a brick if they knew how many there are of them. Us." Eventually he'd get used to the terminology.

The sight of them arriving by the boat load had given her pause. Mainly men and a few women had come. The island, shaped like a large irregular C, swelled with the newcomers. They erected Tents and Hogans up and down the beaches. The farmlands at the north and south tips struggled at keeping up with the demand. Her thoughts turned back to needing disguises.

"Even with the Veil down, it would be suspicious to place an order for robes that large."

"So there isn't anything we could use that is here? No stock piles of stuff?"

Sabrina thought for a moment, looked down at the leather on her legs, and said, "Actually, that gives me an idea."

"What?"

"Fancy a trip to Texas?"

"Are you sure this is the one?" Ora asked, not hiding the irritation in her tone. Did she honestly think Sabrina had led them to four wrong factories on purpose?

"Yes." She prayed it wasn't a lie.

"Better be. I'm starving." Jeremiah held onto her belt. She rolled her eyes, not that anyone would be able to see in the darkness of the Bridge.

"You're always starving, Bullfrog. You need some mighty fine wine?"

"Really wish you wouldn't call me that."

"Would you concentrate?" Ora halted, causing Sabrina to bump into her.

Sabrina shook herself, mentally, but she'd only been to this factory one time. Locations in the Bridge went by memory and connection to people and places. Even if she had the address, it wouldn't have helped. Ora knew all this. It wouldn't do any good to remind her. Besides, Sabrina's own stomach growled.

"Just open the Bridge."

A vibration rumbled underneath Sabrina's feet. The complete darkness faded into something little more than shadow. She peeked out into the darkness of night. Only high streetlamps lit up the large factory. It had a vague familiarity, but couldn't be sure. If this wasn't the correct factory, then they'd abandon the search for tonight. "Can you move us inside?"

"Why?"

"So we can check the inventory."

The Bridge snapped shut, and Ora marched forward. Sabrina's fingers gripped the rope as it slid through her fingers. A second later, the Bridge opened again. More light filtered through revealing the inside of a warehouse. Sabrina couldn't see any workers or security guards. Concrete gray floors ran the long length of the building with steel shelves filled with boxes after boxes. A series of letters and numbers labeling each section revealed nothing to Sabrina.

Ora stepped out of the Bridge, whirled around with her hands on her hips. "You have no idea if this is the right place or not."

Sabrina brought a finger to her lips. "Shhh."

Ora flung her long hair behind her, crossed her arms, and tapped a finger on her forehead. "Fine. Split up. We'll search the boxes. If we don't find anything, we're going home."

Jeremiah formed an X with his forearms jerking them apart. "Split up! Have you never seen scary movies? You never split up!"

Ora smacked herself in the forehead. "We aren't in a scary movie."

"Creepy warehouse. Nighttime. Half the lights broken. That's asking for Jason or Michael to cut us up."

Ora put her hands on her hips. "You should be safe then."

Jeremiah shrugged. "Don't know what she's talking about."

Damien put up his hands in mock surrender. "I ain't got a dog in this fight." He followed Ora down the nearest aisle.

Over the Bridge

Sabrina tossed their words around in her mind, trying to make sense of them. "Who the hell are Jason and Michael? Why would you be safe?"

"Never mind. Let's go." Ora levitated a box from the top shelf, lowering it to the floor, where it landed with a thud. The top split open, and Damien peaked inside. "Bunch of jumpers."

This was going to take forever. Sabrina climbed to the top shelf, maneuvering to the next section, and opened another box. Shirts. The next, black boots. After that, white gowns. The others, too, opened box after box. Nothing. Sabrina opened her mouth to suggest they head on home when a voice called from the ground. "Who goes there?"

Crap! Had no one kept watch?

"Show yourself! I'm armed."

Sabrina shifted her weight, peering beside the row of boxes where Ora squatted, frozen in place.

The unmistakable click of a gun's hammer rang out in the dark. "Now, I mean it. I'm not dying over a bunch of uniforms. Show yourself or I'll call the Pro…police."

The man had been about to say Protectors. Sabrina would've bet anything on it. She stepped to the edge, but out of the range of the man's gun. Magic tingled on her skin. "I'm Lieutenant Sabrina Sun. Protector. I've come for a shipment."

Below, the magic wavered. "Uh huh. Why you sneaking around then?"

Ora glared at her, mouthing, "What are you doing?"

Sabrina waved her off. "I'm coming down. Don't shoot." She pulled the water from the air, surrounding her feet, and lowered herself to the ground. The man kept the gun pointed at her. Middle aged, graying dark hair, and eyes. A halfsie living in the human realm. "Like I said, I've come for our shipment."

He unclicked the gun but didn't lower it. "Now, the way I heard it, no shipments going in or out in months. Since how the Veil is sealed and all."

"Things have been slow."

"That mean the Veil is open?"

Sabrina weighed her options, thinking fast. "Not yet. But those of us on this side have a plan, but as we were on this side, we have to keep it incognito."

He lowered the gun, but only part way, his suspicion still not eased. "That still don't explain why you want Protector leathers."

Sabrina gave the man a knowing smile. "I see I can't fool you. The truth is we've found a way through the Veil, but we don't have any idea what we'll find on the other side. We want the leathers because they're spelled. Better safe than sorry."

He cocked his head, hand still wrapped around the gun, his magic wavering. His control could only be minimal at best.

"I would've come during regular hours, but honestly, we didn't know who we could trust. Does Zachary Taylor still work here?" The whole time they'd been talking, Sabrina's mind searched for the name of the man who'd worked here the last time she'd come.

At this, the man finally lowered his gun. "Yeah. He's my uncle. I'm Theodore Taylor." He reached out a hand. She took his, shaking hard once. "Our stock pile is down here. This way."

Sabrina followed him, sneaking a look upward, and nodded at Ora. Five rows down, Theodore pointed. "They're all down that aisle. How you shipping these out? I didn't see any trucks."

"We wanted to make sure they were here and those entrusted with our leathers were still loyal."

Theodore stared at her.

She scrambled for words. "There are some amongst us that are traitors. Not wanting the Veil unsealed. Figured they'd be better off here unchecked." She shrugged then slipped down the aisle toward the uniforms. For the second time that night, the click of the gun's hammer locked into place. She froze, slowly raising her hands above her head.

"Turn around, girly girl."

She obeyed, magic swirling underneath the surface. She doubted it'd be faster than a bullet.

The black gun pointed at her. Such a small, black, shiny thing that could do some much damage. Theodore's eyes grew as empty as a predator's. With his other hand, he pulled a walkie-talking from the security belt. He pressed a button, which beeped in response. "Uncle Zack, we have company."

The walkie-talkie beeped twice before a harsh voice spoke, "What do you want now, Theo?"

The gun wavered while Theo licked his lips. "I've caught a Protector, and they know how to cross the Veil. Didn't you say the other day you'd blow the whole place up if you had the chance?"

Beep. "Stupid boy. Protectors never go anywhere alone."

Theo's head jerked up, scanning the many boxes. The others remained out of sight.

Sabrina took the opportunity. Water ripped out of the air, slashing down, knocking the gun flying out of sight.

Theo screamed. His dark eyes glowed the faintest red. Flames sparked from his hands. The stench of burned plastic filled the room. He tossed the ruined walkie-talkie aside. "You purebreds think you're so much better than us! We'll see." He raised his blazing palms, taking aim. Sabrina rolled past him. Water rushing behind her. It smacked into Theo. His fire extinguished. He flailed against the water.

Behind her, three thumps hit the ground. Without looking, she knew Ora, Damien, and Jeremiah had joined her. Theo crouched on the ground, panting. He jerked at the noise. "Your Quad? No matter."

Before they could react, he screamed, and flames ignited over every inch of him. Sabrina stumbled backward against the heat. She'd never heard of an Ember doing that.

"Oh God!" Ora covered her mouth with a hand.

Theo's screams transformed from rage to pure agony. His own fire turned against him. The warehouse filled with the acrid stench of burning clothes, hair, and a mingled smell of cooking meat. Theo stumbled, clawing at his face. He crashed into boxes in another aisle. The fire spread as if it had a mind of its own.

Jeremiah shouted, "Stop, drop, and roll!"

Ora and Sabrina raced forward, combining their power to extinguish the flames over Theo. The fire consumed everything in its path, even the oxygen in the air. Sabrina had nothing to pull water from. Ora strained, but nothing she did would put out the fire. Smoke billowed, drowning what little light the emergency lights provided. Sabrina backed away, coughing. She grabbed Ora, pulling her backward. Through hacking coughs, Sabrina said, "We can't put it out."

Ora coughed, sinking to the ground, away from the rising smoke.

Damien and Jeremiah coughed nearby.

"Ora, we have to get out of here."

She nodded and crawled toward the sounds of Damien's and Jeremiah's coughing. Sabrina followed. The fire spread everywhere, killing every sound except for the crackling of flames.

Ora shouted, "Grab hold of me." Sabrina grabbed a hand, while Jeremiah clasped her belt, and Damien took her other hand. Ora stood, bending over, and pulled them toward something. Sabrina hoped it was the Bridge, but she couldn't see anything. They walked and walked, but still the crackling of fire remained. Something had gone wrong!

As if someone flipped a switch, the sounds and smoke disappeared. They remained in darkness, but the familiar, and this time comforting, darkness of the Veil. All of them coughed. "I'm going to try something," Ora said.

Before Sabrina got the chance to ask, the world dipped and swirled. Dizziness and nausea coupled with coughing overwhelmed her. A second later, she fell, but only for a second. She landed hard on something and fell forward, losing her grip on Ora's hand.

Loud metallic banging and clanging accompanied the fall followed by several dull thuds. Her face hit something coarse and cool. She pushed back onto her knees, spitting sand out of her mouth, as the sound of rushing waves reached her ears. The tinge of smoke stuck to her hair and clothes. She coughed again, wiping her mouth, and surveyed her surroundings.

Damien said, "I'll be damned. We're back on the island!"

Over the Bridge

Jeremiah coughed and pointed. "What," more coughing, "are those?"

Sabrina could only stare in amazement. Ora had brought along hundreds of boxes along with the metallic shelves. She'd gotten the Protector's leathers after all.

Chapter Forty-Three
Charlie

CHARLIE SETTLED HERSELF INTO A seat at the newly-erected overlarge Hogan serving as a mess hall. She picked at her food while working on the latest knots she needed to master during training. The last few months had flown by. A year ago, she never would've pictured her life the way it is now.

Waking up at dawn, inhaling breakfast, jogging miles all over this tropical island and tons of exercise along with magic and weapon training.

As her fingers slipped through the rope, she tried to recall which Tempest station she and Arameus would attend after their hasty lunch. Jeremiah rotated through all the stations, and he might join them.

At Tempest station, they practiced tornados, which always gave Charlie the heebie-jeebies. She found it ironic she'd inherited the same core that Corporal Bizard had hurt her with on her first day of college. Perhaps they'd meet in Conjuragic. She'd love to see the look on his face when he saw her manipulate the weather. Her toxic clouds and directing lightening outdid everyone else, and she could fly. Nothing exhilarated her more than the air pushing beneath her feet and sending her soaring hundreds of feet into the air. Ora skipped the flying part every time. No shocker there. She'd always been afraid of heights.

Arameus tapped Charlie on the shoulder, taking a seat beside her, and grabbing a piece of rope. "Hey, gorgeous. How's your day?"

"Not bad. Just thought I'd do this until the meeting."

Over the Bridge

He fumbled with the rope, fixing his gaze on a group of wizards eating at a table nearby.

Charlie abandoned her own rope, rubbing his back. "They volunteered."

He shifted his gaze, focusing on the rope. "I know."

"They're better than the other ones."

"Which would that be? The ones who lost their minds or the ones who refused to volunteer and are now in prison cells?"

Charlie had no answer. "You'd rather she have left them in the Veil?"

He pulled away, and even though she understood, his rejection still stung. "Of course not. I wish we could send them home."

"Then we'd lose the element of surprise. They're not being harmed. If…" She faltered, not wanting to say what was on her mind.

"If what?"

"If you can't even handle this, then how are you going to be able to—"

He cut her off, swiveling in the seat to face her. "Able to what? Kill them? I—I don't know."

Charlie thought it best to drop it for now. "The mock battles are going well."

His shoulders relaxed, and he grabbed her hand, pulling it up to kiss the back of it. "Yeah, we've done sea, mountains, and a team even managed a desert location."

"Too bad we couldn't go through the Bridge to some cities. Too many people."

"Think we're going to finalize the teams tonight."

"Awesome. How many will there be?" She nibbled on the cooling fries.

"Sphere will be the infantry and a separate medic team. Aerial, aquatics, and the pyrokinetics team."

Charlie tossed away the fry. "You're joking?"

"No. It started that way but kind of stuck. Ora's going to ask you to be on the medics team."

Laughter broke out a few tables away. Charlie smiled at a group of Gayden who strolled in for a late lunch. She'd found the Gayden to be humorous, good natured people, and acted as if they never had a care in the world. They sang, and danced, and played music at all hours of the day. They'd even let them celebrate Junkanoo, a special celebration at Christmas. It had been a lovely day, but she missed her grandparents and John. It hadn't helped she caught Ora and Damien kissing.

"Thinking about your grandparents again?" Arameus brushed a lock of hair away from her face. She sank her cheek into his palm.

"Are you still mad at Ora?" he asked.

"I've never been mad at her. She started this whole thing because of John. I knew she'd move on one of these days, but not so soon and with *him*." The note of bitterness in her voice rose with every word.

"If I can forgive him for taking my power, why can't you?"

"Because you almost died. How would you feel if you had to watch me suffering while being able to do nothing and watch the person responsible?"

He pulled her closer, kissing her forehead. "Fair enough. But you know what he went through. We've talked. He's a good man. Besides, Ora hasn't totally moved on."

"What do you mean?" Charlie leaned back, staring at him, and not liking the unhappy feeling she'd gotten. How did he know something about Ora that she didn't?

"Seriously?" He mocked her teenage girl catch phrase. She smacked him in the arm while he laughed. "Those two aren't sneaking off together like we do. They act like strangers at training, and even though they like each other, she pulls away. She loved John, but something's off."

"Like what?"

"She changed overnight at Fox's. Before that day, grief hung around her all the time, and one night, it disappeared."

Charlie hadn't noticed, but she'd been too distracted by Arameus. "How did you pick up on it?"

Over the Bridge

"I'm a Defender. It was my job to read people. Besides, I spent a lot of time with her during her trial. When someone is facing death, all the fake masks fall away, and you can see the real person underneath."

Charlie rolled her eyes. "I guess he's not too bad."

"That's my girl. Besides, you have to admit how they figured out how to have Gayden share power instead of taking it is pretty amazing."

She poked him. "So the volunteers aren't being hurt anymore."

Arameus leaned in and kissed her. A fast, sweet kiss.

"Uhh, why don't you two get a room," Ora teased while placing a tray on the table across from them. She opened a can of Mt. Dew and picked up a fork, digging into chili cheese fries.

Charlie reached over and snatched a fry.

"Yo, Stone!" Finch yelled from the doorway.

"What now?" she muttered, mouth full of fries.

"Meetin' time. Let's go. You too, love birds." He motioned for Charlie to follow him.

The door closed behind him, and Ora rolled her eyes, still eating.

Arameus stood, picking up Charlie's tray. "You all coming?"

"I'm hungry," Ora said.

Charlie waved him on. "We'll be there soon. They don't want her around hungry."

He chucked, walking away. Charlie helped herself to some more fries and Mt. Dew. "Mmmm, so good."

Ora nodded, wiping runny cheese off her lips. The girls said no more, sharing the fries and drink. Just like old times. Charlie followed Ora to drop off her tray, and they left the mess hall heading toward Town Hall. Ora yawned.

"Busy day?"

"Isn't it always?"

"True. So, you think I should be on the medic team even though I'm Tempest?"

"Yeah. You're good with the potions. Besides, we wanted to go to med school. You've got a healing touch."

"That'd make me one of the leaders." Charlie blushed.

"I know. Sorry about that. It's not all what it's cracked up to be."

Charlie didn't want to let on she wanted to be a leader. "You're not mad that you're not the leader?"

Ora scoffed. "Hell no. Only in dumb movies do they make a teenager in charge of an army. But they do listen when I have an opinion, so that's nice."

Finishing up, Ora deposited her tray, and the two of them headed to the meeting.

They ran up the three steps and into the Town Hall. Several sets of voices echoed from down the hall. "Are there usually this many people?"

Ora shook her head, strolling down the long hallway, where the door at the end stood open. "No, usually only a few of us come at any time. Sounds like everyone is here."

The girls ascended the steps to the Defense Tower. Finch stood facing the stairwell, chatting with Perdita. Sabrina finished her conversation with Jeremiah and Arameus as the two entered. Wade and Damien returned from the window to sit down. Healer Roos, a Sphere witch rescued from the Veil, sat away from everyone, hands clasped in her lap, wearing a brown shirt.

"Okay, everyone. Status reports. I'll go first," Finch said as the room quieted. "The infantry has improved on ground tactics. Their communications are stellar, reconnaissance training is completed, and our simulations are spot on. I'd say we're good to go. Wade?"

Wade crossed his arms. "I've been working with our pyrotechnicians to improve our fire missiles. We can send them out with pinpoint precision, but we can also deflect and put out fires. My guys are ready."

He motioned to Arameus, who stood. "Evening, everyone. As you know, our aerial team has focused on weather, including lightening, hail, as well as tornado-force winds to take down our enemies, but more importantly, climate control to include fog for camouflage. We've also been improving on moving people and objects silently through the air, and our long-range abilities to drop a person have been successful. I believe Healer Roos has more to add."

The middle-aged Sphere didn't stand. She'd been one of the first rescued from the Veil to offer to help. The Elders think she volunteered so she can heal the injured Magicians in the war, but she had taken special care when teaching Charlie and the others healing. "We've been improving the spell work of different healing potions. The books and experience that Charlie has provided have helped a great deal. A few are adequate at healing lacerations, broken bones, second degree burns, and the anesthesia potion. I believe it'll be enough to get any wounded out of the line of fire so they can be further treated at a later time." She held her head high. "Any questions?"

Wade coughed. "Yeah, any luck on gunshot wounds or major damage?"

Her face fell. "We've been able to slow bleeding, but major damage, no. As I've told you before, even the best healers need major time to repair those."

Wade nodded, not hiding his disappointment.

Sabrina stood without waiting to be asked. She smirked. "Last, but not least, right?" Quiet laughter flowed around the room. "The aquatics team is ready. Not only can we supply everyone with fresh water, we can pull water outside of bodies, leaving behind a dehydrated husk. Avoid the docks if you can; we're still cleaning up the fish we practiced on. The sea gulls are having a feast." Many chuckled at her words. "Moving on. We've have had moderate success with manipulating the tide, but as you know, the pull of the moon is strong. We can also help underwater breathing for small to moderate groups at a time. As to our recent acquisition, the disguises will be perfect."

She returned to her seat, crossing her legs, blue leather shining. Charlie groaned. She'd never look as good in leather as she does.

Finch asked, "No problems with the raid?"

Sabrina and Ora exchanged a significant look. "Um, no. We were able to get in and out of the factory without incident."

What was that about?

Finch nodded. "Very good. I'm proud of each of you. The maps?"

Sabrina opened a box from behind her, pulled out several rolled-up pieces of paper. She brought them over to the podium and smoothed them out, positioning them to show every building and street in Conjuragic. She also pulled out one for the Haven, the Meadow, and the Sierra. Sabrina, Arameus, Damien, and Jeremiah had been working on those. They gathered accurate information on most every place except for the Willow.

Charlie knew from Arameus the leaders had been discussing the potential plans. Nothing had changed or evolved in weeks. Nothing could be finalized until the agreed upon where and when to cross over. Finch shrugged his shoulders. "So, where do we start?"

Silence followed, but this time Charlie raised her hand. All heads turned to her as she shook her head. "The Haven."

Sabrina stiffened. Finch waved Charlie to step up to the map. "Okay, tell me your plan?"

Charlie swallowed, avoiding eye contract with Sabrina. "The Haven is underwater, deep in the Severn Sea. It's contained. Every other homeland is connected to the city. If we can take the Haven, we may be able to keep element of surprise."

Sabrina rolled out the map of the Haven, and Finch, Wade, Ora, and Arameus all gathered around it.

Sabrina sighed. "She's right."

Charlie pointed to the map. "We'll have to be quick, but if Ora can open the Bridge at different points around the Haven..." Sabrina jabbed the map with a finger. "Like here, here, and here. Those are the locations of the communication centers. We can have the aquatics team submerge the groups and enter at these areas. Then once inside the Haven, we take out communications, so they can't notify the MDA."

Finch ran a finger from the outermost points of the Haven. "After that, we'll force our way into the center of the Haven⨅: the

Eye. Once there, we'll have control of the Haven and a home base during the war."

Arameus tapped spots around the cylindrical shaped Haven. "Also, we'll need to keep a small group outside during the invasion to monitor for anyone leaving to go to Conjuragic and warn the MDA."

Healer Roos scooted in beside Charlie. "We can use the sleeping draft on the inhabitants. That way causalities of civilians will be minimal."

Sabrina's face relaxed. "Thank you," she mouthed to the Healer.

Ora frowned at the map. "There's only one hiccup. This means I'd have to open the Bridge and cross over with our army. Reopen it at the first location, wait for a third of our group to get out, move the Bridge to location two, wait while another third leaves, before moving to the final location to get the rest out. What will the first two groups do while the others are moving? That also doesn't leave us much time. Someone could get out and warn everyone before we even have a chance."

Sabrina asked. "At the raid, you were able to open the Bridge at two different points simultaneously. Why not three?"

Ora stared at her in disbelief. "Sabrina, that was a few people and only a few feet away. This is miles apart with thousands of people!"

A risky idea occurred to Charlie, but if they could pull it off, the pay would be worth it.

"Besides Charlie, anyone got a better idea?" Finch asked.

Charlie said, "What if the aerial team is split into thirds? At each location, the aerial teams can suspend the troops in the air. Then when everyone is in place, the aerial team will take them down. Simultaneously."

"You mean the Bridge will be opened in the sky, hundreds of miles above the sea?" Finch pulled out a cigarette, cradling it in his palm, thinking.

"It could work," Sabrina said.

Ora wrinkled her nose. "So we skydive in?"

Charlie shrugged.

"I hate you." Ora quivered at the thought. "When do we leave?"

"I don't know what else we can do. We're as ready as we can be. I think tomorrow we assign the teams. Give the team leaders a week or two at the most. Then we strike." Finch threw this idea out, and everyone looked around. No one could think of any alternative. "We ain't getting any younger," Finch joked.

Ora turned and looked out of the window at the army. She turned back and surveyed the leaders. Charlie could wield her powers better than even Arameus, but months of training had hardened him. Sabrina was born ready. Perdita hadn't said a word, but Charlie guessed deep down she'd always known this moment would come. Finch, Wade, and Damien looked excited.

Ora's gaze lingered on Jeremiah. "There's something we have to do first."

Chapter Forty-Four
Ora

WE STEPPED THROUGH THE BRIDGE in front of an old run-down house in total disarray. The grass had run wild, covered in weeds with a rusted bike turned on its side. The once-white paint of the siding peeled off in large chunks. Broken blinds hung in the dirty windows. A mud-covered doll in a stained yellow dress lay discarded on the porch. The whole place gave off an air of desperation with a hint of something once loved and well-kept cast aside. Two minutes after we appeared, a van pulled into the driveway. Jeremiah's breath caught in his throat beside me. The van door opened, and a woman stepped out of the driver's side.

The short woman stared. Dull, lanky brown hair hung to her chin, framing her hallowed face. At the sight of her, Jeremiah extended his arms. "Mommy…"

His words were barely a whisper but carried to her by a different magic: the connection between mother and child. Her back stiffened as their eyes locked. Her mouth flew open, grocery bags spilling apples all over the ground. "Jeremiah!" She ran toward him.

"Mommy!" he sprinted toward her. They met in the middle, interlocked in a tight embrace, sinking to the ground. He buried his head in her neck, she stroked his head with tears running down her face. "Oh Jeremiah. Jeremiah. My Jeremiah."

Tears fell from my eyes at this beautiful reunion. I knew tomorrow we would be crossing the Bridge into Conjuragic, and I didn't know how many would lose their lives in this fight. But now after watching this heartache, I knew we must go on. We must fight so this never happens to another family again.

My hand clasped Mom's on one side and Charlie's in my other. We'd came here after leaving her grandparents. The party had to be raging back on the island. Damien wiped his eyes. He'd been too afraid to look for his parents.

Finch coughed, wiping his own eyes. "Dust got my eyes."

"Right."

He turned his back on Jeremiah. "We give him a few hours. If he doesn't want to come back, I get it."

"He'll come," I said. "We leave tomorrow."

Chapter Forty-Five
Ora

I COULDN'T EAT MUCH AT breakfast, but then again, neither could anyone else. I shifted in the uncomfortable purple leather again, wondering how Sabrina had ever gotten used to these uniforms. I finished the braid, tying it off at the end, and flung it over my shoulder. It hung down my back disguising me as a Tempest Protector.

The thousands of Gayden gathered on the beach, the best location for our departure. Charlie and Jeremiah also wore purple. Mom, Damien, and Sabrina disguised themselves in blue. The majority of the army wore the blood-red leathers as most of them resembled Embers with their dark hair and eyes.

Grim faces matched my own. It had been one thing to talk about going into battle. Quite another now that the time had come. Those on the island spent the last evening with their families. The other Gayden went home for a week's leave. The hugs and kisses and goodbyes had been said.

Jeremiah's mother didn't want to let him go again, especially after she found out about Gabe. The memory of her cries still brought chill bumps to my arms. He'd assured her when the war was over he'd move his family to the island. A change had already begun in his childhood home. While Jeremiah, his parents, and younger sisters went out to eat, Damien and Finch mowed the grass and weeded the yard. Mom and I cleaned up the toys and power-washed the house. Naiad magic plus a regular water hose had made a nice fake out. Charlie blew years' worth of fallen leaves from the backyard. Charlie, Mom, and I moved on to cleaning the inside of the house while the men fixed the shutters. His parents thanked us before we'd gone. The haunted look that swarmed his family had lessened in a few hours.

Leaving Charlie's grandparents had been harder. They'd been in hiding at the cabin where they spent their honeymoon. Mom hated to break it to them that we weren't back for good, but hearing from us helped ease some of their worry. We'd given them information to contact us at the island. I wished we could bring them and Jeremiah's family to the island now, but until this was over, I couldn't put them in danger. But at least everyone had gotten to say goodbye, a chance we'd never gotten with John.

Thinking of John, my eyes drifted to Charlie. I couldn't stand it if I lost her too. But she wouldn't stay behind. She caught me looking and shook her head. "Don't worry. I got this, O."

I had to laugh at her boldness. I didn't even waste my breath. She would go no matter what. She, too, had the right to fight for her brother. Healer Roos waved her over.

Mom joined my side and held my hand, exactly what I needed. She always thought of others and knew what they needed, but her own needs faded into the background.

"Nervous?" she asked.

"Very."

She squeezed my hand, hiding her own nervousness, putting me first. The crowd parted as Finch made his way toward me, a rifle strapped across his chest, various knives attached to his legs, and his sword hung on his back. A customary cigarette hung out of the corner of his mouth. "Morning, Stone."

"Morning, Outlaw."

He cracked his knuckles and stretched. "So, you think you ought to say something?"

This took me by surprise. "Say something?"

He lit the cigarette, tangy smoke billowing around his head. "Yeah, like a pep talk. Get 'em pumped?"

He couldn't be serious. He wanted me, the girl who got petrified reading from a book in front of a classroom of thirty people, to get up and make an unplanned motivational speech to thousands of Gayden!

"Wouldn't it be better coming from you? I mean, you're the head of security. You're used to this sort of thing. I wouldn't know what to say." I stuttered like an idiot.

He took once last puff of his cigarette before flinging it onto the beach. "They're fighting for you, Stone. This is your revolution. They need to hear you. You need to be more than a name. They need to see you. Now get up there."

He pushed me toward a dune, and Wade flipped a switch turning on a microphone. I didn't even see the speakers until I heard a high-pitched screech as they turned on. The crowd grew silent as Wade spoke into the microphone. "Morning, everyone. Ora Stone here has something she would like to say."

He thrust the microphone in my hands and turned me toward the crowd. I faced twenty thousand people, and they expected me to talk. My mouth turned to ash, and each beat of my heart banged like a drum in my ears. *Boom. Boom. Boom.* I'd much rather invade the Haven than give a speech. Mom smiled a smile that told me I could do it.

"Umm, good morning."

"Good morning." The words echoed across the beach as thousands of voices answered.

More than a little overwhelmed, my hand shook as I held the microphone to my lips. "Um, I don't know if everyone has heard, but Charlie McCurry, the head of the medical team, along with Healer Roos has developed a sleeping spell. These will be passed out to all of you in a few minutes. All you have to do is throw them at your enemy, and they when they pop open, the enemy will fall into a deep sleep. This will prevent us from causing more harm than necessary."

Everyone stared. Thank goodness I had a microphone because without it, not even those five feet from me would be able to hear me. Finch pursed his lips. Clearly this wasn't what he had in mind, but I had no idea what to say to these people. I didn't know them, and they didn't know me. Not really. How could I get strangers pumped up to risk their lives and possibly die for my cause? As soon as the thought finished, I realized the answer. I couldn't.

"Look I...I don't know most of you, just as most of you don't know me. Knowing what we're going to do today, I found myself searching for reasons to fight. Then I looked at my mother. If you don't know, she is a Geminate, and although she's a Magician, even in Conjuragic, her kind are killed at birth. Next, I looked at my friend Damien Snider, a Gayden like you, who was arrested as a child. A boy of only four when the Magicians sentenced him to death. I could relate because they mistook me for a Gayden. I went through the very same things, and if it wasn't for one of your ancestors, I would've died."

The crowd had grown solemn but hung on every word. Inspiration took me. "There have been countless stories of hate crimes against your people. So today, don't fight for me. Instead, fight for yourselves, fight for your loved ones. Hold the memories of them close, and together, we will fight for our freedom. We will fight for the wrongs done against our people. We will no longer sit idly by while our people are killed or sent into hiding. We deserve to live. We deserve freedom. We deserve to have a name, and together we will become the voice they cannot ignore. We will take the fight to their doorstep. We will not stop until we've been heard and every one of us is free to live our lives in the open. We will become the nightmare they have long feared us to be. We will escalate that fear until we can no longer be ignored. Until they fall at our feet begging for mercy. Only then will we stop and demand to be treated as equals. We'll rise up, better and stronger than before."

The crowd roared, and I joined them. It was time. I stepped down from the dune and joined Finch. He threw out another cigarette. He shouted to be heard above the roars of the troops. "That's what I'm talking about, Stone."

I only nodded. The leaders called out orders to the troops. We were ready. I concentrated, and the Bridge burst open to

Over the Bridge

accommodate the army. Just before I took the first step, Damien spoke in my ear. "Pssst, Ora?"

"What?"

"You look hot."

I couldn't help it. I smiled. I clasped his hand and stepped onto the Bridge, the army right on my heels.

The war had begun.

Chapter Forty-Six
Ora

D<small>AMIEN HELD ONTO MY LEFT</small> hand while Sabrina held the right, leading the way to her homeland. Maneuvering in the Bridge with twenty thousand people slowed the process. Once the last of us stepped inside, the Bridge closed behind us. We moved at a snail's pace. Their nervousness clawed at me. Jiminy's buttery, cinnamon smell helped me ignore their fear. He said, "You can do it."

"Who is that?" Mom's voice sounded frantic. I'd explain about Jiminy later, if we survived. We'd reached our first destination. I opened the Bridge a hundred feet above an ocean. "Are you sure we're in the right place?"

"Yes," Sabrina answered. "The other spots are there and there." I nodded, pretty sure I could get there without her. I nodded, and she gave the order. Arameus, Charlie, Wade, and a portion of the aerial team jumped out of the Bridge with a battle call. They fell straight down but their progress slowed, forming a large circle. The air inside the circle grew hazy as they worked together to form a net. The signal sounded, and the first third of the army jumped out.

I closed my eyes, not wanting to see them fall. Just looking at the flat expanse of nothing but sky made my heart race and my palms sweat. *Why did it have to be heights?*

I peeked. The aerial team slowed the descent. The Tempest wind caught and slowed them, held suspended. The net held. Charlie gave me a thumbs up.

I closed the Bridge, moved to the second location, and reopened it, waiting for Sabrina. She nodded. I'd made it to the right place. The second aerial team flew out and formed the second net. Jeremiah gave me a cockeyed smile as he leaped, arms spread wide, happily screaming. The second half of the army leapt and waited in the net. Only Mom and Sabrina remained from the second group.

Sabrina said, "The last place is there. You think you can do it?"

"Yeah, I got it. Just go." They jumped. In seconds, I closed the Bridge and moved to the final location. The third aerial team jumped, formed the net, and the last of the army sailed past me. "See you soon." Damien squeezed my shoulder and half fell, half jumped. Only me now. Everyone was waiting for me to jump, over a hundred feet in the air, before we could go. "I can't do this. I can't do this." My body froze. Jiminy's warmth touched my back and shoved. I flew forward, legs and arms failing, screaming in terror.

The air pushed against me hard in the opposite direction. The feeling of falling eased. I opened my eyes, not looking down, floating in the air with the rest of the army. The air pushed upward, holding us in place. No one said anything to me, for which I was grateful. Never again. Never ever in my whole life did I want to do that again.

The Bridge closed above me. Finch gave me the okay sign. I touched the comm in my ear. "Team Leader Alpha attempting to make contact."

Sabrina's voice through the ear piece, "Team Leader Bravo here. We're good to go."

Next Arameus said, "Team Leader Charlie reporting. In position and ready."

I grabbed onto Damien's arm with a quivering hand. "Fucking heights!" I touched the comm again. "Tttttt....team Leader Alpha. We're gah...go."

Sabrina said, "Aerial team in five...four...three...two...one... drop."

"Oh shit! Oh shit! Oh shit!"

Damien laughed as the net fell from underneath us.

The aerial teams descended the groups toward the ocean. The bottom fell out from under me. My stomach felt like it slammed against my throat. This was way worse than the original jump. I closed my eyes, grabbed onto Damien, and screamed. I wasn't the only one.

My body clinched, bracing for impact, but the aerial teams pulled back, slowing us before we slammed against the water. Upon our approach, the aquatics team pushed the water from around us, forming a giant bubble, and we sank into the ocean amidst the splashing and gurgling of water.

The gushing stopped as the newly-formed aerial pods held the army descending into the depths of the sea. We sank at a slow, steady pace. Fish darted out of the way underneath the pods. Farther down, a large outline of the crystal city appeared like a large nautilus shell with three distinct areas spiraling from the outer rim toward the center. The whole city glowed with an iridescent blue. The magical energy hummed, vibrating the water, and my magic purred in response.

I'd placed the Alpha pod in the correct position, but if we could see the Haven, the Naiads could see us.

I touched my ear. "Team Alpha to Team Tango, are you in position?"

Wade's voice reached me. "Team Tango in position, no activity on our end."

Relief flooded me. We hadn't been completely sure the communication devices would work underwater. Wade's group made up our look-out team. We'd spread them out in various positions around the Haven, more heavily guarded in the directions closest to Conjuragic.

The area underneath Alpha Pod had no activity. Teams Alpha, Bravo, and Charlie dropped into radio silence until we'd reached the striking position unless any activity started. Little late now to worry if we'd oversimplified our plan to invade the Haven at the three entry points, and each team worked our way along the long hallways toward the Eye at the center. The camerae, or living chambers, veered off the hallways. Each team had to clear each area as we advanced forward, heading toward the communal area called the Eye.

Over the Bridge

The pod descended and we'd almost reached our position. I switched channels to speak only to my team. "Team Alpha. Battle positions." The feeling the group gave off teetered on the edge of panic, but with my order, an eerie calmness stole over the group.

At last the pod reached its destination. "Team Alpha, we're a go. Three...two...one...attack!"

Our pyrokinetics team sent a blast at the entrance. The crystal wall exploded, and water rushed in. Our bubble pushed toward the entrance, and the Gayden sprang outward.

Screams and crashes of spells hitting the walls reverberated down the hallway. Farther ahead in the crystal city, flashes of light lit up the ocean outside like the fourth of July. The last of the Gayden left the pod.

Damien and Finch covered me as I resealed the crystal wall. The walls dripped ocean water into puddles all over the floor. My feet skidded as I maneuvered around the hopefully unconscious Naiads.

Damien, Finch, and I jogged along the long, tortuous hallways, checking cameras as we passed. Each cell was either empty or held an incapacitated body. The crystal walls shined bright giving everything a bluish hue all around.

On and on we went finding no one to fight. The emptiness bothered me more than if it had been filled with people. Screams, loud bangs, and crashes sounded all around, but there was no one here. We rounded a hallway.

Three people—two men and a woman—threw down a barricade of ice on the floor. My leather boots screeched as I ground to halt to avoid the icicle spikes. In one move, the ice thawed and flung back at them. It took them by surprise. The water collided against their chests, pushing them backward into the wall. Still stunned, Finch tossed Charlie's bags full of sleeping potion at them. The bags exploded, raining aerated potions over them. As they inhaled, their eyes flitted closed, and they sunk to the ground. Damien bound them with magic before we moved on.

Two minutes later, another group jumped out of a camerea. Seven men and one child. Before they could react, I threw a sleeping bag like a baseball. The bag smacked the man in the center dead in the face. Two other bags hit the group. Eight bodies crashed to the floor. My power slipped around their wrists. It locked them together with an audible click. Farther up the spiral, we caught up with the rest of our team.

"Section A, Part One is cleared," said a Gayden whose name I didn't know.

"Great, keep going!"

Sabrina chimed in my ear. "Section B, Parts One and Two are cleared. We're headed for Part Three. Then to the rendezvous point."

The deeper we penetrated, the more crowded it became. Most of the fighting occurred ahead of me. I passed bloody bodies, quite a few of them Gayden. No time to stop and check on them. The group relayed back Part Two had been cleared. I put my hand to my ear. "Team Alpha, Section A, Parts One and Two cleared. Team Charlie, report."

I ran, feeling the heavy weight of the silent comm, heaving three sleeping spells, and a gust of wind at a group who managed to slip past the others.

"Team Charlie, do you copy? Where are they?" Finch's lips pursed in a thin line. He didn't like this any better than I did.

Charlie's voice blared in my ear. "Team Charlie. Section C, Parts One and Two cleared. Arameus is down. We…" Static. "…to Part Three."

Arameus!

We'd entered Part Three.

To my right, a darkened alcove caught my attention. Swerving from the group, I jogged inside it. Damien yelled, "Ora!"

I continued alone. Down the darkened alcove, a small door lit up around the edges. This one had been missed. I knew it. My power jetted in front of me. The door swung open wide. Hundreds of Naiad children stared back at me. Bookshelves lined the walls. Desks turned on their sides. This must be a type of school.

I hesitated. The children didn't waste any time. Several of them cast spells toward me. I threw myself to the side to avoid them. One hit me. The water so thin and fast it sliced through my arm like a blade. I screamed as it ripped through the soft flesh. Hot pumping blood poured down my arm. They must have hit an artery.

The kids stared, stone-faced and unafraid. Dozens of them raised their hands. This was how I would end. Taken down by children.

Damien rolled into the room. His power took hold of mine. With our combined power, hundreds of sleeping bags burst in the air. Gusts of potion exploded over the children. They fell as if in slow motion.

Damien pulled me to my feet. I screamed, clutching the injured arm. Waves of nausea rolled over my stomach.

Finch stuck his head in the door. With one sweep of his hand, he cleared the room. "Come on!"

Damien's power still mingled with mine, burning hot on the wound. The frantic pumping of blood halted. The wound remained, but I wouldn't bleed to death. I grabbed what looked like a ripped blanket. While running, I yanked off a long strip. My power pulled away from Damien, wrapping the bandage around the wound and tying it. The pain rippled through my body. I managed not to stumble.

Finch held up his hands. We halted, panting. "Part Three's cleared. We're in position to raid the Eye."

"Team Alpha in position."

"Team Bravo in position."

"Team Charlie in position."

Finch nodded.

I pressed the comm. "On my order. Go!"

The three teams burst into the Eye at the same moment. The remaining Naiads had retreated here as we'd invaded their home. Like red ants, the Gayden rolled inside. Gunfire rang out. We'd ran out of sleeping bags! This had to end. Fast!

The world descended into a commotion of activity and violence. I dodged water and ice as my magic aimed at anything blond.

Thought melted away. My body ran on auto-pilot. Act and reacting to the chaos. Time held no meaning. We could've fought for hours or minutes.

Far above us, crunches and crackling rippled. The sounds grew louder. A visceral part of me recognized the meaning. The crystal walls in an underwater city, that could mean only one thing. We were in deep shit!

Risking injury, I looked up. Like a fractured mirror, the ceiling split in a hundred directions. With each heartbeat, it spread. Water sprayed into the building. In an instant, the danger from above became far greater than anything else. The fighting ceased as all eyes cast upward. The crystal exploded into a million pieces. The sea poured in.

Naiads and even some of the Gayden held their hands above their heads. Their magic combined, forcing the water away. The Sight opened. The magic blazed. But as more and more of the sea forced inside, it wavered.

Someone shouted, "Do something!"

"The sea is too strong!" Sabrina screamed.

The damn broke. Water filled in. The Gayden and Naiads swept away. Many lost underneath the rolling waves. Charlie struggled on a beam. With a scream, she disappeared underneath the water. Finch, Mom, Damien were nowhere to be seen.

The weight of the water pushed against me, making it almost impossible to keep standing.

The deep well of power inside me boiled. Infinite like the invading sea, my power exploded out of me. The two forces clashing. The inferno inside rising higher and higher. A bright white light of power encased me. It ascended. The Eye glowed bright as the sun. The sea quivered and halted against the force of it. Silence overtook the Eye. Nothing happened for a split second. Like the calm before a storm.

With a surge of power, no longer singular, the sea rose. Higher and higher. Out of the Haven. Naiads and Gayden alike had joined me. Hundreds of faces stared upward. Hands raised high. Eyes closed. Together for the first time in history.

The crystal walls reformed like a large jigsaw puzzle, this time infused with the sea and intertwined magics. The ceiling solidified. Strong than ever before.

Over the Bridge

The danger had passed. The Naiads stared at me with uncertain eyes—a mixture of fear and irreverence. They raised their hands in defeat. Every Naiad surrendered. We had won. The Haven was ours.

Chapter Forty-Seven
Ora

SABRINA BOUND THE NAIADS.

"Team leader Alpha to Team Tango. The egg has hatched. Report."

"Team Tango. Had some action on our end. Captured a few stragglers but none got through."

I sighed in relief. No more fighting today. "Great. Come on in, boys."

The aftermath revealed a sea-soaked floor, the shattered remains of tables, chairs, broken glass, and bodies littered everywhere. Most of the Gayden struggled to their feet. Coughing and sobs echoed in the enclosed area.

Sabrina, white faced, strolled to my side. "We have to begin Phase Two."

I nodded, not really paying attention as my gaze swept the Eye searching for Mom, Charlie, Arameus, any of them. My heart thundered. Where were they? Panic rose unlike anything I'd felt in battle. Charlie had said Arameus was down. Down as in hurt or dead? Arameus, my first friend in the magical land who stood by my side from the beginning, might be hurt or dead. My friend who fought for me when no other Defender would touch my case. Who went in search of my mother and John after he thought I died. I owed him so much. I couldn't ever thank him enough.

A mantra sped through my mind in rapid succession. *Mom. Charlie. Arameus. Damien. Jeremiah. Finch. Mom. Charlie. Arameus. Damien. Jeremiah. Finch. Mom. Charlie. Arameus. Damien. Jeremiah. Finch.*

All of a sudden amidst the sea of strangers, Mom rose to her feet. I dashed toward her, dodging people, and I almost knocked her down as I hugged her. She gathered me in her arms. Relief like I'd never known coursed through my veins. The bittersweet relief of the reunion didn't last long. The others were still missing.

Sabrina screamed at me from across the room, "Ora, Phase Two!"

Sabrina stood where I'd left her, with her hands on her hips, glaring. From farther across the room, a man's voice shouted, "Sabrina?"

Her head whipped toward the voice, and her faced paled. "Simeon!"

Phase Two forgotten. She dashed toward the owner of the voice, a young man with red hair, wearing purple robes. They crashed into an embrace, and I looked away in embarrassment as they kissed.

I asked, "Isn't that?"

Mom squeezed my shoulder. "The man she is in love with."

"Ora!" Jeremiah helped a limping Damien. Mom and I sprinted toward them.

Jeremiah said, "Finch went down Section A to begin Phase Two."

I wrapped one arm around Jeremiah, taking extra time and care with Damien. "Have either of you seen Charlie?" They shook their heads.

My entire body felt numb and quivered. I touched my ear. "Charlie, do you copy?"

Silence.

Static sounded. Then a voice spoke through the earpiece. "Hello. This is Healer Roos. Can you hear me?"

"Yes, I hear you."

"I'm with Charlie. Her comm is broken. We're with Defender Townsend."

Nausea clenched and knotted my stomach. "Is he alive?"

"Yes. He has several injuries but should make it. We're working with him now."

Thank you. Thank you. Thank you.

"Where are you?"

"Section C between Parts One and Two."

Mom motioned for me to follow her as we left the Eye, entering Part C. We raced down the long crystalline hallways that shimmered like mother of pearl. The beautiful lights mocked the travesty in the midst of this chaos. It'd be a shame to get caught now. "Teams, begin Phase Two."

Charlie knelt on the floor along with Healer Roos. Arameus pushed himself from the floor, wiping a bloody towel over his head, the injury healed. Tears ran down Charlie's cheeks.

A large laceration coursed down her left eye and cheek. Blood and tears stained her face, and wet hair clung to her neck and back.

I sank to the floor, wrapping my arms around Charlie, as she clung to me, sobbing. When she'd finally calmed, I pulled back, hugging Arameus. Now that I had a chance, I wasn't going to lose it. "Thank God you're okay. I can't begin to tell you how much you mean to me. You've done so much for me and my family. I can never thank you enough."

He squeezed my hand. "You would've done the same for me." He wiped the blood from Charlie's face, leaned forward, and kissed her softly.

Static rang through the comm. "Yo, Stone, you going to get to work?"

I rolled my eyes, pushing to my feet, and waved to my friends. "Don't get your panties in a twist, Outlaw."

The delivery team and I stepped through the Bridge back into the Eye. Sabrina tilted her chin in the air. I nodded, letting her know all had gone smoothly. She turned her attention back to her sister. Mom, Charlie, and Damien accompanied me to the island. Sabrina stood and marched toward us, head held high, eyes constantly sweeping the room. Back in Protector mode.

Over the Bridge

"Phase Two is complete. All the non-essentials are across the Veil and placed in the prisons. The seals are holding, but the Gayden are guarding them."

She crossed her arms behind her back. "Phase Three is well underway. We've cleaned up majority of the Haven. The Gayden have taken over the living quarters, and we have the Eye up to 90% operational." Simeon, the handsome Tempest, joined her. Her arm fell, and they clasped hands. He smiled, but it didn't reach his lips. He gave off an air of embarrassment.

I offered my hand. "Hi. I'm Ora Stone."

He didn't move but stared at my hand. Sabrina nudged his shoulder. "She's fine. Trust me."

His sweaty palm gripped mine. "I'm Simeon Weston."

"So." I wiped my hand on the leather, which did nothing about the sweat. "You're a Tempest. What were you doing at the Haven?"

He flushed. "I, um…"

Sabrina finished for him, "He's been coming here helping my family."

Sabrina's demeanor changed dramatically after the attack. Her family hadn't been harmed today nor when I'd destroyed the Unity Statue. The damage to the city hadn't been as devastating as we'd thought. Hundreds died, and many buildings had been damaged, but it wasn't a total loss. Life in the city dwindled for the first few weeks, and most stuck to their homelands, but they rebuilt several buildings, and their world continued.

Sabrina's family chose to stay here with her, despite the dangers, but Sabrina wouldn't give up trying to convince them to go to the island. Her father was an entirely different story, but we'd have to deal with that later.

Charlie stepped forward. "I'm Charlie McCurry. Human turned Tempest."

"Uhh, nice to meet you?" Simeon stumbled over his words. I doubted he'd ever met anyone quite like us.

Sabrina chuckled, an odd sound from her, and patted his arm. "I'll fill you in later."

"This is my mother, Perdita Stone." Mom stepped forward. Simeon jumped backward staring wide-eyed at Mom.

"Wait, did you say your mother?" His reaction confused everyone.

"Yes."

"But aren't you Evelyn Hamilton?"

What was he talking about?

She flushed. "Not exactly. That was an alias to get here so I could rescue my daughter."

Simeon gaze flicked between the two of us. "So, is Jack your brother?"

"What? Who's Jack?"

Mom's face fell. "Jack was also an alias. His real name was John, and he was Ora's boyfriend and Charlie's brother. He came with me to help."

"Then why did you leave him behind?" Simeon asked.

Charlie stiffened. "Because he died during the escape."

He shook his head, brows furrowed. "Jack's not dead. He's been living here since you left. He told everyone you broke into their hotel room and used them as hostages so you could escape. He managed to get away, but you took his mother, Sabrina, and Arameus across the Veil as your prisoners."

"What?" Mom, Charlie, and I said together.

"John's alive?" Charlie's hand rose to her chest, hope and sadness mingled in every syllable.

"Yes. You didn't know?"

"No!" Charlie and I shouted.

He stepped back. "He managed to get away because he said you'd given him a potion to remove his identity crystal. It didn't come out fast enough and put him into a deep sleep. When he woke up, you were gone. He told the Quads his mother's crystal must have been removed, allowing you to take her across the Veil."

The memory of John's lifeless eyes flashed in my mind, and I shook my head. "He was hit by a boulder. I saw his body. I saw his eyes open and lifeless. I saw it!"

Over the Bridge

Sabrina inhaled sharply. "Of course! If the crystal had been tampered with or the time ran out, he would've froze. No life, no breath, and any damage from the boulder could've been repaired before he was revived."

Charlie sobbed.

Mom wriggled her hands together. "Oh, thank goodness."

Horror and happiness raged in me like a great battle. He was alive, but I left him behind. I swear I didn't know he hadn't died. Hot tears fell down my cheeks. *How will he ever forgive me?*

Aryiana's words sprang in my mind. *I'm sorry child. The boy you knew is dead.* Had she read the future wrong or was John truly with Strega?

A throat clearing jerked me out of my thoughts. My eyes fly up to see Damien. "What's going on?"

Charlie cried out, "John's alive."

Damien's eyes didn't leave mine, but something in them broke at the news.

Loud music like an orchestra sounded all around.

I asked, "What's that?"

Simeon pointed to the ceiling. "The Council has been having nightly announcements."

The ceiling turned opaque.

"Can they see us?"

Sabrina answered. "No."

The High Council appeared on the opaque screen. They looked the same as during my trial, but more people flanked them. "Who are they?"

Sabrina leaned closer to me and whispered, "Those are their advisors."

"Witches and Wizards of Conjuragic. Not much has changed since yesterday," the Naiad Council woman said.

A collective wave of relief passed through my group. They didn't know we were here.

"What's her name again?" I asked.

"Cilla Souse, and her husband is Talon. Naiad High Council."

Cilla continued. "We're continuously working to fix our city and as you know have repaired most of the buildings. The Unity Statue is still a loss. No matter how much we work with it, the Great Mothers' magic cannot be restored. The Veil remains sealed. But our teams are working night and day to attempt to reopen it so we can be reunited with our loved ones."

Damien nudged Sabrina. "Hey, what's that man's name?"

I didn't hear her reply as my attention focused on Cilla. "As soon as the Veil is unsealed, finding the escaped Nip, Ora Stone, will be top priority. She'll pay for her crimes. I assure you."

I gulped as Damien tapped my shoulder, each strike harder than the one before. "Ora."

"What?" I snapped.

Damien dropped the bomb. "I know who Master is."

SNEAK PEEK

Into the Fire
The Conjuragic Series
Book 3

Chapter 1
Strega

"**Master, you called for me?**"

"Ahh. Strega, you're better?" Master bent over his desk scribbling at various papers, not bothering to look at her.

"Yes, I'm improving." Strega rubbed her back where the rocks crashed upon her as she ran from the collapsing buildings. Damn that girl.

"Have you been able to transform again?" Master raised one eyebrow, appearing non-chalant, but Strega knew better than to underestimate him.

"Yes, Master." She wouldn't disappoint him again. The last punishment had been brutal. Not that she deserved any less for allowing the girl to escape.

He swiveled around in the chair, gliding to his feet with a natural grace she'd never be able to replicate. "Show me."

Her nose wrinkled for only the faction of a second. This was really going to hurt. Her human form quivered preparing for the transformation. Her screamed morphed into a wailing screech interlaced with cracking of bones and rearranging sinew. Moments later a tiny black tailless cat perched on its haunches staring up at the blond man.

He flashed an award winning smile that didn't reach his eyes. "Excellent." He gestured and the cat expanded as if inflated, bones snapping, fingers pushing past the claws. Nausea passed through her from the pain. Hate aided the pain. If she ever saw that girl again she'd end her.

"Come." He didn't wait to see if she followed. There was no

question of that. With his hands together as if in prayer he strolled the length of the Pyre on bare feet. He flung his dark blue robes outward to keep them from acquiring ash while he perched upon his make-shift throne. Deep within the volcano, beads of sweat poured down her back. She disliked being here. Her earliest memories were of this place. The endless, insufferable heat, dim light, and pain. Pain in every possible. She clasped her hand behind her back, waiting, careful not to displease him.

"Now my pet, tell me what happened."

"Master. The girl wasn't a Nip. She's like nothing I've ever seen. She drew power from all cores, merged them into one, and that's what destroyed the Unity Statue."

Master's lips pulled into a thin line. His interlaced fingers paled under the angry grip. Anger pulsated off him in waves. "You mean no one helped her. She destroyed the Unity Statue all by herself?"

Strega gulped as the sweat morphed into cold chills of fear. She wouldn't be the first of his experiments to be lost in one of his rages. "Yes, Master." Bending at the waist, she stared at his dirty toes, holding her breath, not knowing if she'd be dead in a few seconds.

Master breathed in and out, slow, monotonous, as he wrestled an idea in his mind.

"There's something else Master." Strega braced herself for what she must tell him. He would be even angrier because she'd let them escape, but if he found out from another her punishment would be much worse.

"What is it Strega?" His tone hinted at boredom, but this ruse didn't fool her. He paid attention to every word, every gesture or eye movement. Her Master missed nothing.

"She wasn't just with the human, her Defender, and the traitor Protector."

"Oh."

"She was also with one of the Geminates who escaped you long ago." Her words whispered.

His anger erupted without warning or mercy. His water whip slammed upon her scarred back in wave after wave of stinging agony. A single scream echoed off the walls. She bit down on her tongue hard, bringing blood, while she balled her hands into tight fists, knuckles white. He wouldn't tolerate her screams. Her years with him had taught her that much. She reigned in any sound, refusing to let the wail leave her lips. The Nip magic inside her struggled to break free, to take his magic, pull it within herself, to claim it as her own, but that would mean death. His mercy alone allowed her to live. Blow after blow landed, striking her back, legs, and buttocks. One more, she told herself, and waited her punishment to end. Just one more. One more.

The water whip fell to the ground in a puddle, mingling with the constant, warm, thick droplets of blood from her newest wounds. Angry fingers dug into the soft flesh under arm, yanking her upright, dragging her back to his office. Master jabbed a finger at the pictures of the Geminates who'd escaped him so long ago. "Which one?"

Her finger hovered over the picture of the younger version of the blonde woman she saw with Ora Stone the day the world changed.

Master released her. He spun away from her, leaned over his desk, long white fingers tapping on the blacked wood. He laughed. "Of course."

Strega stumbled backward, pulling on all her strength to remain standing.

Master faced her, blue eyes reflecting neither warmth nor depth. "Gather all your brothers and sisters. I'll not stop until she's mine."

"The Geminate, Master?"

"No. The girl."

"Yes. Master." Strega bowed, the pain in her back caught in the back of her throat, but she held it back, tasting blood.

When she straightened Master pointed a finger in her face. She hadn't even heard him approach. "She'll come to me unharmed. If you touch her, I will kill you. Slowly. Understood?"

Her chin lowered to the floor. "Yes, Master."

"Strega, my pet, you're going to get your revenge. It'll be so much sweeter than her blood on your hands."

What could he possibly mean?

"How"'s the boy?" Master tilted his head to the side.

She hid her confusion about the change in conversation. "Healing. But his questioning is growing more intense."

"Excellent. Excellent. I believe it's time for you to go on a little rescue mission and make a new—friend."

A shadow entered the office, interrupting them. The Master smiled. "Corporal Bizard. How good to see you. This is Strega. One of my most trusted partners."

The young Tempest dipped his head, but said nothing. His glare told her all she needed to know about Master's new ally. He might be here, but his hatred of Nips oozed from his very pores. He would abide her presence, but only because the Master allowed it. He hated her on sight. "I'm not a Corporal anymore. Remember." He didn't bother hiding the bitter tone from the statement. The stench of resentment wafted off him. Something she'd never have been able to pick up if she hadn't spent years in animal form.

She flicked a glance to see what Master would do about the Tempest disrespectful attitude. The corners of his mouth turned upward only a fraction, but none of it reached his eyes. He'd get his revenge for the insult, but not at this moment. Master was calculating in all things.

"An injustice was done to you, young Jabez. A justice I will help you right. Which is why you are here." Master put one arm around Jabez and the other around her caressing the new lacerations in her skin. "Now let me tell you both what we're going to do."

About the Author

LEANN M. RETTELL was born and raised in West Virginia but now lives in North Carolina with her husband, three children, two crazy dogs, and two aloof cats.

She is the author of the Conjuragic Series and the upcoming Dream Thief Series published by Falstaff Books.

She has dreamed of being a writer since she was a little girl. Never give up. Dare to dream and believe in magic.

Sign up for newsletter updates and never miss a thing!
https://leannmrettell.com/newsletter/

Made in the USA
Lexington, KY
04 May 2018